Keep Me Warm at Christmas

brenda novak

Keep Me Warm at Christmas

mira

Recycling programs
for this product may
not exist in your area.

ISBN-13: 978-0-7783-1216-1

Keep Me Warm at Christmas

This edition published by arrangement with Harlequin Books S.A.

For questions and comments about the quality of this book, please contact us at CustomerService@Harlequin.com.

Mira
22 Adelaide St. West, 40th Floor
Toronto, Ontario M5H 4E3, Canada
BookClubbish.com

Printed in U.S.A.

To the following members of my book group on Facebook:

Elizabeth Cronin, Maureen Fink, Roberta Peden, Virgie Lane,
Robyn Sneed, Marie Christensen, Sheila Chin, Lynn Hill, Pam Record,
Cathy Eberly, Starr Roybal, Ginger Lyman, Liz Schneider,
Leslie Henning, Janice Rigby, Barb Ackerman, Amy Ikari, Ali Hird,
Carolyn Broderick, Sonia Connon, Lori Sang, Juanita Whisenant,
Shari Ashmore, Flavia McCutcheon, Annjanet Foeckler, Sonya Steele,
Cora Hannold, Patricia King, Marilou Frary, Jeanne Keller,
Donna Ingram, Wendy Keel, Janice Shaw, Tracy Goodsell,
Julie Bodie, Denise McDonald, Sheila Wise, Tina Meyers,
Susan Frobish, Patti Lyn, Susanna Klein, DeeAnn Kraft, Nalria Gaddy,
Rosalind Dickinson, Mellissa Hewitt, Pennie Schlepp, Marilyn Hendry,
Nicki Hitchiner, Christina Taylor, Jessica Strayer, Kirbi Smith,
Tammi Kendall, Denise Schaer, Jodie Roberge, Cindy Reynolds,
Laura Meyer, Maryann Anderson, Deb Latham, Barbara Selman,
Georgia Harrell, Lisa Angus, Lezli Robin, Tanya Jackson, Tammy Bell,
Ann-Louise Smith, Judy Johnsen, BranDee Wenzl, Kay Luker,
Darla Pinkerton, Doris Ortiz, Sherry Thomas, Heidi Williams,
Robin Austin, Jimette Ross, Terri Heywood, Cathy Woods,
Nicole Duvall, Jessy Hogue, Doris Barks, Dawn Tenud,
Nancy Jordan, Gloria La Para, Marie Newman,
Bonnie Hazard, Andra Baley and Cathy Garrison.

Your friendship—and that of *so* many others in the group
I didn't have room to list here—has enriched my life.
Thanks for your tremendous support!

Keep Me Warm at Christmas

CHAPTER ONE

Thursday, December 16

Tia Beckett ran a finger along the jagged scar on her cheek as she gazed into the mirror above the contemporary console on the living room wall. She'd taken down almost every mirror in her own house as soon as she came home from the hospital—broken them all and tossed them out. But she couldn't do the same here. This wasn't her home, and there seemed to be mirrors everywhere, each one projecting the same tragic image.

She leaned closer. It must've been the windshield that nearly destroyed her face.

She dropped her hand. After a month, her cheek was still tender, but she continued to examine her reflection. The woman in the mirror was a complete stranger. If she turned her head to the left, she could find herself again. The shiny black hair that framed an oval face. The smooth and creamy olive-colored skin. The bottle-green eyes with long, thick eyelashes. The full lips, which were her own, not a product of Botox injections. All the beauty that'd helped her land the leading role in Hollywood's latest blockbuster was still there.

But when she turned her head to the right…

Her stomach soured as she studied the raised, pink flesh that slanted in a zigzag fashion from the edge of her eye almost to her mouth. The doctor had had to piece that side of her face back together like a quilt. He'd said there was a possibility that cosmetic surgery could improve the scars later, but that wasn't an option right now. After what she'd been through already, she couldn't even contemplate another surgery. It'd be too late to save her career by then, anyway.

Who was this poor, unfortunate creature?

Her agent, her fellow cast members for *Expect the Worst*, the romantic comedy in which she costarred with box-office hit Christian Allen, and the friends she'd made since moving to LA said she was lucky to have survived the accident. And maybe that was true. But it was difficult to *feel* lucky when she'd lost all hope of maintaining her career just as it was beginning to skyrocket.

A knock at the front door startled her. Who could that be? She didn't want to see anyone, not even her friends—and especially not the press. They'd been hounding her since the accident, trying to snap a picture of her damaged face and demanding an answer as to whether she would quit acting. That was part of the reason she'd readily accepted when Maxi Cohen, the producer of her one and only film, offered to let her stay at his massive estate in Silver Springs, ninety minutes northwest of LA. He and his family would be in Israel for the holidays, so he needed someone to house-sit. That was what he'd said. What she'd heard was that she could hide out for a month and be completely *alone*. And she wouldn't even have to pay for the privilege. She just had to care for the houseplants, feed and play with Kiki, the parrot, occasionally drive each of the six vehicles parked in the airplane-hangar-sized garage and make sure nothing went wrong.

She also turned on the lights in the main house at night—

Maxi didn't yet have them set up on a timer, like those in his yard—so that it looked occupied since she was staying in the guesthouse, which was smaller and more comfortable. But that was probably unnecessary. There wasn't a lot of crime in Silver Springs. Known for its boutique hotels, recreational opportunities and local, organic produce, it was sort of like Santa Barbara, only forty minutes away and closer to the coast, in that there were plenty of movie moguls and the like who had second homes here.

Still, he couldn't have left Kiki without a caretaker. And safe was always better than sorry. He also owned an extensive art collection that could never be replaced, so she figured he was wise to have someone watch over it, just in case.

Whoever was at the door rapped again, more insistently. Maxi had given the housekeeper and other staff a paid holiday. Even the gardeners were off, since the yard didn't grow much during the cold, rainy season. The entire estate was essentially in mothballs until Maxi returned. And no one Tia knew could say exactly where she was. So why was someone at her door? How had whoever it was gotten onto the property? The front gate required a code.

"Hello? Anyone home?" A man's strident voice came through the panel. "Maxi said you'd be in the guesthouse."

Damn. Those words suggested whoever it was had a right to be here, or at least permission. She was going to have to answer the door.

"Coming," she called. "Just…give me a minute." She hurried into the bedroom, where her suitcase lay open on the floor. She'd arrived in Silver Springs two days ago but hadn't bothered to unpack. There hadn't seemed to be much point. There didn't seem to be much point in doing anything anymore. She hadn't bothered to shower or dress this morning, either, and she was wearing the same sweat bottoms, T-shirt and socks she'd had on yesterday.

Yanking off her clothes, she pulled on a robe so that there'd be no expectation of hospitality as she scurried back through the living room. Still reluctant to speak to anyone, she peered through the peephole.

A tall, slender man—six-two, maybe taller—stood on the stoop. His dark hair had outgrown its last haircut and stuck out beneath a red beanie, he had a marked five-o'clock shadow, suggesting he hadn't shaved for a couple of days, and a cleft chin almost as pronounced as that of Henry Cavill. He was a total stranger to her, but he had to be one of Maxi's friends or associates, and she should treat him as such.

Bracing herself—human interaction was something she now avoided whenever possible—she took a deep breath. *Please, God, don't let him recognize me or have anything to do with the media.*

The blinds were already pulled, so she turned off the lights and cracked the door barely wide enough to be able to peek out with her good side. "What can I do for you?"

His scowl darkened as his gaze swept over what he could see of her. He must've realized she was wearing a robe, because he said, "I hate to drag you out of bed at—" he checked his watch "—two in the afternoon. But could you let me into the main house before I freeze my—" catching himself, he cleared his throat and finished with "—before I freeze out here?"

Assuming he was a worker of some sort—she couldn't imagine why he'd be here, bothering her, otherwise—she couldn't help retorting, "Sure. As long as you tell me why I should care whether you freeze or not."

The widening of his eyes gave her the distinct impression that he wasn't used to having someone snap back at him. So... maybe he wasn't a worker.

"Because Maxi has offered to let me stay in *his* home, and he indicated you'd let me in," he responded with exaggerated patience. "He didn't text you?"

"No, I haven't heard from him." And surely, what this man

said couldn't be right. Maxi had told her that she'd have the run of the place. She'd thought she'd be able to stay here without fear of bumping into anyone. She'd been counting on it.

"He was just getting on a plane," he explained. "Maybe he had to turn off his phone."

"Okay. If you want to give me your number, I'll text you as soon as I hear from him."

He cocked his head. "You'll...what?"

"I'm afraid you'll have to come back later."

"I don't want to come back," he said. "I just drove six hours, all the way from the Bay Area, after working through the night. I'm exhausted, and I'd like to get some sleep. Can you help me out here?"

His impatience irritated her. But since the accident, she'd been so filled with rage she was almost relieved he was willing to give her a target. "No, I'm afraid I can't."

He stiffened. "Excuse me?"

"I can't let some stranger into the house, not unless Maxi specifically asks me to." Even if this guy was telling the truth, forcing him to leave would not only bring her great pleasure, it would give her a chance to feed Maxi's parrot before hiding the key under the mat. Then there would be no need for further interaction. He wouldn't see her, and she wouldn't have to watch the shock, recognition and pity cross his face.

Pity was by far the worst, but none of it was fun.

"If I have the code to the gate, I must've gotten it from somewhere, right?" he argued. "Isn't it logical to assume that Maxi is the one who gave it to me?"

"That's a possibility, but there are other possibilities."

"Like..."

"Maybe you hopped the fence or got it from one of the staff?"

His chest lifted in an obvious effort to gather what little patience he had left. "I assure you, if I was a thief, I would not present myself at your door."

"I can appreciate why. But I'm responsible for what goes on here right now, which means I can't take any chances."

"You won't be taking any chances!" he argued in exasperation. "If anything goes missing or gets damaged, I'll replace it."

What was there to guarantee that? "The art Maxi owns can't be replaced," she said and thought she had him. Maxi had told her so himself. But this stranger said the only thing that could trump her statement.

"Except by me, since I'm the one who created most of it in the first place," he said drily.

"You're an artist?" she asked but only to buy a second or two while she came to grips with a few other things that had just become apparent. If he was one of the artists Maxi collected, he wasn't some obscure talent. Yet…he couldn't be more than thirty. And he certainly didn't look too important shivering in a stretched-out T-shirt, on which the word *Perspective* was inverted, and jeans that had holes down the front.

"I am," he replied. "And you are…the house sitter, I presume?"

She heard his disparaging tone. He wondered who the hell she was to tell him what to do. He thought he mattered more than she did. But that came as no surprise: she'd already pegged him as arrogant. She was more concerned about the fact that Maxi might've referred to her as a menial laborer. Is that the way her former producer thought of her now? It was only a few months ago that she'd been the most promising actress in Hollywood. Certainly she'd attained more fame than this snooty artist—when it came to having her name recognized by the general public, anyway.

But what did it matter how high she'd climbed? She'd fallen back to earth so hard she felt as though she'd broken every bone in her body, even though the damage to her face was the only lingering injury she'd sustained in the accident. "I'm house-sitting, yes. But, like you, I'm a friend of Maxi's," she said vaguely.

Fortunately, he didn't seem interested enough to press her for more detailed information. She was glad of that.

"Fine. Look, *friend*." He produced his phone. "I have proof. This is the text exchange I had with Maxi just before his plane took off. As you can see, he says he has someone—*you*—staying in the guesthouse, but the main house is available, and I'm welcome to it. If you'll notice the time, you'll see that these texts took place just this morning."

Her heart sank as she read what he showed her: I have someone in the guesthouse. Just get the key from her.

"How long are you planning on being here?" she asked.

"Does it matter?" he replied.

It *did* matter. But this was Maxi's estate, and they were both his guests, so she had an obligation to treat him as well as he was accustomed to being treated. "Just a minute," she said and muttered a curse after she closed the door. *There goes all my privacy.*

She got the key from the kitchen drawer before cracking the door open just wide enough to slip her hand through. "Here you go, but I'll need your phone number so I can coordinate getting inside the house when I need to."

"The main house? Why would you need to get inside that?"

"I take care of the plants. As easy as that may sound, in a house that's over fourteen thousand square feet, it's no small job. And I have to take care of Kiki."

"Kiki?"

"Maxi's parrot."

"Maxi didn't say anything about a parrot."

"Well, he has one, and parrot-sitting requires more than throwing a handful of birdseed in a bowl." Maxi had taught her how to take care of Kiki the day before he left. Then he'd observed her for several hours, just to be sure she could do the job. Parrots could be finicky, and he knew Kiki wouldn't like him leaving. "I was also going to dust and vacuum once a week to keep things up, since the housekeeper is on holiday. But if you'd rather take over those chores, I can show you how to do it all."

"Nice try," he said. "Who are you—Tom Sawyer's sister? I'll let you handle the parrot and the rest of it. And don't worry. I won't get in your way."

She continued to hang back so he couldn't see her face. "You'd rather have me invade your space?"

"I won't mind as long as you're quiet. That bird isn't going to be too loud, is it? Because I typically work at night and sleep during the day."

She barely refrained from rolling her eyes. The tortured artist was such a cliché. "She sleeps at night, so she should be quiet while you create your latest masterpiece. During the day you might hear her speak or squawk or whatever."

"She speaks?"

"She says a few phrases. Maxi used to have a dog, so she learned to bark, too."

He narrowed his eyes as if he wasn't quite sure she was being straight with him. "Sounds annoying."

"It's the reason he didn't replace his dog once it passed. But you don't have anything to worry about. She lives in an aviary in the middle of the house that goes up through both stories. The plants and the glass walls capture most of the noise, so you shouldn't hear much—not unless she's upset."

"How often does that happen?"

"She's an animal. Emotional episodes aren't scheduled. If we keep her happy, it might not happen at all."

"Good to know. I'll make you a copy of the key." He turned to go but she spoke again.

"You don't feel it would be presumptuous to copy someone else's house key?"

"Not if I'm going to be staying for a few months. I consider it a practical matter. Why? Would you rather try to pass it back and forth between us?"

Her heart sank at learning he'd be living on the premises for more than just the weekend, but she tried to focus on the coordination sharing a key might require. "No. A copy will be fine."

"That's what I thought," he said and cracked the first smile she'd seen him wear. He was getting in the house right away and would have his own key, and she'd be taking care of the bird. That he was gloating annoyed her, but she had to admit that his smile absolutely transformed his face. He was much more handsome than she'd wanted to acknowledge—in a dark-lord-of-the-underworld sort of way. She thought of all the beautiful people she'd encountered in Los Angeles and believed he could easily hold his own.

She'd been able to compete in that arena once, too. As far back as she could remember, people outside the tight-knit Mennonite community in which she'd been raised had gushed about her beauty, even though her parents had done everything they could to downplay it. They and the other members of their church believed it put her at risk of losing her soul through the sin of vanity. But she didn't have to worry about that anymore. She'd lost all the beauty she'd once had.

"Welcome to Silver Springs," she said, her voice as frigid as the wind whipping at his clothes. He hadn't bothered to put on a coat before climbing out of the car. Getting the key hadn't been as quick as he'd obviously expected.

Instead of being offended by her response, he chuckled as he strode off. She didn't even know his name. But that was fine with her. If he did anything wrong, Maxi could deal with it. She didn't plan on interacting with him again.

His presence only meant there was now someone on the property she'd try to avoid.

CHAPTER TWO

"There's something wrong with that woman," Seth Turner grumbled as he stalked back to his car to get his luggage. She'd acted so strangely. Instead of opening the door wide enough to introduce herself, she'd hung back so far he couldn't even see her face. Maybe having a stranger come to the door had frightened her. But she hadn't acted frightened, exactly. He'd gotten the feeling it was something else. And she'd kept up the odd behavior even after he'd proven himself a friend of Maxi's. What was up with that? When Maxi told him there was someone on the property who could let him in, he'd thought it would be a *good* thing. He'd assumed this person would be a caretaker, someone who would watch over the place while Maxi was gone, allowing Seth to focus exclusively on his work and what he'd come to Silver Springs to accomplish. He hadn't expected to share the property with one of Maxi's friends, especially not one as prickly as himself.

How long are you planning on being here?

He'd heard the disappointment in her voice. Neither of them wanted company. That was apparent.

But even with her living only fifty yards away, he didn't have a better option than to stay here while he could. He didn't want to be in a hotel for an extended period. He didn't want to stay with his brothers. Two of them owned homes in the area, but they each had a wife and kids. How could he squeeze in with them? He'd have no place to work. And he certainly didn't want to go home to his mother's house, not with everything she did to celebrate the holidays. He'd be faced with the scents of pine and gingerbread, the unrelenting cheer of Christmas carols and the sight of an elaborately decorated tree every time he came into the house. There'd be no way to avoid those things. He'd agreed to help out at New Horizons Boys & Girls Ranch, the boarding school for troubled youth Aiyana had founded, but he refused to get involved with anything else. He especially didn't want to be available to his mother 24/7: that would come soon enough, when Maxi returned and he *had* to move home. Aiyana was too worried about him right now, and feeling the weight of that concern only made life more difficult. He'd cope with this Christmas like he had every Christmas since Shiloh's death, by doing all he could to avoid the festivities that made her loss that much more poignant.

At least he'd have the main house to himself.

Most of the time, anyway.

His phone signaled an incoming call. After unlocking the house, he dropped his luggage in the entryway so he could see who was trying to reach him.

It was his mother.

He punched the Accept button before he could miss Aiyana's call. He loved her more than any other person in the world—since Shiloh had passed away—which was why he'd agreed to come home and mentor several of her students. She felt strongly that a special few had the talent, as well as the desire, to do what he did, which was all fine and good, but he had a sneaking suspicion she'd scheduled it at this time of year on purpose, so that he wouldn't spend Christmas alone.

That should've bothered him; he didn't like it when she meddled in his life. But he was sort of glad she'd done this. Closeting himself away in his house, where he had a studio that overlooked the Pacific Ocean, was starting to get to him.

Maybe Aiyana could tell he was sliding into a dark place. His mother was nothing if not attuned to the needs of others. She always seemed to know when he was in trouble, even when he denied having a problem.

"Hey, Mom."

"How close are you?"

"Just arrived."

"Thank God."

"What do you mean? It was only a six-hour drive."

"That may be true, but the way you run yourself ragged, I had no idea if you'd even slept before starting out."

He didn't comment on the sleeping aspect of her statement. He'd always struggled with insomnia. It'd been several days since he'd had more than a few hours of sleep, so the drive had been much more difficult than he was making it sound. "I'm fine. Don't worry. I'm going to nap for a few hours before you come over."

"Good plan. By the way, I have the art supplies you shipped to my house. Cal and I will bring that stuff over to you in his truck."

"I really appreciate it. There was no way it would all fit in my car."

"*You* barely fit in that car," she said, joking. "Anyway, it's not a problem. Cal's an old cowboy. He's used to hauling things."

"Cal's a good guy. I'm looking forward to seeing you both tonight."

"Eli and Gavin and their families are coming, too."

"Good."

"I've missed you—and I'm excited to see the house."

It was a gloomy, overcast day. He flipped on the light and

found himself standing in the middle of a giant marble entryway with twenty-foot ceilings. A huge chandelier hung over a pedestal table featuring a soapstone sculpture he'd created himself, and two flights of stairs made with black iron railings, one on each side, curved up to a second story. The aviary that housed the bird was on the other side of his *Young Man Dreaming*.

"It's nice," he said. "I can't believe you've never been here."

Maxi was one of Aiyana's biggest benefactors. He donated huge amounts of money to help keep the school running, which was how he'd first become aware of Seth's work. Seth also contributed to the yearly fundraiser. His mother auctioned off a piece of his work at the end of the night as the grand finale, and Maxi had bought several of those pieces, as well as others—some paintings, too—directly from him.

"Why would you be surprised? Maxi and I talk on the phone occasionally, and we're always friendly if we see each other in town, but I don't know him quite as well as you do."

Seth didn't know him all that well, either. Maxi emailed him or called once in a while. He was always interested in what Seth was doing next. But their relationship mostly revolved around Seth's work. They'd never hung out together. Since Shiloh's death, Seth hadn't really hung out with anyone.

He didn't correct her, however. He just hoped she wasn't offended that he'd chosen to stay here instead of with her. He hated the thought that it might make her feel bad, but he'd known he wouldn't be able to hold out for the entire three months she needed him if he didn't have a place where he could retreat. Being around his family, seeing his brothers so happy and busy with their wives and children, only made him feel empty by contrast. And last year he'd learned just how much Christmas could exaggerate that effect. "You'll love it."

He thought of the woman staying in the guesthouse but decided not to mention her. He'd run to the store, before he slept, and have a key made. Then he'd walk it over and forget about her—as much as he could.

"Okay. Eli and Gavin are eager to see you, so call me when you get up."

"Sounds good." He had seven brothers he'd grown up with since he turned fourteen, but none were genetically linked to him. The one thing they did have in common was that they all came from tragic backgrounds, and Aiyana had adopted each one of them after they'd first been a student at her school. Only Eli and Gavin, the two oldest, still lived in town. They worked at New Horizons with Aiyana. The rest were spread out, pursuing their own interests or going to college, but most would be returning for Christmas within the next two weeks. "I'll see you soon."

"Seth?"

He could tell by the change in her tone that she had something serious to say. "Yes?"

"I ran into Shiloh's mother the other day."

His throat immediately tightened. "And?"

"She asked if you were coming home for Christmas."

He suddenly felt exhausted, as if he'd spent the entire day fighting an intense battle instead of driving a car. Maybe that was because every day was a battle for him.

Closing his eyes, he drew a deep breath. "I'll have to pay them a visit."

"That would be nice." There was a slight pause. "Would you like me to go with you?"

Definitely not. That was something he had to do alone. But it wasn't going to be easy to face his late wife's parents. Because they'd wanted her to finish her degree and marry someone else, someone with less baggage and more potential—not a penniless, struggling artist with no plans of going to college—they'd been furious when she'd dropped out and moved to San Francisco to be with him. At the time, he'd been determined to prove that he was the best thing for her. But they'd been right. Had Shiloh remained in school, she'd probably still be alive.

"That's okay." He didn't need his mother complicating what would already be a difficult visit. "I've got it."

"You sure?"

By the time Shiloh died, he'd achieved some success in the art world, which had enabled him to build a decent relationship with her parents—decent enough that he felt obligated to see them.

But he almost wished they still hated him. It would make things easier now. "I got it," he said.

Tia parted the drapes and craned her neck to be able to see the driveway. The Porsche Taycan driven by her new property mate was still parked where it had been since he'd knocked to say he was leaving the key on her doormat.

Damn. She'd been hoping Maxi's new guest would go out again—for groceries or something—which would give her the opportunity to traipse over to the main house. She had to take care of Kiki. Maxi had said the bird needed daily company. He was afraid his beloved pet would fall into depression without consistent companionship, and Tia was supposed to make sure that didn't happen.

But she didn't want to run into the man who was staying there now.

She bit her lip as she tried to decide what to do. Maybe she could slip inside, take care of Kiki and get out without being heard. It wasn't just her face. She didn't want to be recognized, didn't want to field the questions that seeing her would inspire. And she didn't want him telling anyone she was in town, because then she'd feel like she had in LA: that there were people lurking around, trying to get a photograph they could sell. It made her feel besieged, unable to escape or move about freely.

How could Maxi have invited someone else to stay? She'd

felt safe from the curiosity of the world here, but that security had lasted for only two days.

Was she making too big a deal of it? The man she'd spoken to didn't seem the type to care too much about fame. If he was that popular, he was famous himself, at least in some circles. Maybe who she was and her connection to Hollywood wouldn't matter to him, and he wouldn't tell anyone about it.

After the success of *Expect the Worst*, she doubted it would go that way, but one could always hope…

She checked the clock. Nearly seven. She needed to get over there. She'd already put off Kiki's care as long as she felt comfortable.

She went into the bathroom and covered her scars with bandages as though she'd just come from the hospital. The big white gauze squares were unsightly, but not as unsightly as what lay beneath. And the bandages hid how much her face had changed, so if Maxi's friend *did* recognize her and he decided to say something to someone, he couldn't reveal *too* much.

If she were lucky, she wouldn't even encounter him. That was the goal.

But when she stepped out, she found three more cars in the drive: a Cadillac Escalade, a Ford Explorer and a pretty Tesla. What was going on? Was this guy already throwing a party?

Maxi should be more careful about the people he allowed onto the property while he was out of town. But because she'd already gone to the trouble of covering the damaged part of her face and she needed to take care of the bird, she didn't turn back as she was tempted to do. She told herself that it was a good thing her new neighbor had company. If he was distracted, she had a far greater chance of getting in and out without being noticed.

Pulling her sweater tighter around her body—she'd been gaining weight with all the emotional eating she'd been doing— she hung back behind the vegetation until she could confirm there wasn't anyone in the yard. Then she hurried along the path leading to the main house and tried her key at the back door.

It didn't work. Of course.

With a sigh, she ducked her head and marched purposefully toward the front.

"Activity at the front door."

She froze the second the computerized voice of the security system announced her presence. But no one came to find out what was going on. She could hear voices in the kitchen/living-room area, and the conversation didn't even pause. Either no one had heard the security system, or they couldn't be bothered with it.

Breathing a sigh of relief, she moved swiftly to the aviary and entered through the small side door by the elevator—the only part of Kiki's home that wasn't glass.

Although she was an animal lover, she'd never even seen a live parrot, not up close. Being responsible for such a large and expensive bird made her a little nervous. She'd read on the internet that parrots had a strong bite, especially this breed, but Maxi had assured her that his macaw was tame. He'd insisted that as long as Kiki received the care she needed, she wouldn't get aggressive.

Tia could only trust that was true. It would be just her luck to be attacked by the darn thing.

She searched the trees. When she didn't spot Kiki right away, she nearly panicked, thinking the man who was staying here had accidentally—or on purpose—let the bird out. But then she spotted the bright red plumage and the yellow and blue feathers of Kiki's lower wings. The parrot was perched on one of the highest branches of the center and largest tree, which was surrounded by thick bamboo shoots, vines and ferns. Along the ground, there were boulders and even a small pond. Maxi had spared no expense.

"Uh-oh, here she comes," the bird said, startling Tia. It was almost as if Kiki was outing her for being in the house.

"Shh." She put a finger to her lips.

"Shh," the bird mimicked. "Be quiet."

Apparently, this wasn't the first time she'd ever been shushed. Maxi had probably told her to be quiet a thousand times when she was barking like a dog.

Tia glanced around to make sure no one had heard the noise. Kiki sounded loud inside the atrium, but Tia knew the sounds were somewhat muted beyond the glass. Maxi had seen to that when he planned the enclosure.

Seeing nothing alarming, she crouched behind the foliage and filled Kiki's bowl. "Here you go. It's time to eat."

"Time to eat," the parrot responded, punctuating those words with a squawk before repeating them a second and a third time.

When Tia stepped away from the feeding dish, Kiki flew down to enjoy the fruit, nuts and seeds that were her dinner. Maxi had said she ate ten to fifteen percent of her body weight each day and, for the most part, could have anything healthy that humans could eat, but Tia wasn't going to take any chances. She planned to stick strictly to what Maxi had provided.

As Kiki pecked at her food, she watched Tia out of the penetrating small eye on the left side of her head. Kiki knew Tia was a stranger, so Tia wasn't planning to get too close. Not yet, anyway.

While waiting for Maxi's pet to finish eating, Tia remained huddled in the corner in case someone in the house decided to peer into the aviary. She couldn't see any faces pressed to the glass, but the aviary had been built such that it could be seen from many rooms. Even if it hadn't provided a home for such a spectacular pet, it would be an awesome sight with the way Maxi had brought the outdoors into his house.

Maxi had given Tia a Koosh ball to toss to Kiki. He said she played fetch like a dog and that retrieving it would help keep her stimulated. Tia hadn't brought it out yet, though. Maxi had said Kiki loved it so much, she wouldn't eat her dinner if she saw it.

"That's a good girl," Tia said.

This time Kiki didn't create an echo, and Tia shifted to sit cross-legged in an attempt to get more comfortable. When Tia learned she'd be caring for a parrot, she'd done some studying and learned that these birds could live to be fifty years old. That was surprising, but it was equally surprising to read that it was difficult to determine the sex of a parrot. Physical examination didn't make it obvious; it required a DNA test.

Had Maxi ever had Kiki tested? Or had he decided—from her beauty or something else—that he'd simply assume she was a female?

"Are you really a girl?" she whispered to the bird.

"Pretty girl," the bird responded, adding a sharp whistle. "Pretty girl."

Shoot! Again, Tia looked around, expecting the man she'd met earlier to be peering in at them.

But she didn't see anyone. Maybe whoever was at the house had already looked their fill and they were doing something else now. She was pretty sure they were eating.

She stayed in the atrium with Kiki for over an hour. Maxi said ninety minutes would be ideal, but she was too nervous to hang out any longer. She played fetch with Kiki, gave her some pumpkin seeds, which Maxi said she'd love, and decided to get out while she could. But the bird started to whistle as soon as she got up.

"Pretty girl. Pretty girl," Kiki said, over and over.

Tia guessed Kiki could sense that her playmate was about to leave and didn't want that to happen. She was making so much noise that Tia was hesitant to open the door.

"Shh," she said again, but that only started the bird saying, "Be quiet. Be quiet." *Squawk.* "Be quiet."

Tia tossed the Koosh ball to the other side of the atrium and let herself out as the bird swooped down to get it.

"Shh, be quiet," she heard Kiki say as she closed the door.

Tia had just reached the front door when she heard voices— and they were getting louder.

She hadn't wanted to be seen before. But she *definitely* didn't want to be seen now, for all the same reasons and one other— she'd let herself in without knocking. They hadn't set up a routine, and he'd given her the key, so she felt as though she had a way to justify her actions. But she was still loath to run into him, so she ducked into the first room she could reach without making any noise.

It was a bedroom suite, but it wasn't one most people would choose if they had their pick of all seven bedrooms in the house, which was why she was so surprised to find a suitcase on the floor.

Oh, no! She'd chosen the room where Maxi's friend was staying.

She could hear the man she'd spoken to earlier tell his visitors—a collection of adults and some children, judging by the jumble of older and younger voices—that it'd been great to see them.

She'd been right to get out of the entry hall even if she had ducked into his bedroom. They were leaving—she would've run into them, no question.

Her heart pounded as they made plans to see each other tomorrow and finished their goodbyes. They seemed to be relatives of some sort, but she wasn't focused on deciphering the specific connections between them. She was trying to figure out a way to escape.

There was a door that led into a private garden. She remembered that. But she also remembered it was enclosed with a high wall and no gate.

She was deliberating on whether or not she could make it to

the back entrance when silence fell, but then footsteps began to cross the marble entryway, once again coming in her direction.

No way would she be caught in his bedroom! With nowhere to go to escape and no time in which to find a good hiding place, she dropped to the floor and slid under the bed.

CHAPTER THREE

Seth's eyes slowly scanned the room. She was in here somewhere. After he'd heard the computerized voice of the alarm system announce that someone had come into the house, he'd seen movement in the atrium. He'd assumed it was the woman he'd met at the guesthouse—who else could it be?—and thought she'd eventually come out and say something to him. But when he'd nearly encountered her in the entryway while walking his family to the door, she'd darted away, her long black hair flying behind her. And he knew where she'd gone because his bedroom suite was the only room close by.

What could she possibly want *in his room*? And what was Maxi thinking, having someone so strange take over the care of his property?

He was about to call out to let her know the jig was up. He had no idea if she was in the bathroom, had snuck out to the private garden—although the alarm would probably have notified him if she'd used a door to the outside—was hiding in the closet or what. But just as he opened his mouth, he glanced in the full-length mirror next to the TV and saw the bottom of her sneakers.

She was under the bed.

Rather than let her know he was on to her, he decided to teach her a lesson by trapping her under there for a few more minutes. And just to make her as uncomfortable as possible, he got his razor from his suitcase and stripped down to his boxers before sitting on the end of the bed to watch TV while he shaved. This was what he'd be doing if she weren't around. If she was going to hide in his room, she had to understand that she might see more of him than she ever cared to.

He liked imagining how much it must've made her squirm when she heard the plop of his clothes hit the floor and could barely hold back his laughter. He was diabolical. The skittish creature he'd met had to be *dying* to escape. He thought the noise of his shaver might make her feel safe enough to crawl out and try to sneak back into the entryway, at which point he'd let her know she could come over to take care of the bird and the plants at designated times but could not invade his privacy by sneaking around the place.

Pretending to be searching for a good show, he flipped through television channels while he shaved and continued to keep an eye on the reflection in the mirror.

Her feet moved as she inched toward the edge of the bed closest to the door. She was getting ready to make a dash for it. He smiled to think how easy it was going to be to catch her.

But when she didn't dare to try and he was finished shaving, he grew tired of the game.

Having earlier hauled the sculpture he'd created all the way up to the gallery/office on the top floor, along with some canvases and other painting supplies, he wanted to grab a shower before he started work. So he put his razor away, turned off the TV and left the room as though he was going into the kitchen.

Surely, she'd bolt now, he thought and hid on one side of the doorway.

He didn't have to wait long. She came out of the room almost immediately. But when he stepped over to confront her, she was running so fast she barreled right into him.

Tia felt like she'd just hit a brick wall. Pain exploded in her right cheek, which wasn't fully healed to begin with, and she stumbled back. She would've crumpled to the floor if Maxi's new guest hadn't caught her by the shoulders.

"What were you doing in my room?" he growled.

He was so much taller, she found herself staring at his bare chest and, somehow, through the fog of pain, remembered him taking off his clothes. She was afraid to look down for fear he'd taken off everything. But it was hard to be too concerned about nudity, his or anyone else's, when her face felt like it was on fire. She struggled to blink back the tears that sprang up while trying to get some of the bandages, which had come loose in the collision, to stick like they had before. "I—I came over to take care of Kiki. You know...you know that's my responsibility."

"Is it your responsibility to sneak into my bedroom, too? Why'd you do that? Are you some kind of thief? What's wrong with you?"

She tilted her head back to look up at him—and that was when the bandages and, probably, the tears registered. She knew because she could see the shock that came over his face.

"Oh, my god!" he exclaimed. "I'm sorry. I didn't mean to hurt you. Are you okay? *What happened to you?*"

"N-nothing!" Still rattled from the unexpected blow, she jerked away and stumbled to the door, leaving it standing open as she fled.

"Holy shit." Seth stared at the square of pale yellow the porch light formed on the marble floor. He felt like a total jerk—and sort of ridiculous standing there in his underwear. The game he'd been having so much fun playing suddenly just seemed cruel. No wonder she'd hung back in the darkness when he appeared, unannounced at her door. No wonder she'd tried to slip in and take care of the bird without notice. She didn't want to be seen. And he could understand why. Something terrible had happened to her. Before she'd managed to cover her cheek, he'd caught a glimpse of the red, angry scars underneath those bandages, and he knew her injuries hurt, because he could see the tears filling her eyes.

"I'm such an idiot," he said with a groan. But…why hadn't Maxi warned him? All the man had to do was send a quick text.

Tempted to go after her, he took two steps toward the door. He wanted to make sure she understood that he really *was* sorry. But he doubted she'd talk to him. He couldn't imagine she would ever want to see him again.

After shutting the door, he returned to his room, where he found his pants and dug his cell phone from his pocket. He hadn't heard from Maxi since he'd been told he could stay on the property. He needed to talk to him.

Drawing a deep breath, he hit the Phone icon. It'd been long enough since they'd communicated that Maxi should've been able to fly halfway around the world by now.

But what time zone would he be in? Would he be awake and available?

Seth paced at the foot of the bed while he waited for the phone to ring.

"Hello?"

Relieved that Maxi had answered, he stopped moving. "There you are."

"What do you mean?" Maxi asked. "I only just got off the plane. Thanks to some congestion on the runway, we were stranded on the tarmac for hours, and we missed our connection. So now we're stuck at Charles de Gaulle Airport and can't get out of Paris for another eight hours. God, I hate flying. They make it as miserable as they possibly can, don't they?"

"Who's staying in the guesthouse?" Seth demanded without comment.

After a moment of silence, Maxi said, "I already told you. Tia Beckett's staying there. Why?"

"You never gave me a name. Who is she?"

"You don't know?"

Confused by this answer, Seth shoved a hand through his hair, which was getting so long it fell nearly to his shoulders. "How would I?"

"Do you live under a rock? She starred in my last film, *Expect the Worst.*"

"So she's an actress." Seth didn't get out much, and he certainly wasn't familiar with what was going on in Hollywood or the movie industry. He didn't care about any of that. But the title of the film certainly seemed appropriate to this situation.

"Yeah. Why?" Maxi asked. "Is something wrong?"

"We haven't exactly gotten off on the right foot," he admitted. "What happened to her face?"

"Oh, that. I thought I mentioned it. She was in a car accident shortly after the film's release. Ran a red light about a month ago."

"Was she drunk?"

"No. Alcohol wasn't involved. But it just about destroyed her face. You can imagine what that would do to an actress. She'll never look the same, no matter how much cosmetic surgery she gets, and that means she'll be unlikely to get the parts she would've gotten otherwise, which is unfortunate. She's talented. Really talented. I fully expect her to get an Oscar nod for my film. And I believe she deserves it."

Seth cringed as he remembered asking her if she was the house sitter. "And this talented actress is here, *taking care of your parrot*?" No one would expect that, would they?

"She needs somewhere to stay until she can get back on her feet."

"You mean to hide."

"You could put it that way, I guess. She's a big deal right now. The paparazzi have been in hot pursuit, and they'd love nothing more than to snap a picture of her injured face and sell it to the tabloids."

Seth pictured Tia's huge green eyes. Together with her dark coloring, they were spectacular. The second she'd met his gaze he'd realized that he was looking at something rare and beautiful.

"I'm providing her with some privacy so she can at least get through Christmas," Maxi was saying. "The holidays are hard after a loss."

Seth certainly understood that.

"And it's nice of her to feed Kiki while I'm gone. My wife feels Kiki will be good for her, too, and I agree. They'll provide each other with some companionship. It's not like a bird cares that Tia's no longer the beauty she was a month ago."

Seth pinched the bridge of his nose as he imagined what she'd been through. "It would've been good to know what I was getting into."

"I don't see how it makes any difference to you," Maxi said. "She's staying in the guesthouse. You're staying in the main house. I'd have you switch, so that she doesn't have to come there to take care of Kiki, but you were excited to have my office for your work. There's no space for what you do in the cottage. And it's not as if I can move Kiki. I—"

"Of course not. I would never expect your pet to be put out of her home," he broke in. "We'll make it work. Don't worry."

"Except that I'm already a little worried. What happened between you two?"

Seth should've been more generous in his thoughts and assumptions, should've waited until he knew more before drawing so many conclusions. But he'd gotten so little sleep lately and was dreading the holidays so much, he'd taken his frustrations out on her. "I just…bumped into her and accidentally hurt her, and I feel bad about it."

"You *hurt* her?"

Remembering the tears swimming in those incredible eyes made him want to kick himself. "Yeah, I thought… Never mind. It was a misunderstanding. But you forgot to let her know I was coming so…could you text her and tell her that… that I'm a friend and not as bad as she thinks? Let her know I feel terrible about our little accident." It wasn't actually an accident. He'd caused it. But he hated to own that. "Tell her I'd never purposely hurt her?"

"Okay. No problem. I got caught up and forgot about it, that's all. I'll do it right now."

"Thanks. I appreciate you letting me stay here, by the way. The house is spectacular," Seth replied, but it was difficult to focus on anything else when he had the image of Tia Beckett's terrible scars fixed in his mind.

Not many things would be worse for an actress, especially one who was just becoming famous.

Tia filled an ice pack and held it to her face while lying on the couch. That little episode had been a disaster. Not only had she *not* been able to get in and out of the main house without being noticed, she'd also made the whole thing worse by attempting to hide. Maxi's guest had stripped down, and she'd been under his bed like some kind of sick voyeur.

She was embarrassed for not simply stepping up and owning who she was and what'd happened to her instead of sneaking around, but the consequences loomed so large in her mind and she felt so fragile, she probably would've taken the same risk even if she had it to do over again.

Her phone signaled an incoming call.

She wasn't going to answer it. She didn't even want to look to see who it was. She was sure it would be Maxi wondering why she'd been in his friend's bedroom. No doubt the artist next door had called right away to report her. She'd seen how angry he was when he caught her; he'd had a right to be angry.

What was she going to tell Maxi, who'd been so good to her? Would he tell her to go back to LA?

Maybe she should. She had no business here.

But she liked Kiki. Having something to care for gave her a sense of purpose that distracted her—for a short time, anyway—from the terrible thoughts that tortured her these days. Thanks to Maxi, she'd been set up in a situation she'd thought she could tolerate.

And then he'd gone and invited someone else to stay on the property...

"What's happening to me?" she asked herself as the phone stopped ringing. She'd fallen into a nightmare and couldn't wake up. And yet she'd been so careful to avoid getting caught up in the drugs, alcohol and sex scandals that ruined so many careers, especially in Hollywood. The last thing she'd wanted to do was to prove her family, friends and other church members—all those who'd been judging her for leaving—right. When she'd landed the lead role in *Expect the Worst*, her father had quoted Mark 8:36: *For what shall it profit a man, if he shall gain the whole world, and lose his own soul?*

She heard a text come in and ignored that, too. But after another thirty minutes, she had to glance at her phone. If it was Maxi, she felt too guilty ignoring him while she was staying on his property.

Sure enough, he'd been trying to reach her, and when she hadn't answered his call, he'd resorted to a message.

Are you okay? Seth said there was an incident, and he feels terrible about it. He wants you to know he's sorry and that he would never hurt you intentionally.

Putting the ice pack on the towel she'd gotten to absorb the condensation, she sat up to respond. She didn't know how much her new property mate had told Maxi, but Maxi didn't seem to be upset.

Or was that still coming?

Who is he?

Seth Turner. A phenomenal artist. Made the sculpture in the entryway when he was only eighteen. He usually focuses on the stages of a young man's life, and the way he does it is so insightful. I've never seen anyone else be able to use negative space the way he does.

She assumed *negative space* referred to the parts of the sculpture that weren't really there but were sort of assumed.

I have a whole series of his work in the library upstairs, Maxi added.

She didn't really care about Seth's work. She didn't care much about anything these days except finding a hole she could crawl into.

What's he in town for? A gallery showing?

She hoped it was something like that. Then maybe he'd change his mind about staying longer and leave after the show was over.

No. His mother lives in the area. Her name's Aiyana Turner. She founded New Horizons Boys & Girls Ranch 20something years ago.

Boys and girls ranch? What's that?

It's a boarding school just outside of town for troubled kids. Aiyana does a lot of good for a lot of people.

So Seth's home for the holidays?

Yeah. He said he was going to teach an art class at the school for his mother, so he's probably home for that, too.

She sighed. Teaching sounded long-term.

I don't want to get in his way, she wrote. Maybe I should head back to LA.

Definitely not! He won't bother you. That's what he wanted me to tell you. And there's no way I'd trust him with Kiki. He's a great guy—don't get me wrong—but I can't see him taking care of a parrot.

A tear rolled slowly down her good cheek—until she dashed it away. She couldn't stay here. Not with Seth Turner around. But she didn't feel as though she could abandon Kiki.

She couldn't face returning to Los Angeles, either.

Briefly, she considered going home to Iowa. Her mother and father lived on a small farm, like almost everyone else of their faith. She could go back there, but she knew what she'd face. "I told you it was a mistake to go to LA," her parents would say, and maybe she'd never summon the courage to stand against them and leave again. That community was so closed off from the rest of the world, it was like an alternate universe.

Besides, her sister and her sister's husband had lost their house and barn in a fire, and her parents had taken in their entire family, which included five kids under the age of ten. Tia wasn't even sure there'd be a place for her to sleep.

No, she couldn't go home. She'd shrivel up and die if she

had to weather their disapproval—the disapproval of the entire Mennonite community—on top of what she was going through already.

You'll stay, won't you? Maxi wrote.

She stared at those words. Certainly dealing with one temperamental artist would be easier than going back to LA, where the accident happened and there was a much greater threat of the paparazzi catching up with her. Easier than returning to her parents' small farmhouse forty miles outside of Cedar Rapids, too.

Sure.

Thank you. I know it doesn't seem like it right now, but everything's going to be okay.

She sent a thumbs-up to make him think she believed that. But right now it didn't feel as though anything would ever be okay again.

After putting her phone on the coffee table, she curled onto her side and put the ice pack on her face. She had a headache from colliding with Seth Turner, and the pain in her face seemed to radiate into her brain, but that was probably more from the nasal pressure and congestion caused by crying.

She was just drifting off to sleep when she heard pounding on the door. "Tia, it's Seth."

Her heart skipped a beat as she came back to full awareness. He knew her name and probably who she was—thanks to Maxi. But surely he didn't expect her to answer. Even if he did, she wasn't going to get up, let alone let him in. He could stand out there and knock for hours in the cold for all she cared. When she was feeling better, she'd get his number from Maxi and text him to work out a schedule. Then she'd go over to take care of Kiki when he was out of the house or busy working.

There was no reason their paths had to cross, not if they were careful.

"I know you probably don't want to come to the door, and that's okay. But I thought maybe you could use a hot meal." There was a pause before he added, "It's good old-fashioned comfort food from a little diner in town called the Eatery. I think you'll like it. I got the fried chicken with twenty herbs, garlic mashed potatoes and gravy and the best gluten-free corn bread you've ever tasted."

She wanted to say, "That's okay. I'm good." But she didn't trust her voice not to crack, and she was afraid responding would only start a dialogue between them.

Besides, he didn't need to bring her food. She'd had more than enough calories today. All she'd been doing was eating. She hadn't had the energy to make anything tastier or healthier than a peanut butter and jelly sandwich since she'd been released from the hospital, so it had been mostly snack food, but it wasn't his responsibility to feed her.

She held her breath while she waited to see what he'd do next. Maybe he'd get mad, take the food and stomp off. She hoped he would. Then he'd know to stay away from her, and their cohabitation would be easier.

"I'm leaving it here by the door." Surprisingly, he didn't seem mad. He sounded patient, considering he'd just caught her lurking in his bedroom while he was undressed.

After that, she heard nothing. She listened carefully, but when several minutes of silence passed, she decided he must be gone.

Pulling up the blanket she'd dragged out to the couch earlier, she stared at the painting on the wall across from her. Black and white, with a simple, thin metal frame, it was conceptual, not a lifelike representation, but it appeared to be a woman caught in the throes of a scream that no one else could hear. As if to

emphasize the anguish she was feeling deep in her soul, there
was a dash of red filling her wide-open mouth.

Yes, Tia thought. I understand you because you're me.

CHAPTER FOUR

Friday, December 17

The school had grown quite a bit since Seth had attended New Horizons. Not only was there a girls' side these days, the boys' side had a new computer lab, which was quite extensive, a community center for social events and a section of campus devoted to animal husbandry, where he could hear the bleating of sheep and the lowing of cows. The auto shop wasn't new, but it had been updated, and he was looking forward to when the school would be able to add an arts and humanities building. That was partly why he'd agreed to return and tutor a small class of handpicked students who showed artistic potential. He planned to do some fundraising while he was here, so the building he dreamed of could become a reality, and he knew it would be much easier to draw money and attention to Silver Springs if he was on campus. With what he could raise and what he was willing to contribute himself, he hoped they'd be able to break ground this summer.

"You're quiet today," his mother commented as they walked across campus together. Although he wouldn't start teaching until after the holidays when the new semester began, she was excited to show him his classroom. "Is something wrong?"

"No, nothing," he replied, but he couldn't quit thinking about Tia Beckett. He'd spent much of the night wondering how badly she was hurt, if he should assume she was okay or if he should walk back over to the cottage and try to reassure himself.

In the end, he didn't go over because she'd made it clear she preferred to be left alone. He preferred to be alone himself since Shiloh died. So he understood. But...did she have anyone else who was checking in on her? Showing they cared and helping her through this rough patch?

Maxi had indicated that Tia wasn't from Silver Springs, so Seth couldn't imagine anyone *here* was keeping a close eye on her.

"Are you nervous about teaching?" his mother asked.

Truth be told, he wasn't looking forward to it. That type of thing was so far out of his comfort zone. And he wasn't convinced the elusive *extra* that'd made him successful could be taught. He'd started when he was only eighteen, with almost no training. To him that meant it had to be at least partly instinctual.

But that wasn't what he said. Unwilling to admit, even to her, that he was anxious about teaching, he said, "Why would I be nervous?"

"Because you don't like being the center of attention. It's not your thing. I almost feel bad for asking you. I wouldn't have if I didn't think it'd be good for you as well as the students."

He sent her a sidelong glance. "Thanks for the opportunity."

As she chuckled at his sarcasm, he noticed that the lines bracketing her eyes and mouth were growing deeper. His diminutive mother, with her long black hair almost always worn in a braid down her back, her brightly colored clothing and heavy turquoise jewelry, was finally starting to age. But she still had that sparkle in her eyes that seemed to make everything okay.

He wasn't sure how she stayed so unfailingly optimistic in the face of what she'd seen, working with so many troubled youth, but she pulled it off beautifully. "I predict you'll thank me when it's all said and done," she said. "Working with these kids is so rewarding."

"I'll settle for *worth it*," he said drily. "*Worth it* should be attainable."

Still laughing, she slid her arm through his. "And the assembly? Will you do that, too?"

She'd asked if she could gather the whole student body together—or what was left of it since the kids who got to go home for Christmas would be gone by then—to hear him speak about his career and his work. That was when they planned to announce the winners of the art contest he'd sponsored just after school started. If someone won who was gone, they could check the website for the list or learn once they returned to school, but she wasn't going to hold off because she always did her best to entertain those who had nowhere to go and make the holidays fun for them, too. He wanted to support her in that, but he wasn't anxious to speak in front of such a large group, since probably half the student body would still be around, any more than he was excited to teach next semester. "You know I will."

"You're just not happy about it," she said, joking.

They'd reached the classroom so he didn't bother to comment as she showed him inside. "This is where you'll be teaching," she said. "I've had Gavin remove the chairs and desks and set up these stations."

Seth walked slowly around the room. His brother had already covered the carpet with a tarp, too. "And the girls' class?"

"Rather than sacrifice two classrooms, I'll have the girls report here."

"Allow them to cross onto the boys' side?" he teased as if it was some big, dramatic thing. "That's unusual, isn't it?"

"We have dances and joint assemblies with the girls, so it's not *too* remarkable. You'll teach the boys on Mondays and Wednesdays and the girls on Tuesdays and Thursdays. And who knows? If you're happy with the way things are going, maybe you'll extend the class or do a second session to finish out the semester."

He scowled at her. She hated that he was living so far away, had been trying to get him to return to Silver Springs ever since Shiloh died. *Why are you still in San Francisco in that mausoleum of a house by yourself? You need to be around people. You need to start living again. Come home where you have a family who cares about you.*

"Don't get your hopes up." He held his hand in the classic stop gesture. "I told you I can't stay any longer than what I've already committed to. I have a gallery showing coming up and need to get ready for that. It's important. But I'll give you one term."

She nodded, seemingly satisfied—for the moment. He knew this subject would come up again. "Fair enough," she said.

"Did you get the list of student supplies I sent you?" he asked.

"I did, and I already got the order in, so everything will be here when we start the new semester."

"Good, because I want to focus on something else while I can."

"And that is?"

"Raising money for the humanities center I've been talking about."

Her eyebrows slid up. "You're going to do that now?"

"Why not? Might as well get started while I'm here. It's the end of the year. The kind of people who would be in a position to help might also be looking for a tax break." Maybe by Christmas he'd be so deeply immersed in the project he'd scarcely notice the holidays, and this year wouldn't be quite as empty as the others. He was just as eager for that as he was to get the center started.

"If you really want it, I have no doubt you'll get it," she said. "Once you make up your mind, nothing can stand in your way."

Except himself. He'd long been his own worst enemy. "We'll see."

After they left the classroom, he took Aiyana to lunch at her favorite Italian place off campus so they could have some time alone together. Then he dropped her off at the school and swung by the grocery store, where he gathered fresh fruits and vegetables, hummus, plant-protein wraps, POM Juice and other items to fill the fridge and cupboards at Maxi's. He didn't want to have all his meals delivered. He was making a renewed commitment to eating healthier and exercising.

He was just coming out of the store when he caught sight of Shiloh's mother trying to get one cart separated from another at the other entrance. Although she hadn't noticed him, that could easily change.

He needed to call her and Graham and go visit them. They'd be offended if they found out he was in town and he hadn't let them know he was coming. But he dreaded that encounter.

So he stood there, waiting to see if Lois would turn around— and was nearly rammed from behind by an older gentleman who was trying to wheel an overloaded cart to his car.

"What're you doing in the way?" the old guy snapped, his scruffy gray eyebrows knitting above a hawkish nose.

Seth didn't respond, but he stepped to one side, and by the time he looked up again, Lois was gone.

When Seth got home, he grabbed the groceries from his back seat but hesitated before carrying them into the house. What was Tia Beckett doing? Had she already been over to feed Kiki?

He doubted it. It was only midafternoon. Judging from what she seemed to have been doing yesterday at this time, he guessed she was still sleeping. He had a feeling that was about all she'd been doing since the accident, which wasn't a good sign.

He thought about going over to check on her but ultimately shrugged off his concern. They hadn't bumped into each other *that* hard. And she wasn't his responsibility. He was only in town to appease his mother, to teach at the school that'd brought him a family and to raise enough money to build a humanities center so that he could give back to the woman who'd given him so much. That was it—besides work, of course. He had deadlines to meet. Those deadlines were everything to him, what helped *him* keep going since he'd lost Shiloh.

Which was why it was odd that, after he put away the groceries and went up to the large office that comprised a large section of the top floor of Maxi's house, he couldn't seem to focus on what he was creating. He liked the sculpture. A contemporary piece commissioned for an office in the business district of San Francisco, it was a businessman hurrying to work with his briefcase falling open and pages and pages getting caught in the wind—to represent the change caused by the digital revolution and how the old ways were disappearing in the face of progress—and he felt a great deal of pressure to get it done. The attorney who'd commissioned it called almost every week, asking when it would be ready. But instead of seeing the finished piece in his mind's eye, like he usually did when he set to work, he kept picturing Tia Beckett's green eyes brimming with tears as she'd looked up at him last night.

Frustrated that he couldn't let go of the distraction, he finally dropped his chisel and hammer and stalked over to the window. He could see the roof of the guesthouse from his vantage point—the front and back wall of the office was made of glass—but seeing her roof didn't tell him anything.

Forcing himself to return to his work area, he put away his tools and cleaned up. He was supposed to have had plenty of time and space to create while he was here. Sure, Maxi had mentioned that he had someone staying in the guesthouse, but he hadn't acted as though it would be a big deal. He hadn't even told Seth her name—or about the damn bird that was beginning to squawk.

"Pretty girl… Pretty girl."

Kiki wasn't loud. But he could still hear her. That was irritating enough.

"There she is." Squawk. "Pretty girl."

"You gotta be kidding me." Grabbing his laptop, he carried it to the desk in the center of the room. What was Tia Beckett normally like? Had she been odd before this whole thing happened?

Perhaps learning more about her would put his mind at ease, he thought and typed her name into a search engine.

Tons of links popped up, along with clips and ratings for *Expect the Worst*. He watched a couple of the clips first. Romantic comedies weren't his favorite. Since Shiloh had died, he eschewed love songs, too. But the film was obviously a success. Critics likened the movie to *Silver Linings Playbook*—a realistic but funny take on two damaged people who manage to find love—and most said it compared favorably. During the first few weeks, it had garnered much more at the box office than projected, some of which had been attributed to Tia's performance.

Once he'd read all he wanted to know about her role in the movie and the movie itself, he searched for information on the accident. There was some early speculation that drugs or alcohol had been involved, which made him wonder if Maxi knew what he was talking about—until he found an article on the website of a local LA news station.

Actress Tia Beckett, 27, of Expect the Worst *fame, was involved in a traffic accident late last night. After suffering extensive injuries, she was taken by ambulance to the hospital, where she is reported to be in stable condition. The driver of the other vehicle was also taken to the hospital for related injuries but has already been released. According to the police report, Ms. Beckett ran a red light while traveling to Beverly Hills from LAX. Alcohol and other substances were not a factor in the accident.*

"Were *not* a factor," he read out loud. Maxi had been right, after all.

Seth scrolled farther down the listings his query had produced and found her biography on Wikipedia.

She'd been born and raised in a small town in Iowa. The youngest of three, she'd left home as soon as she turned eighteen, took a bus across the country and arrived in LA with only ten bucks in her pocket, where she got a job hawking tickets for a comedy club while staying in a three-bedroom house with eighteen other people in what sounded like some kind of hippie commune. While there, she started taking acting classes. *Expect the Worst*, directed by Peter Wagoner and produced by Maxi Cohen, was her first feature film, but she did have some shorter-format credits: commercials and music videos and the like.

He went to her IMDb and clicked through the pictures he found online. Thanks to the incredible beauty of her eyes, Tia had been compared to Elizabeth Taylor. But in his mind, the comparison ended there. Tia had her own unique look, and it was far more exotic than Elizabeth Taylor's.

As he stared at one photograph, his favorite of what he'd seen so far, he shook his head. Tia had been beautiful, all right—fresh-faced and innocent. What'd happened was a tragedy on so many levels.

So…why hadn't she headed home after the accident? He felt she should be spending Christmas with her family, where someone could look after her. Did her parents and siblings realize she was completely alone? That she was hiding out in her producer's guesthouse in California when he wasn't even home?

Did they care?

With a sigh, he closed his laptop and rocked back. He had to go check on her. He was getting so worried he couldn't make himself hold off any longer.

Ignoring Kiki, who was saying *Shh…be quiet* in between barking like a dog, he jogged downstairs and marched out the front door and over to the guesthouse. He was in an untenable situation, he decided. He didn't want to live like this—worried about someone he didn't even know—for the next two months until Maxi returned and he moved over to his mother's house.

The food he'd bought was still on her doorstep. That was the first thing he noticed. "You couldn't have put it in the fridge?" he grumbled.

Except he was pretty sure she'd left it there for a reason. She was sending him a message: *I don't need you. Leave me alone.*

"Fine. I *will* leave you alone." He grabbed the bag, intending to go back to the main house. But he hadn't taken more than two steps before he reconsidered. If he didn't at least speak to her, he'd stew about it all night.

He was going to knock whether she liked it or not.

He hit the door hard enough to make sure it would wake her up if she was still sleeping. "Tia? It's Seth. Are you in there?"

That was a dumb question. Her old, beat-up car was parked in the driveway and didn't look as though it'd been moved since he'd left for New Horizons this morning. Why would she go anywhere? She was loath to let anyone see her.

"Can you please answer me? Kiki is squawking. I think she might need something."

"I'll be over to check on her soon."

Aha! Mentioning the bird had elicited a response. "I'm sorry about what happened when…when you came over yesterday. I heard the security system announce activity at the front door and thought you'd say something or just let yourself out again. I never expected to find you in my bedroom. But…never mind. I overreacted, for sure. Let's just say… I wasn't aware of your situation."

No response.

"Are you hungry? The food I brought is still out here. Maybe you're picky about what you eat, like me. Typical restaurant food isn't all that healthy."

Again, no answer.

"If I bring you something else, will you eat it?" he called through the door.

"No. Save your money" came her reply.

That wasn't the answer he'd been hoping for, but it sounded as though she was just on the other side of the wooden panel. At least he'd drawn her to the door. "Why not?"

"Because I'm not hungry. And you have other stuff to do like…create another giant sculpture or something."

That sounded flattering, he thought sarcastically. "You don't like my work?"

"I have no opinion on it."

But she'd seen it. One of his best pieces sat on a pedestal in the entryway of the main house—and there were more sculptures and paintings in other rooms. There could even be a piece or two in the guesthouse. Seth didn't know because he'd never seen it. This was his first time on the property. But he didn't say anything. "Okay. I'll let you get back to…to whatever it is you've been doing. I just wanted to make sure you were okay."

"I'm okay," she said flatly.

It was the right answer, but he could tell she was lying. She wasn't even *remotely* okay. She was drowning in depression. All the classic signs were there. He just didn't know what to do about it, except maybe… "I know someone who…who might be able to help you," he said.

"Help me do what?" came her disembodied voice.

"Feel better."

"Are you talking about a surgeon who can fix my face? Or a shrink who might be able to fix my mind? Because I think both of those things are impossible at this point."

"I was actually talking about my mom," he said simply.

"Your *mom*?"

He chuckled. "Granted, it sounds funny, but she…she knows

how to take care of people. And she's kind of a big deal around here. Everyone loves her. She's done so much good."

"Kudos to her for what she's been able to accomplish. But please don't call her. Don't call anyone. I'd really appreciate it if you didn't even let on that I'm here."

Because she was trying to disappear. That was what concerned him. How long would it take her to bounce back? *Would she bounce back?* Hollywood was replete with tragic stories of unstable actors who resorted to drug abuse and/or suicide. "Of course I'm not going to alert the press or anything like that. My mom would never say—"

She cracked the door open and peeked out with one eye, surprising him enough that he fell silent. "Don't get her involved," she reiterated. "Please. Promise me."

Seth wasn't out to make things any worse for Tia Beckett, but he was enough of a businessman to recognize an opportunity when he saw one. He had a bit of leverage in this situation, after all. "Come over tonight, and let me make you dinner, and you'll have my promise."

"No way," she said immediately.

With the lights off and the blinds drawn, it was dark in the cottage, as he'd expected, and she wouldn't open the door enough that he could see more than a sliver of her. "You have to feed and play with the bird, don't you? I just want to see you eat something, so that I can work."

"I'm not stopping you from working."

He was pretty sure she was wearing the same robe she'd had on yesterday. She wasn't getting up and getting dressed. She didn't seem to be doing much of anything. "Actually, you *are* keeping me from my work," he said. "I can't concentrate with you over here, feeling sorry for yourself."

"Go to hell," she said and shut the door.

He'd provoked her on purpose to see if she still had some fight in her and was relieved to find that she did. If she was going to recover, she'd need every bit of it. "Fine. But if you won't start acting like a normal person, I'll have to call the newspaper in the morning and let them know that the famous actress Tia Beckett is right here in Silver Springs," he called out.

"Do that and I'll leave," she called back to him. "Do *you* want to take care of Kiki while Maxi's gone?"

"Do you want the paparazzi waiting at the gate?" he countered. If she wouldn't take care of herself, he had to do *something.* As the only person who was aware of where she was and what she was doing—the only person nearby, anyway—he was sort of responsible for what happened to her.

He knew how bad it could get if she lost *all* hope, and he certainly didn't want to deal with that.

When she said nothing, he turned to look back at the main house. It would serve her right if he gave up and followed through with what he'd threatened. He could hire someone to come over and care for Kiki. But he couldn't help feeling sorry for Tia. So he offered her one last chance.

"It's just a meal," he said. "What will that hurt? I already know who you are, what happened in the accident and that this is where you're hiding from the world. I've already seen the scars you were trying to cover with those bandages yesterday, too. So there's nothing to be lost and everything to be gained by accepting my offer. All you have to do is assure me that you're okay, that you're taking care of yourself and eating, and I'll leave you alone."

She didn't answer.

He knocked again. "Tia? What's it going to be?"

Her words, when they came, were muted. "I'll be over later," she said grudgingly.

He smiled. He'd won this round. "Come at eight. I'll have dinner ready."

CHAPTER FIVE

Tia checked the mirror. She'd showered and dressed in a pair of black slacks and a cream wraparound sweater with pearl earrings, and she'd pulled her hair back in a low ponytail. She'd also put on some makeup, for the first time since the accident, and covered the damaged part of her face with bandages, just as she had last night. She couldn't stand the sight of her own scars—and if Seth had somehow missed how extensive they were, she wasn't going to give him a second chance to view them.

She understood what was resting on tonight. This was how he planned to assess her mental and physical well-being, so he'd know whether she could be trusted to stay on her own. If she wanted the peace and quiet—and privacy—she'd come to Silver Springs to obtain, she needed to convince him that she was coping with her recent tragedy.

That meant she'd have to rely on her acting ability now more than ever. Fortunately, she possessed the talent, and she was willing to put on a show it if it meant keeping Seth Turner from bothering her in the future.

After grabbing her coat, she forced herself to step into the cold, dark night. The fact that she'd cleaned up should reflect

well on her. That was one of the details he'd probably be assessing—one of the few indicators he had to judge by—so she'd
been determined to check those boxes.

She *could* get out of bed; she *could* get dressed.

In her mind, that was half the battle. Maybe it was even more
than half. It'd been so difficult to put on makeup when scars
covered so much of her face. What was the point? Makeup could
only improve her appearance by so much.

But now that her cheek was once again covered and she'd
managed the Herculean effort it had required to get ready, she
planned to do all she could to pull off the rest of the evening
and salvage the next month. According to Maxi, Seth Turner
was no small name in the art world. She'd received a text from
her former producer gushing about how fortunate she was to
get to know him.

She believed Maxi was trying to spin their winding up together on his property in a positive way so she wouldn't be mad
at him. But that text had reassured her that Mr. Turner had
much better things to do than watch over someone he didn't
even know.

One night. *This* night. That was all it would take to overcome this new obstacle.

She hoped.

When she reached the main house, she didn't know whether
to knock or let herself in. She had a key, and they both expected
that she'd come and go often while taking care of Kiki, but they
had yet to set up a schedule so that their paths would never cross.

So to maintain a polite facade and add support to his stated
plan, she knocked.

Almost immediately, his voice came through the speaker by
the doorbell. "Come on in."

She didn't need her key; the door was unlocked.

As soon as she stepped inside, she encountered the sculpture
in the middle of the entry. She'd seen it before, of course, but

she was so eager to procrastinate encountering her host that she took a longer look at it than she ever had before.

She had to admit that it was special in the same way the painting across from the couch in the guesthouse was special. That painting was probably Seth's, too, she realized. Now that she looked carefully at this piece—a man taking flight because of something he was thinking, presumably a dream or a goal— she recognized the similarities, even though they were different mediums.

His work evoked so much emotion. It was almost the personification of emotion. What he could do with a few clean lines and a smooth, spare shape, with very little detail, was impressive.

The lights were on in the kitchen, where she assumed he was busy cooking. The scent of sausage, basil and oregano drifted out to her. She loved Italian food, but her stomach was churning too much to feel any interest in eating tonight.

"Well? What do you think?"

She startled at the sound of his voice and looked over to find him watching her from the doorway of his bedroom. She hadn't expected him to be there. That part of the house was dark. He must've just finished changing or something and was on his way back to the kitchen. "I don't know anything about art."

"Isn't that the point? You don't have to know anything to enjoy it."

She could've told him that it made her feel something profound—that she couldn't avoid feeling whatever he was depicting when she looked at his work. The painting in the guesthouse hit her like a sledgehammer, as it was meant to.

But she refused to pay him the compliment. She wasn't here to flatter him. She was here to take care of Kiki and, she suspected, reassure him that she wasn't going to commit suicide while staying in the guesthouse next door. "How much is something like this worth?"

He shrugged. "A lot."

"Then, you don't need me to tell you it's good."

"Money isn't the only measure, is it?"

"You don't care about money?"

"It becomes a lot less important when you have enough of it."

She had to agree. She had enough right now, too. But what she'd made from the movie wouldn't last for the rest of her life. At some point, she'd have to figure out what to do next, and she cringed to imagine how people would stare and whisper if she had to work in public—as a waitress or in retail or sales or whatever. She'd draw attention for who she was no matter what she did, would never be able to return to the anonymity of a regular person. One day she'd probably be pictured in a small inset on the cover of the tabloids reporting on bigger stars: *Tia Beckett now working at Target!*

Imagining the future, which had seemed so bright only a month ago, made her want to crawl right back into bed. "Not everyone can retire at...what, thirty?" she said.

"Twenty-eight," he corrected.

"Success came quickly for you."

"I started right out of high school."

She'd started young, too, which was now part of the problem. She had no safety net. "You're a lucky man."

"It might look that way."

"It's not true?"

He didn't clarify. "I watched a few clips of your movie," he volunteered instead.

She winced. She couldn't even think about *Expect the Worst*, not without feeling the loss of all the parts she'd anticipated getting after the success of her first big role. It wasn't just the money and the fame. When she was acting, she was doing what she loved most. Her dreams had been destroyed in the same instant as her face.

"I don't want to talk about the movie," she said firmly. "I don't even want to hear you mention it—or I'll have to leave."

His eyebrows slid up. "Got it. No problem. That's actually a good thing, since I don't know much about the entire industry." He came toward her. "Can I take your coat?"

She preferred to keep it. No doubt it would be easier to leave at the earliest opportunity if she remained ready. But it was premature to think of leaving. She had to spend time with Kiki, and there was no use carrying her jacket around the house.

"I hope you don't have any dietary restrictions," he said as she relinquished it despite her initial reluctance.

"No."

He walked over to the closet. "Good. I would've called to check, but I was afraid if I gave you the chance to change your mind, you would." That captivating smile curved his lips again, the one that made it impossible not to notice how attractive he was. But she didn't return it. She wasn't here to make friends. She just wanted to get this over with as soon as possible.

"You'd have to have my number to call me," she pointed out. And she knew *she* hadn't given it to him.

He hung up her coat. "I have it."

"How?"

"How do you think?" he asked as he led her into the kitchen. "Maxi."

He indicated a chair at the table near the window that faced the pool and deck, but she chose to remain standing. "Didn't he give you mine?" he asked.

"He might've texted it. I haven't checked my phone."

"You've been busy," he said.

When she realized he was teasing her, she shot him a dirty look.

Instead of getting offended, he laughed. "I'm giving you a hard time. Would you like something to drink?"

She craved a drink in the worst way, but she knew alcohol would only make her relax, and she needed to remain vigilant, in total control. "I'm okay."

He uncorked a bottle of chardonnay with an expensive-looking label before pouring himself a glass, and she was so jealous watching him take his first sip, she relented. What could one glass hurt? She didn't have any alcohol in the guesthouse—and that had been intentional. There'd been no alcohol in her house growing up, and she hadn't gotten into it very much since, but she didn't want to face the temptation to self-medicate. "Actually, I'll have a little." She narrowed her eyes at him. "You won't think I have a problem with alcohol if I have one glass, will you? That isn't part of the test?"

He chuckled. "Relax. I'm the last person you have to worry about."

"Then, why am I here?" she grumbled.

He handed her a glass. "I guess I feel it's my responsibility to make sure you're okay, seeing as I'm the only one who has any contact with you."

"How do you know there aren't others?"

He seemed hopeful when he said, "Are there?"

Not really. She'd spent the past month ignoring her friends and fighting with her family. But it was none of his business. And she would've told him so—except, if she couldn't make this situation work, her alternatives were even less attractive. *You can do this*, she reminded herself. *Just play your role.* "Of course."

"Can you prove it?"

She took a sip of wine. "How?"

He held out his hand. "Show me at least one text exchange in the past twenty-four hours with a friend or family member that proves someone is keeping track of you."

She blinked at him. *Oh, my god, he's serious.* "I would, but I don't have my phone with me." She was relieved to be able to say that. The last thing she wanted was for him to see her latest exchange with her mother.

Fortunately, she really *didn't* have her phone. Before the accident, she'd been tethered to technology just like everyone else.

Now she rarely even bothered to look at it. Not only was she afraid to hear from those she loved, the internet was anathema to her. She was afraid she'd see something about herself, or even the movie, and fall apart.

"And you expect me to believe that's normal behavior for you?" he asked.

"Why not? Not everyone carries their phone when they're going next door to dinner. It's polite to leave it behind."

"And I'm sure that's why you did it," he said facetiously.

"You don't believe me?" She could tell he didn't.

He leaned in, studying her face.

Instantly self-conscious, she took a step back. "What are you doing?"

"Is there some…medical reason you have to wear those bandages?" he asked.

She lifted her hand to make sure they were still sticking to her cheek. "No. Why?"

"I'm wondering why you'd bother."

"You know why I'd bother."

"But I'm already aware of what's under them, and no one else can see you. Aren't they uncomfortable?"

"Not as uncomfortable as the alternative," she said, dropping her hand.

He sighed as his gaze lowered. She got the impression he was assessing her body to see how it might've changed since the accident. She couldn't discern any sexual interest, but it still made her self-conscious. Although no one could call her fat, she'd seen actresses ridiculed over five pounds.

"What?" she said, defensively.

"You're going to get through this," he replied. "With time."

What he'd said was intended to be nice. She wanted to believe him. But the fact that she'd made the A-list, something very few people ever attained, only to have it ripped away from her before she could really run with it, was so heartbreaking she felt sick inside.

Sinking into the chair he'd offered her earlier, she put her head between her knees and squeezed her eyes closed. She knew this wasn't the best way to reassure Seth Turner that he had nothing to worry about. But she had to stave off the anxiety and panic that was welling up, because having a nervous breakdown in front of him would be worse.

"Are you okay?" He rested a hand on her back. It was a light touch meant to show compassion and reassurance, but it felt as though his palm would burn a hole right through her sweater.

When she could, she jumped to her feet and cleared her throat. "I'm going to feed Kiki before we eat," she announced as if nothing had happened.

"Can't it wait?" He used the hand that still held his wineglass to gesture at the food. "Our dinner's ready."

"It'll only take a minute. I'll play with her later."

He didn't respond, and he didn't try to stop her. Relieved for the chance to escape him, even if it was only for a few minutes, she fled the kitchen and let herself into the aviary, where she flattened herself to the wall that wasn't made of glass and gulped in big lungfuls of air.

Damn it. This wasn't how she'd planned for the evening to go. She'd wanted to walk in, play her part and leave successful, if not triumphant.

But Seth Turner wasn't that easily fooled. He was intense, complicated. And she suspected he had a brilliant mind to go with his handsome face. The emotional depth of his art certainly seemed to support it. The perception required to create what he had created showed he wasn't one to accept anything at face value.

She couldn't make him believe she was okay—even though she wanted to.

Maybe she'd lost her acting ability, too.

★ ★ ★

As Seth watched Tia eat the pasta in garlic sauce he'd made with sausage, tomatoes and mushrooms, he couldn't help noticing that her bandages were coming loose. They couldn't withstand the movement of her jaw while she talked and chewed, but she kept pressing them back to her cheek to make them stick.

He wished she'd just take them off. Were the scars really that bad? He had a hard time believing they wouldn't improve over time or that a good plastic surgeon couldn't make a big difference.

"Would you please quit staring at me?" Tia lifted a piece of the crusty sourdough he'd purchased to go with the pasta. "You wanted to make sure I'm eating. Well, here I am, eating."

"I'm not staring at *you*," he said. "I'm staring at those bandages. They're falling off."

"That's my problem."

"It's distracting."

She shifted uncomfortably. "Sorry, but you're the one who wanted to do this."

He wouldn't have had to do it if she hadn't been acting as though she was tempted to walk off a cliff. But he didn't point that out. "Why keep messing with them?"

"Put yourself in my shoes, and I think it'll be pretty easy to answer that question."

"Fine," he said with a shrug. "If you prefer to be uncomfortable, suit yourself." He stabbed a few rigatoni with his fork. "Are you planning to go home for Christmas?"

"No."

Damn. He knew how hard it was to get through the holidays after a major tragedy. That was why *he* dreaded Christmas each year. "Why not?" Then her family or someone else would have to take care of her. She needed some emotional support, whether she would admit it or not.

"I'd rather stay here."

Of course. But he didn't think that was best for her. He was the only one here to make sure she was okay. "Alone? Won't that upset your family?"

"They're already upset."

They were? Why? And how badly were they behaving? Were they mistreating Tia, or was Tia rebuffing their attempts to help her? He wanted to ask, but he knew she'd probably take exception to him probing any deeper into her personal life. Her answers were clipped for a reason.

"Do you have a husband or a boyfriend?" he asked. Maybe a love interest would step up to help her.

"No. I went through a messy breakup while filming the movie—the guy I was with was way too controlling—and haven't dipped my toe back into the dating pool since. Now I think it'll be a long time before I do."

He put down his fork. "Tia, you're still incredibly beautiful." He meant that, but he could tell by her doubtful expression that she assumed he was patronizing her.

"Can we talk about something else?" she asked. "You know a lot about me, but I know almost nothing about you, except that you're an artist." She took another bite of pasta. "You're here by yourself, so… I take it you're not married?"

He decided not to mention that he had been married. Shiloh had died so soon after the wedding it hardly counted. And losing her was still too difficult to talk about. "No."

"Were you born here in Silver Springs?"

He washed his food down with a swallow of wine. "You haven't looked me up online?"

"Like you did me? No. I'm currently unplugged. So all I'll know about you is what you tell me."

"That's unusual in today's world." And sort of pleasant for someone who valued their privacy as much as Seth did. "Are you steering clear because you're afraid of what you might find about yourself?"

"Wouldn't you be?"

"Yes." She was famous enough that total strangers would be speculating on what'd caused her to run that red light and whether she'd ever return to acting.

He guessed she wasn't very interested in watching TV, ei-ther—except maybe the streamed stuff—since the various en-tertainment news programs would be talking about *Expect the Worst* and whether it should be nominated for an Academy Award. Feeling as though she couldn't participate even if she or the movie was to be nominated would be difficult.

"For what it's worth, I think you're doing the right thing there," he said.

She picked up her wineglass. "You've seen what everyone's saying about me online? How bad is it?"

He chose his words carefully. The last thing he wanted was to thrust her any deeper into depression. "Your fans are con-cerned about you. That's all. They want to see you in another movie, so you need to heal as quickly as possible."

She blinked at him. "If you think I'll ever be able to land another decent part, you're crazy. I won't even be able to do commercials, not looking like this."

"You don't know what the future holds."

Her jaw clenched. "It doesn't hold more acting. I know that much."

He felt stupid for even suggesting it. He was out of his ele-ment, didn't know what to say to make her feel better. But there was no way to minimize what she'd lost, so he'd only looked foolish trying. "Maybe you'll find something else you enjoy."

When her eyes met his, he saw the pain inside them and couldn't help feeling some empathy. "What would you do if you couldn't paint or sculpt anymore?" she asked. "Would you be able to find something else?"

He had to concede that point. He couldn't even imagine how terrible it would be to lose his career. He'd had only two great loves in his life: art and Shiloh. Or maybe three. He loved his adopted family, too. But he couldn't survive losing his ability to create. "I don't know," he admitted.

She put down her wine and began to shove her pasta around her plate. "I appreciate your honesty."

He topped off his glass and offered her a refill, but she refused. "So…you're from Iowa?"

"I am. What about you? Did you grow up here?"

"I was born in Denver."

"What brought you to Silver Springs?"

He ripped off a piece of bread, which he dipped in olive oil and balsamic vinegar. "New Horizons."

"That's a school, right?"

"It's a reform school."

Sitting back, she folded her arms. "What'd you do to get shipped off to a reform school?"

He didn't care to remember those years, so he quickly summarized. "Anything and everything I could to cause trouble."

"Then, it was nice of your mother to move here, too." Her eyebrows came together. "Or…wait. I think Maxi told me your mother founded the school."

"My birth mother put me up for adoption when I was six. Aiyana Turner, the woman who runs New Horizons, adopted me when I was a freshman."

"So where were you between the ages of six and however old you were as a freshman?"

"I was being bounced around the system—when I wasn't in juvie."

She seemed a great deal less defensive than she'd been so far when she said, "You seem to have recovered nicely."

"I owe that to Aiyana." Maybe his experience growing up was why he was so concerned about Tia. He'd been that person who needed someone—definitely wouldn't be where he was without the care and concern of the woman who'd taken him in and given him the love and structure he'd needed to build a better life.

"She must be quite a woman."

"She is."

The security system announced activity at the front door, startling them both. He wasn't expecting anyone…

He got up to go see what was going on, but his oldest brother strolled into the kitchen before he could get more than two steps from the table. "Eli, what—"

"Well, hello," Eli said to Tia, his eyes widening in surprise as soon as he saw her and realized that he'd interrupted dinner.

Seth felt Tia cringe. He was surprised she didn't try to duck under the table the way she'd tried to hide in his room last night. The last thing she wanted was to let other people know she was in town, which was why he didn't introduce her.

"You couldn't have knocked?" he said to his brother instead. He now regretted giving his family the code to the gate out front, but he'd done that before he found Tia hiding in his room, never dreaming it would be a problem.

Eli spread out his hands. "Why would I? I had no idea you'd finally started dating again."

"This isn't a date," Seth said.

"It looks like a date to me," Eli responded with a grin.

In the early years, Eli had been remote. He'd been dealing with his own issues. But the older and happier he got, the more he liked to tease and goof around. Seth usually gave as good as he got—they needled each other whenever they were together—but tonight wasn't the time. "We're just sharing a dinner," Seth told him.

Still grinning, Eli walked over and sampled the bread. "Then you won't mind if I join you."

"Where's your family?" Seth expected Cora and the kids to come bounding into the house any second.

"At home. I went out to get some ice cream so we can make

sundaes, and I bumped into—" his gaze shifted to Tia before returning to Seth "—someone."

The way his voice dropped when he said *someone* sounded foreboding, but Seth was so distracted he had no idea what Eli was talking about. Regardless, it would have to wait. "Okay, we'll discuss it later."

"I doubt you'll want to put it off any longer," Eli murmured. "That's why I swung by on my way home. You weren't answering your phone. Shiloh's parents know you're in town, man."

"You ran into Lois?"

"Graham. And he was clearly unhappy that they haven't heard from you. You need to call them."

Seth had stretched his luck too far. "Okay. I will."

A perplexed expression claimed Eli's face as he looked at Tia again. "Hey, don't I know you from somewhere?"

Tia didn't answer. She froze like a deer caught in head-lights, so Seth took Eli's arm and pulled him back toward the entrance. "Listen, can I call you later? You wouldn't want that ice cream to melt."

Eli laughed. "Okay, I can tell when I'm not wanted. So this *is* a date?" He lowered his voice to a whisper so that Tia wouldn't be able to hear him. "Where'd you meet her? Online? Had to be, since you never leave the house. But…why does she have all those bandages on her face?"

Tia suddenly shot out of the kitchen and skirted around them, surprising them both. "Your brother can stay. I—I have to get back, anyway. I'll take care of Kiki later," she said and hurried into the cold, leaving her coat behind.

Eli turned to watch her. "Where's *she* going?"

"To the guesthouse," Seth replied. "She's staying there for a couple of months."

"I didn't realize there was anyone else on the property. I mean, I saw what must be her car when we came yesterday, but I assumed it was one Maxi left behind."

"That car has to be something she picked up dirt cheap when she totaled hers, because it's nothing Maxi would ever own. And she's not just anyone, Eli. That's Tia Beckett, the movie star who was in the car accident a month ago."

Eli looked stunned. "Oh! That's why I recognized her! Cora dragged me to see the movie she was in, and I read about her accident. So she damaged her face? How bad is it under those bandages? She was beautiful in the movie. I mean…wow."

Hesitant to say anything about her scars, especially because he hadn't seen the full extent of them himself, Seth pursed his lips. "I'm more worried about what's going on inside her head. She's struggling."

"Of course she would be. Damn…" He raked his fingers through his hair. "I was being a jackass when I came in. I'm sorry."

"You didn't know."

Resting his hands on his hips, he continued to stare at the guesthouse, even though Tia was now inside. "You think she's going to be okay?"

Seth rubbed his chin. "I don't know. Christmas is coming."

"What does that have to do with anything?"

"Things get harder when everyone else is happy and celebrating."

Eli studied him. "For her or for you?"

"For both of us," he admitted.

CHAPTER SIX

Tia regretted going over for dinner. Now there was someone else in Silver Springs who knew she was here, and who could say how many people he'd tell? His wife, for sure. Then his wife would tell her friends and family, they would tell a few more people, and the word would spread from there.

In this small a town, she could only imagine how fast the news would travel.

Would she still feel safe?

Once again, she considered going back to LA. But when she remembered the frenzy of reporters that'd besieged her condo after she was released from the hospital, she couldn't bear the thought of it. Neighbors who'd been fine before had suddenly become as intrusive as the press, and they used any excuse they could to knock on her door. When she wouldn't answer, some even tried to peek in the windows or enter uninvited.

Fortunately, she'd been smart enough to keep her doors locked at all times, but the mere attempt jangled her nerves. She'd cringed every time she heard the handle rattle. Everyone claimed they just wanted to check on her, make sure she was okay, get her whatever she needed. But that was an excuse to act as they would normally never act.

She didn't know whom she could trust. There were too many who craved a picture, or at least a glimpse of her. Too many who wanted to make a few bucks selling her photo to the tabloids…

Her condo didn't provide enough privacy. She should've bought a house instead, and would have except she'd been waiting for the film to come out so she could ascertain its success. Her paycheck for *Expect the Worst* wasn't nearly as big as an established actress would get, but it was the most she'd ever made, and she'd planned to stretch it as far as possible, just in case.

A fool and his money are soon parted.

Her father loved that aphorism. He'd always been cautious when it came to money, something he'd instilled in her. The whole community had been ultraconservative. Even if he hadn't prevailed upon her to be penny-wise, she'd gone hungry too many times since she'd left home to take much of a risk.

She stared in the mirror as she peeled off the bandages and couldn't help but grimace at her own unsightly flesh. Was it really only a few short weeks ago that she'd believed she'd continue to star in major motion pictures and her financial worries were behind her? That there would be no more coupon-clipping? No more dollar menus or accepting almost any job just to make a buck? Her agent had received calls from some of the biggest producers and directors in Hollywood.

The possibilities had seemed limitless, until it had all ended in one careless moment.

"Ugh." She stretched her mouth to ease the residual discomfort from the tape before slumping onto the couch and pulling the blanket up over her shoulders. She was *so* tired, which made no sense because she hadn't done anything that required much energy.

She was about to put on a movie to provide background noise while she fell asleep when Seth knocked.

"Tia?"

Determined to ignore him, she squeezed her eyes closed.

"Tia, answer me," he said.

"Go away!" she barked.

"I'm not going away, so you might as well open the door."

She had a feeling he was even more stubborn than she was, but she'd already taken off her bandages, so she wasn't about to let him in. "Not tonight."

"Do I have to text Maxi to see if he has an extra key?"

"To *my* house?"

"Why not? You have a key to mine."

"That's different. I have to go over there to take care of Kiki. You said you didn't want to do it."

"There's an equally good reason for me to have one to your house."

Her jaw dropped in outrage. "No, there isn't! He would never give it to you!" She hoped.

"If he thinks it's safer for me to have it, he will."

She had to agree. If Maxi believed it was for her own good, he'd provide the key without a second thought. "Damn it! I'm fine!" She threw off the blanket and marched to the door, barely cracking it open so she could hide behind it. Sure enough, Seth had his cell phone out. "What do you want?"

"To reassure you. My brother isn't going to tell anyone you're here."

"Right. Of course he won't."

"I mean it," he said. "You don't have to worry about him. He's the most trustworthy man on the planet."

Even if Seth's brother *did* talk, Maxi's property was gated. She could still feel secure, couldn't she? It wasn't as if she could go out in public, anyway. Wearing a beanie and sunglasses wouldn't cut it when she had bandages covering half her face. Those bandages would draw too much attention.

She'd just stay in the guesthouse and order food and other

staples via her phone. Then it wouldn't matter what happened in the outside world. Although it made her feel more vulnerable to know that there were now people out there who might give away her presence—meaning reporters and obsessive fans might try to get onto the property—she was better off here than in LA. At least the people here were outside the fence. "I want to be left alone," she said. "Seriously. You don't have to worry about me."

"You never finished your dinner."

"I've had enough to eat."

His frown made it clear he was Displeased. "Okay, then, you forgot your coat."

"You could've brought it over with you. But no worries. I'll get it later."

"Why not now?" he pressed. "We weren't done. I bought tiramisu for dessert."

"I'll have to skip it," she said in exasperation. "I already took off the bandages, okay? And I don't want to put them back on."

His scowl grew darker. "Can we just get over this right now?"

"Get over what?"

"The need to hide your scars from me. You're going to be coming over every day to play with Kiki and once a week or however often to water the plants. It's inevitable that we'll bump into each other now and then. Are you going to bandage up your face every time you walk over, just in case?"

She hadn't really thought about it, but she supposed she'd have to. She'd feel too exposed, otherwise. "Probably."

"Wouldn't it be better if we got comfortable with each other instead?"

The idea of letting down her guard appealed to her. It took so much effort to maintain those barriers, to wall *everyone* out. A certain amount of lost freedom and privacy went along with fame. That was to be expected. But she had the negative side to fame without the hope of future success to offset it. She wouldn't be famous—she'd be infamous.

She couldn't leave off the bandages. She had a hard enough time looking at herself, let alone allowing someone as attractive as Seth to look at her. "It's only for another month or so. Then Maxi will be back, and we will both be moving on."

"A month is a long time. That's thirty days. Thirty applications of those bandages."

"It's not your problem."

"I guess I don't understand why it has to be a problem at all."

He was even more stubborn than she'd thought. "I'm going to text Maxi right now and tell him he'd better not give you a key," she said.

"Seriously? Hiding is a waste of time and effort. I don't give a damn what you look like."

"I'm not saying you do. It's just…you don't understand how bad it is to…to lose what I've lost."

"I understand that you're only making it worse."

She hesitated, oddly tempted to give in and get it over with—much like ripping off a Band-Aid. But she ultimately couldn't bring herself to go through with it. "I can't."

"Fine, have it your way," he said but as he lifted his hands in a "whatever" gesture, he bobbled his cell phone, and she instinctively darted out to help him catch it.

She managed to grab it before it cracked on the cement. She almost couldn't believe she'd made such a great save, and, for a second, she was excited and relieved. But when he nonchalantly took it back from her, she realized he'd dropped it on purpose.

"The scars aren't that bad," he said as he slid his phone into his pocket. "You need to get over it."

She gaped at his back, which was all she could see, since he'd started toward the main house.

"I—I can't believe you just did that," she stuttered, angry enough to follow him in spite of her reluctance to leave the house. "That you would…would make me believe I had to save your phone!"

"I didn't make you believe you had to save anything. I just dropped my phone," he said without turning back.

She took a few more steps. "What if I hadn't caught it? It would've shattered on the ground, and that…that's an expensive fix!"

"I wouldn't have bothered to fix it. I would've just bought a new one."

Of course. He was rich. He could do that. Why had she felt the need to help him? "That was mean! You're a…a jerk!" she yelled from partway between their two dwellings. "An…insensitive person!"

He didn't even break his stride. "If those are the worst things you ever call me, I'll be happy," he yelled back.

She would've called him worse, but she couldn't think of what would be appropriate. He hadn't really done anything wrong, except see what she hadn't wanted him to see. He was the first person, besides her doctor, to know how extensive Tia Beckett's scars really were. What could she call him for that?

"You arrogant, stubborn, overly assertive…*ass*!" she yelled, unwilling to go any farther.

She could hear him laughing. "Be careful, or I might think you like me," he said.

"I *don't* like you! I hate you!"

When her voice broke on a sob, he finally stopped and turned around, and she was surprised by the compassion on his face. Although he'd been laughing a moment earlier, he was perfectly serious now. "That's fine," he said. "You can hate me all you want. But I just did you a favor. Now you won't have to mess with those bandages when you come over every day, because there's nothing to hide. I've already seen your face, up close, and it's no big deal."

She couldn't stop the tears that rolled down her cheeks. "It *is* a big deal. I look like a monster!"

"No," he said. "Nothing could destroy the beauty of your eyes."

The compliment made her feel slightly better. He sounded sincere, as though he wasn't just saying that to be nice. But she wasn't going to let him know how much those words meant to her. She was still too mad at him. "Whether or not you saw my face should've been *my* choice!" she insisted.

"And you're the one who made that choice," he said.

With a sniff, she wiped her eyes. "You're an ass," she said again, but this time even she could hear that her voice was more subdued.

Apparently he was done being serious, because he grinned at her. "You're probably not the only one who thinks so. Anyway, you can thank me later."

The second Tia couldn't see him, even from the back, the smile slid from Seth's face. He let himself into the house, closed the door and leaned against it. "Holy shit," he said on a long exhale. Tia was right—her beautiful face was destroyed. She'd never get another acting part. And it was only a matter of time before some brazen journalist managed to snap a picture of her. Then those scars would be plastered all over the tabloids for the world to see, and she'd become the brunt of ruthless jokes and endless speculation.

He cringed to imagine what that would be like for her, especially because he was no longer convinced plastic surgery would help.

"Poor thing," he muttered.

"Pretty girl… Pretty girl," Kiki was saying. Although it wasn't loud, her parrot voice came through the glass walls of the atrium and echoed against the ceiling, seemingly mocking his thoughts. Tia had once been more than a pretty girl. She'd been stunning. But now…

At least he'd been honest about her eyes. A man could drown in those eyes. They were mesmerizing.

But people wouldn't be talking about her eyes if pictures ever leaked online. They'd be talking about the terrible scars, and he was already afraid of what some might say. People could be so cruel. He knew because they'd been cruel to him, once upon a time, when he was just a defenseless boy.

I know why you don't have any parents—it's because no one could love you.

And this, said in a whisper by so many of his foster families: *How could a mother give away only one of her sons? What does that say about him and his behavior?*

Trying to block out the echoes, he used his phone to text Eli. Just in case I didn't make a big enough point of it, you can't tell anyone Tia is here, okay? No one. Including Cora. It's important.

Sorry, dude. Already told Cora came his brother's response. She's my wife. I tell her everything. But I'll make sure she knows it's a secret. We can trust her.

Seth liked Cora, but what if she confided in a friend, maybe even someone at New Horizons where she worked as a teacher? It would go through the school like wildfire. "Damn."

Did you call Lois and Graham? his brother wanted to know.

Seth groaned. He'd chosen to focus on Tia instead, not only because she needed help and there didn't seem to be anyone else in her life to provide it but also because he welcomed the diversion. It was so much easier to deal with someone else's problems.

But he'd already put off contacting the Iveys for too long.

Doing it now, he wrote and ambled into the kitchen, where the remains of the dinner he'd made were waiting for him. He was tempted to clean it up first but made himself take a stool at the gigantic marble island and scroll through his phone to find his mother-in-law's contact information.

Hey. I'm in town to do some fundraising for an arts center at New Horizons and would love to see you and Graham while I'm here. Let me know if you have time.

He saw the three dots that signified she was reading his text and responding, but he waited several minutes, and her response never came.

Muttering a curse, he rested his head in his hands while imagining Shiloh in the room with him. "Well, babe, I might've pissed them off again." He knew it was crazy to talk to his wife as though she was still alive, but she was such a part of him that even after three years, it was almost impossible to accept that she was gone.

A few minutes later, he checked his phone again.

Nothing.

Fortunately, when Tia went over to spend time with Kiki two hours after her yelling match with Seth, she didn't run into him. She could see that the lights were on upstairs, so she assumed he was up. But she figured he was deeply immersed in his work, because she never heard from him while she played with Maxi's parrot. Classical music came through a stereo system that filled the house, which was more soothing than she would've expected, and after the first hour, she began to relax and feel as though the soul-crushing events of the past month weren't pressing in on her quite so insistently.

Being inside the protective walls of the aviary, enjoying such an incredible creature, proved to be a nice reprieve. One she desperately needed. She hesitated to give Seth the credit for this improvement, but she suspected he deserved at least some of it. The constant vigilance and care it required to hide her face had been a bigger deal than she was willing to admit. Now that he'd seen her, she could release that, and they could go on about their business, as he'd suggested, without worrying about it.

For the first time in a long while, she could breathe without experiencing such a terrible tightness in her chest.

Of course, it wasn't only being able to forget about the bandages. His reaction to her scars had helped, too. He hadn't recoiled in shock or horror. He'd shrugged. That was it. He seemed to possess a certain depth of understanding that made her trust him. No matter what he did—and he'd definitely surprised her once or twice already—she believed he wouldn't purposely hurt her, wouldn't sell her out to the press or anything like that.

"Say *I love Tia*," she told Kiki, trying to teach the bird a new phrase.

Kiki eyed her dubiously, as though she wasn't interested in expanding her speaking repertoire.

Tia held up a pumpkin seed. "I love Tia."

Kiki didn't mimic her, but she did lean forward and steal the pumpkin seed before Tia could pull it away.

"Hey, what a cheat!" Tia cried out and actually laughed, probably for the first time since the accident.

She kept trying to train Kiki, thinking it would be funny for Maxi to hear his pet pay her homage long after she was gone, but after another hour, she grew tired of the effort. She didn't seem to be making any progress, so she decided to leave.

She was feeling better, but she still didn't want to run into Seth. She was afraid he'd say or do something to make her mad again—or remind her of the things she'd been able to forget in the past hour. Over all, she could dub this a good night, by current standards, and she wanted to cling to that incremental improvement for as long as possible.

Besides, even though going without her bandages was as liberating as he'd said it would be, she preferred he not see her face again so soon. She needed time to get used to the idea. It was a victory just to have come over without them. She felt it would be better, for tonight anyway, if it ended there.

She almost grabbed her coat, but she was so afraid the closet door would squeak she decided to get it another time.

She was still smiling, despite the harsh bite of the wind, when she reached the guesthouse. But then her phone buzzed.

When she pulled it out of her pocket, she saw that it was just a push notification from one of her apps, although she had missed a text, much earlier, from her mother:

No one here has heard from you in several days. Are you really going to treat your family this way?

Tia sighed. Just when she'd finally been feeling a bit better…

CHAPTER SEVEN

After Seth heard Tia leave, he rinsed his brushes, even though he hadn't been working long, and went down to the kitchen. He still had dinner to clean up, but he wasn't in any hurry to get started.

Spotting the open bottle of wine on the counter, he poured himself a glass and carried it out back. He could smell a storm coming, but it hadn't started to rain yet, and he was used to chilly weather. San Francisco could be freezing, even in the summer.

The pool was constructed with natural rocks and a water feature that flowed constantly over one side. It had steam rising off the top, so he knew it was heated and was tempted to get in. But the hot tub would be even warmer. He would've gotten into that for sure—except he hadn't brought any trunks.

He'd probably neglected to bring other things, too, which he'd discover as the days went by. Shiloh had been the one to keep their lives organized and on track, and he still hadn't adjusted to living without her. She'd left such a big hole in his life he could never fill it, so he didn't even try.

His wife had also been more social than he was. Without her

creating connections and dragging him into relationships, he'd have even fewer friends than he did now. He was surprised he had *any* left, after three years. He'd shoved everyone away, except his immediate family, who wouldn't let him.

God, he missed Shiloh. Everything would be different if she was still here.

Leaning back to stare up at the starless sky, he remembered the day he first met her. It was at the party of some rich boy at one of the private schools for kids whose families loved them enough to spend a fortune on their education. When word got out that there'd be no parents to chaperone, students from almost every high school in the area attended—even his, although those who went to New Horizons were typically not invited. They were the poor kids, the ones who came from broken homes or no homes at all, the ones who caused trouble and weren't expected to *amount to much.*

In other words: the disreputable and undesirable.

Seth wouldn't have gone that night if his brother hadn't needed a wingman. He'd made it a point to avoid the wealthier kids. He'd considered them to be spoiled and clueless if not stuck up. But if he hadn't gone that night, he might never have met Shiloh. Although he didn't really believe in love at first sight, he had no other way to explain what happened the minute he saw her. He'd known instantly, at seventeen, that she was the one he wanted to spend the rest of his life with.

She hadn't been interested in dating him, however. She'd had a boyfriend at the time—one her strict parents approved of because he went to the right school, had a football scholarship to UCLA and attended the same church they did. Seth still wasn't sure why Shiloh messaged him on social media once that relationship ended. He suspected she'd done it to rebel against her parents' tight control, because she knew what she was getting into from the beginning—knew he'd spent eighteen months in juvie for driving the getaway car for some friends who'd tried to rob a bank. All the kids knew that. It was what her ex played on most to try to win her back.

Taking another drink of wine, he walked over and rolled up his jeans so that he could stick his feet in the hot tub. He had no business whiling away the hours out here, thinking about Shiloh. Missing her only made him grow maudlin. And he needed to finish "The Businessman" so he could start the piece he owed the Monterey Bay Aquarium. He was thinking of making that one a representation of the mad passion of Captain Ahab from *Moby Dick* and needed to decide exactly how he'd capture Ahab's obsession through a strictly visual medium.

But he couldn't concentrate. This felt like the many nights he'd spent the year after Shiloh died, walking the empty halls of their house for hours on end, as if he might find her in one of the rooms.

If he was being honest, however, it wasn't just Shiloh standing between him and his ability to create tonight. It was Tia. He found her new face so intriguing that he wanted to paint her, which was crazy. It was a waste of time to even think about how he'd approach something like that. She'd never agree, even if he promised he wouldn't sell it.

"There you are. I've been shouting your name through the entire house. I wouldn't be surprised if the bird started imitating me."

Seth twisted around to see his mother coming through the back door. "What are you doing here?" He checked his watch. "It's late."

"I know what a night owl you are. So I decided to stop by and say hello."

"You mean *drive over*?" he said as she came toward him. "There is no *stopping by* when you live on the other side of town and it's nearly midnight."

Once she reached him, she playfully swatted his arm. "Stop it. It's a Friday night. I don't have to get up early in the morning, and I didn't have to come that far. I love having you in town. I plan to take full advantage of it and see you as often as possible."

"I appreciate that. I do," he said. "But I'm still not buying that this visit was spontaneous."

"What are you accusing me of?" After removing her high-heeled boots, she lifted her skirt and stepped into the water with him.

"You've spoken to my big brother, and he told you what happened earlier. *That's* what motivated the visit."

She wouldn't look him in the eye. "Eli and I work together. We talk all the time. You know that."

Seth set his wineglass to one side. "But I told Tia he was trustworthy, Mom."

"Eli *is* trustworthy."

"I used to think so, too, but first Cora and now—"

"He knows who he can tell and who he can't," she broke in, as if that was all that mattered.

Seth laughed. "So four people are now aware that Tia Beckett is staying in town instead of just one. How is that keeping her secret?"

"The two people Eli told are as trustworthy as he is," she pointed out. "That's how."

Seth rolled his eyes. "So did you come over hoping to catch a glimpse of her? Do you even know who she is?" His mother wasn't one for movies. She worked too hard and spent every extra minute trying to support her family or help someone else who needed a hand or a listening ear.

"I admit I'd never heard of her before. But I looked her up." She tossed her long braid over her shoulder. "Gorgeous girl."

Seth lowered his voice even though there was no way Tia could hear him. "Not anymore."

A pained expression formed deep grooves in Aiyana's forehead. "How tragic."

"It is. I feel terrible for her."

"How's she coping?"

"She's hiding out in the guesthouse and won't come out except to take care of Maxi's parrot."

"Eli said she had dinner with you."

"That was—" he stretched his neck "—somewhat coerced."

She nibbled at her bottom lip as she considered the situation. "I have to say, it was brilliant of Maxi to give her some responsibility."

Seth was grateful for that, too. It forced Tia to emerge from her self-imposed dungeon at least once a day. But he doubted Maxi had put Tia in charge of Kiki for Tia's sake alone. "I think he saw it more as a win-win."

"What about her friends and family? Are they checking on her? Does she have any emotional support?"

"Not that I can tell."

"Then, we need to do something."

He cocked a remonstrative eyebrow at her. "*You* can't do anything because you're not even supposed to know she's here, remember?"

She didn't seem satisfied with that, as he guessed she wouldn't be. "She needs a good therapist."

"I would agree, but she'd first have to get to a good therapist, and I don't see her doing that, not when she won't leave the house."

"Why couldn't the therapist come to her?"

He remembered opening the door while at the guesthouse and forcing Tia to let him see her scars. He'd intended that to be a good thing but now worried that it hadn't been. He wasn't a psychologist. He was just a pragmatist. Maybe he'd done exactly the *wrong* thing, which was why he'd listened so closely to be sure she came to take care of Kiki.

Fortunately, she had… "I don't know what her financial situation is."

"She had to have made some money on that film."

"But who knows what she's done with it—or how long it will have to last her. Judging by her car, she doesn't have much."

His mother sighed as she stared into the steam rising from the churning water. "What should we do?"

"I'm keeping an eye on her."

"Of course you are," she said, shifting her focus back to his face, but her smile faded as she added, "But what about you?"

"What about me?"

"Eli also mentioned he ran into Shiloh's father at the ice-cream store."

"That's what he said, but I don't understand how they know I'm in town. I just got here."

"Graham told Eli a neighbor saw you."

Of course. He'd gone to the grocery store, and he'd taken his mother to lunch. Anyone could've seen him. "You told me to call them. I just…"

She reached over to squeeze his arm. "I know. It's not easy."

"They hated me for so long." Sometimes it was difficult to forgive them, because of how hard their disapproval had been on Shiloh. He'd been afraid being caught in the middle would tear her apart. And it wasn't just in the beginning. The tug-of-war lasted until well after they were married.

"They couldn't see past your record, that's all. But once they got to know you—"

"My record?" he interrupted. "I was only thirteen when I helped rob that bank."

"I know. I see it that way, too, especially because you were roped into it by much older boys. And the execution of the robbery was…well, more comical than they perhaps realize."

Seth couldn't help chuckling at that statement. Because he'd refused to go inside the bank, he'd been designated the driver, even though he was younger by several years and didn't have a license. He'd been so filled with adrenaline by the time they came running out, he'd floored the gas pedal the second they got in, lost control and crashed into the ATM.

"I'm sure Weasel and Zach don't think it was funny," he said. Although they'd also been underage, only sixteen and seventeen, they'd been prosecuted as adults because they'd used a toy gun that looked far too real.

Aiyana shook her head. "The crazy things we do."

"No kidding. And for what? Had we gotten away with it, we would've split all of five hundred and thirty-two dollars. I still don't know why I let them talk me into that."

"You were angry," she said.

He didn't correct her; what he'd said was only a figure of speech. He actually did know why he'd done what he'd done. He'd just heard from his biological brother for the first time, and what he'd learned had caused such pain he'd been trying to destroy himself once and for all, just so he could stop *feeling*. He'd fully expected to get caught when they robbed that bank, could remember hoping the police would shoot him.

Instead, the branch manager had yanked him out of the driver's seat, and several patrons had tackled his two partners—a friend's brother and their neighbor—as they tried to run away. And for the next year and a half, he'd been treated as though he was such a worthless piece of shit he'd regretted the fact that he hadn't been shot.

"But look at you now," his mother said. "You weathered that in addition to everything else you had to go through as a child. And you've weathered losing the person you loved most, too. I'm so proud of you."

"Come on, Mom, tell the truth," he said. "You're worried about me, which is why you've tried everything to get me down here."

She didn't bother to deny it. "And here you are."

"Yes, here I am, where I can't even work, thanks to my property mate."

"I don't feel sorry about that. All you've been doing for the past three years is work. It's not healthy. You need to start living again, need to spend more time with people."

"I *will* be spending more time with people. I'm going to be fundraising while I'm here and will soon be teaching an art class for you, remember?"

Her gentle smile reminded him of how healing her love had been. By the time the state sent him to New Horizons, after he got out of juvenile hall, he'd been so starved for love he probably would've acted out again. But her calm, steady and determined heart had made all the difference.

She was the real reason he'd come back. He'd come because she'd wanted him to.

"Those things might not be as important as this," she said, motioning toward the guesthouse beyond the fence that encircled the pool area.

"*This* as in Tia?" he asked in surprise.

She dropped her hand. "She needs someone, Seth."

"That person isn't me," he said. "I didn't sign up for that."

"But you've been through some very difficult things yourself."

"My situation is completely different."

"It's not," she insisted. "Suffering is suffering. And who understands suffering better than you?"

Maybe if he'd been able to get clear of the jagged rocks of life himself, he could take on Tia. After he married Shiloh he'd thought he was there, finally knew what happiness was. But that had all changed the day he lost her. With so many of his own issues, how could he ever save Tia or anyone else?

Tia had been staring at her mother's message for the past hour. She'd tried to write back several times but always deleted it. How could she explain how hard she was fighting just to get through each day? That she'd felt as though she was being tossed about on very rough seas with no way of finding safe harbor?

She couldn't withstand her family's criticism on top of that. She knew they wanted her to admit she'd been wrong for leaving in the first place and to come back, but she could never be satisfied living the way they did. She felt claustrophobic just thinking about getting caught in Kalona for the rest of her life. Did it make her a bad person that she wouldn't sacrifice her own wants and desires to please her parents and continue to be part of the community they felt was so important? That she couldn't fit into the same mold as her sister and brother?

How many times had her parents told her she had no business trying to be an actress in the first place? They considered Hollywood a den of the profligate, the wanton and the greedy, had told her all along that such a wicked place would destroy her soul. And for what? According to them, acting didn't contribute anything meaningful to life. Her chances of success were one in a million, anyway.

At least she'd proven them wrong on that count. She would've been successful, could've been if only she hadn't had that accident. But *I told you so* garnered her nothing, because it was their *I told you so* that rang loudest and clearest. They were still angry they'd lost control of her, in spite of the pressure they'd put on her to stay.

Her chest was growing tight again.

Dropping her head in her hands, she began to rub her temples. She wished she could tell her mother that she wasn't ignoring her family, she was just putting the pieces of her life back together. But her mother heard only what she wanted to hear and saw only what she wanted to see. Gloria believed Tia wouldn't be in her current situation if only Tia had listened, and Tia couldn't argue with that. It wouldn't have happened if she hadn't come to California.

I'm sorry, she wrote, hoping it would somehow help. But she knew it wouldn't even as she hit Send.

Nothing could turn back the hands of time.

CHAPTER EIGHT

Saturday, December 18

Tia woke up with a crick in her neck. She'd fallen asleep on the couch while holding her phone. She'd known better than to expect an immediate response from her mother. By the time she'd answered Gloria's text it had been almost midnight California time and two hours later in Iowa. The difference in time zones meant her mother would be up now, however. Gloria always woke with the sun. Almost every good Mennonite did.

A sense of impending doom hung over Tia like a dark cloud as she risked a glance at her phone. Sure enough, her mother had responded.

When are you coming back to Kalona?

To Gloria, being sorry meant Tia would finally obey her parents, and that included returning to Iowa. But how many times had she told her mother that she was helping out a friend? That she *couldn't* come home?

After Christmas.

You're going to miss the holidays? We were hoping to have a memorial for Uncle Wilson now that things have calmed down. You don't want to be part of that?

She hadn't been there for his funeral because she'd still been in the hospital when Uncle Wilson died after a protracted battle with cancer. It wasn't as if she'd arbitrarily chosen to stay away— although, if she was being completely honest, there was a small part of her that was relieved to be able to hide from her family during that sad event. Her mother had flown out right after the accident to see her in the hospital. Tia had been so heavily drugged at the time she hadn't yet had to face her mother with all of her faculties intact. Gloria hadn't stayed very long. She'd felt too out of place and uncomfortable in the big city. It was the first time she'd ever stayed in a hotel or been on a plane.

Tia had hoped to be much stronger when she did have to face her mother, and her father, too. But Gloria was essentially screaming *You screwed up* again. *Now, prove you love us by doing penance.* Which meant admitting defeat by going home. Gloria had always used guilt and shame to manipulate her children, which was one of the reasons Tia had been so eager to get away.

With a sigh, she combed her fingers through her tangled hair. She couldn't deal with this. She'd been foolish to let her mother engage her to begin with. She'd decided days ago that for her own sanity she had to step back from *everyone*—most especially her family.

She was about to turn off her phone, which was almost out of battery anyway after sleeping with it all night, when it dinged.

"Mom, *please*. Leave me alone," she cried to the empty room. Desperation welled up—what she'd been trying to avoid by coming to Silver Springs—but she couldn't keep from glancing at the message.

Fortunately, it wasn't her mother. It was Seth.

Breakfast is ready.

Breakfast? She stared at those three words, trying to decide what to do. If she didn't go over, he might come get her. But if she *did* go over, he'd expect her to come without her bandages.

She knew from the freedom she'd experienced last night that he was right. She needed to lower her defenses and be herself with at least one person. And since he was a stranger—one who wasn't connected to the movie industry or fandom—it was easier with him. But still. Associating with anyone right now was a huge challenge.

It took her so long to decide, he sent another text.

Food's getting cold.

He was certainly persistent. She had to give him that. I'm coming, she wrote.

While listening for the security system to alert him to Tia's entry, Seth finished making her omelet, slid it onto a plate and poured fresh-squeezed orange juice into two glasses. This morning, when he'd gone out for a run, he'd noticed several citrus trees laden with oranges on the property, so he'd picked a bagful.

As he went to the stove to get the fried potatoes, he finally heard the mechanical voice he'd been expecting. "Activity at the front door."

"Morning," he murmured as footsteps sounded behind him, but he didn't turn. He'd decided to act as casual as possible, figured that was probably the best way to handle this first encounter after what he'd done at her door yesterday. He wanted to make sure she felt safe, and he couldn't imagine anyone in her

situation would enjoy being the subject of too much attention
or even attention that was too highly focused.

"Smells good," she said, but her voice sounded tentative
enough to suggest that she wasn't convinced she'd made the
right decision in coming.

He almost made a joke that it would be her turn to cook
next. But he knew it would fall flat. She couldn't care for anyone right now, even herself. He'd been in her shoes once upon
a time, in the months after Shiloh died, so he understood.

Besides, he sort of liked doing the cooking. It gave him something to think about besides work and how badly he missed his
wife. It also meant *he'd* eat a more complete meal. For the past
three years, he'd subsisted mostly on what he could find root-
ing around in the pantry or fridge—hummus and vegetables,
crackers and cheese, cold cereal, bread and peanut butter—or
what he could order from a restaurant. He missed the meals he
and Shiloh used to prepare together, the recipes they'd used,
the conversation and togetherness.

"Hope you're hungry," he said.

"Wow. You went to a lot of work," she responded.

With the spatula he'd used to dish up the potatoes, he gestured at her chair, an unspoken invitation to take the seat next
to the wall, where her damaged cheek would be turned away
from him. He hadn't been able to catch a glimpse of her entire
face yet—she had her head bowed and her hair was falling forward—but he hoped she'd left her bandages at home. As far as
he was concerned, they'd already cleared that hurdle; he didn't
want to backtrack. "The best thing on the table is the juice,"
he said as he returned the pan to the stove and divested himself
of the oven mitt he'd used to carry it. "Give it a try."

A chair scraped the floor, and she sat down as he searched
the fridge for some ketchup.

"You're right," she said after a moment. "It's delicious."

"Sometimes it's the simple things in life that make all the difference."

"If you say so," she grumbled, and he chuckled at her response. He knew at this point what she was going through: *nothing* seemed as though it would help.

Once he joined her at the table, he still couldn't see her face full on, but he was pretty sure she wasn't wearing any bandages. He considered that a step in the right direction. She had to accept herself as she was. In his opinion, that would be her first step out of this thing. "You sleep good?"

"Not too good. You?"

It was hard not to crane his neck to take another look at her damaged cheek. He hoped he was remembering those scars as worse than they were. But she was being careful to keep her face averted, so knowing how important it was to ease into this encounter, he reached for his glass. "Sleeping has always been difficult for me, which is why I typically work at night."

"Why do you have trouble sleeping?"

He took a drink of juice and set his glass down. "I don't know. Neither do the doctors. They've given me plenty of sedatives through the years, though."

"The pills don't work?"

"I refuse to take them." He'd been too afraid he'd become dependent. He knew if he went down that rabbit hole, he might never get out.

"Then, how do you get enough rest?"

"I sleep for a few hours around four or five in the morning. If that's not enough, I occasionally fall asleep watching the news before dinner."

"Maybe I'll have to adopt your schedule," she said. "During the day, it doesn't seem as though I can get out of bed. But at night, I wander through the house obsessing about everything."

He could only imagine how long the nights must be for her. She didn't even have work to distract her. "If you're going to adopt my schedule, you need something to keep you busy during the dark, lonely hours."

She finally turned to where he could see all of her face. "I'm an actress. What am I going to do?"

He'd been right in assuming she wasn't wearing any bandages. That was so brave he couldn't help being proud of her. He considered mentioning that as proof that she was more resilient than she realized.

But he doubted she cared to talk about that. And she didn't know him very well, so it might seem like an odd statement to say he was proud of her. Figuring it would be easier if he just didn't say anything, he returned his attention to his plate. "Tomorrow you can go running with me. The exercise would be good for you."

She obviously hadn't expected that answer. "Did you say *running*?"

"Yes. As in jogging, working out."

"How often do you do that?"

"Today was the first time in a long while." She wasn't the only one whose life had spun out of control. He needed to let go of the past, too, and plot his own journey forward. If meeting her had done anything for him, it had made him take a long, hard look at himself. He couldn't tell someone else how to get beyond tragedy if he couldn't overcome it himself.

Eager for her to taste the omelet he'd made, he glanced over to see if she'd started in, but she'd put down her fork and knife. "You run in the cold?" she asked. "It's freezing outside."

"Not if you're working out hard enough." After the first mile, he'd had to tie his jacket around his waist. And he'd been dripping with sweat by the time he was done.

"I'm not going to be running *that* hard," she said.

"Then, you can bring a sweatshirt."

She reclaimed her fork. "No way."

"You won't bring a sweatshirt?"

"I'm not going running."

"Why not?"

"Because someone might see me."

"You can't let that stop you."

"Yes, I can."

"It'd be really good for you."

"I'll go to a gym when I'm ready."

"I don't enjoy staring at the wall while I work out. Just can't do it. Drives me nuts." He grimaced. "And I see gyms as germ receptacles."

"Great. Thanks for that mental image," she said as she took her first bite.

He smiled at her sarcasm. "Fresh air. Sunshine. You can't get either of those in a gym. Plus, vitamin D. Most Americans are seriously deficient."

"Maybe that's true. But it's safer in a gym."

"*Safer?* How?"

Her eyebrows went up. "Do you know how many women have been attacked while jogging on some lonely trail?"

"Which is why you run with a buddy," he said once he'd swallowed.

She cut another bite. "I guess you've never heard of the Zodiac Killer."

"I've heard of him, but I can't remember what he did."

"Killed couples for no reason, right here in California." She took another bite of her omelet. "And have I mentioned that he was never caught?"

Seth remembered the story. The Zodiac Killer had actually operated up north, near San Francisco, where he lived. But that was years and years ago. "There's an exception to every rule. That's not going to get you out of running," he said jokingly.

"In case you didn't hear me the first time, I can't be seen outside," she said. "I could be recognized."

She had to face the public eventually. She had to pull herself out of the dark hole she'd fallen into before it got any more difficult. "That's what hoodies are for."

"I don't have a hoodie."

"Fortunately, I have one you can borrow." He winked before indicating her plate. "So…are you going to tell me how you like the food?"

She seemed mildly surprised that he was interested enough to ask. He was a little surprised himself. In spite of how closed off he'd become over the past three years, he was intrigued by this woman and the situation she was in.

"It's good," she said. "Thank you."

"What do you normally have for breakfast?"

"Lately? Doritos and Coke when I want to be healthy and Hostess Ding Dongs when I don't."

He stopped eating. "You've got to be kidding me." Even when he'd been in the depths of despair, he hadn't eaten *that* badly.

"It's a slow way to die, but it'll do the trick eventually. I read a newspaper article not long ago about a man who died from eating too much black licorice, so anything's possible."

He gave her a pointed stare. "That's not funny."

"Stop it. I'm not suicidal. It was joke, okay? And trying to kill yourself with black licorice is sort of funny."

"Why aren't you with family or friends? This is when you need them most." He said that as if family was everyone's automatic go-to, but after Shiloh died, he'd pulled away from his own family, which was why his mother had been pressuring him to come home.

"The dynamic there is a little…complicated right now."

Had that started with the accident? They had to be worried about her, didn't they? Or maybe they didn't act as though they cared. "What happened that day? Didn't you see the traffic light?"

She stared down at her food. "All I remember is catching

a glimpse of a white van speeding toward me after it was too late to stop."

He let his breath seep out slowly. "It might be smart to get some professional help, Tia."

"Are you talking about a shrink? Therapy won't restore my face or my career."

"Talking to someone might help you cope with your losses." Again, he felt like a hypocrite. He hadn't gone to a therapist after Shiloh died, even though it might've helped. "And while you're already upset, I should prepare you for something else."

Going rigid, she looked toward the entryway as if he might've lured her here to surprise her with the paparazzi, who would be busting in any minute. "What is it?" she asked apprehensively.

"My mother knows who you are and that you're in town."

"You said you wouldn't tell anyone." She didn't sound happy about this, but some of the tension left her body, suggesting she was relieved it wasn't worse.

"*I* didn't," he said. "My brother did."

Her eyebrows snapped together. "The most trustworthy man in the world?"

He made a sheepish face. "Hyperbole. Anyway, I'm sorry. I don't think Eli realized he couldn't tell the family."

"So the word is out."

It was a fatalistic statement, not a question. "No," he assured her. "Nothing like that. I just... I wanted you to know because she might try to reach out to you, even though I asked her not to."

"What does she want? A picture? An autograph?"

"Neither. The only movie star whose name she can recall off the top of her head is Tom Cruise. Or maybe Clint Eastwood. She just wants to help. I told you before, she's good at that sort of thing, good with people."

"I remember. But...she doesn't even know me."

He smiled. "She barely knew me when she decided *I* needed her. But without her, I'd probably be in prison right now."

"You were a child. I can understand why she might step in. I'm an adult. I don't see how she can help."

"Love, patience, understanding, friendship. We could all use more of those things, regardless of age. She's not overly intrusive. She'll just check on you now and then. See how you're doing. And she might try to get you to come over to the house—especially if you're going to be alone for Christmas."

She gave him a skeptical look. "Won't the rest of your family be there on Christmas?"

"Yes."

"Then, I'll pass. But… I guess I wouldn't mind meeting her."

"Okay," he said. "I'll bring her over later tonight and save her the trouble of trying to figure out another way to make contact with you."

CHAPTER NINE

Tia couldn't believe she'd agreed to allow Seth to bring his mother over to the guesthouse. The more people she associated with, the greater the chances of the press finding out where she was. Two different tabloids had already offered her a sizable amount of money to provide them with an exclusive interview and pictures. But they were crazy if they thought she could tolerate a photo shoot.

Even if the press didn't become a problem, there could be local fans who would resort to extreme measures to invade her privacy. And she was too fragile for that. The panic that welled up at the thought that it wasn't safe to open her door nearly paralyzed her.

On the flip side, remaining inside the guesthouse alone all day, every day, with nothing constructive to do, wasn't healthy, either. She was drifting further and further from the person she'd once been, after she'd adjusted and found herself in LA, and all the people she loved. That was never more apparent than when she checked her phone and saw all the texts of concern she couldn't bring herself to read from friends she'd met in acting school or while making the movie.

Focusing on the fact that the last two encounters she'd had with Seth had been positive, she refused to allow herself to call him and cancel. To ensure she didn't, she plugged her phone into the charger in the bedroom before curling up on the couch and turning on the TV.

She intended to take only a short nap so she'd have the energy to clean up the place. But the next thing she knew, someone was knocking on her door.

"Tia? Hello?"

It was Seth. Groggy and discombobulated, she reached for her phone, patting the blanket she'd used to cover herself until she remembered leaving it on the charger. She couldn't check the time, but it was obvious she'd overslept. The light that crept around the edges of the blinds during the day was gone.

How long had it been?

Seth hadn't set up a specific time for her to meet his mother. He'd just said *tonight*. But it had been twelve thirty when she returned from the main house. She must've slept the entire afternoon.

"Tia?" Seth's voice came through the door again.

"Shoot," she muttered as she eyed the candy and junk food wrappers that littered the coffee table and floor and the dishes that were stacked high on the counters and in the sink.

"Tia?" This time it was someone else—a female. "It's Aiyana Turner," the voice went on. "I hope you don't mind giving me a moment of your time. I promise I would never do anything that would compromise you in any way."

Although Seth's mother sounded sincere, and Tia didn't doubt her motives, a heavy dose of skepticism remained. Why had she allowed this meeting? What could Aiyana Turner really do?

No one could help her.

But it was too late to cancel. They were at her door.

Scrubbing a hand over her face—then wincing at the tenderness that remained in her cheek—she got to her feet and crossed the room. "Sorry, I…uh…fell asleep," she said through the door. "Can you…can you give me a minute?"

"Of course," the woman replied. "We'll wait right here. Take all the time you need."

"Thank you. It…it won't be long."

"Okay, honey."

Such an endearment shouldn't have meant anything coming from a total stranger, and yet the way Seth's mother said it made it feel like a caress.

Still trying to shake off the last vestiges of sleep, Tia used the bathroom, brushed her hair and did what she could to fix her makeup. Touching up her mascara and eye shadow seemed futile when she couldn't believe anyone would be able to focus on anything other than her scars. But going through the motions gave her a moment to collect herself.

When she was done, she cast one final glance at the frightening image she saw reflected back at her and hurried out to open the door. Silver Springs rarely got snow, but it was chilly in December, and she felt bad for making them wait outside.

"Hello." She'd decided not to take the time to cover her cheek with bandages, but Aiyana gripped her hand and looked into her eyes as if she didn't even notice the scars.

"It's so nice to meet you," she said.

Seth's mother was only about five-two. With long dark hair, kind brown eyes and a plethora of smile lines around her mouth, she had small hands to go with her petite body. Her orange nail polish looked beautiful next to her dark skin and matched the print of her vibrant, loose-fitting dress. She looked comfortable but well put together at the same time, and she smelled like gardenias.

"It's nice to meet you, too," Tia said. "Seth has a lot of good things to say about you."

"He has a lot of good things to say about you, too," she responded, her smile widening.

Although Tia was reluctant to let them into the house, since she hadn't been able to get it cleaned up, Aiyana's manner put her at ease. Seth's mother didn't seem to care about her fame or her scars or even what the house looked like. Tia got the impression Aiyana saw only another human being in desperate need of a friend, and her interest came off as so genuine that Tia couldn't help responding to it. "Would you like to come in?"

"If you feel comfortable letting us, we'd love to." Aiyana lifted a canvas bag with a cute logo on it. "I brought you a few things from around town I thought you might like."

"You didn't need to bring me anything," she said.

Aiyana waved her words away. "It was my pleasure."

Accepting the bag, Tia opened the door wider to admit them.

Aiyana came through first, the scent of gardenias growing stronger as she passed by. Seth cast Tia a grin as he followed.

Tia couldn't help smiling back at him. As angry as she'd been when she realized he'd be staying on the property with her, she was starting to like him.

After leading them into the living room, she set her gift sack aside and bent to pick up some of the wrappers and other trash while they sat down.

"Have you ever been to Silver Springs before?" Aiyana asked, completely ignoring the mess.

"No, I'm afraid this is my first visit." Tia dumped what she'd collected into the wastebasket before sitting across from them and taking the items Aiyana had brought her out of the bag. There was a box of fresh-baked sugar cookies shaped like Christmas ornaments from a place called Sugar Mama, a fresh loaf of crusty sourdough bread from Millie's Bakery, a bottle of California pressed olive oil, a bottle of balsamic vinegar and two large pomegranates.

"I picked those pomegranates from my own tree," Aiyana said.

"Wow. It's all wonderful. Thank you." She carried the items to the kitchen counter.

"Once you've tried Sugar Mama's cookies, you'll be hooked," Seth predicted.

"A friend of mine owns the store," Aiyana explained. "You can find her shop right on the main drag. And Calista's Winery, where I got the olive oil and vinegar, is always fun to visit."

"Mom's lived here for over two decades," Seth told her. "She definitely knows her way around. And she's friends with literally everyone."

"It's not that big a place," Aiyana chimed in modestly. "But if you ever decide to try some of the restaurants in town, be sure to let me know. I can guide you to the best Chinese or Italian or Thai or whatever you like."

"I doubt I'll be circulating much." Tia was taken aback that Aiyana would even suggest her being seen in public.

"I hope you won't miss the entire Christmas season."

That was kind of the point of coming here, but Tia didn't say so. Aiyana was now leaning forward to make sure she held Tia's attention as she added, "I hope you won't let *anything* hold you back."

The razor focus of her eyes belied her warm smile. She was implying that what happened next was up to Tia and Tia alone, and Tia knew she was right. That was why she'd quit covering her scars, why she'd joined Seth for dinner and then breakfast this morning, why she'd agreed to this meeting. It had very little to do with Seth trying to strong-arm her by threatening to call the paparazzi. She could've refused and, as unappealing as it sounded, continued to hide from the world. But she knew he was right, too: Although those things were difficult for her, she knew she had to at least *try* to accept her new reality and embrace a normal life again, before she lost the ability to do so.

Seth and Aiyana were trying to throw her a rope. She just wasn't sure she'd be able to catch it.

"I'll do my best," she said.

Aiyana sat back and began to tell her about how she knew

Maxi, the good he did for the school, how much he loved Seth's work and that Seth would be teaching at New Horizons after Christmas.

Tia enjoyed chatting with them. It was like letting some fresh air and sunshine into the room. After about twenty minutes, she found herself offering them coffee or tea and insisting they share the cookies.

Aiyana and Seth both agreed to tea, and Aiyana joined Tia in the kitchen to help prepare it.

By the time Seth and his mother were ready to leave, Tia was feeling better again. The talking and laughing and camaraderie made such a difference. For an hour, she hadn't been able to dwell on the tragedy that had stolen her career and disfigured her face, and when Aiyana turned at the door and pulled Tia into a big hug, Tia found herself squeezing Seth's mother just as hard in return.

"I had such a wonderful time getting to know you," Aiyana said. "I hope you'll allow me to visit again."

Tia didn't want her to leave. She was afraid the darkness and despair of her situation would close in on her again. "Of course. Come by whenever you'd like."

"Wonderful. I'll do that." Her eyes twinkled, reminding Tia of Mrs. Claus as Aiyana squeezed Tia's hand before slipping her arm through her son's and letting him lead her away.

Tia watched them go before closing the door. She'd thought Seth and his mother's visit would be awkward and difficult.

But nothing could be further from the truth.

"So? What do you think?" Seth asked once he and Aiyana were in the main house. "Is she going to be okay?"

"That's hard to say," his mother replied. "But she seems like a really nice young woman. It's so unfortunate that this happened. Did she tell you what made her run that stoplight in the first place?"

He sank onto the sofa, and she sat in the leather easy chair not far away. "She told me she doesn't remember."

"She probably doesn't. It's obvious she hit her head pretty hard."

"Maybe there's nothing *to* remember. It's not uncommon to miss a traffic signal."

"Generally, that's true. But in LA—where there's so much traffic?" she asked skeptically.

"Even in LA. She could've been messing with the stereo, eating, or checking something on her phone. She could even have sneezed at the wrong time."

Aiyana grimaced. "I hope she wasn't texting."

"Regardless, we've all accidentally run a red light at least once in our lives. What happened to her could've happened to anyone."

"The consequences of this are so severe," his mother said, shaking her head in sympathy. "I wanted to ask about her family, but I figured that conversation was better saved for another time."

"I get the impression her relationship with them is...difficult," he admitted.

"What has she said about them?"

"Nothing specific. But she doesn't plan on going back to Iowa for Christmas. I know that."

"She couldn't leave Silver Springs even if she wanted to, could she? She has to be here to take care of Maxi's parrot."

"I could manage Kiki for a few days. It's that she doesn't *want* to go."

"What about her friends? People she's worked with? No one is staying in touch with her?"

"Hard to say, Mom. I just met her myself. It might be difficult for her to talk to those people at the moment."

"Movie stars are so dependent on looks—at least the type of leading roles she must aspire to are."

"Being around other industry people would only remind her of what she's lost," he agreed.

"And it's possible she doesn't know who she can trust."

He shifted to get more comfortable "What do you mean?"

"I'm referring to the paparazzi. From what you've told me, Tia's famous enough that photographs of her face, ones that reveal all the scars, would sell for a high price."

"What kind of a friend would sell her out?"

"A greedy one," she said. "And we can't let that happen."

He smiled at her. She had the kindest heart he'd ever known. "We won't."

"Have you been able to reach Shiloh's parents yet?" she asked, changing the subject.

He hated talking about Lois and Graham. Now that he'd made a success of himself, they acted as though they'd always embraced him. They never referred to all the bullshit they'd put him and Shiloh through, but there'd been a period during which her parents' disapproval and threats to disown her had nearly destroyed their marriage—mainly because he had no contact with his biological family and knew how isolating and lonely losing a family could be. He didn't want to put her in that position, so he'd pulled away, started walling her out.

Fortunately, she'd called him on it, and they'd gone to counseling, which had helped. He needed to learn how to open up and trust, the therapist said, but emotional intimacy still wasn't easy for him.

Shiloh had insisted she loved him more than anything and would not leave him no matter what he did. He'd needed her to prove that. It wasn't fair, but it was the only way he could get beyond his insecurities.

So where did his obligation to her parents end? Now that they felt slighted over his not contacting them immediately, could he just let himself walk away?

That would be easiest. He wished he never had to speak to

them again. But he owed Shiloh more than that. And if he was going to be in Silver Springs for the next several months, he was bound to run into them. He preferred those encounters not be unpleasant. "I left them a message," he told his mother.

"One they haven't returned?"

"Not yet. They're probably...busy."

"They've always looked for insult or injury. I don't know how you managed to build a relationship with them."

"I got rich," he said simply.

She opened her mouth as if his response surprised her. He thought she might try to defend them. But she pressed her lips back together.

"They never thought I was good enough for her," Seth explained. "But once I became well known, they couldn't tell enough of their friends that their daughter was married to Seth Turner."

"You've done a lot for them."

More than he should have. He'd probably been trying to buy their love, since he couldn't get it any other way. He'd paid their mortgage for several months when Graham got sick and couldn't work. He'd replaced their old car because the repair bills that were coming in were more than what the vehicle was worth. He'd even given them paintings and sculptures as gifts they'd then sold to pay off debt. They didn't understand or appreciate his work. They only liked the prestige of being associated with him—and the money they could get from him.

"They've always been difficult, even for Shiloh," he admitted. His late wife had apologized for them many times and told him that it didn't matter what they thought. But it mattered to him. The rejection he'd suffered when he was put up for adoption at six years old made him desperate to find the acceptance and unconditional love he'd been denied. He'd done everything he could to win them over, and they'd taken advantage of his need. It wasn't until Shiloh died that he recognized it wasn't really him they'd finally embraced.

Aiyana tilted her head, studying him.

"What?" he said at the speculative look on her face.

"I'm so proud of you," she replied. "I couldn't have a better son."

He wished he'd been born to her. She'd done everything she could for him, and it had made a world of difference. But what he couldn't tell her—and wouldn't tell her because he never wanted her to think he was ungrateful—was that no amount of love could make up for the fact that his own mother hadn't wanted him enough to bring him back home. He was the only child she hadn't rescued in the end. Not only had she changed her mind about his older brother and reclaimed him, she'd changed her mind about his younger one, too.

So the question that burned uppermost in his mind, and would give him no relief, was *Why not me?*

CHAPTER TEN

Ray Kouretas had never been to Silver Springs. He was a city boy born and raised in Carson, east of Interstate 110 in the Los Angeles area, which was blue-collar through and through. The hygge vibe that was so prevalent in this community couldn't have painted a bigger contrast. And he didn't particularly like it. He couldn't relate, didn't feel comfortable here.

What was with these people? Were they totally out of touch with what real life meant for the lower socioeconomic classes? He had bigger things to worry about than whether his water had been filtered, whether his vegetables were non-GMO *and* organic and whether the hamburger he'd had for dinner supported an industry that significantly contributed to global warming. He didn't want some wealthy retiree wearing Birkenstocks and drinking kombucha lecturing him on the dangers of smoking, let alone the carcinogens in animal protein. And he sure as hell had no interest in hiking, biking or doing yoga. The people here had outlawed chain stores, for crying out loud. He couldn't even get a Big Mac in this place.

Dropping his duffel bag on the floor, he sank onto the bed in the room he'd rented in a mission-style hotel. It was a much nicer room than he was used to, but all the places to stay out here were expensive. And he didn't have a lot of time to mess around. He needed to get Tia's photograph, and he needed it bad.

He hoped it would be worth the effort he was putting into it. He was going to be pissed if his informant was wrong, especially because he'd had to tell his editor he was certain he could get the shot just to get the chance to follow up on the lead.

He pulled his phone out of his pocket to check his messages. His editor was on his ass again.

Have you found her yet?

Barely got here, Eddie. What, do you think I can just snap my fingers and she'll appear?

It's not that big a town, is it?

Jesus! It was a Saturday night. Didn't the guy ever stop working?

No, but there are 7,000 people in the area, and she's not exactly strolling down Main Street. She's in hiding, remember? Otherwise, we'd be too late already. Someone else would've gotten what we want.

How long will it take to find her?

How should I know? A few days?

Let me remind you that the magazine's paying your expenses. This is not a fucking vacation.

Irritated, he called his lousy editor an idiot before texting back. I get that. I'm not here for the hell of it. My informant knows what she's talking about.

Then, have her give you the damn address.

She doesn't have the address.

Can she get it before we get scooped?

We won't get scooped. I'm the only one who has any idea where Tia Beckett is.

He'd given up a night out drinking with his buddies to work, which showed commitment, but he didn't mention that. The sacrifice was nothing less than any good tabloid editor expected when a hot tip promised a big story.

How do you know?

He didn't. He was bullshitting, but a paparazzo had to do what a paparazzo had to do. Otherwise, he'd never get the support he needed, not from the cheap-ass rag he worked for. And after he'd screwed up last month and reported something he hadn't fully fact-checked, causing *The Lowdown* to be slapped with yet another lawsuit, he was on Eddie's shit list.

This was his way of getting off it.

Because I've been doing this for twenty years, and I've learned a thing or two. She's legit.

What relationship does she have with Tia Beckett?

She won't say.

Then, how do you know she's legit?

Shit, Eddie. I can just tell, okay? Even if you doubt that, I'm already here. Let me do my job.

I hope you do it a lot better than you've been doing it lately. I wouldn't want to have to fire your ass at Christmas.

But Eddie would do it. The threat was real.

I'll let you know as soon as I have something, he wrote back.

He waited to see if Eddie had a response to that, but nothing came. "Bastard," he mumbled and called the number he had for the informant who'd reached him at his desk yesterday, out of the blue.

A female voice answered. "Hello?"

"It's me," he said.

"I know."

She didn't sound particularly happy to hear from him, but she was the one who'd started this thing. "I'm in Silver Springs. Now what?"

"What do you mean? I told you, I don't know *exactly* where she's staying. You'll have to find her."

"You sure she's still here?"

"I'm positive. She's not going anywhere. She's taking care of a friend's parrot while he's on vacation in Europe."

"Did you say *parrot*?" he asked.

"Yes."

"What...is he a fucking pirate? Why would anyone have a parrot as a pet?"

"Do you really have to use that kind of language?" she asked.

He rolled his eyes. Those who took exception to bad language were ridiculous. Words were completely neutral. Saying that some words were bad was like choosing one color to be bad but accepting all the rest as good. It was something imposed by society that didn't really exist. But he'd dealt with people like her before, and he needed her, so he said, "I'm sorry, but

if you're playing with me, you won't get one red cent. I hope
you know that."

"I'm not playing with you."

"Then, call her up and ask her where she's staying."

"I can't do that!"

"Why not?"

"Because when the photographs come out, I don't want her
to know I had anything to do with it."

She could call him out for his *language* while betraying a
friend, cousin, work associate or whatever? "So you're doing
this strictly for the money," he said.

"Of course." She spoke quickly to confirm it, but he got the
impression there was something else at play, something more
personal. As long as he got what he wanted, however, he didn't
care. "Okay. I'll let you know what I find. And if you can get
me any more information, please do. We'll have a lot better
chance if we make quick work of it."

"I'll do what I can, but...you'll pay me, right? How do I
know you'll really pay me?"

"You don't have to worry about that. Not if you do your
part."

"I've brought you this far, haven't I?"

He was doing all the work. That was the thing. He'd pay her
a little, but there were a lot of excuses he could use to whittle
down the amount they'd initially discussed. "Close isn't good
enough," he said. "But I'll see what I can do."

He hit the End button. If he was going to find Tia Beckett,
he needed to get out and visit the nightclubs and bars. If the
most buzzed-about Hollywood star since Jennifer Lawrence was
in town, someone would be talking about it.

Tia heard the sound of a car engine and peered out the window to see Aiyana leaving in her sedan and Seth getting into
his expensive Porsche. She wondered if they were going to Ai-

yana's house or if Aiyana was going home and Seth was going
out. He'd lived in Silver Springs when he was younger. He
could have friends here. He definitely had family.

After they were gone, she walked over to the main house to
take care of Kiki and tried, once again, to teach the bird to say
I love Tia. She repeated the phrase ad nauseam, but Maxi's parrot had no interest in even attempting to copy her.

"How did you learn what you say already?" she muttered,
frustrated by her lack of success.

Kiki barked like a dog but didn't repeat any of the phrases
Tia knew she could say. The bird mostly kept a close eye on
the ball, obviously hoping Tia would throw it. Maybe she remembered the dog barking while playing catch.

Tia played with Maxi's parrot for quite some time before
she let herself out of the aviary. She listened to see if Seth had
returned, and when it became clear she was still alone in the
house, she considered going upstairs to take a peek at whatever
it was he was working on. She was curious to see his process.

But there weren't any plants up there to give her a good excuse to intrude on his privacy. And she didn't want him to
come home and catch her. Being found where she shouldn't
be—*again*—would be awkward indeed.

Since the guesthouse was starting to feel more like a prison
than a refuge, she ambled around the yard, picked a few oranges
and then some grapefruit.

There was a lock on the pool gate to keep kids who happened to be on the property safe, but she knew the code. It was
the same as the one required to get onto the property in the
first place. After putting down the fruit, which she planned to
grab on her way back, she punched in the numbers, let herself
through and settled on a chaise to watch clouds drift across the
moon.

Although it was cold out, she had on a thick sweater. She
inhaled deeply, drawing in the smell of the citrus trees nearby

and the stronger scent of chlorine from the pool. She could heal in this place, couldn't she? When she didn't allow herself to think about her family, or her career, or her face, she almost felt like herself again.

But then she would see a mirror or get a message from home, and reality would intrude...

Determined to hold off that moment of reckoning as long as possible, she got up and bent to test the temperature of the water in the hot tub. Maybe she'd get in. Just because she'd given up the main house to Seth didn't mean she had any less right to the pool and Jacuzzi.

After going back to get her bathing suit, she spent half an hour in the hot tub. But once that was over, she was looking down the barrel of another long, lonely night. She couldn't bear to turn on the TV. Streaming one show after the other was all she'd done since the accident. There was nothing left to watch. But she had to keep busy or the regret and pain would get the best of her as it had every other night.

After a shower, she dropped onto the couch, pulled out her phone and finally started to listen to the voice mails she'd ignored over the past month.

Barbie Kowalski, a woman about her age she'd met in acting school, had tried several times to reach her. Tia had lived with Barbie for years, before Barbie moved in with her boyfriend. "God, Tia. Where are you? Why won't you respond to me? You must be going through hell, and I'm so sorry. I love you, girl."

She loved Barbie, too. Barbie had been the one to drive her home from the hospital. Barbie and her boyfriend had also helped her purchase a cheap, nondescript car, since hers had been totaled, and she hadn't wanted to spend a lot on a vehicle if she was only going to end up flying home to Iowa. But Tia hadn't talked to her since she'd told Barbie she'd be house-sitting in Silver Springs for the holidays. She'd been afraid any more detailed information would bring Barbie out to check on her, and she'd just wanted to be left alone.

As she scrolled up and down, picking and choosing which voice mails to listen to, she heard messages from several people who'd worked on the film with her. Christian, her costar, had called a couple of times.

"Hey, I'm really sorry about what happened," he said, his voice deeper than almost any she'd ever heard. "Call me if you need to talk. Johnny and I would love to have you over, if that's even a possibility."

She really liked him and his partner, but she didn't want him to see her like this. The same thing held true for her other film-industry friends. They'd also tried to wish her well, but she hadn't responded, and they'd moved on with their lives. She hadn't been close enough to those people for them to do much else.

Maxi, however, was a notable exception. "You're not shutting me out, Tia. Answer the damn phone." Next call: "Answer your phone, or I'm going to hunt you down. I'm worried about you." Next call: "I'm watching the news, and I can see the paparazzi trying to break down the gate at your condominium complex. What the hell is wrong with people?" Next call: "I'll be in LA on Friday. I'm coming to see you whether you like it or not."

She smiled as she remembered how he'd made good on that promise. He'd sweet-talked someone in the complex into letting him through the gate by pretending to be a potential buyer for one of the units, at which point he'd gone around back, hopped the fence to get to her patio and banged on the slider. "Tia, it's Maxi. Open the fucking door," he'd said, and she'd done it.

That was when he'd offered her the use of his property in Silver Springs.

She deleted those messages and moved on.

Her sister: "Is it true? You're not coming home? You haven't learned your lesson? What more does God have to do to direct your footsteps?"

Wincing, Tia deleted that one. She and Rachel had always struggled to get along, and what'd happened not long before the accident hadn't brought them any closer.

Rachel again: "Seriously? You're not even going to answer my call? What kind of sister are you?"

She wasn't as bad as Rachel made her sound. She'd done a lot to help her sister. The way it had worked out wasn't *her* fault.

Unable to listen to any more from Rachel, she deleted the rest. They were all the same—and simply too hard to hear.

Unwilling to return *any* calls, she sent a few text messages to those who'd wished her well and was just thanking Christian and Johnny when she received a message from Maxi.

Are you and Seth getting along okay? You're still at the house, right? How's Kiki?

Seth and I are doing fine. Kiki is great. Hope you're enjoying yourself, she wrote back. She thought that would be it, but a few minutes later, she got another text from him.

That was a little too easy, Tia. What's the real story? You hanging in there?

Trying, she messaged back.

You have more to offer the world than a pretty face.

Except that her career and her dreams depended on her face. But what was the point of insisting it was the end of the world? It was only the end of the world for her. For everyone else, life went on as usual.

She sent him an emoji blowing a kiss so that he'd let it go and wouldn't press her anymore. Then, because she didn't want to think about all the messages from her sister she'd just deleted carte blanche, she went onto the internet and searched Seth Turner's name.

Various pictures popped up. As she scrolled through them, she couldn't help but admire his high cheekbones, strong chin and pretty eyes. He came off as dark and brooding even with his hair short and combed off his face, but he was definitely attractive.

His bio said he was an American sculptor and painter who'd been discovered at a young age, that his work was popular among critics and art collectors alike because he was able to convey so much with so little—something she'd noticed herself. His first painting to sell for over a million dollars was called *Brothers* and depicted the love/hate relationship that could so often exist between siblings.

As she stared at it, two figures—who could've been male or female—seemed to be trying to cling to each other even as something unseen was tearing them apart.

She tried to find a picture of the screaming woman that was hanging across from the couch to see if it was, indeed, Seth's work and wasn't surprised to find that it was. *In Her Head* had sold for a quarter of a million dollars.

"Wow," she said on a long exhale. Seth was rich. *Really* rich. If he made that much off each piece, he had to be.

"Well, good for him." She would've clicked away, except that when she scrolled down, she noticed the Wikipedia biography continued with a section labeled "Early Life."

He'd told her he was born in Denver. But there was a lot he hadn't said. His childhood hadn't been easy. His mother had gotten pregnant and dropped out of high school. His father, who'd been a classmate, had dropped out, too, after which he worked odd jobs until he became a plumber. Seth was born about that time, and they added one more child before the marriage broke down. After Seth's father left the family, his mother fell on hard times. She and her three kids became homeless and had to live out of a car for a few months, after which his mother decided she couldn't care for her children any longer.

No wonder he'd been in and out of *juvie*, as he'd called it, when he was growing up and had gone to a school for troubled youth.

What had a young Seth been like? And what had led to the time he'd spent in juvenile hall?

She tried searching with other keywords in an attempt to find out and discovered an interview he gave right after he launched his career, during which he made an oblique reference to being involved in something where two other kids had been tried as adults and gone to prison.

"That sounds serious," she murmured to herself. He didn't seem like a criminal...

She continued to look through the pictures she found online but stopped scrolling when she found one of Seth with a beautiful blonde who was almost as tall as he was. They appeared to be at a big charity gala or some other function. He wore a tux, and the woman, who was wearing an evening gown, had her hair done with old-fashioned finger waves, making her look like a 1950s movie star.

"Who's *that*?" Tia clicked on it to be able to read the caption. *American artist and sculptor Seth Turner and his wife, Shiloh.*

She rocked back. "*Wife*? You told me you weren't married." So...why did he lie? And where was Shiloh now?

They had to be divorced, she decided. Most people would have said so. But maybe he hadn't wanted to get into it.

She searched the name *Shiloh Turner*, just to be sure, but found they hadn't divorced.

Seth's wife had died three years ago—only two days before Christmas.

CHAPTER ELEVEN

Seth sat at The Blue Suede Shoe, a popular bar in town, with his brothers, Gavin and Eli. They'd come over to play pool. Earlier, Eli's wife, Cora, had been to a Christmas Tea with a group of teachers from New Horizons and had decided not to come. She was getting the kids to bed and relaxing at home. But Aiyana had agreed to babysit for Gavin's wife so that Savanna could join them after she returned from a shopping trip. She was running late because she was fighting traffic, trying to get back from LA.

"So… Eli told me that Tia Beckett is in town," Gavin said as they drank a beer while watching a program that showed one video snippet after another of hilarious skateboarding, bicycling or other accidents.

"He *what*?" Seth turned to glare at Eli. "What part of *Don't tell anyone* don't you understand?"

"I haven't told anyone," Eli said, instantly defensive.

"No? You mean other than Cora and Mom and Gavin—"

"They're family," he interrupted. "That doesn't count."

Seth rolled his eyes before leaning in and lowering his voice. "She's terrified the paparazzi will find her and start hounding her again. This town might feel safe to us, because we've never experienced anything like having people camp outside our homes, hoping to get a picture they could sell, but to her, it's a serious threat."

"No one in our family's going to tell anyone," Eli assured him.

Gavin cast him a sheepish look. "Except… I've already told Savanna."

"Oh, hell," Seth said.

Eli and Gavin laughed, but Seth didn't think it was funny. He glowered at them both until they quit.

"Come on. Our wives won't tell anyone. You trust every person who knows," Eli said.

Seth couldn't argue with that. But still.

"What's she like?" Gavin asked. "Is she as gorgeous in real life as she is on the big screen?"

He hesitated before saying, "The accident did some damage."

Eli seemed surprised. "I saw a few bandages on her face, but she wasn't paralyzed or anything. And most wounds heal. Hers will, too, won't they?"

They would heal, but the scars they left behind would never go away. It'd been a month since the accident, and from what he'd seen, there couldn't have been much improvement. But he supposed anything was possible. It was early yet. "Maybe," he replied.

"Savanna and I liked her movie," Gavin said. "It was funny but poignant and sort of real."

"She's got some talent." Eli grinned. "And no one's as pretty as Cora, but Tia's got gorgeous eyes."

"They're incredible," Seth agreed. "That hasn't changed."

A stir over by the bar caught their attention. Several people were talking at once, and whatever they were discussing seemed to be generating more and more interest, because a crowd was forming.

"What's going on?" Gavin asked.

Seth shook his head.

Eli stood. "Let's go see."

Seth wasn't particularly interested when he followed his brothers to the other side of the room. He didn't live here and couldn't imagine whatever it was would concern him. He ordered another drink while Eli and Gavin tried to learn what all the commotion was about. Seth was tempted to tell them it didn't matter, that they should go play another game of pool because he had to get home and start work soon, when he heard Tia's name.

"What'd they say?" he asked Gavin, suddenly as interested as they were.

"I couldn't hear, but I see a friend over there," Gavin said. "I'll ask Ben if he knows." He nudged his way through the group. "What's going on?" Seth heard him ask some guy with a full beard.

Ben gestured at a slouchy-looking guy in a flannel shirt over a white T-shirt and a pair of baggy jeans that had big cuffs at the bottom. "This guy was just asking if we've seen Tia Beckett, the movie star. He claims she's in town."

Seth caught his breath, hoping Gavin wouldn't do anything to give Tia away.

"The one who was in that accident?" he heard Gavin say.

"Yeah," his friend replied. "Have you seen her? Because I sure haven't. I'd remember that."

"I haven't seen her, either," Gavin said. "What about everyone else?"

After the rest of the people in the group shook their heads or mumbled a negative response, Gavin addressed the guy in the flannel shirt. "How do you know she's here?"

"That's what I was told." He pulled some business cards from his pocket and started handing them out. "If you see her, would you give me a call?"

"What do you want with her?" Eli asked as everyone took one.
The guy looked up. "We have some business together."

"So you know her."

A smile curved his lips. "Yeah, we're friends."

Seth wanted to believe this guy was truly a friend, since Tia desperately needed one, but he didn't get that feeling. He was too old to be the ex-boyfriend she'd labeled as *controlling.* And the fact that he didn't take care of himself made Seth doubt he was an actor.

Was he a paparazzo? Part of an industry that made money off the fame of others?

Seth couldn't wait for Gavin to return with the dude's information. He was eager to see if there was a company or something else, besides his name, to indicate who he was.

There wasn't. The card read only *Ray T. Kouretas* and provided a number.

It was late when Seth returned to the house, but he could see light gleaming around the blinds in the guesthouse as he got out of the car, which led him to assume Tia was still up. He wondered what she was doing; she'd mentioned that nights were long and hard to get through. Since they were often the same for him since Shiloh died, he felt for her.

He considered knocking to tell her what he'd heard at The Blue Suede Shoe. If anyone beyond his family learned she was in town, word could easily get back to Ray Kouretas. The man wasn't making any secret of the fact that he was looking for her. She had no ties to this area—no family or history here—so people would have no reason not to tell him if they saw her, especially because those in Silver Springs generally tried to be accommodating. But she was struggling to get back on her feet as it was. He didn't want to make her recovery more difficult. She was already being cautious. What more could she do?

Besides, he didn't really know who this Ray Kouretas was,

so it could be a mistake to spook her. He might do it for no good reason.

He let himself into the main house, where Kiki greeted him by barking like a dog. Having a parrot that imitated a dog might be a good way to scare off any would-be intruders, but that made it no less annoying.

"It's fine, Kiki. It's just me," he shouted and shoved his coat in the closet before grabbing his laptop.

As soon as he settled into the recliner in the living room, he signed onto the internet and typed *Ray Kouretas* into Google.

Several links came up, but none looked promising. There was a LinkedIn account and a Twitter account for a man who went by the same name, but the small round picture attached to each didn't fit the guy at the bar.

Seth tried other queries—*names of the paparazzi, how the paparazzi get jobs, places where paparazzi sell photos*—to learn how the industry worked. He thought this guy's name might pop up somewhere. But the best article he found said that most members of the paparazzi didn't reveal their names. They kept a low profile because what they did was so invasive and contentious. They had to remain anonymous to avoid backlash.

Seth was also surprised to learn that a good paparazzo could make half a million dollars for one picture, depending on the subject, the clarity, the timeliness, and so on. Most didn't make nearly that much, of course, but they didn't have to get up and go to work every day, either. They could follow whomever they wanted, whenever they wanted and hang out and drink coffee or talk on their phones while waiting for an opportunity to make a buck or two. All they needed was a good photo every once in a while, and they could earn a living.

Was Ray trying to take pictures he could sell?

If so, there was nothing on the internet connecting him to that line of work. But that didn't necessarily rule him out.

Seth shut down his laptop, then stared at the business card

Gavin had passed along to him. Maybe he should just call Ray and see what the guy had to say.

He checked the clock. It was after eleven, but Kouretas had been at The Blue Suede Shoe when Seth and his brothers walked out. Even if he'd left shortly after, chances were good he wouldn't be asleep quite yet.

After blocking his number, he bowed his head and examined the grain of the hardwood floor beneath his feet as the phone rang.

"Hello?"

Music blared in the background; Ray was still at the bar. "Are you the one looking for Tia Beckett?" Seth asked without preamble.

"I am," he said. "Have you seen her?"

"I might have."

"Where?"

"What's in it for me?"

There was a slight pause before the guy said, "You'd be doing her a big favor."

Seth began to pace. "Come on. You expect me to believe I'd be doing *her* a favor?"

"Can you give me the particulars? Exactly where she's at and when she might be going out?"

"Maybe."

"Just a sec." The music faded before going silent, suggesting Kouretas had just stepped outside the bar. "How much are you looking for?" he asked a moment later.

Seth had no idea what to say. He was just leading this guy far enough along that he could be certain of his intentions. "Half."

"Half of what? I don't even know what I'll be able to get."

"It'll be a lot, though, right? For the first picture of Tia Beckett after her big accident?" If that wasn't what Kouretas was after, this was where he'd make the correction…

"There are too many variables," Kouretas replied. "I don't even know if I can get a good shot."

Bingo. He was a paparazzo, all right. "What if I can get you one?"

"If you can tell me where she is, and you can make it possible for me to get the shot—*a good one*—I'll give you ten percent of whatever I make."

"Ten percent?" Seth scoffed. "Dude, you'll get nothing without me."

"I don't need you that badly. I know she's in town. I'll just keep looking until I find her."

"How do you know she's in town?"

"I have it on good authority."

Who the hell was giving this guy his information? "What if she's leaving soon?" Seth asked.

He laughed. "She's not."

"How do you know?"

"She's house-sitting for some rich dude while he spends the holidays abroad, and she's taking care of his parrot. Am I getting warm yet?"

Seth felt his stomach tense. "She was, but now she's going home to spend Christmas with her family."

"Sure she is," he scoffed. "Who is this?"

Seth wanted to say he was someone who would never let Kouretas get what he wanted. But that would only give away the fact that he was now scared for Tia—and if Ray smelled blood in the water, he'd keep circling until he *did* get what he wanted. "Someone who knows where Tia is and who's willing to make a deal."

"You won't give me your name?"

"You don't need my name. And if you don't want the information I have, I'll just go to someone else who'll pay more."

Seth sensed a change in attitude. "Don't do that," Ray said.

"I'll go twenty-five percent. But that's the best I can do. There's already someone else in the deal."

"Then, have whoever led you this far take you the rest of the way," Seth said and hung up.

Who could've told Ray where Tia was? She didn't seem to be communicating with *anyone*. But he wasn't with her all that often. Maybe he didn't really know. This proved there had to be at least one person who knew she was in Silver Springs—and that person didn't seem to be very trustworthy.

With a sigh, Seth went to his bedroom, where he could peer out at the guesthouse. He could still see a glimmer of light around the windows. He was once again tempted to walk over and warn Tia. But there was no reason this couldn't wait until morning. Why make the night any longer or harder?

He sent her a text message, just to touch base. You okay?

Although he checked his phone periodically as he worked over the next several hours, he never received a response.

It was dawn when he was finally exhausted enough to sleep. Before dropping into bed, however, he looked out the window and saw that her lights were *still* on and couldn't help wondering what she was doing.

"Breakfast is ready!"

Tia dragged herself out of the depths of sleep. Someone was banging on her door. Again.

"Tia?"

Seth. Of course. What was this—*Groundhog Day*?

She groaned as she rolled over. She'd fallen asleep on the couch again. The last thing she remembered was watching rerun after rerun of *The Office*—which was about the only thing that could cheer her up these days.

"Go away!" She tried to go back to sleep, but the next thing she knew, she heard Seth singing Christmas carols outside her door. *Deck the halls with boughs of holly...*

"What are you doing?" she called. He couldn't even sing!

"Just sending a little Christmas cheer your way," he called back. "I managed to sleep for a few hours, so I happen to be in a good mood. You?"

She sat up and stared daggers at the door. "No, I'm not in a good mood. And I don't want any Christmas cheer. What's wrong with you? Can't you just leave me to my depression?"

He laughed. "Nope. It's that time of year. If I have to enjoy it, so do you."

She suddenly remembered reading that his wife had died at Christmastime not too long ago. Was that why he hated the holidays? "What do you want from me?" she asked.

"I made breakfast. The least you can do is help me eat it."

"No breakfast for me."

"You have to be hungry."

"Hunger has nothing to do with it. I'm getting fat."

"Because you're eating junk food. If you eat *real* food, you might be able to lay off that stuff."

She doubted it, but she'd do anything to stop him from singing when he began to belt out *Joy to the World*.

"Okay! Stop it," she yelled. "I'm coming."

"Great. See you in ten minutes. Otherwise, I might have to come back and sing *The Twelve Days of Christmas*, and you know how long that song is."

She managed a grudging smile. "I'll save us both the agony. But you're going to have to give me a minute. You woke me up. I haven't even showered."

"Just pull on that ratty robe and come over," he said.

"Ratty? Did you just call my robe *ratty*?"

"You have ten minutes before I start singing again."

She frowned at the empty box of Andes Chocolate Mints she'd found in a cupboard and devoured last night. She needed to have some groceries delivered.

"See you soon!" he called just when she'd thought he left.

"Are you going to do this every morning?" she asked.

"I might. But today we have something important to discuss."

She wasn't sure she liked the sound of that. "What could we have to talk about that's *important*?"

"I'll tell you when you come over."

"Is it something I'm not going to like?" she asked, getting to her feet.

"I'd rather not answer that question. It's going to be okay. Just come over."

"You said I could have ten minutes," she grumbled and shuffled to the bathroom so she could at least comb her hair and brush her teeth.

CHAPTER TWELVE

"What is it you want to tell me?" Tia asked as she came through the front door.

Seth motioned toward the table. She was wearing yoga pants, a long sleeve athletic top and tennis shoes, and had braved the short walk from the guesthouse without a jacket. She'd mentioned something about getting fat, but he didn't think she was overweight. "We'll talk about it after you eat."

Kiki started to squawk excitedly, so Tia stopped at the aviary to tap on the glass and say hello. "How are you, Kiki? You're such a beauty."

"Pretty girl, pretty girl," Kiki said.

"Yes. You are a pretty girl," Tia confirmed.

As Tia came into the kitchen, she eyed the egg burrito on her plate with some detachment, but once Seth encouraged her to dig in while he finished making his own, she didn't even pause to talk.

"Apparently, you were hungrier than you thought," he said wryly.

She glanced over at him. "Don't read anything into this. I do *not* want to encourage you to wake me up every morning."

He stuffed his tortilla with eggs, sausage and cheese and added plenty of salsa. "Judging from what I've seen so far, *someone* needs to." He grinned to let her know he was teasing and put his own plate down before holding up the pitcher of orange juice he'd squeezed earlier. "Juice?"

She lifted her glass. "Goading comments aside, this *is* pretty good," she said grudgingly. "Why are you being so nice to me?"

He laughed at the suspicion in her expression, but he figured he couldn't blame her for being skeptical of kindness. He was skeptical of it, too. "Because you can't let what happened to your face destroy your life. You have until Christmas. Then you need to get back to living again. I figure you can start by taking a few baby steps—like coming out to eat and exercise."

She eyed him speculatively. "You're almost a hermit, and you're giving *me* advice about getting out?"

Assuming it was Maxi who'd told her he wasn't particularly social, he filled his own glass before putting down the pitcher. "I get myself up, I eat, I exercise, and I work. I'd say that puts me a mile or two ahead of you."

"You just started exercising," she pointed out. "You already told me that."

"At least I've done it," he grumbled. "Once."

She laughed, and he couldn't help laughing with her.

"Besides, a hermit doesn't do gallery showings." He'd often pointed to that when Aiyana began to press him to start dating or seeing his friends again.

But Tia didn't let him get away with it, either. "Making a few exceptions here and there for work doesn't count. That you don't have more support for your argument is concerning."

"Being a little eccentric is good for my image."

"That's how you view yourself?"

"That's how I hope others view me." He preferred they not see more than what he expressed in his art, because as far as he was concerned, he was *too* normal, had all the same needs and desires as other people no matter how hard he tried to quash them.

"Then, you might have your wish. You've been characterized as a *tortured soul*."

"Sounds like Maxi has had a lot to say about me."

"I haven't been talking to Maxi," she said. "I looked you up online."

When he finally sat down across from her, he was careful not to stare at the scars on her face. He was curious enough that he wanted to examine them more closely, but they didn't bother him. Maybe it was because he'd never known her any other way. "You braved the internet on *my* account? I'm flattered."

"Don't be," she said with a scowl. "I was just curious."

"I'm disappointed."

"Because…"

"I'm no longer shrouded in mystery."

She didn't comment on his sarcasm. "Why didn't you tell me you were once married?"

He'd poured her some coffee while she was saying hello to Kiki. Now he slid the cream and sugar over to her. "Because it's no longer relevant."

As she watched him start to eat, he could tell she had something on her mind. "What are you thinking?" he asked.

"Would you mind if I asked just one thing about her?"

He knew who Tia was referring to—and preferred she didn't. "Whatever you want to know, I'm sure it's on the internet."

"I couldn't find this. But never mind." She went back to her own meal. "I'm sorry for being so nosy. It's none of my business."

Feeling the added distance between them—distance he'd put there just now—he sat back with a sigh. His psychologist, back when he had one as a ward of the state, had told him he had to lower his defenses and open up, and he knew he'd just done the opposite. "Go ahead and ask."

"No, it's okay."

"Come on. It's only fair. I know more about your situation than you'd probably like me to," he pointed out.

"That's true," she admitted.

"So I'll give you one question."

She took a sip of her coffee. "Fine. But if it's too hard to answer, I'll understand."

"I'll manage," he said drily.

"I was just wondering how Shiloh died. I mean, she was so young. Was it cancer or an accident or something like that?"

Shiloh's death wasn't an easy subject, but Tia hadn't been able to hide her problems from him. She'd even let him invite his mother over to meet her, which couldn't have been easy so soon after the accident. "Have you ever heard of cat scratch disease?"

She set her cup in its saucer. "No."

"I'm not surprised." What'd happened was so crazy and unlikely he couldn't help feeling robbed. Cats scratched people every day. Very few of them died because of it. "If a cat licks an open wound on a human or bites or scratches deeply enough to break the skin, it can cause a bacterial infection that can travel to the brain or the heart."

Lines showing sympathy creased her normally smooth forehead. "I didn't even realize that could be dangerous."

"Neither did I. Most people—those who aren't already immunocompromised—have no trouble overcoming it. But there's—" he stared down at his food, which suddenly tasted like cardboard "—always the exception."

"So…was it her cat or your cat—a pet—that made her sick?"

"We didn't have one cat in particular because we were always so overrun. She'd made it her life's mission to save the feral cats in our neighborhood, and one scratched her deeply while she was trying to capture it."

"You'd think antibiotics would be able to take care of that," she murmured.

He got that response a lot, which was why he found it so difficult to face Shiloh's parents. He couldn't help assuming they believed the same thing—that it should've been easy to save her—and blamed him for her death.

Had he been home when she got sick, she probably would've survived. That didn't make the situation any easier. "You would," he agreed. "But there were…extenuating circumstances."

When she acted as though she'd let it go at that rather than press him, he realized he was still being too guarded and made an attempt to push even further beyond his comfort zone. "Okay. Here's the story. I had a gallery showing in New York at the time. Shiloh had more cats than usual—one she was nursing back to health—and several meetings with potential families to place them in homes. So she decided not to come with me."

"That's when it happened?" she asked softly.

"That's when it started," he corrected. "I was two days into my trip when she said she wasn't feeling well."

"Did she tell you she'd been scratched?"

"No. She'd been scratched so many times before, she probably didn't think it was worth mentioning, and I certainly wouldn't have known to be alarmed." The regret he felt for not being more aware, for not acting sooner, tore him up inside. If only he'd known to take her illness more seriously. "Anyway, I told her to see a doctor, but she insisted it was just the flu or some other virus and promised me she'd go in if she wasn't feeling better by morning."

Tia bit her lip. "Don't tell me she didn't go in…"

He frowned. "She wanted to wait for me to take her. When I boarded the plane, I still assumed it wasn't serious. But when I got home I could tell something was terribly wrong and drove her straight to the hospital."

He paused, but Tia didn't break in. He could tell she was trying to give him the time he needed to finish this difficult story.

"And by then it was too late. Her brain had started to swell, and…" He'd thought he was firmly in control of his emotions. He was well-practiced at shoving them deep inside. But when his voice threatened to crack, he fell silent.

Without saying anything, Tia reached over to lay her hand lightly on his. "I'm so sorry, but I… I appreciate you telling me. It puts what I'm going through into perspective. Here I am, feeling sorry for myself over a scarred face, when you've been coping with something much worse."

"What you're going through can't be easy, either," he offered. "Don't beat yourself up."

He could tell she was about to pull away. She'd only meant to convey a bit of compassion. But he was oddly reluctant to lose contact with her. It'd been so long since he'd been touched by a woman.

The moment he shifted so that he could run his thumb over her smaller, more delicate fingers, her gaze lowered to their hands. She seemed mesmerized by the sight, but after a few seconds, he forced himself to let go and return to his meal. He couldn't allow himself to care about Tia or anyone else. Caring never worked out for him.

"Sorry," she said.

He wasn't sure what she was apologizing for. For being bold enough to touch him in the first place? Or for enjoying those few seconds?

Had she enjoyed them? Because he certainly had—although he couldn't help feeling he'd just betrayed Shiloh. Maybe it was illogical, but even three years after her death, it somehow mattered that he remain loyal to her. "There's nothing to apologize for," he said to compensate for his sudden withdrawal, but even then he sounded so gruff he added, "I didn't mind. I think maybe we're both starved for human contact."

He regretted those words as soon as they were out of his mouth; they embarrassed him, made him feel too exposed.

"About that thing I had to tell you…" he said, hoping to escape what had become an awkward moment.

Tia had a hard time shifting gears. The leap of attraction that had flared when Seth was holding her hand had caught her completely off guard. She'd never had a serious relationship last longer than a couple of months. She'd been too highly focused on her career, and she hadn't met anyone she'd felt that strongly about. She'd assumed she'd pay a high price for that now and would probably be alone for years. Because of the accident, she couldn't even imagine dating.

And then she'd touched Seth, and he'd turned his hand over, sending a lightning bolt of awareness through her that still left her feeling strange. "Right," she said and folded her hands in her lap because she suddenly didn't know what else to do with them. "What is it?"

"There's a man in town."

"A man?" Her mind still wasn't fully engaged.

"A member of the paparazzi," he clarified.

She felt her eyes widen. This definitely drew her back to reality. "How do you know?"

Seth looked uncomfortable. She got the impression he didn't want to tell her. No one liked to be the bearer of bad news. But he obviously felt compelled. "Last night he was at The Blue Suede Shoe, a popular bar in town, asking if anyone had seen you."

She covered her mouth. "No!"

"I'm afraid so."

Her mind raced as she tried to figure out how the paparazzi could've tracked her down, especially so soon. "How could he have known *already* that I'm here?" She'd figured word would leak out eventually—if she ever worked up enough nerve to go into town, or to one of the wineries as Aiyana had suggested—

but she hadn't been spotted by anyone in Silver Springs yet, except Seth, his mother and his brother.

"I have no clue."

"Did you speak to him?"

"Not at the bar," he replied. "But he was passing out his business card to anyone who would take it, so Gavin grabbed me one, and I called him after I got home last night."

"You didn't!"

"I did. I wanted to be sure of who he was and what he wanted with you."

"And? Did he admit to being part of the paparazzi?"

"Essentially. I did what I could to throw him off your trail by saying you'd be leaving in the next few days. But he wasn't buying it."

"Why not?"

"Whoever told him where he could find you also told him you're taking care of a pet parrot through Christmas. He just doesn't know for whom, or he wouldn't have been asking if anyone has seen you. He would've been asking where Maxi lives."

That made sense, but how did this paparazzo get so far so fast? "I can't remember telling anyone about Kiki. You know what it's been like for me. I rarely even look at my phone." But she had to have mentioned the parrot to *someone*, or this wouldn't have come up.

"Do you have any idea how many people in this town are familiar with Maxi's pet?"

She rubbed her temples as she tried to think. "I have no clue. I guess we could ask Maxi. But I can't imagine he ever takes Kiki out, so even if he's mentioned her, I'm not sure many people will remember."

"I can tell you he doesn't talk about her much. I didn't even know about her, and I was coming to stay at the house."

"Who could've given me away?" She was talking more to herself than Seth, but he lifted his hands in a defensive position.

"Just so you know, it wasn't me or Eli or anyone else in my family. If it *was* one of us, this dude would've been knocking on your door, not asking around the most popular bar in town."

"I'm not accusing you," she said. "I'm just…dumbfounded. I've had such limited contact with my friends since the accident. It couldn't be any of them."

He got up and grabbed a business card from the counter, which he slid across the table to her. "This is the guy," he said. "Do you recognize the name?"

She stared at the bold black lettering: *Ray Kouretas*. "Never heard of him."

"You haven't told anyone you're here?"

"Barbie, my friend, knows I'm here," she replied. "But I can't believe *she'd* give me away."

"She knows you're house-sitting for Maxi?"

"I don't remember giving her Maxi's name, but I might've said I'd be pet-sitting for my producer."

The beard growth on Seth's face rasped as he rubbed his chin. "I got the impression that Kouretas is paying for the information he's receiving. Does your friend need money?"

Barbie lived an unorganized life, couldn't seem to stay ahead. But she'd been doing better since getting with Mike. She loved him so much. And she had a heart of gold. "Like most people, she could use it," she admitted. "She's a struggling actress who hasn't been lucky enough to get the kind of break I did. Not yet, anyway. But she would never sell me out."

"Then, there has to be someone else."

"There isn't. I haven't talked to *anyone*—just Barbie, my parents, and my brother and sister. And I can't imagine my family would give me away." A sick feeling started in the pit of her stomach as she heard herself speak and realized that wasn't really true. "Or…maybe they would."

He looked surprised by this admission. "What do you mean?"

She hated talking about her family. She knew, in their own

way, they meant well. They just looked at the world so differently—allowed what she'd term *superstition* to guide their actions—and Tia had always hungered for bigger and better things than living in such a small, religious community, where her beliefs were dictated by her parents. "They're…disappointed and worried and angry," she explained.

"Because…" he prompted.

"They didn't want me to leave Iowa, didn't agree with my choice to become an actress, didn't believe I'd continue to be the kind of daughter they could be proud of." Or they were afraid she'd succeed and prove them wrong. Her father definitely didn't like to be wrong. "Sometimes I get the impression my sister might be sort of glad this happened."

It was a difficult admission, and it elicited the response she'd expected. "You can't be serious!"

Except she was. "She has five kids with a husband she doesn't like all that much, and right now they're living with my parents. For a while, my life must've looked pretty darn glamorous next to hers."

"So she's jealous."

It was more complicated than that, of course, but she felt jealousy was a big part of it. "That's all I can figure."

"Have you two ever been close?"

She watched him add a splash of cream to his coffee. "Not really. We're too different."

The spoon clinked against the cup as he stirred. "How old were you when you left home?"

"I moved to LA as soon as I turned eighteen."

His eyebrows slid up. "All by yourself?"

"I didn't have any choice."

"Did you know anyone in SoCal?"

"No. I just wanted to be an actress—and knew I'd suffocate if I didn't escape right away."

"There's nothing wrong with being a wife and mother."

"Absolutely. I agree. I just…" How much should she tell him? Not everything, she decided. "I wanted to see the world. To break free and experience more than I would ever be able to there. But Rachel accused me of abandoning the family. And once I landed the movie part, she started telling everyone I thought I was too good for them. What she said caused a lot of damage and has made it that much harder for me to get along with our mother. Rachel's always tried to drive a wedge between us."

"I'm sorry to hear that. But surely your family would never leak your whereabouts to the media, not after all you've been through." He sounded sympathetic and cautiously hopeful at the same time. "That's a line most families would never cross."

Tia wanted to agree with him. But her family wasn't like most. She knew he'd be shocked to learn how just how different her childhood had been. Deep in her heart she could see her mother doing almost anything to force her back home. If her scarred face appeared on magazines at every checkout counter in the country, where else could she hide? And she could see her sister doing it because misery loved company. Rachel was jealous that Tia had managed to break away, and even more jealous that she'd dared to chase her dream. "I don't want to think it could be my family, either," she said, especially because the media didn't know about them. No one did. If this had come from her family, her family would have to have reached out to the media—not the other way around. "But I would suspect my sister before Barbie."

He shook his head but finally started to eat in earnest. "Well, now that you know Kouretas is looking for you, you'll have to be more careful when you talk to Barbie. Your family, too— in case they're gabbing to others. Word has to be getting out somehow."

She toyed with what was left of her burrito. "Maybe I should leave Silver Springs."

Seth looked up. "And go where?"

"Home to Iowa, I guess."

"I don't think you should go back to your family," he said. "You're too fragile to land in the middle of a situation that sounds as toxic as the one you describe. And I don't want you spending Christmas locked up alone in LA."

She supposed it should've bothered her that he would presume to have such a strong opinion when they barely knew each other. But it felt good to have someone care enough to be protective. "I can't stay here. It's only a matter of time before—"

"Being spotted and photographed will be a threat no matter where you go," he broke in.

"It'll be much less of a threat in Iowa."

"You don't think this guy could hop on a flight as easily as you can?"

That wasn't likely, but only she knew why, and she wasn't about to say. "The more they need to spend, the less likely that will be," she said to deflect the question. "Most of them live day-to-day."

"If this guy believes there's enough money in it, who knows what he'll do? I think you should stay right here. I'll make sure, even if Kouretas figures out where you are, that he doesn't get onto the property."

"I don't want to put you in that position," she started, but he waved her off.

"It's not as if there's a whole pack of paparazzi trying to bust down the gate. I can handle one guy."

CHAPTER THIRTEEN

Because they couldn't go running—not with Ray Kouretas in town—Seth suggested they go swimming.

"I'm not a good swimmer," Tia said.

"You don't have to be good," he responded. "It's just for exercise. Plus, we have a heated pool. Might as well make use of it."

He thought she was about to refuse, so he pushed a little harder. "You have to fight," he said softly. "What you're going through won't go away, and it won't fix itself, but you can fight through it. Actually, you have no other choice. You either beat it, or it will beat you."

She stared down at her feet for several seconds before lifting her head. "You mean I have to adjust to my new reality."

He felt terrible for her. But the more he was around her, the less the scars from the accident bothered him—and they hadn't bothered him much to begin with. Although he could see why they'd be a big deal to her, surely they didn't have to ruin the rest of her life. "The future doesn't have to be as bad as you think, even if it doesn't include acting."

"You have no idea how hard it is to even hear that," she said.

"I do," he assured her. "But you're healthy and strong and

smart and talented…" He could've added that she was beautiful, too. He'd said it before. But now it felt different. Something had shifted at the breakfast table when she'd taken his hand, and he couldn't figure out how to make it go back.

"Thanks for the encouragement," she said. "But I'm worried about Ray Kouretas, and I just…don't have the energy to work out today."

"Don't let Kouretas bother you. Come swim with me." He bent his head to peer into her face. "What else do you have to do?"

Making an expression that conceded the point, she said, "Okay."

Once again, she could've mentioned that he wasn't very good at following his own advice. The past three years, he'd focused far too much on what he'd lost, even though, unlike her, he still had his job and was able to support himself doing what he loved.

But it was always easier to see what other people needed to do. It was also easier to cope with his own problems when he was focused on someone else's. Tia had given him a renewed determination to set a better example. Ironically, considering how he'd felt about her the day they met, he was glad she was here. Otherwise, nothing in his life would've changed. And he'd desperately needed…something.

Seth was waiting in the pool when Tia returned fifteen minutes later. His dark hair was wet and slicked back, highlighting the bone structure of his face, which was inarguably masculine and yet classically beautiful, especially his cheekbones and strong jaw.

But she didn't want to think about beauty—his or anyone else's—not when she'd been robbed of hers.

"Is the water warm enough?" she asked, shivering against the cold as she stripped off her towel.

"It's perfect," he said and immediately pulled his gaze away from her, pushed off from the side and started swimming.

Surprised that he wasn't a little more welcoming, considering she'd made the effort to come over at his insistence, she dipped her toe in to test the water and was relieved to find that it was at least eighty degrees. "Oh, you're right," she muttered in relief and hurried around to use the steps.

Seth cut cleanly through the water, flipping over at the opposite end of the pool each time he reached it with a natural grace she knew she did not possess in the water. "It feels great, right?" he asked when he finally stopped and hung off the edge.

She got the impression he was hesitant to come too close, which was odd. He hadn't acted that way before. But maybe that moment at the breakfast table had made him conscious of her in a whole new way. It had certainly made her conscious of him—and reluctant to get her hair wet in front of him. She knew having it slicked back the way his was would show her scars in the worst possible light. "Surprisingly good."

"I told you." He cocked an eyebrow. "But sitting on the steps isn't swimming."

"I'm working up to it," she said drily.

He chuckled. "How about you start now?"

And let him see her face without her hair to help cover it? She didn't want to do that, and yet…she had no idea why it would matter so much to her. Regardless of what'd happened at the kitchen table, her love life was over. Who would want her now?

Although she knew that was self-pity talking, and people found love despite scars and other physical differences all the time, she felt *so* ugly. And physically, Seth was far above average. "I think I'll wait and see if I warm up to the idea."

His smile slanted to one side, making him even more attractive—to the point he gave her butterflies. She was beginning to have an unexpected response to him—one she would never have believed she could feel in her current situation—which was a little disconcerting. She couldn't allow herself to get infatuated with a man who was now so much better-looking than she was, not to mention that he was still in love with his dead wife. She didn't want to be nursing a broken heart on top of everything else.

For a moment, she wondered if she'd made the wrong decision coming out here. She shouldn't have done it, didn't want him to see her looking any worse. But she was already in the water, and she didn't have a chance with him, anyway, so there wasn't any point in leaving. As he'd implied, she had to accept her new reality. The least she could do was put forth the effort to get some exercise.

Once she started to swim, and he didn't seem horrified by what he saw, she decided she'd made a good decision. She was actually *happy* to be out of the house, she realized. The steam rising from the water created an interesting effect, and Seth acted less remote as time went by, especially once he started coaching her on how to swim freestyle. She wasn't any good at it, but concentrating on it gave her a break from everything else, and that was such a relief that she wasn't ready to stop when he did.

"Can you dive?" she asked as she climbed out of the water.

"That's not one of my talents," he replied. "Why? Can you?"

"I'm better at diving than swimming," she bragged, but she didn't do much to prove it once they started competing. She tried to do a somersault, but it'd been so long since she'd done one that she sort of freaked out in midair and wound up landing awkwardly and making a big splash.

Once he helped her out and learned she hadn't hit her face and was fine, Seth couldn't quit laughing. "Show me again how you do that?" he teased, so she shoved him into the pool.

"Now look who's laughing," she said, but that only made him come after her.

Although she tried to run away, she was being careful not

to fall on the wet cement—something he didn't seem too worried about—so it wasn't difficult for him to catch her. She felt
his arms close around her and squealed just before he lifted her
off her feet.

She could tell he expected to toss her in that easily, but she'd
grown up with an older brother who'd tried to do the same
thing, at the swimming hole they all used, on more than one
occasion. Grabbing his wrist at the last second and holding on
for all she was worth, she pulled him off balance and into the
water with her, and they both came up sputtering.

"I can't believe you got me *again*!" he said, pretending to be
angry, and dunked her, but that only made her determined to
dunk him back.

They play-fought and laughed and play-fought and laughed,
wrestling in the water until Tia was so exhausted she thought
she might drown. She managed to drag Seth under one last time,
but when they came up, she had to hold on to him to keep from
sinking, since he was tall enough to stand and she wasn't. He had
his arms around her, too. She didn't know why—maybe to hold
her up. But the front of her was smashed up against the front
of him, and neither one of them seemed eager to change that.

Although they were both breathing hard from the exertion
and the laughing, all levity faded the instant their eyes met. The
color of his irises deepened to a dark chocolate color, and his
gaze fell to her mouth just before he kissed her.

His kiss couldn't be categorized as timid. It wasn't what she'd
call soft or gentle, either. But it was extremely satisfying. He
crushed her lips beneath his as he drew her tongue into his
mouth and didn't stop kissing her until she had to break away
to catch her breath.

Then he looked as startled as she was—and probably more
uncertain. She liked what'd happened. She wanted more. And
yet…neither of them were in a good position to let this get out
of hand.

What was he thinking?

She wanted to ask, but before she could say anything, his arm swept her to the edge of the pool where she could hang on as he got out. Then, without a word, he grabbed his towel and walked into the house.

Seth's heart was thumping against his chest. He'd had to get away from Tia before he dove back into the pool. There was love, and then there was sex. He craved one of those things, but it wasn't the one that would be good for Tia, not when she was this fragile. When he couldn't get into a relationship with her, she'd think it was because of what the accident had done to her face, but nothing could be further from the truth. He knew he'd never be able to get over Shiloh and definitely didn't want to make Tia's life any worse.

He thought maybe she'd come in and demand an explanation. Why he'd kissed her in the first place. Why he'd walked away without saying anything. But she didn't, and for that he was grateful. He had no idea what he'd say. He hadn't been himself since that short interlude at breakfast, because he hadn't been able to quit thinking about how much he'd enjoyed her touch and wanted more of it. So once he had her in his arms, instinct had taken over, without any permission from his brain.

Trying not to dwell on how good Tia had tasted—the mere acknowledgment felt *so* disloyal to Shiloh—he got in the shower, where he knew he was safe from a confrontation, and let the water pound down his back.

Afterward, while drying his hair, he couldn't help listening for sounds of movement in the house above the whir of the blow-dryer.

He couldn't hear anything. *Thank God.*

What would've happened had he stayed in the pool? he wondered. But the answer was easy. He would've removed her suit and his basketball shorts. No question. The thought of her bare body sliding under his as he pressed her up against the side of the pool and—

Yanking his mind away from *that* precipice, he drew a deep, steadying breath. Lust had always seemed like such a shallow emotion. At least, it was portrayed that way. Who knew it could be powerful enough to nearly bring him to his knees?

"Help me out, Shiloh," he said while staring at his reflection. But she'd never felt more distant than she did in that moment. And the only way he could siphon off the sexual energy flowing through him was to start a new painting, one that hadn't been commissioned but captured the desire, the wild turbulence and the deep-seated anger he felt—at his mother, at his childhood, at the loss of one of the few people who'd ever truly loved him, and at the fact that his body craved something his mind and heart couldn't let him have.

Tia was a little shaken after Seth left. She'd been feeling more like herself than she had since the accident. She'd even begun to let go of her self-consciousness and fear and believe that Seth didn't really see or care about her scars.

And then *wham*. What'd happened to them when they'd come up out of the water that last time? Had *she* instigated their kiss?

She didn't think so, but she'd certainly been a willing participant.

She had to admit she was sort of disappointed that he'd pulled away. Since the accident, sex had been the furthest thing from her mind. She was prepared to go years without even dating. But his kiss had definitely reminded her of how wonderful it felt to be close to someone in that way—when it was the right person and the right time. And now that sex was back on her radar, she couldn't seem to stop craving it.

Why had he gone inside without a word? What was he feeling? Regret? Was he wracked with guilt because of his love for his late wife?

Maybe he regretted inviting her over to eat and swim…

She had no way of knowing, because he didn't come back out, and she wasn't about to go after him.

With a long sigh, she got out of the pool, dried off and went back to the guesthouse through the gate so that she wouldn't have to go through the house. But after she changed and showered, she didn't know what to do. She didn't feel like lying around and watching TV for yet another day. She wanted go out, see the town and get dinner like a normal person. That kiss in the pool had taken her mind off the accident. But what would take her mind off that kiss?

Nothing, if she continued to stay inside the house, pacing like a caged tiger.

For the first time in what seemed like forever, she experienced a burst of energy at the prospect of being mobile again, enjoying the holiday decorations, playing some Christmas music in the car, maybe even buying a peppermint latte or a sugar cookie at that place in town—Sugar Mama—Aiyana had mentioned.

But it was the middle of the day. Someone could recognize her and potentially report the sighting to Kouretas. Besides that, since the accident, she was afraid to get behind the wheel. It'd taken a great deal of self-talk and willpower to drive from LA to Silver Springs, and if she had to brake quickly, she nearly broke into a cold sweat.

So she played a game on her phone, tried to watch another episode of *The Office* and scoured the cupboards looking for the supplies to bake cookies—without success—before she grew so bored she gave in and used thick makeup to disguise her face as much as possible. She was an actress. She could pretend to be someone else, couldn't she? And she had to overcome her fear of driving, couldn't let that debilitate her any more than what the accident had done to her already.

Pulling out her sunglasses to hide her eyes, she put on a

hoodie, even though she'd claimed not to have one when Seth first suggested she go running with him, and headed out.

It was cold enough that everyone would be wearing coats and hats and hoodies. She'd made herself as nondescript as possible, but still. With Kouretas blabbing about her being in town, putting everyone on high alert, she couldn't take any chances. She wouldn't be able to get out of the car like she suddenly longed to do—couldn't go shopping or get something to eat. But she could drive around, gain her confidence back as a driver and see the area. She couldn't imagine anyone would recognize her in a hoodie with sunglasses covering most of her face. People would have to look at her carefully to be able to recognize her, and there'd only be one or two opportunities to do that, maybe at a stoplight.

The town wasn't big enough to keep her busy for long. But even after she'd driven through it a few times, slowly and carefully to compensate for her fear, and wound around the Topatopa Mountains that helped form the narrow valley that sheltered Silver Springs, she wasn't ready to go home.

She could think of only one more option.

After pulling off to the side of the road, she searched for New Horizons Boys & Girls Ranch on her phone and called the number.

"New Horizons," a female voice chirped.

Tia could hear Christmas music playing in the background. "Is Aiyana Turner in?"

"Yes, she is. May I tell her who's calling?"

Tia couldn't use her real name. The woman might recognize it. "Tell her…tell her it's Seth's new friend from the guesthouse."

"One moment, please."

Thankfully, it wasn't long before Seth's mother came on the line. "Tia? How are you? Better, I hope."

Tia drew a deep breath. It was good just to hear Aiyana's voice, which was weird since they'd only met once. "I'm fine.

I'm…in the area and was wondering if…well, never mind. It's a workday, so you're probably busy. I was just hoping I could come by sometime."

"Of course you can come by! Since you're in the area, come now."

The welcoming reassurance felt so nice. "Are you sure? I don't want to bother you if this is a bad time, especially because I—I can't allow myself to be seen by anybody else—not unless I want an unflattering picture splashed across the tabloids, and I'm definitely not ready to deal with that. So maybe we should just set a time, after dark, when it'd be safer for me to stop by?"

"That won't be necessary. Seth might've told you I live on campus, but my house is distanced from the other buildings. Where are you?"

Tia leaned over her steering wheel to take a look at the wrought iron arch that marked the entrance to New Horizons. "By the turnoff."

"To the school?"

"Yes."

Aiyana laughed. "That *is* close. Just take the loop until you see the big yellow house with the wraparound porch. It'll be after the administration building, set off by itself. You can't miss it. I'll meet you there."

Tia took a deep breath. As excited and relieved as she'd initially been to reach out to Aiyana, she was suddenly running out of enthusiasm for taking this risk.

But she liked Aiyana. Now that she'd come this far, she wanted to follow through.

"Thank you. I'll be there in a second."

Seth stood back to examine his work. It wasn't often that he had such a vivid picture in his mind of what he wanted to create that he was able to do it, start to finish, in one day. The frenzy of energy required to work that fast, before he could lose any of his vision, left him drained afterward, and today was no differ-ent. But as he stood back to consider the piece he'd just finished, there was little he felt the need to change. That was unusual. He was such a perfectionist that there was always some small or even large tweaks he wanted to make. But in creating the contemporary rendering of what Tia's entry into his life meant to him, he seemed to have said everything he needed to say.

He just hoped she never saw it, or, if she did, that she didn't recognize herself in the figure he'd created with calming blues and alarming reds. The reds represented her situation, her drive, her disappointment and the physical reality of the life-altering crash with its resulting scars. The blues represented her young age at the time, the hope she'd felt and should still feel and a certain humanity he could sense in her, even though he didn't know her very well.

It was the duality of the painting he liked, because it also represented what he felt toward her: the sympathy, the friend-ship, the well-wishes of the blue juxtaposed to the desire and sexual frustration of the reds.

"I'm done," he said, even though he was alone, and tossed his brushes aside before yawning and combing his hair back from his face with his fingers. He didn't want to think anymore. He didn't want to feel anymore, either. He'd always felt too much. And he found the tension between the past and the present as exhausting as the painting mania of the past six hours.

He'd been living on too little sleep for too long and was going to bed. His brushes were expensive, but he didn't even have the energy to wash them out. He suddenly didn't care if he had to replace them all.

He was just going down the stairs when he felt his phone buzz in his pocket. Others had tried to call or text him while he was working, but he'd been too engrossed to even look at his screen. He was tempted to ignore this, too, but he had to take his phone from his pocket to charge it when he went to bed, anyway, so he glanced down to see what he'd missed.

There was nothing from Tia.

He'd sort of expected that.

His mother had tried to reach him a couple of times. Eli had invited him over for dinner. Gavin had sent him a message saying they needed someone to dress up as Santa for his kids, which was more of a joke, since Gavin knew that was something he would never do. Maybe he'd pay for a Santa, but he wouldn't pretend to *be* a Santa.

Then there was the text that'd just come in. It was from his mother-in-law.

I'm making Shiloh's favorite dinner. Would you like to join us?

He cursed as he came to an abrupt stop. Of course they would reach out to him tonight. He didn't want to go over to their house; he wanted to sleep. But if he didn't accept the invitation, especially after being late to notify them that he was in town, they'd be offended again.

They were giving him the chance to smooth over that small gaffe and were probably testing him to see if he still loved their daughter enough to make tonight a priority, no matter the late notice.

That there always had to be more to it rankled. He wished he could say no without feeling any remorse later. But maybe he should accept and get it over with. It would go a long way toward keeping the peace while he was in town, and he knew it.

So, with a sigh, he leaned against the railing and typed his response. What time?

CHAPTER FOURTEEN

If Aiyana was surprised that she'd stopped by, Tia couldn't tell. Seth's mother was *that* gracious.

"I'd love to introduce you to my husband, Cal," she said as she met Tia on the porch after hurrying over from the school. "But I'm afraid no one's home at the moment."

"Is he working, or out of town, or…"

Aiyana unlocked the house and ushered her inside. "He owns a cattle ranch about ten miles from here. That's how we met. For years, he's provided the beef for this school at rock-bottom prices. When I first moved here, it would've been so much harder for me to get a start without his support in that and so many other ways, including his pull with the city council."

"Sounds like a great guy."

"He is," she said without hesitation. "When I tell everyone he practically gave me whatever the school needed, he says he knew it would be the best way to my heart. But I don't believe that's the only reason he did it. He's just covering up the fact that he's a sucker for a good cause."

Although Tia chuckled at the joke, the sprawling campus looked state-of-the-art, and something like that didn't come into existence without a lot of work, effort, money and deter-mination. She had no doubt Aiyana had put everything she had into New Horizons—and that Cal had indeed known how im-portant the school was to her. "How long have you two been together?"

"For years," she said. "But we didn't marry until last De-cember."

That sounded sort of unconventional for someone of Aiyana's generation. "When did you first come to town?"

"Oh, boy. It's been well over two decades."

"Then, he must be a patient man."

Aiyana laughed. "Yes. I'm very lucky he didn't give up on me. I was so stubborn. I did everything I could to push him away—until I finally realized I was only sabotaging my own happiness."

"You raised the boys on your own?" Tia couldn't imag-ine adopting eight troubled kids as a single parent, but Aiyana must've managed.

"I could've used Cal's help, and I probably should've taken it. He did what he could from a distance. But I was too afraid of the commitment, of how he might impact my life, of hav-ing someone tell me not to adopt when I wanted to or possibly interfere with my vision for the school. All I could see were my goals, I guess." Her voice softened with affection. "I really don't deserve Cal."

Tia smiled. "I bet you're perfect for each other."

"Well, either way, I wised up." Aiyana gestured at an over-stuffed chair in a huge living room that contained three re-cliners, the biggest flat-screen TV Tia had ever seen and more than one gaming console. The gaming consoles had their cords wrapped neatly around them and were stored on the bookshelves that took up the whole of one wall, other than the TV, but Tia could easily imagine the chaos that must ensue when Aiyana had her big family around.

"While you relax, I'll put on some tea," Aiyana said. "Or would you rather have hot cocoa or coffee or something else?"

Tia had left the house planning to enjoy what she could of the season, so she chose something she probably wouldn't have chosen otherwise. "Hot chocolate, please."

"Wonderful. I think I'll have a cup, too. Would you like some peppermint in it?"

"That would be nice. Thank you."

While she waited, Tia gazed at the large Christmas tree in one corner, visible from two windows on the outside. She didn't think she'd ever seen so many ornaments on one tree. There was a garland with lights and ornaments decorating the mantel and stuffed elves arranged on several of the bookshelves, as well.

Aiyana came back a few minutes later with a tray that held two mugs, whipped cream bobbing on the top, and a plate of cookies. "I made these last night and thought you might like some."

The cookies were dipped in white chocolate and topped with crushed candy canes. "I've never seen this kind of cookie before. Is it a family recipe?"

"I guess you could say that. I've been making Candy Cane Cookies for so long I don't remember where I got the recipe."

Tia nearly groaned in delight at the taste. They were soft and thick like a sugar cookie, with the crushed candy cane on top adding a minty crunch. "Wow! These are delicious."

"I'll have to send some home with you. And maybe you can take a plate to Seth. I made extra because they're his favorite—when he's not being a Scrooge and refusing to enjoy the holidays," she added with an impatient roll of her eyes.

Tia lowered her half-eaten cookie so that she could talk with an empty mouth. "I know that his wife died at Christmas."

Aiyana sobered. "Yes. Three years ago. It was tragic. Shiloh was such a wonderful person."

"He obviously loved her a great deal."

"When Seth falls, he falls hard. And he's as loyal as they come."

Did that mean he'd never be able to get over his wife? Tia took it that way—and yet he'd just kissed her in the pool. She supposed that was why she'd made her way over to his mother's. Not only was she lonely and looking for companionship from someone she could trust, she also craved greater insight on her new neighbor. "How long were they together?"

"Since high school. She was his first serious girlfriend, but they'd only been married a short time when she got sick."

"I'm sorry that happened."

Aiyana's lips curved into a sad smile. "So am I. I miss her, but he's the one who has really suffered. He lost her right when he was making great progress with putting his past behind him. I'd never seen him so happy."

"His past—you mean when his mother gave him up?"

"Yes." She took a sip of her cocoa. "He was six years old when he was essentially abandoned, old enough to remember it—and feel every bit of the rejection."

"I read about that on Wikipedia," she admitted.

"Did Wikipedia mention his two brothers?"

"It did. The article said after his father left, his mother couldn't support the family, so she turned the children over to social services. But that's about it."

"That's probably for the best. Seth is so private. I'm sure he's glad there's not a lot of information out there about his early years."

"So…he was separated from his brothers, too?"

"Not in the beginning," Aiyana said. "Seth's first set of foster parents tried to take all three boys, but they returned Seth and his older brother, Brady, after just a few months."

"Returned them!" Tia cried. "Why?"

"They said it was too hard to take on all three. They wanted only the youngest. But losing his mother and then his little brother hit Seth hard. He started to act out, which caused him to be rejected by his next family, too. And this second family kept Brady, his other brother."

Tia swallowed hard. "So then he was on his own."

"Yes." Aiyana's cup clinked as she put it on its saucer. "But I'm afraid that isn't even the hardest part. Later, he learned that their mother changed her mind and rescued Derrick and Brady within two years of giving them up."

Tia's stomach dropped. "But she didn't reclaim Seth? Why not?"

A pained expression deepened the lines in Aiyana's face. "I have no idea. He was the middle child, the easiest to overlook. That's all I can imagine, because he is such a wonderful person."

"That must've crushed him."

"It did," Aiyana said. "It's made him very leery of love. Now maybe you can understand why he'd hang on to Shiloh so tightly."

Tia didn't know what to say. She'd been so miserable she'd assumed he couldn't possibly understand what she was going through, had assumed he'd had an easy life—until she read about his wife, anyway. And now she was learning this, which painted an even clearer picture.

"Would you like another cookie?" Aiyana held out the plate.

"One is enough. But thank you." Tia thought of Seth trying to get her to improve her eating and start exercising and felt a wave of affection she did not want to feel—not in addition to the excitement that had overcome her when he was kissing her in the pool.

"I hope you don't mind me confiding in you about Seth's background," Aiyana said. "I'll be honest—I'm only doing it because I hope the two of you can become friends. I know you both need one."

"He's been good to me," she said and took another drink of her cocoa before adding, "Can I ask you one thing?"

"Of course."

"Does he have any contact with his mother?"

"No. Even if he could forgive her, I can't see him associating with her."

"She let him down too badly."

"Exactly."

"Wow. I'm so sorry for what he's been through." Tia had issues with her own parents, but nothing on the same scale. At least they'd kept her and provided for her.

"It wasn't my intention to make you feel sorry for him," Aiyana clarified. "I was just…hoping to help you understand why he might be a little guarded."

The memory of him getting out of the pool and going into the house played again in Tia's mind. Had he reacted that way because he'd actually liked the kiss, too? Liked it but didn't want to like it? Or was it something else? "I appreciate that."

Aiyana's phone rang, and she took a moment to dig it out of her purse. "Speak of the devil," she said and hit the Accept button. "Hello, son."

Tia waved to get Aiyana's attention and gestured not to mention that they were together. She'd agreed to take him some cookies, so he'd realize after the fact, and that was fine. He was the one who'd introduced her to his mother. Tia just didn't want it to get awkward.

Aiyana nodded to signify she understood. "I'm good," she said into the phone. "And you?… Tonight?… It won't be *that* bad, will it?… You have the right to say no. You sound exhausted… Of course, but… Okay. Try to enjoy yourself." She grinned at Tia. "By the way, how's Tia doing?"

Tia wished she could hear Seth's response, but she couldn't. She heard Aiyana say, "She'll get back on her feet eventually," before telling him to have a good time, after which she disconnected.

"Everything okay?"

"Yes. He said you seem to be doing better than you were at first and that your scars aren't as bad as you think."

Tia liked hearing that, especially from Seth—not that she cared to examine why. "I keep trying to tell myself that others won't notice my scars as much as I do."

"They won't," Aiyana insisted. "You're still a very beautiful woman."

But no longer movie-star material. She could never have what she'd had, even after demonstrating her acting ability—unless she was willing to accept bit parts. Maybe she'd have a chance there, and maybe that would satisfy her one day, but that day wasn't now. It was too far to fall. "As I said, Seth has been kind to me. I hope I can help him, too."

"Just remember, he's as stubborn as a mule—like me," Aiyana added with a laugh.

Tia set her cup and saucer on the coffee table. She didn't want Aiyana to regret accepting her visit by overstaying her welcome. "I'd better go so you can get on with your evening. But thanks for having me. I just…wanted to get out of the house and didn't know where else to go."

"You can always come here."

That sounded so sincere it helped soothed the rawness inside her. "Thank you."

"Before you go, did Seth tell you that there's a man in town who's looking for you?"

"He did. If I'm lucky, the guy will give up after a few days and go back to LA or wherever he's from."

"Fingers crossed there. But…have you ever thought about… Never mind." She waved her words away. "I'm sure you know what's best."

"What were you going to say?" Tia pressed.

"It would be hard to even consider this, but…what if you provided a picture to the tabloids yourself? They're going to get one eventually, you know. Why let them make a prisoner of you—to the point you feel you can't even go out of the house? If you provide the picture, you might be able to get something for it, some amount of money that would help compensate for what you've been through—not that money ever could, but you have to admit it would be better than nothing—and then you'll be able to dictate what picture is used."

"I've considered it," Tia admitted. Lord knew she could use the money. She had to support herself somehow after her savings dried up. She'd be smart to make the most of the fame she had. But she couldn't bring herself to do it right now, not at Christmas. "I'm just not ready yet."

"I understand," Aiyana said, as if that was that, and stood up.

Tia and Aiyana were almost to the door when it burst open, and Eli walked in. He was already yelling "Mom!" and barely managed to stop before crashing into them.

"Whoops! Sorry," he said. "Hi, Tia."

Eli was almost as handsome as Seth—but not quite. Tia was beginning to believe there wasn't another man out there as handsome as Seth, which was almost as concerning as how much she'd liked that kiss in the pool. "Hello."

He looked around the living room. "Where's Seth?"

"It's just me."

He didn't act as though that was odd, didn't even ask how she knew Aiyana. He was probably used to strangers seeking his mother out, because she offered so much love and support to everyone.

"He told you about that guy at the bar last night, right?" Eli said.

"He did," Tia replied. "You don't happen to have any idea of where Mr. Kouretas might be staying, do you?"

He scratched his head while he considered the question. "There are a lot of boutique hotels in the area, but someone like that, who's hoping to grab something quick and leave, would probably go for the obvious."

Aiyana spoke up. "The Mission Inn."

Eli nodded. "That's what I think, too."

"You're talking about that Spanish-style hotel in the heart of town," Tia said, seeking confirmation. She'd seen it while driving around earlier.

Eli gave her a skeptical look. "Yes, but don't tell me you're going to go looking for him."

"No. I don't have the nerve. Not yet. And I'm not sure he's the guy I'd approach even if I was ready to expose my new face to the world. I just wanted to know where he is...in case, I guess."

"In case..."

"In case she decides to beat him at his own game," Aiyana supplied.

"Got it." He stepped aside so that Tia could get out but stopped her at the last moment. "Hey, are you heading back to Maxi's?"

She didn't want to. The guesthouse suddenly seemed lonely and depressing. But she couldn't think of anywhere else in town that would be safe. And it was almost time to feed Kiki. "I am."

"Great. I have something for Seth. I was going to take it to him, but he said he was going to see Shiloh's parents."

"They live in the area?" Tia asked.

"They do," he said. "So...would you mind taking it to him for me?"

"Oh! And the cookies!" Aiyana exclaimed. "I almost forgot."

Tia didn't know if she'd be seeing much of Seth. He might be eager to avoid her in future. No more meals. No more exercise. No more advice. But if he was going to be out of the house tonight, she'd just leave whatever his family had for him on the kitchen table.

"I'd be happy to," she said, and Aiyana hurried to put a plate together while Eli went out to his truck and brought back a small statue of a mother and baby.

"I accidentally knocked this off the table the other day and cracked it," he said ruefully. "I'm hoping Seth can fix it so that I don't have to tell Cora."

Tia immediately recognized the artist but asked anyway. "Seth made this?"

"He did. It was a gift for Cora when our first baby was born."

As modern as the rest of Seth's work, the small statue represented a mother cradling her baby. Although both faces were featureless and the entire statue was made of a smooth white substance, the simplicity of the piece made it understated yet powerful. "It's beautiful," Tia said and couldn't escape the thought that the love and protection Seth had managed to depict so well was probably something he'd always envied.

Seth's eyes felt like sandpaper. As if he wasn't tired enough, his in-laws had the heat cranked up so high he'd taken off his coat *and* his pullover sweater and still felt like he might melt.

"You love my shepherd's pie, don't you?" Lois said as he waited for her to serve dinner while watching TV in the living room with Graham.

Seth struggled to keep his heavy eyelids from closing of their own accord. "I do," he said, but that was true of almost any kind of old-fashioned comfort food. He perceived those dishes as something a loving mother would make her family, and he'd always longed for the kind of mother who would gather her kids around the dinner table instead of driving them over to a fast-food joint.

Graham used the remote to lower the volume on the TV. "How's work been going?"

Seth struggled to resist the memory that had suddenly emerged from some dark corner of his mind—his birth mother blowing the smoke from her cigarette out the open window of the driver's side of the car while he and his brothers devoured

Happy Meals and tried to trade each other for a different toy. "Good," he said. "I've been busy."

"Maxi buying many pieces?"

"Maxi always hits me up to see what I'm working on, but these days I've mostly been doing commissioned pieces—for parks, buildings, state and local governments and the like—so I haven't had much to sell him."

"Doesn't that take all the fun out of it? To have to create something that someone else has commissioned?"

"Not really," he said. "There are parameters—it has to fit the setting and purpose—but I can use my imagination from there." And he could always do what he wanted on the side. It had just been a long time since he'd felt as inspired as he'd been today when he'd painted Tia. The outpouring of creative energy reminded him of how it used to be when he started a new project. But as happy as he was when he could do exactly what he wanted, he was grateful to be successful and wasn't going to complain just because he had to please someone other than himself.

"Seems like it would be restrictive," Graham said.

"Sometimes it is. But it's a good thing to be able to pay rent and be able to eat, you know?" he said in a joking tone, alluding to the practical side of his career.

"Oh, don't tell me you're struggling with bills. We know you've made a fortune, don't we, Mother?" Graham said, loudly enough that Lois could hear him in the kitchen.

"Graham, you're not supposed to say things like that," she admonished, but Seth could tell she was used to her husband making statements that were a little embarrassing.

Although Graham didn't seem to pay her any mind, he changed the subject. "So you're going to be teaching at New Horizons?"

"I am."

"How'd that come about?"

"My mother has some students she feels could benefit from the extra attention."

"Then, you'll be in town for a while."

"Just one term, through February."

"That's asking a lot from someone who's as famous as you are, isn't it? Your time is valuable."

"I'm happy to help. As you know, she's done a lot for me."

"A lot more than your real mother, eh? From what Shiloh told me, she was a piece of work. Who gives their children away? Do you ever hear from her?"

Now Seth understood why he'd been avoiding Graham and Lois. They knew too much about him, couldn't help treading on sensitive ground. "No."

"What about your brothers, the ones she took back?"

"No." Seth could've elaborated, could've told Graham that Derrick and Brady had both tried to reach out to him in recent years. But Seth hadn't been responsive. He couldn't bring himself to associate with them. They had so many shared memories he wasn't part of. Just talking to them took him back to a time when he'd felt completely unloved and rejected.

Even if he could get beyond that, he was afraid they might also try to bring Sandy back into his life.

"That's too bad. I bet now they regret how they treated you, eh?"

Why now? Because he had more to offer these days? Seth couldn't help cringing at the comment, because he knew what Graham was thinking: that they'd screwed up, not because he was a person worth knowing and loving but because they could not tap into his wealth. Graham looked at him and saw dollar signs.

"I think they're happy enough with their own lives," he said to get his father-in-law off the subject.

That seemed to work, but then Graham looked over at Shiloh's senior picture, which was sitting on the side table, and his eyes filled with tears. "I sure miss her," he said.

Seth didn't want to feel what he was feeling. He didn't want to be where he was. And he definitely didn't want to think about Shiloh on a day when he couldn't seem to forget Tia and that heated kiss in the pool. No matter how hard he tried, that kept coming to mind, even here.

Unable to stop himself, he shot to his feet. "I'm so sorry, but suddenly, I'm not feeling well. If you'll excuse me, I think I'd better head home."

Lois stepped out of the kitchen, a large mixing spoon in one hand. "You're leaving?" she said in apparent shock.

"I'm not feeling so great," he reiterated. "I'll have to call you later. And next time, I'll take you both to dinner so that you don't have to cook."

"No problem," Graham said. "Of course if you're not feeling well, you should go lie down. But…"

"But?" Seth said when he stretched his collar and stopped.

"I know it's a bit out of the blue now that you're rushing off. We haven't really had a chance to get into it. But we were going to see if you could help us out a little."

Seth's skin began to crawl. "Help you out?"

"The pool-supply business has been slow, so I had to borrow some money to get us through. The loan's due this week, and I know the asshole who lent it to us will make our lives miserable if we can't pay him off. So I was wondering if…if we could borrow it from you and pay you back as soon as we get on our feet."

So that was what this was about. They'd been mad at him until they realized they needed him again. "How much is it?" Seth asked as he grabbed his coat and sweater.

Graham shoved his hands in his pockets while trying to affect an expression of chagrin. "Fifty thousand dollars." He laughed awkwardly while Lois looked on, her eyes filled with hope. "Can you believe it?" he added. "It's been a really rough year."

That was what he'd said the last time he'd come to Seth for money. And yet he still had a boat sitting in his driveway. "You haven't paid back what I gave you last time," Seth pointed out.

Graham's eyes widened as if he didn't think Seth should require that money back. "Because we haven't had it. You know how it is for us working-class folks."

They could've at least made the attempt. Or come to him to explain the situation. But they hadn't even mentioned it, even though the date they'd promised to get him the money had come and gone months ago. They wouldn't make good on this new loan, either. They saw Seth as being so rich he'd never miss it.

Seth almost said yes. He would've given it to them if Shiloh were alive—for her sake. But this time, something wouldn't let him do it. "I'm sorry you've gotten yourself into another tight spot," he said. "But I'm afraid I can't help you this time."

"Why not?" Lois blurted, obviously shocked.

"Because our relationship is starting to revolve around money."

Graham followed him to the door. "What are you saying?"

"I'm saying no," he reiterated.

"You're not feeling well. I understand. Let's wait and talk about it tomorrow. Should I give you a call?"

"No. Not unless you're interested in me for something other than my money." The words were out before Seth could stop them, but he didn't try to take them back.

"What are you accusing us of?" Graham exploded. "Not all of us can make millions of dollars just for slapping a bunch of paint on a canvas. It's not like you're good at what you do. You don't even put faces on your people!"

"Graham, he said he wasn't feeling well. Let's...let's just wait until tomorrow," Lois said, obviously not wanting to overreact in case he'd change his mind, given a little more time. But Seth knew there'd be no going back from this point. She'd only invited him over and cooked him a meal because she was hoping he'd bail them out once again.

"Too bad our daughter's not around to see you treat us like this," Graham spat.

"She was too good for me," Seth admitted. "But she was too good for you, too."

CHAPTER FIFTEEN

Tia thought she'd have the house to herself, at least for a while, so she was surprised when she heard the door slam with enough force to shake the walls. A startled Kiki squawked, and Tia turned in the atrium in time to see Seth stalk into the kitchen. He'd walked right past her, didn't seem to realize she was there.

He must've caught sight of her out of the corner of his eye at the last second, however, because he suddenly backed up and froze.

Tia felt like she'd been spotted by some predatory animal—a big cat who was sizing her up and measuring…what? She couldn't tell, but if she had her guess, Seth was upset about something.

The intensity of his gaze made her skin prickle. His face could've been made of stone for all the expression he allowed it. But she could read pain and confusion in his eyes. *That* he couldn't hide.

Something had changed tonight. What was it?

Refusing to be the first to look away, she stared right back at him. It felt like he was challenging her, although she didn't know how or why. Would he come in and tell her to go?

She thought he might—until he walked into the kitchen as if he hadn't seen her to begin with.

She finished up with Kiki and let herself out. She was going back to the guesthouse. She assumed he didn't want to be sociable, or he would've poked his head in and said something.

But everything she'd learned about him wouldn't allow her to walk away. He hadn't abandoned her to her demons these past few days. He'd tried to make sure she got something to eat, encouraged her to get out and exercise. He'd even brought his mother over, thinking Aiyana might be able to help her.

What if he needed her to do the same for him, needed *someone* to stay and fight to get the message through that he had intrinsic value and that it went far deeper and was more fundamental than the fact that he could create beautiful art.

Taking a deep breath in case he rejected any attempt she made to help him, she followed him into the kitchen only to find that he'd thrown the coat and sweater he'd been carrying on the couch and the doors to the backyard were standing open, allowing a biting wind to sweep into the house.

"Seth?" she called as she approached the opening.

He didn't answer, so she peered tentatively out into the yard. "Seth?"

Again, she received no response, yet she was fairly certain he could hear her. He was sitting on a chaise by the pool, staring off toward the mountains, wearing nothing but a T-shirt, jeans and tennis shoes.

What was he doing out there? It was cold, and it smelled as though it was about to rain.

Rubbing away the chill bumps standing out on her arms, she went back and pulled on his sweater before carrying his jacket outside. "Will you put this on?" she asked softly.

When she spoke, he didn't even look over.

She touched his shoulder. "Please?"

His gaze finally shifted. She got the impression that he was fighting some internal battle and that the stakes were high.

He took the coat and put it on without saying a word, but she guessed he was only complying so that she wouldn't continue to prod him. He didn't seem to feel anything on the outside.

Maybe that was because he was feeling *too much* on the inside…

"Are you going to tell me what's wrong?" she asked.

"It's nothing," he replied, his words clipped, and he once again stared off toward the mountains as though his mind was a million miles away.

He obviously expected her to accept that answer and go— and yet she couldn't leave him like this, not knowing what she knew about him after visiting Aiyana.

Instead of pressing him to talk, she sat down behind him on the chaise.

He didn't seem to mind her proximity, so she slid even closer, seeking the warmth of his body while trying to give him a little of hers.

When he didn't react to that, either, she slipped her arms around his waist and held him against her.

It was a bold move—nothing she'd ever done to anyone else she'd known for such a short time—but he was like a statue, had withdrawn completely inside himself, and she didn't know how else to reach him. She hoped she'd at least be able to give him some comfort through physical contact.

After a few seconds, he said, "It's cold out here. You'd better go in."

She might've taken that suggestion if he'd put any conviction behind his words. But it'd taken him so long to speak up. He didn't really want her to leave; he just didn't expect her to stay. From what she'd heard, too many other people had walked away from him already—right when he needed them most.

"If you can take the cold, so can I," she said jokingly and rested her good cheek against his back.

"Why are you doing this, Tia?" He sounded tired.

"Because I want you to know I'm here," she said. "And because holding you feels pretty damn good."

If he was going to get up and stalk off, she figured he'd do it now. Instead, he surprised her by reaching around to bring her in front of him, where he could look into her face, but sitting so close meant straddling his hips, which was an intimate position, as exciting as it was unexpected.

"You should go in," he said again, but the way he rested his forehead against hers indicated he wanted the exact opposite.

"I won't leave you out here alone," she said simply.

"It's cold."

"Not if I stay close to you."

"If you don't go, you might get more than you bargained for," he warned.

Their mouths were so close she could feel his breath fan her cheeks. She could also smell his cologne: it was a scent she liked. "Which would be…what exactly?" she asked.

"I think you know."

She could guess. How long had it been since he'd been with a woman? Three whole years? Since Shiloh?

It'd been a long time since she'd made love, too. Maybe that was why she couldn't resist pressing her lower body firmly against his. "I'm not worried," she said, suddenly breathless because she could feel his erection.

"Maybe you should be. I don't want to be responsible for hurting you, especially at such a vulnerable time."

He moved as though he'd set her aside so that he could get up, but she caught his face between her hands before he could. "I'm a big girl, Seth. I can decide what I want—and be responsible for my own actions."

Once again, his gaze lowered to her mouth. "But I don't think you understand my limitations."

"You're not open to a relationship. Is that the limitation you're talking about?"

He nodded, but he kept staring at her lips as though they were all he could really think about.

"Consider me warned," she said and slid her hand around his neck to bring his head down to hers.

When he had first come outside, Seth hadn't been able to feel the cold. He'd been dead inside. But that was no longer true. Now there was a fire growing in his belly that made him feel very much alive and provided more than enough warmth.

Still, he had to think about Tia. Although she was wearing his sweater—and he couldn't help imagining her in it without anything underneath—he knew it wasn't thick enough to ward off the cold.

He managed to quit kissing her long enough to ask if she wanted to go in. But she didn't seem to be worried about the cold any more than he was. She didn't even answer. She just went right back to kissing him—deep, openmouthed, hungry kisses—so he supposed that was his answer.

She didn't stop him when he started to take off her clothes. He craved her bare skin against his worse than he could remember craving anything in a very long time. "Thank you," he murmured as soon as her warm breasts came up against his chest.

Briefly, the vision of the painting he'd created earlier rose in his mind. This was what had inspired the swirling reds he'd used so heavily: they represented desire more than anything else.

She was trembling. Just in case it was from the cold, he led her into the hot tub and supported her back with one arm as he lowered his head to pull her nipple into his mouth.

The testosterone flooding his system made him feel invincible, strong enough to lift a house. But more importantly, he

finally had a constructive channel for his emotions. And he was
so caught up, so desperate for that release, he had to lift his head
to try to catch his breath or it would all be over in seconds. He
told himself to slow down, but she seemed to be in as much of
a hurry as he was. She immediately guided him between her
legs, which was exactly where he wanted to be.

That brought up the issue of birth control, however. He had
no condoms, not even in the house. He hadn't bought a pack
in years; he hadn't been with anyone since Shiloh died.

He opened his mouth to tell Tia they would have to do something else, but birth control must've occurred to her at the same
moment, because she answered his question before he could even
ask it. "Don't worry," she whispered, her voice slightly hoarse.
"I can't get pregnant. And I don't have anything."

"Neither do I. But…you're on the pill?"

"Sort of."

He wasn't sure exactly what that meant. He just trusted her
enough to believe she wouldn't lie to him, not about this. In-
finitely relieved, he allowed himself to accept her invitation—
and as he pressed inside her and felt her body slowly accept his,
he couldn't believe how incredibly good it felt.

She groaned as he began to thrust, letting him know she was
as caught up in their lovemaking as he was, which only excited
him more. Once again, he tried to calm down. If he closed his
eyes, he thought he might be able to last longer. But he didn't
want to miss the expression on her face—the way she was looking up at him with such heavy-lidded eyes, the steam condensing on her skin like dew, her lips parted with expectation.
With the moon casting a silvery glow over her bare shoulders
and breasts, he couldn't help thinking that she was beautiful,
in spite of the accident.

He wanted to tell her so—sincerely. But he knew she'd never
believe him. And that wasn't a discussion for right now. She
seemed to have forgotten about her injury. Why would he ever

remind her? He didn't want to be reminded of his own scars, which were far less visible but every bit as real.

As the hot water sloshed up against the sides, he did his best to gauge what she was feeling. He tried to read the clues her body was giving him, too, so that he'd know when he could let go. But he didn't have his usual control. After what'd happened with Shiloh's parents earlier tonight, he wasn't mentally prepared for this type of encounter.

When he stopped moving in an attempt to keep from going too far too fast, she gave him the sweetest smile he'd ever seen.

"It's okay," she whispered, and that was all it took to snap the last of his restraint. At her encouragement, he began to drive into her harder and faster and harder and faster and harder and faster until he was acting with the same wild abandon that had overtaken him at his easel earlier.

And when his release arrived, his whole body shuddered in relief.

Tia woke in Seth's bed. Holding perfectly still so that she wouldn't rouse him, she listened to the sound of his slow, steady breathing. She couldn't tell what time it was, but it had to be early. Five? Maybe six? She couldn't see any light creeping around the fancy automated blinds in the bedroom, but that could be due to storm clouds outside. It was the rainy season, after all.

She angled her head in an attempt to make out Seth's face. He had his arm slung across her waist as if he feared she might otherwise slip away from him. She would've laughed at that idea, but when she thought about how he'd lost his mother and his brothers and then Shiloh, she could understand why he might feel the need to physically hang onto the people in his life.

She couldn't make out the stubble on his cheeks and chin, but she knew it was there. She'd felt his beard growth against her neck, her breasts, even her thighs. He had to be the sexiest man she'd ever known—and he was unquestionably a good lover.

Just the way he kissed was fulfilling. But it was the vulnerability he'd exhibited last night that'd really endeared him to her.

She was tempted to reach out and smooth his hair back so that she could see more of his face, but she knew for sure that would wake him. She understood why his mother worried about him. He didn't get enough rest.

Moving slowly and carefully so that he wouldn't feel it, she fingered the scars on her cheek and tried to imagine what he'd thought when he looked at her last night. She was used to men gazing at her with open admiration. But she couldn't imagine anyone looking at her like that now.

She *had* to look grotesque. What she saw in the mirror couldn't be a lie. Normally, that would've made her too self-conscious for a sexual encounter, but his need had been more important than her vanity.

He was also in love with another woman, so maybe her appearance didn't matter. Maybe he'd just needed a warm and willing body to distract him from the torture of his mind.

So what happened before he got home that upset him so badly? He hadn't told her. They hadn't talked much. After they got out of the hot tub, he'd led her into the house, where they'd showered together. Then he'd pulled her into bed with him and used his mouth to make sure she wasn't left disappointed before falling asleep almost immediately.

It hadn't taken her long to drop off with him. It'd been a relief not to have to spend another endless night alone. Their relationship was temporary—he'd made that clear—but she was grateful for the intimacy and the companionship all the same. If nothing else, they were both filling a need.

"What are you doing awake?"

Startled by the sound of his voice, she pressed a hand to her chest. "You scared me. I was trying not to disturb you, so you'd be able to get some sleep."

"Don't worry about me. I'm fine."

Again, she had the impulse to smooth back his hair, but she was no longer sure touching him in that way would be welcome. Was last night an isolated incident?

She had no idea what his conscience would allow. "I'd better get back to the guesthouse," she said and tried to get up to go find her clothes, but he stopped her.

"It's early yet. *Very* dark and cold outside."

"*Very?*" she echoed with a laugh because he'd dramatically emphasized the word.

"So dark and cold you'll regret it the minute you leave the house."

"Even if I'm going such a short distance?" she teased.

He kissed her neck. "Trust me. It'll be miserable."

She couldn't help moving her head to give him better access and closed her eyes as his mouth moved up toward her jawline. "What's my other option?"

"You could stay here," he whispered right before using the tip of his tongue to outline the rim of her ear.

"And do what?"

When his eyes latched on to hers, she couldn't look away. "Let me show you."

As his hand slid up her bare thigh, she felt a corresponding quiver in her belly, but the fact that she reacted so strongly to his touch made her nervous. Sharing a night together was one thing. Becoming emotionally dependent was another. She didn't want to risk getting too close to the fire.

"You're thinking too much," he told her. Then he kissed her mouth, using his tongue in deliciously wonderful ways, as he moved his hand higher and higher.

And once he reached his target, she could no longer come up with a good reason to refuse him.

Tia wasn't in his bed. Still groggy from a deep sleep, deeper than he'd been able to sleep in a long while, Seth lifted his head and listened to see if he could hear movement in the house. He hoped she hadn't left. But there was only silence.

"Damn," he muttered. The contrast of having her warm body tucked up against him and then waking up alone made him feel strangely bereft.

After a stretch, he reached for his phone—but it wasn't there. He'd left it outside with his clothes. Afraid that it'd rained since, he yanked on a pair of boxers and some sweatpants and ran barefoot through the house to reclaim it.

But he didn't get all the way to the door. As he passed through the living room, he spotted his clothes folded neatly on the couch. His phone was right there, too, on top of the pile.

Thank god. Tia must've brought them in when she'd retrieved her own clothes.

He touched the screen and felt a surge of relief as it lit up.

He'd received several text messages, but he didn't check to see what they were or even who they were from. He didn't want to hear from anyone, didn't want to be dragged back to reality too soon. He was going to put on a pot of coffee and enjoy feeling more relaxed and satisfied than he had in a long while before launching into his day.

The coffeemaker hadn't quite finished, however, when he heard the intercom buzz, signaling that there was someone at the front gate.

He'd given his family the code to get in, so he didn't think it could be any of them. According to his phone, it was after ten. They'd all be at work right now, anyway.

Maybe Tia had ordered groceries or breakfast or something…

With a yawn, he made his way to the console and pressed the button. He wished he could check the camera positioned there, but it wasn't working. "Hello?"

"Yes, um, is this… Maxi Cohen?" Although the voice Seth heard cut in and out, something about it put him on edge.

"No, it's not," he replied. "What can I do for you?"

"Is Mr. Cohen there?"

Seth refused to give out any information, not until he knew who he was dealing with. "Are you a friend of Maxi's?"

"Not really. My name is Ray Kouretas. I was hoping I could have a word with Tia Beckett."

Shit. Kouretas had found where Tia was staying *already*? Seth supposed he shouldn't be surprised. Kouretas had known she was taking care of a parrot. Not many people had such an unusual pet. "I'm sorry, there's no one here by that name," he said.

"I was told she's pet-sitting for Maxi Cohen. This *is* his residence, isn't it?"

"It is, but I'm the one who's staying here and caring for the parrot."

"So you're saying…my information is incorrect?"

"That's exactly what I'm saying," Seth told him. "The woman you're asking about isn't here."

"Look, just so you know, I don't mean her any harm. I'd like to talk to her. That's all."

There was no way Seth was going to trust this guy. Tia had been through enough. "I told you she's not here."

"Come on, man. There can't be two parrots in Silver Springs."

"How do you know?"

There was a long pause before Kouretas said, "Wait a second. I recognize your voice. You're the guy who called me, right?"

Seth had been hoping the distortion that went along with using an intercom would keep Kouretas from realizing that they'd spoken before. But he would've been more surprised if Kouretas hadn't put two and two together. A good paparazzo would have to be a decent investigator, too, or he'd never get what he was after. "I am."

"Then, maybe we can make a deal. You were interested before."

"I'll consider it if you'll tell me who gave away the fact that she was in Silver Springs to begin with," he said.

"I'm afraid I can't reveal that information."

"Then, I can't help you."

"Wait! I know she's on the property. All I need is one good picture. Just tell me what you want in order to make that happen."

Seth felt his hand curl into a fist. "The only thing *I* want is for you to take a hike—and don't come back."

"Can't you—"

"If you don't leave right away, I'm afraid you and I are going to have a serious problem," Seth broke in.

This time he got no response. Seth wanted to believe the dude was getting into his car and driving away, but he'd seen on TV how persistent the paparazzi could be. They didn't take no for an answer. They couldn't—not if they wanted to be successful at the job.

He paced back and forth in the giant marble entryway for several minutes, waiting to see if Kouretas would try to buzz him again.

The intercom remained silent, but that only made Seth more nervous. Was Kouretas climbing the fence right now, trying to get onto the property?

Surely, he wouldn't go that far. Or…would he? How brazen would this guy be? Although trespassing was illegal, what recourse did they really have? Seth didn't know the ins and outs of the law when it came to dealing with the paparazzi. But he understood enough about the legal system to know that it wasn't easy for a wronged party to pursue the remedy he or she deserved. The most he could do to protect Tia would be to call the cops, and they would…what? Escort Kouretas off the property? Who was to say he wouldn't just come back? And what if they didn't arrive until after Kouretas had taken the photograph he wanted? Tia would have to sue him, and there was no way she had the mental fortitude to do that, even if she had the resources it would require.

With a curse, he hurried to his room, threw on a sweatshirt, stuffed his feet in some tennis shoes without bothering to put on socks and jogged outside.

It was a gray, overcast day. The Christmas lights Maxi had on the front of his house and along the fence twinkled through the fog. He started toward the gate. But Maxi owned something like seven acres. Even if Kouretas wasn't near the driveway, it didn't mean he was gone. He could be climbing the fence somewhere out of sight—behind the garage, for instance.

There was a small door beside the gate. Seth used it to walk out and look up and down the road.

He didn't see any vehicles, but Kouretas wouldn't be likely to make his intentions plain by leaving his car parked out front. He'd move it somewhere else first, or wait at the end of the street, hoping Tia would eventually emerge, and he'd get the opportunity he was hoping for that way.

"What are you up to?" Seth murmured. He had no idea what to expect. And since he couldn't be everywhere at once, he decided he'd better warn Tia.

After taking a final look over his shoulder at the empty road, he jogged to the guesthouse and banged on her door.

It took several minutes to rouse her, but when she finally answered, he could tell she'd been sleeping. "Don't tell me we're going running," she said when she saw him in sweats.

He would've laughed, except his mind was still on Ray Kouretas. "No. Well, maybe later. I just thought I'd let you know—" He caught himself. While he wanted to warn her, he didn't want to freak her out. Especially after last night. She seemed to have found some solace in him, just as he'd found some in her. How could he destroy her peace of mind, when nothing had really changed? She knew Ray Kouretas was in town. "I just... I wanted to thank you for last night," he said.

Her eyebrows shot up in surprise. She had to be wondering

why he'd banged on the door like it was some kind of an emergency. "No problem."

The blush that went with those words made him chuckle. He'd embarrassed her. "It was nice," he added. "*Really* nice."

Her blush deepened, as he'd known it would. "Thanks, but we don't have to talk about it," she said.

He laughed in spite of Ray Kouretas. He'd just have to keep an eye out and make sure she remained safe. "Okay, well, I'll let you go back to sleep."

"That's all you wanted?" she said. "To tell me I was good in bed?"

He loved that she was willing to tease him back, despite being slightly embarrassed by the topic. "That's no small thing."

"Well, you weren't too bad yourself," she said quickly and started to close the door. He could tell she was eager to get behind it. But he didn't want to let her go.

"I have one more question," he said.

She cleared her throat and opened the door a little wider. "What's that?"

"Last night, while we were in the hot tub, you said something about only 'sort of' being on the pill." He shoved his hands in his pockets. "That came off…a little questionable."

"I can see why. I've been on the pill since I was fourteen for reasons other than birth control. But the pill *is* birth control, so we were covered."

What other reasons could there be for taking the pill? He wanted to ask but felt as though that was probably none of his business. They hadn't risked a pregnancy. That was all he needed to know. "Okay."

When their eyes met, he was tempted to try to kiss her again. She looked slightly rumpled with her wavy dark hair falling in an unruly mass about her shoulders, and those large eyes, framed with long lashes, were peering up at him. The scars on her cheek were there, of course. They were red and angry and terribly unfortunate. But her coloring, her gorgeous hair and beautiful eyes, along with the oval shape of her face, created a pretty picture in spite of them.

And he already knew how soft her skin was.

If only he could part her robe and slip his hands inside...

Maybe he would have acted on that impulse had his phone not signaled a text.

She gestured expectantly toward his pocket. "I think someone's trying to get hold of you."

Since she'd noticed, too, he pulled out his phone for the obligatory check.

Are you coming to brunch?

Apparently, his mother had been trying to reach him all morning. He'd missed several messages from her. Dallas and Emery had shown up this morning to surprise her for Christmas. They'd come early because they were going to Boston to spend the holiday with Emery's mother and grandmother, so Aiyana had decided to take the day off and had made a big meal.

Can I bring Tia? he wrote back. There was no way he could leave her on the property alone—not with Kouretas skulking about.

Of course, came Aiyana's immediate response.

"My brother and his wife are in town, so my mom's made brunch," he said. "She wants me to invite you." It didn't happen in quite that way, but he thought Tia would be more likely to agree if she thought it was Aiyana's idea.

When Tia still hesitated as though she'd refuse, he guessed she was worried about being spotted. But if she was well covered and her scars weren't visible, even if Kouretas did get a few shots they wouldn't be worth anything. "We'll make it so that no one will be able to recognize you until after we get inside my mother's house."

"It sounds like a family thing," she said. "I don't want to intrude."

"It'll be good for you to get out and start interacting with people. This gives you the chance to start with a small, friendly gathering."

She bit her bottom lip. He imagined she was picturing what it might be like to meet his brothers and their wives and children and hoped, if any of his nieces and nephews were going to be there, they wouldn't make a big deal about the scars on her face. If they did, it could get awkward for everyone, but he honestly thought a small gathering of trusted individuals would be a good way for her to start mixing with others again.

"We won't stay long," he promised by way of encouragement.

She flashed him a quick smile. "Okay. Why not?"

"Perfect. Do you have a baseball cap?"

"No, but I do have a hoodie. I lied before because I didn't want to go running."

He rolled his eyes. "I've got a ball cap. We'll make use of both."

"No need. I'll wear a beanie instead of either, as well as a scarf I can use to cover the lower half of my face," she said. "What time do we need to leave?"

"As soon as you can get ready."

"Give me thirty minutes."

"Okay, but don't come out until I ring the doorbell."

"What?"

That probably sounded odd, but he knew about Kouretas finding the house, and she didn't. "I want to make sure you're disguised well enough. That paparazzo's in town, remember?"

She made a face. "How could I forget?"

CHAPTER SIXTEEN

A wave of apprehension rolled over Tia as they left the sanctuary of Maxi's property. She was wearing a puffy ski coat over her clothes with a scarf and beanie, as well as a pair of sunglasses, so she wasn't necessarily afraid of being recognized and confronted by Kouretas. At least she was no longer inside her condo with an army of media crowding the gate, drawing all kinds of attention and making her feel vulnerable and outnumbered. Besides, she had Seth with her; she finally had the advantage. It was more that this would be her first social gathering, and one that would include the family of the man she'd just slept with. She and Seth were both adults. What they did was their own business—as long as it didn't hurt anyone else, of course. She understood that. But these people knew and loved his late wife and might perceive Tia as an interloper if they suspected anything physical was going on. They also knew that Seth still loved Shiloh, so they'd wonder what she'd been thinking. They might even feel sorry for her.

That just made it awkward. She didn't belong in this group.

Tempted to ask if they could turn back, she glanced over at Seth. He hadn't bothered to shave and was also wearing a beanie with his coat, which was unzipped over a waffle-knit shirt he wore with a pair of chinos. Driving with one arm slung over the steering wheel of his sleek sports car, he looked far more comfortable than she felt. She thought he'd make a good advertisement for Porsche, but she knew she shouldn't allow herself to admire him too much. Her emotions were scrambled from the accident and its aftermath, which made her vulnerable. After the crazy, thrilling and even tender night she'd spent in his bed, she could easily get too caught up in him and wind up in an even worse situation after her stay in Silver Springs came to an end.

That was another reason she had no business going to this brunch with him.

She opened her mouth to suggest turning around but couldn't bring herself to pose the question. It was almost noon. The time it would take for him to return her to the guesthouse could easily mean he'd miss the family meal.

She should've tried harder to refuse in the first place. While the idea of an outing appealed to her, especially after how long she'd been cooped up, she could've driven to Santa Barbara or somewhere else for the day.

Although…driving was always a daunting challenge since the accident. Not only that, but where would she go and what would she do once she got there? Wander around alone on a cold beach?

"Quit fidgeting," he said, giving her a mock scowl. "You're going to be fine."

"How do you know?" she retorted.

He turned down the stereo, which was playing "The Show Must Go On" by Queen. "Because I'm here to make sure of it."

She recalled how he'd pulled his Porsche as close to her doorstep as the walkway and landscaping would allow and rushed her out of the house and into the passenger seat of his car as though he was her new security detail. "Why are you even trying to take me with you?"

His eyes slid her way. "Because we're friends."

Friends *and* lovers—after last night. They called that Friends with Benefits, didn't they? She barely refrained from rolling her eyes. She'd never dreamed she'd find herself in such an arrangement. According to her parents, and what she'd been taught, premarital sex was a sin—even for two people who were in love.

But it was just one night, she reminded herself. They'd both needed someone. And now it was over. She wasn't going to beat herself up over it. Better to let it go, pretend it'd never happened.

"What're you thinking?" he asked.

She turned her head to gaze out at the passing scenery. "Nothing."

"I can tell that's not true."

She didn't attempt to bolster the lie. He kept checking the rearview mirror, so she twisted around to see why. "Is something wrong?"

"Nothing."

"You seem worried that someone might be following us."

"You trusted me enough to come out, so I'm being cautious, just in case."

She checked again, but there wasn't even a car there. She was too nervous to focus on anything except meeting more of Seth's family, anyway—so nervous that as they drew closer to New Horizons, she started jiggling her leg.

He put his hand on her knee to stop her. "Will you calm down?"

She didn't want to like the warmth or the weight of his hand as much as she did. After last night it felt somewhat familiar—and far too welcome, which only made her more anxious. "No," she said simply. "Who's going to be there?"

"You know who's going to be there. My family."

"*All* of them?"

"My four younger brothers won't be in town until closer to Christmas."

"So it's just the older ones? And their wives and children?"

He took his hand off her knee as he turned under the New Horizons arch, and the coldness that rushed upon her in its absence felt grossly disproportionate. "I don't know. We'll have to see."

"Just give me an idea," she pressed.

He rolled his eyes as though she was being ridiculous. "Fine. We'll go over them one by one. Gavin might be there. He does the grounds and maintenance for the school, so he might be able to shuffle his duties around a bit."

"And Eli?" She didn't mind Eli, since she'd already met him, but Seth shook his head.

"I doubt it. Eli will most likely be running the school, since my mother's not there."

"Eli and Gavin have wives, don't they?" She remembered hearing a handful of children the night Seth had first arrived. It was doubtful that they all belonged to one person.

"Yes, but Cora teaches, so it's unlikely we'll see her, either. Savanna could be there, if she doesn't have something else going on."

"So four, maybe five people?"

"Tia, you're making too big a deal out of this."

She probably was, but the scars on her face suddenly felt like they were on fire. She flipped down the visor so that she could see herself. Fortunately, the scarf did a decent job of concealing the damage, but she couldn't leave the scarf on inside the house…

"Relax." He flipped the visor back up. "We're going to have a nice meal."

She was overreacting, but she was a celebrity. Most people were excited to meet her. She didn't want to disappoint them if they'd seen the movie and expected her to look like she had before.

She didn't want to feel their disappointment, either. She felt enough of her own.

After Seth parked in front of Aiyana's large yellow house, he came around to her side of the car and opened the door. "Let's go."

She stared miserably at their ultimate destination. "Do we have to?"

He chuckled, but she felt his hand at her elbow as soon as she got out, all the way until they'd climbed the steps of the wide front porch. He only dropped it when he opened the door. "I hope you saved some food for us," he called out as he walked in, waved her through and shut the door.

"Look who it is!" Aiyana hurried from the kitchen to give her a hug. "I'm so excited you decided to come. Can I take your coat?"

"I got it," Seth told her and held out his hand to Tia.

Tia reluctantly stripped off her jacket and nudged his hand away when he left it there as though he expected her to pile her beanie and scarf on top of it, too.

"You keep that stuff on, you're going to melt in here," he murmured under his breath, but that didn't change her mind. She took off her sunglasses and shoved them in her purse but wasn't willing to relinquish the rest quite yet.

Aiyana stepped back as three other people drifted in from the kitchen. "Dallas, Emery, Gavin, this is Tia Beckett."

Gavin had long dark hair and a beard, kind eyes and a gentle manner. "Nice to meet you," he said.

Dallas allowed his wife to shake her hand before he did. He was almost as handsome as Seth, but he had a completely different build. While Seth was tall and slender, taller than Gavin and Dallas, Dallas was more compact, with powerful-looking shoulders. His wife was a petite woman with big blue eyes and long blond hair. "Thanks for allowing me to crash your party."

Emery gave her a warm smile. "You're welcome here."

That none of them seemed remotely surprised that the leading actress of *Expect the Worst* was standing in their living room indicated Aiyana had prepared them.

"Have a seat." Dallas gestured at one of the recliners, but Aiyana slipped her arm through Tia's and drew her to the kitchen.

"Actually, why don't the four of you visit in here while Tia and I finish up? You wouldn't mind helping me, would you, Tia?"

"Of course not." Relieved to be able to escape the attention she would otherwise have received, Tia left Seth with his brothers and Emery.

"You look beautiful, even with that scarf hiding half your face," Aiyana said once they were alone. "But it might be hard to eat with that thing on," she teased.

Tia unwound the scarf but left it hanging from her neck so that she could cover up again if she felt the need. "I'm sorry. Getting used to my new...*look* isn't easy."

Aiyana flipped the pancakes she had cooking on a griddle. "I understand. You're incredibly brave to come out at all. How're you feeling today? Any better?"

The memory of Seth's naked body against hers in the hot tub last night flashed before Tia's mind's eye. That had helped a great deal, had enabled them both to work out some frustration and anger and not feel quite so alone. But she didn't want to dwell on it. "Better," she affirmed.

"You know, Emery's father is a gifted plastic surgeon. He lives in Boston these days, but he worked in Los Angeles for years. Although he won't name names, word has it he's worked on many famous people. At some point, you might want to have him take a look at your face. There might be something he can do."

"Thanks, but I'm guessing that will be quite expensive, and I'm not sure that would be the smartest way to spend my money, given the situation. I had to back out of several projects in the

days immediately following the accident, so I'm essentially un-
employed." Even if she took the gamble and spent the money,
there was no guarantee cosmetic surgery would help. That was
what her doctor had told her. He'd said she could spend a fortune and end up making things worse—or at least create a face
she no longer recognized.

"I see. Well, there will be time to decide later."

Except, when later finally came, she would've lost all of her
momentum in Hollywood. Comebacks after a long drought,
especially those that included an altered face—even if it wasn't
quite as bad as it was now—were unlikely. "Yeah," she agreed,
simply because it made her sick to face the truth, and she preferred to avoid the rougher realities for now.

Aiyana had Tia carry the food—the pancakes, an egg soufflé
and some bacon—to the table as she called, "Come and get it!"

Seth was the first one through the doorway. He arched an
eyebrow at Tia as if to ask if she was okay, and she forced a smile.
She'd known this wouldn't be easy, but it was good to get out
and to talk to people again. Wallowing in her disappointment
certainly wasn't making it any better.

Aiyana insisted on putting on some Christmas music before
they could eat. Tia guessed Seth wasn't excited about it, but his
mother came up behind where he was seated at the table and
dropped a kiss on his cheek as if to ask him to indulge her. And
he briefly covered the hand that rested on his shoulder with
his, as if he'd give her anything. Tia loved witnessing that exchange—and wished she had as caring a relationship with her
mother as he had with Aiyana.

Seth caught her watching them, so she focused on passing
the syrup Aiyana had placed closest to her.

"Seth tells us you're babysitting a parrot," Emery said. "What's
that like?"

Tia accepted the eggs Seth was handing to her and scooped

a small amount onto her plate. "It's kind of fun. Kiki's not only beautiful, she's incredibly smart."

"Can she say anything?"

"I've heard a few phrases. She says *pretty girl* quite a bit. Then there's *Shh, be quiet*. And she barks like a dog."

Gavin laughed. "I heard her the other night."

"Drives me nuts," Seth grumbled, and they all laughed.

"That would be annoying," Dallas allowed.

"Apparently she's not partial to humans," Tia said. "She's willing to learn from any species."

"What made Maxi want to get a parrot?" Emery asked. "Do you know?"

"He told me he has a friend in South America who has one," Tia replied. "He loved it so much he decided to build an atrium so he could get one for himself."

"I heard caged birds can get lonely and depressed and start pulling out their feathers," Dallas said.

Emery nudged her husband. "Spoken like a man who prizes his freedom above all else."

"I don't love it more than you, honey," he said with an exaggerated wink, but Tia could tell what he said was true, which made her feel as warm and happy as when she'd witnessed the interaction between Seth and Aiyana. She'd been so consumed with her career and achieving her dreams. Maybe there were still enough good things left to her in life that she could be happy herself.

"Kiki has it pretty good," she told them. "The atrium is huge and always the perfect temperature. And I got the impression Maxi spends a lot of time with her. That's why he wanted someone there while he was gone—not just to feed her but to play with her."

"It must be cool getting to know such an exotic bird," Gavin said.

Aiyana took a seat at the head of the table. "I'm not surprised she's thriving. Maxi never does anything halfway."

"What do you do for a living?" Tia asked Dallas, intrigued by Emery's earlier reference to her husband loving his freedom.

"Dallas is a professional rock climber," Gavin piped up. "He has a sponsor and everything."

Dallas nudged his brother. "Don't sound so surprised when you add that part."

"You look as fit as he does," Tia said to Emery. "Do you climb, too?"

"I go out with him sometimes, but not professionally. I'm nowhere near as good as he is and don't even attempt the really hard stuff."

"You've come a long way in only a year," Dallas said.

Tia couldn't put it off any longer: she had to unwrap her scarf to take her first bite. But once she did, no one seemed to pay her any additional attention, so it wasn't as uncomfortable as she'd feared. Aiyana must've warned them about the damage to her face when she'd prepped them for her visit because they took her scars in stride, just as they did her presence, and that helped. "You've only been climbing for a year?" she asked Emery.

All eyes turned her way, but again, no one acted as though they saw anything too shocking. Emery merely used her fork to gesture at her husband. "Only since I hooked up with this guy last Christmas. Before that, I was a news anchor in LA—"

"I thought you looked familiar!" Tia broke in, starting to feel more and more comfortable in this group. "I admit I don't watch much TV, but I must've seen you at some point."

"Do you think you'll ever go back to reporting the news?" Gavin asked his sister-in-law.

"I enjoyed my job, so I would never say never." She turned her attention to Tia to explain. "I write a travel blog these days, from a climber's perspective, and post some of the crazy pictures we get with the GoPro."

"And she's wildly successful," Aiyana added.

The pride Aiyana felt at Emery's accomplishments was evident in her voice, and based on Emery's smile, she heard it, too. "Thanks, Mom," she said. "I'm surprised by how big my following has become, so that's fun," she added for Tia's sake. "I love interacting with the community I'm creating. I might even enjoy what I'm doing now more than what I was doing before, which surprises me. I was so set on that career path."

"You can do this job in your pajamas," Dallas pointed out.

She grinned at him. "You just like that it leaves me free to traipse around the world with you."

"Damn right," he said, and everyone laughed.

The conversation moved to Gavin, the new tennis courts he was helping build at the school and the fact that his wife, Savanna, was overseeing a homeschool program for kids in the area. She was going to stop by the brunch, but she'd got caught up.

Eli stopped in at the end of the meal. He said hello to Tia as he grabbed a paper plate and piled it high with pancakes, eggs and bacon, but he treated her just like everyone else. That Seth and his family didn't make her the focal point of every conversation and hadn't even brought up the movie or her accident made her feel like an average person—like she was one of them—and that was a nice reprieve.

By the time Eli and Gavin rushed out to return to the school, Tia had all but forgotten about her lost career, her scars, Kouretas being in town—even the fact that she'd slept with Seth last night—until after she'd helped Aiyana with the dishes and went into the living room, where Seth was chatting with his brother and sister-in-law. Although they'd offered to help clean up, too, Aiyana had shooed them out, allowing only Tia to stay with her, which made Tia feel even more at home. She could tell Aiyana was keeping her close whenever possible.

Seth glanced up when she approached the three of them and

asked if she wanted to sit down, but as soon as she accepted his invitation, she caught sight of the pictures on the mantel. Front and center was an eight-by-ten of Seth and Shiloh at their wedding, smiling happily for the camera: two gorgeous people who looked totally happy and absolutely in love.

That was when she realized, as relaxed and welcome as she'd begun to feel, she'd been right in the beginning—she didn't belong here.

"You're quiet," Seth said as they drove back to Maxi's.

"I'm tired. You woke me up this morning, remember?"

He chuckled. "It was almost noon."

"I know. I'm joking."

She didn't reference the fact that he'd kept her up most of the night. He wondered what she was thinking about that. He hadn't let himself think about it too much. It made him feel disloyal to Shiloh, but he'd be lying to himself if he tried to say he didn't enjoy it. "Brunch seemed to go okay."

She kept staring out the window. "Brunch was great. You have a wonderful family, and they obviously love you very much."

It was starting to rain. Fat drops hit the windshield with a solid splat. "Then...what is it?"

He saw her chest lift as she drew a deep breath. "Nothing," she said. "I need to plan out a new life, so I'm just trying to do that."

"What do you think you'll do?"

"I'd like to stay in the movie industry. I can't help how much I love it. I've spent my whole life dreaming of being an actress. So...maybe I'll become a director."

He switched on the wipers. "Is that feasible? What would it entail?"

"It wouldn't be easy, but it's possible. First, I'd have to go back to school and get a bachelor's in film."

"How long would that take?"

"The standard four years."

"How would you get into the industry once you graduated?"

"There's more than one way, but I'd probably try to become an assistant to an established director."

Lightning flashed in the sky, and thunder boomed a few seconds after. The temperature was dropping, but it was so warm inside the car, the windows were starting to steam, so he switched on the defroster. "How hard is that?"

"Very hard."

"Do you think Maxi would put in a good word for you?"

"I hope so, but I'm not convinced it'd be right to even ask him. No doubt he's got enough people at him for those kinds of favors."

"Maybe he'd be happy to do it. He knows you're a talented actress. He told me you deserve an Oscar for your performance in *Expect the Worst*."

That drew her attention away from the window. "Maxi said that?"

"He did." Seth stopped at the light at one end of town. "The nominees will be named shortly, won't they?"

"In January."

"Are you excited?"

"Not really. I'm sort of dreading it, to be honest."

"Why?"

"If I'm nominated, I won't feel comfortable showing up to see if I win. And if I'm not nominated, I'll feel like that was my only shot."

"Maybe as an actor. But you could get one for directing. A lot of actors go into directing, right? Angelina Jolie, Kevin Costner, Bradley Cooper, Denzel Washington. There have to be others."

She sent him a sly glance. "I thought you didn't know much about the movies."

"I don't. If you'll notice, those names have been around for a while," he said with a chuckle.

"True." She began playing with the ends of her scarf. "Your mother thinks I should give the paparazzi the picture they want. Arrange it beforehand and make whoever I choose pay me for it."

After he'd taken a moment to consider the idea, he nodded. It wasn't hard to see Aiyana's wisdom. "Sounds like a good idea to me. Are you leaning that way?"

"I am."

"Right away or after Christmas?"

"After Christmas. I need a little more time."

She'd already been through so much. That she had this on the horizon made him feel protective of her. Maybe people wouldn't be mean to her face, but he could easily guess that some of those on the internet would be cruel. No doubt there would be many jokes at her expense—probably quite a few memes, too.

Sadly, there wasn't anything he could do to stop all that. He might be able to hold off Kouretas for a while, but she couldn't hide forever.

He could give her Christmas, however—and he intended to do just that. "There's no rush. Take the time you need. You'll know when you're ready."

She nodded as though she was relieved that she had the respite she needed.

But as soon as they pulled up to the gate at Maxi's place, they found Kouretas, sitting in his car, waiting for them.

CHAPTER SEVENTEEN

Tia's heart began to pound the second she saw the man blocking Maxi's driveway. He was wearing a fedora and sheltering his camera inside a heavy trench coat as he got out into the rain. "Oh no," she said, almost involuntarily.

Seth's eyes narrowed. "Don't worry. I'll get rid of him." After putting the car in Park, he climbed out and slammed the door.

"What do you think you're doing?" she heard him say, his voice dim but audible. "You can't block the driveway."

Kouretas said something in return. Tia couldn't make it out, but it must not have been nice, because Seth exploded, "Get the hell off the property!"

"I'm not on anyone's property," Kouretas argued, words Tia could hear because he was now raising his voice, too. "I can be here. *Anyone* can be here. This is a public easement."

Tia didn't want Seth to have to deal with this. Kouretas was *her* problem. Her hand lifted to the door latch, but other members of the paparazzi had harassed her so much at her condo that the prospect of confronting this guy made her sick inside. Even when she was ready to bear the shame and humiliation of allowing her new face to grace magazines everywhere, she hoped she wouldn't have to do it with *this* guy. That he would threaten her sanctuary when she needed it most angered her too much.

Seth pointed at Kouretas's car and stalked menacingly toward him. But, surprisingly, Kouretas didn't back off. He stood his ground and started gesticulating while shouting that he wasn't doing anything wrong and there wasn't anything Seth could do about him being where he was, regardless.

It got so bad that Tia felt she had no choice except to get out. It wasn't fair to make Seth deal with the situation. What if the two men got into a fight? Seth hadn't signed up for anything like this.

After making sure her face was covered, she opened the door. "Go," she yelled at Kouretas before it could get any worse, but the bottom of the scarf got caught by the door as she came around it, yanking it down for a moment, and she could tell he caught a glimpse of her cheek because his eyes went wide.

"Holy shit!" he said. "Your face *is* fucked up."

The anger that welled up nearly brought her to tears. There was no escape from what she was going through—no way out and no way to counter the threat he and others posed. She'd grown up a nobody from a Mennonite family that was more devout and superstitious than educated, yet she'd never felt more impotent. "You have no right to be here," she said.

"I have *every* right to be here," he argued. "We all gotta eat. What difference does it make to you, anyway? Someone's gonna get a picture of the mess that accident made of your face. Might as well be me."

Seth wheeled around to confront her. "Get back in the car. Now." Although he spoke much more gently to her, there was no mistaking the authority in his voice. "I can handle this," he said, but that short change in Seth's focus was all Kouretas needed to pull out his camera.

He started snapping pictures immediately. Tia could hear the click of the shutter again and again—until Seth ripped it out of his hands and smashed it on the pavement.

"What'd you do?" Kouretas gasped, incredulous. "How dare you! That was a two-thousand-dollar camera!"

"Move your car," Seth ground out. "Or that camera's not the only thing I'll break."

Kouretas's eyes nearly bulged out of his head. "Now you're threatening me?"

Seth stepped forward while hitching a thumb in her direction. "You don't think *she* finds what you're doing threatening? Give her a break, for god's sake. She's been through enough."

Kouretas gaped at the pieces of his camera. "I'm going to the police!"

"Be my guest," Seth responded. "Just don't ever come back here. Do you understand?"

"You'll be spending the night in jail!" Kouretas said as he scrambled back into his car.

"It won't be the first time."

Seth had spoken that last bit under his breath, but Tia heard him.

Kouretas fired up his engine, giving it more gas than necessary. The sound alone was enough to frighten Tia, but Seth merely propped his hands on his hips and glared at the paparazzo, which was probably why Kouretas swerved toward him, nearly hitting him before skidding onto the road.

Seth kicked the back end of his car as he tore off, but fortunately, the ugly encounter ended there.

"Oh, my gosh!" Tia pressed a shaking hand to her chest. "I can't believe that just happened."

"I had it handled," Seth said. "You should've stayed in the car."

He obviously wasn't pleased with her attempt to help him. "I didn't want you to get into a fight on my account," she said.

"He deserved what he got."

"I'm afraid the police won't agree. *Now* what do we do?"

"Nothing."

She bent to gather the pieces of the camera. "He's going to report this."

"Let him."

"What if they arrest you?"

"They won't. They'll make sure there wasn't anything worse going on. Then they'll tell him to sue me for the camera."

"And if he does?"

"I'll get him a new one."

"*I'll* buy him a new one," she said. "He wouldn't have been here if not for me."

Seth waved her off. "You weren't the one who broke it."

"But you broke it because of me."

"I'm responsible for my own decisions."

She remembered saying something similar to him last night—although in a very different context—and wondered if he was referring to that. She wasn't going to ask, though. "I'm sorry."

"Don't be." They'd been out in the rain long enough that their hair was getting wet, causing his to curl at the ears and the nape of his neck. "That dude is a douchebag."

"That's the way most of them are," she grumbled as they got back into the car. "It's sort of a prerequisite of the job."

A muscle moved in Seth's cheek as he pulled up to the keypad, punched in the code and drove through the gate and down the winding drive to the cluster of buildings where they were staying.

"I'm sorry," she said again as they got out. It wasn't a very good ending to their brunch at his mother's house, but the accident and its aftermath was part of her reality these days, and there was nothing she could do to change that.

He stopped her before she could hurry over to the guesthouse. "You know he'll just come back, don't you?"

She sighed. "He'll try."

"That was a bold move. Who knows what he'll resort to next."

She nibbled on her bottom lip as she imagined Kouretas lurking around, trying to catch her out and about. She wouldn't be getting in the hot tub again, she knew that much. The backyard was too exposed. "He might flirt with the law, but I doubt he'll break it outright." She said that with more conviction than she felt. Even if he didn't come onto the property—although she wouldn't put it past him—he could use a telephoto lens to get the shot he wanted, which made her feel cornered. She was just weighing how far he might go when Seth shook his head.

"I wouldn't take anything for granted. Especially now that he's found you, and you're mostly alone. Why don't you get your things and move into the main house with me?"

Surprised, Tia sheltered her face from the rain. *"What?"*

"I won't be able to protect you over there. You need to move into the main house so that you're closer, and he has to deal with me if he wants to get to you."

Taking care of an injured and paparazzi-harassed movie star was probably the last thing he'd expected he'd be doing when he'd arranged to stay at Maxi's. She didn't want to put him in that position. "It'll be fine," she said. "I'll be careful."

"You can't stay in all the time, Tia. It's not healthy, and you know it. Even if you try, you have to come out once a day to take care of Kiki. What if, next time, he's waiting outside your door, and I'm inside the main house sleeping or painting or whatever?"

The possibility did make her uneasy.

"There are plenty of bedrooms in Maxi's house," he continued. "With Kouretas around, why do you have to stay in the guesthouse?"

"I don't," she said. "I only moved over there because it's smaller and more comfortable."

"Trust me, the main house is comfortable, too."

Thinking of the beautiful blonde in the wedding picture she'd seen at Aiyana's, Tia swallowed hard. If she moved to the main house, it would be far more difficult not to wind up back in Seth's bed. While she'd told herself she understood his limitations, it wasn't fun to realize that he'd probably been thinking of Shiloh the whole time—that she'd just served as a stand-in.

"It makes perfect sense," he insisted.

"I guess it does," she admitted. "But—"

"What?"

"I don't want to invade your privacy or…or get in your way."

"The house is fourteen thousand square feet, Tia—the size of a small office building. I think there's plenty of room for both of us."

It was the biggest house she'd ever seen, but it had only one kitchen and living room. The rest of the house was made up of bedroom suites, a movie theater, a wine cellar, a huge pantry, a music room, a library and the giant office that also served as a showroom for Maxi's incredible art. She and Seth were bound to run into each other again and again, even if they were trying to avoid it. "I know that."

"So you'll move over?"

Unable to come up with a good reason not to, she nodded as though it wasn't a big thing. But after last night, she was almost more afraid of Seth—and what he made her feel—than of Kouretas.

If she wasn't careful, he could hurt her much worse.

Seth offered to help move her things, but Tia had brought only one suitcase, and she hadn't put a lot in it. When she'd been getting ready to leave LA, she couldn't think of anything except escaping her condo and the dogged attention she was receiving. She'd had the presence of mind to grab the basics, her swimsuit and a few pairs of sweats, yoga pants and T-shirts. But that was about it. She hadn't been able to imagine having the need for much else, not when she was supposed to be staying alone on such a large, fenced property and taking care of a parrot.

She *still* couldn't believe that Maxi had invited Seth to stay with her. But he had the right. And she could understand his perspective. His home was available. Why not help both friends?

After she gathered her clothes and folded them neatly inside her suitcase—far more neatly than when she'd packed at her condo—she spent some time cleaning. Until today, she hadn't cared enough to even pick up her trash, so she considered having the ability to perform this simple task a sign of improvement.

While she worked, she checked her phone several times, wondering if she should call or text her family. She'd ignored almost all of their attempts to reach her since the accident— had received several texts just today that'd gone unanswered.

From her sister: Really? You're not talking to us? Do you think God is pleased with who you've become?

From her mother: I understand that you're upset, Tia, but I don't understand why you won't come home. You need to do what's right before you lose God's favor entirely.

She considered all the things she had to say but knew she couldn't distill it down into a text, and there was no way she wanted to talk on the phone. She wasn't strong enough yet. She needed to continue to heal and get back on her feet before she tried to navigate those complicated relationships.

When she let herself into the main house, the security system announced her presence, but most of the rooms were dark now that the sun was setting, and she couldn't hear or see Seth.

Where was he? She stood in the entryway with one hand on her roller suitcase, wondering if she'd made the wrong decision in allowing him to talk her into this.

But then he appeared at the top of one side of the curved staircase.

"Do you care which room I pick?" she asked when she saw him.

"Not at all," he replied. "Would you prefer to be on the main floor or upstairs?"

It wasn't difficult to make that decision. "I'll go with the second story. That way I won't ever have to feel as though someone might be trying to peek in the window."

"Understandable."

He jogged down and took her suitcase. "You pack light, for an actress," he said jokingly as she followed him back up.

"I admit I wasn't myself when I left LA."

He strode down the wing opposite the office, which eventually dead-ended at the massive master suite. "You've been up here before, right? Which room suits you best?"

"I guess any of those that overlook the pool."

He stopped at the first door. "This one fits that description."

"Perfect."

As he put her suitcase inside, she thought about the reason she'd decided not to stay in the main house in the first place. She was afraid she'd feel too lost wandering through its many rooms. And as much as she was growing to like Kiki, living with a parrot had seemed a little off-putting. She'd been afraid that hearing the bird speak in the middle of the night might freak her out.

But now that Seth was in the house, that had changed. This was suddenly where she felt the most secure—when it came to breaches of her privacy, anyway. She figured she was *more* at risk in other ways, which meant she'd have to be careful.

"You're not upset by what happened with Kouretas, are you?" he asked.

"I'm not happy that he found me, but I'm okay. I'm more worried about what it might mean for you. I'm afraid the police will be knocking on the door any minute."

"If they do, I'll take care of it." He gestured toward the office. "Well, if I'm ever going to finish the piece I'm working on, I'd better get back to it. Make yourself comfortable."

"Thanks. I'm going to water the plants, then feed and play with Kiki."

"Sounds good." He started to walk away but turned back. "I hope you feel okay about staying here. After last night, I don't want you to think I'm trying to take advantage of the situation."

"Not at all. I know we both understand that last night was just a...a time out from our regular lives, a moment when we both needed a little comfort." She felt her face heat as she thought that they'd received quite a bit more than comfort. There'd been a lot of pleasure, too—so much that it was going to be difficult for her not to sleep with him every night for the rest of their stay. "An anomaly," she reiterated.

"Right." She got the impression he had more to say, and she was curious to hear what was on his mind, but he didn't come out with it. After hesitating for another moment, he gave her a nod and left.

Once he was gone, Tia sank onto the bed. She couldn't feel safe in the guesthouse. Not with Kouretas proving to be such a determined adversary. But was she any safer here?

She supposed that depended on her definition of *safe*.

Seth knew Tia probably assumed he was working on the commissioned piece for San Francisco he'd mentioned to her before. But he couldn't quit thinking about last night and the way she'd tasted and smelled and felt against him. Now that he'd made love to her, he had to change the painting—to add more depth and texture—or it wouldn't feel right to him anymore. As obsessive as he could be about his art, he knew he wouldn't be able to focus on anything else until he fixed it and hoped that channeling his emotions—the regret and the guilt he felt along with everything else—onto canvas might dispel some of the tension inside him.

As he worked, he became aware of the fact that his painting was becoming decidedly more erotic, which surprised him. He hadn't painted a naked woman in years. His usual passion—for anything—had been so muted since Shiloh died. He'd felt as though he was living in a bubble, so insulated from the rest of the world that nothing seemed particularly sharp or in focus, except for the pain of losing the love of his life. He'd been living a gray, lonely existence since she died, but he had to admit part of that was his fault. He'd purposely isolated himself so that he wouldn't have to deal with anyone else's questions or concern.

But his libido had come roaring back. To cope with the sudden surge of testosterone, he had to create something that would help him remember every detail of last night, down to the satiny feel of Tia's skin, so that he wouldn't continue to obsess about it. After having no interest in any woman for three years, he suddenly seemed to have focused all of his latent desire on Tia.

Using her wasn't the answer, however.

The buzzer signifying someone was at the gate went off an hour later.

After setting aside his brush, he jogged downstairs so that Tia wouldn't feel as though she had to answer it. But he could tell she'd heard it, too. She came out of the aviary and stood nervously in the entryway.

"Do you think it's the police?" she asked.

"Probably," he replied.

"I admit I was holding out hope Kouretas wouldn't really go through with filing a report. The paparazzi typically don't like the police. They're rarely on the same side."

Seth pressed the intercom button. "Can I help you?"

"It's me."

"Kouretas?" he said in surprise.

"I came back to make you an offer."

"I'm not interested."

Kouretas ignored that response. "I won't go to the police if you'll let me get a couple of pictures. I can use my cell phone,

be done in seconds. Then, you won't get in trouble, we'll forget about the camera, and I can get out of here."

"No," Seth said, unequivocally.

"Seth—" Tia started, concerned that she was again putting
him in the middle, but he immediately waved her to silence.

"Come on, man," Kouretas said. "You don't want to me to
go to the police, do you? That was an expensive camera."

"I understand that, and I'm happy to pay for it. I've got your
business card. I'll send you a check."

"I'd rather have the picture."

"You're not going to get it, so you might as well accept that
and leave."

"Okay, then. I guess I'll just have to do what I have to do."

"As long as you stay away from Tia, you can do whatever
you want," Seth said.

There was silence after that. As Seth let go of the intercom
button, Tia said, "I don't want to cause you all this trouble.
Should I just give him the picture?"

"No. He has his answer. He needs to accept it."

The intercom buzzed again. Irritated to think that Kouretas
would be so persistent, Seth pressed the button. "You'd better
leave us the hell alone!" he snapped.

"Excuse me?" The voice at the other end of the intercom
wasn't that of Kouretas. It was a female voice, one he easily recognized because it was Lois, Shiloh's mother.

Seth's heart hit his chest once, then twice, hard, before he
could summon a response. "I'm sorry. I thought you were someone else."

"The guy who was just here?"

"You met him?"

"I pulled up as he was storming off. He asked me if I could
get him in the gate."

"You've got to be kidding me. Is he still there?"

There was a moment of silence. Then she said, "Yes, actually. He's sort of watching me."

"He's not coming in. Make sure he knows that."

"He says you have a woman in there with you—a movie star. Is that true?"

Seth dropped his head in his hands. He wanted to be done with Shiloh's parents. They'd caused enough pain—and yet he felt silly even thinking such a thing. Why did he care?

He wasn't sure why. He just did, and he always had, which had given them way too much power.

"Seth? Are you still there?" Lois prompted when he didn't respond.

Although Tia didn't speak, he could feel her watching him. "I'm here."

"Can I come in?"

"You can't let that guy or anyone else come through with you."

"I won't." She spoke with enough conviction to convince him.

"Okay," he said. "I'll come out and get you."

CHAPTER EIGHTEEN

Tia went upstairs while Seth spoke to the woman who'd come through the gate. She'd been surprised when he told her his visitor was Shiloh's mother, probably because he hadn't acted very excited to see her. He didn't say anything negative specifically—she'd had only his body language to judge by—but that had been telling enough.

She tried not to listen to the voices that were rising up from the living room below, but the vaulted entry acted as a megaphone, and when the conversation started to get heated, she couldn't help being drawn to the banister.

"You said you came over here to make amends," Seth said.

"I did" came Shiloh's mother's response.

"Until you learned that I'm not alone. Then you acted as though I'm somehow cheating on Shiloh."

"Of course I didn't mean it that way. I know you no longer owe her your fidelity. I—I was just shocked that you have a woman here with you. That's all. In Silver Springs, as if…as if this wasn't where you met Shiloh. I mean, it's where *we* live, for crying out loud."

"You have no idea how much Shiloh meant to me—how

much she still means to me. But Tia isn't the reason I won't give you the money, so why would you accuse me of that?"

"Because you've never had a problem helping us out before!"

"I didn't realize what was going on before! I don't want to be viewed as an ATM."

"We don't view you as an ATM. It's just… We thought you'd want to help us out—seeing that we're family."

Seth's voice dropped, but Tia was so reeled in by the conversation, she found herself straining to hear the rest. "That's the cruelest form of manipulation, and you know it," he gritted out. "Before I had money, you didn't want anything to do with me, did everything you could to tear my marriage apart. So forgive me if I don't have a lot of trust where you're concerned."

"Maybe we weren't excited about you at first, but…how were we to know you'd become a famous artist?"

"Did I have to become a famous artist to earn your approval?"

"You had to become *something*! You weren't anything to start with. We only wanted what was best for our daughter."

"You think rejecting me and making her feel as though she had to choose between us was a *good* thing? You cut her off for six months once you learned we'd eloped. It wasn't until my mother told you I'd landed my first gallery showing that you finally called."

"I don't remember it that way," she said, but even Tia could tell Lois was trying to cover for her past behavior.

"Well, I do," Seth responded. "And that you're so oblivious—or uncaring—of the damage you caused makes me resent it."

"*Any* mother would be worried about her daughter getting involved with someone who…who has a criminal record," Lois spat. "You tried to rob a bank, for goodness' sake. You may think that's nothing, but it's not."

"I never said it was nothing. But I was only thirteen when I got in trouble, and there were a lot of extenuating circumstances."

"There's no excuse for illegal behavior!" Lois insisted.

"I'm not excusing myself. I'm saying you didn't even try to get to know me. Shiloh told you I wasn't a bad person, but you thought I'd never amount to anything—"

"And if not for a little luck, we would've been right!" Lois yelled. "Just because people are stupid enough to pay you huge amounts of money for your so-called art doesn't mean I don't see it for what it is—*garbage*. That you're now rich and famous doesn't change who you really are."

Tia's hand flew to her mouth to cover her gasp. Those words were the sharpest of arrows, and she could only imagine how painful they were for Seth.

Once the echo of Lois's outburst died away, silence ensued, and when Seth finally spoke, Tia could barely hear him. "You have some nerve denigrating my work and then asking me for the money it provides."

"I—I didn't mean anything against your work," Lois said, trying to retrench. "I'm just saying…it's not like you're a brain surgeon or something. You're no better than we are. We were just trying to take care of Shiloh as any good parents should!"

"*I* was taking care of her," Seth bit out. "I would've died for her. That's what you didn't understand. We never asked you for anything, even when we didn't know where our next meal would be coming from."

"She would never have been at risk if not for you. You weren't *capable* of taking care of her, and you proved it. If she had stayed in school, as *we* tried to convince her to do, she'd still be here," she shouted and marched to the door, slamming it behind her.

Lois had shot into the entry hall before Tia could step back, out of sight. If Shiloh's mother had merely looked up, she would've been spotted. But Lois had been too eager to get out of the house.

Seth, however, who'd followed Lois into the entryway, turned and saw her standing at the top of the stairs almost immediately, as if that was where he'd expected her to be all along.

"I'm sorry," she murmured. "Are you okay?"

He rubbed his forehead as though he had a headache.

"Seth?"

"I'm fine," he insisted as he came up the stairs, but those words were so mechanical she knew better.

Tia was tempted to put her arms around him. She wanted to hold him and tell him that Lois must be blind. Both he and his work were magnificent. Maybe she would've done it, but he didn't give her the chance.

Nodding politely as he passed, he went into the office, and she knew she wasn't welcome to follow him when he closed the door.

Tia went back to the aviary to finish up with Kiki and stayed longer than usual, trying to give Seth the uninterrupted time he needed. After she was done playing with the bird, she got a book from the house library and tried to entertain and distract herself by reading. She couldn't wait for Seth to emerge from the office, however, and kept tapping her foot and watching the clock as the hours passed.

By eleven, she was growing so agitated that she was beginning to pace. She'd made dinner, but when she'd gone up to knock on the office door, he'd told her he wasn't hungry. She imagined him working feverishly, but it was equally possible that what'd happened had made it difficult for him to paint. She could tell by the pallor of his face when he'd come up the stairs how much Shiloh's mother's visit had hurt him.

Finally, she couldn't take the wondering and the worrying any longer and went back to knock on the door. "Seth?" she said softly.

No answer.

"Seth?" she repeated, a little louder.

Still nothing. So she tried the handle.

It was locked. Why would he need to lock the door? Growing even more concerned, she hurried to her room, got a bobby pin out of her makeup bag and was able to bend it such that she could insert it into the lock and open the door.

Inside, the only light hung above the desk. It cast a pale gleam over the middle of the room but didn't reach all the way to the edges. Obviously, Seth wasn't working. She could see large covered objects and uncovered canvases and tables with paints and brushes and chisels and sanders scattered about, but she couldn't see any of it in any detail, and she didn't spot Seth until she'd wandered to the back of the room. Then she could make out a large, lanky body draped over a couch.

Her heart jumped into her throat—until she touched him and found him warm and breathing.

When he stirred, she said, "Thank goodness," and sagged in relief.

His eyes opened, and he stared up at her with the same hollow expression she'd seen him wear as he'd slowly climbed the stairs after Lois stormed off.

"Are you okay?" she asked. "You scared me."

He didn't answer.

"Lois, or whatever her name is, was completely wrong about you," she whispered. "You can't believe her."

"I wish things could've been different—from the beginning," he finally said. "But more for Shiloh's sake."

What about him? After a childhood like his, he was probably used to being shunned, probably thought he must deserve it in some way. "From what I heard, they're just blind."

"No, Lois was right. I did try to rob a bank."

She'd guessed it was true; he hadn't tried to deny it. "At thirteen? What made you do it?"

"I was stupid."

"Did you use a gun?"

"No. I didn't even go in. I was driving the getaway car for a friend's older brother and his buddy. I honestly didn't care about the money. I was just…so self-destructive at that age, I guess."

He said it as though he didn't understand why he would be. But Tia guessed he'd been crying out for help, trying to make someone care. From what she'd learned so far, no one had given a damn about him until Aiyana came along. "We all do stupid stuff when we're hurting," she said and, probably because kissing him was all she could think about, lowered her mouth to his.

She meant only to give him a soft kiss to convince him of her sincerity. She didn't think he'd accept anything more than that, so she was more than a little surprised when his hands came up right away, his fingers slid into her hair and he not only returned the kiss, he deepened it so quickly and so hungrily she got the impression he'd been starving for exactly this.

The shadows in the room were so heavy that Seth couldn't see much of Tia's face or body. It was the curves and lines he'd created while painting her that swam through his head as he propped himself above her on the thick Turkish rug covering the hardwood floor and tried to measure everything through touch and sensation alone. He wanted to drink in every detail, to commit her entire body to memory, so that he could make sure he'd accurately captured the essence of her in his work.

At least, that was what he told himself. He wanted to believe this was no different than last night, nothing more than a casual encounter for the sake of comfort and release, with the added benefit of inspiring new work that demonstrated more passion than he'd been able to summon in recent years.

But deep down, he knew tonight was different. It meant more than it should, and that made him feel as though Lois was right—he *was* betraying Shiloh.

At one point, he almost pulled away from her. He would have, if Tia hadn't let go of him the second he panicked. He couldn't see her scars in the dim light as she stared up at him with her arms resting above her head and her hair fanned out on the carpet. But even if he could, he didn't think it would change his mind. To him, she looked perfect. Her chest was rising and falling fast—they were both breathless—and her lips were still wet since he'd just broken off a kiss. She had every right to ask him why he'd suddenly pulled away, but she didn't. She didn't put any pressure on him at all. He could tell she sensed that he was on the verge of bolting, but instead of trying to convince him to stay, she just waited to see what he decided.

Her immediate acceptance that he might have to abandon this encounter unexpectedly made getting up and walking away even harder. He could've made himself forego the pleasure. He'd been celibate since Shiloh died. But Tia had something else he craved, something beyond the physical, and he couldn't put his finger on exactly what it was. Maybe it was that he understood and could identify, almost too well, with how difficult it was for her to allow someone else to get close to her right now, and that kinship drew him to her.

Whatever it was, instead of withdrawing, he dipped his head to kiss her again. She parted her lips and accepted the kiss, but she didn't put her arms back around his neck. In his mind, that signaled that he'd spooked her.

"I'm sorry," he whispered.

"You don't have to be sorry," she whispered back. "But… I don't want to continue if you're not sure you want this."

He closed his eyes as guilt wrestled with need. He'd always craved more love than he could get, had always been left wanting. Except when he was with Shiloh. Those years with her had been the only time in his life he'd been able to assuage that old ache.

"I want it too badly. That's the problem," he said and sank into her in relief when he felt her arms finally clasp tightly around him again.

★ ★ ★

Tia woke on the floor, tangled up in Seth, beneath a fur throw that had been on the couch.

She realized where she was quickly enough. The light glaring through the windows on either side of the huge room made that obvious. But it wasn't until she heard, for the second or third time, what'd awakened her that she understood they were no longer alone in the house.

"Seth?" a male voice called as whoever it was came charging up the stairs.

"Someone's here!" she whispered in alarm.

Seth covered a yawn. "What's wrong?" he mumbled, still half-asleep.

Pulling away, she jumped up and scrambled to collect her clothes. "You have to get dressed."

"Hey, where are you?" came the voice again. "You home?"

Once he heard the person, too, Seth said, "It's Gavin" and sprang into action. But he'd barely managed to shove his legs into his jeans—was still buttoning his fly—when his brother walked through the door Tia had left standing open when she'd come in herself last night.

"Whoops!" Obviously embarrassed to find them only half-dressed and Tia with her back to him, struggling to get her yoga pants on, he whipped around to face the other direction. "I, uh, I'm sorry. I'll be downstairs," he said and left as fast as he could.

"Do all of your family just…walk in?" Tia asked once Gavin was gone. Eli had done the same thing, she remembered, when she was over for dinner.

"It's my fault," Seth explained. "I shouldn't have given them the code to the gate. I just…didn't have any reason not to at that point."

And she was supposed to be staying in the guesthouse, so

they'd have no reason to think they might walk in on something they shouldn't.

"They aren't used to worrying about interrupting anything
like this with me," Seth added as he found his shirt. "I haven't
been with anyone since Shiloh."

Tia had wondered from the beginning if that was the case,
and the way he'd acted last night had pretty much confirmed
it. He'd seemed able to give himself a pass the first night, but
he felt more guilt making love a second time. "I guess this *is*
an office," she said as she grabbed her bra off the floor. "It's not
like he barged into your bedroom."

Gavin hadn't seen as much as he would have had he not been
yelling at the top of his lungs while looking for his brother. But
he *had* seen enough to let him know what'd been going on.

Seth yanked his shirt over his head and combed his fingers
through his hair in an attempt to get it to lie down. "I didn't
lock the front door after Lois left. I didn't even think of it.
That's on me."

"It was still daytime when she left. I didn't think of it, either." That surprised her a little now, given Kouretas's visit to
the front gate and his second attempt to get onto the property
when Lois arrived, but Tia didn't really expect him to walk into
the house. That would be going too far even for someone like
him, especially when Seth was around. But it was more than
that. She'd been too consumed with how terrible Seth was feeling to be concerned for herself.

"Are you okay?" he asked, before starting toward the door.

"I'm fine," she said. "Go talk to him. But I think I'll go take
a long shower. I'm not eager to face him."

"Sorry for the unwelcome surprise," he said with a rueful
expression. "I don't blame you for not wanting to come down."

She let him go first, then peered over the banister to make
sure the coast was clear before darting into her bathroom and
locking herself in.

★ ★ ★

"Dude!" Gavin said as soon as Seth walked into the kitchen. "I'm sorry. I had no idea."

"You could've rung the bell." Seth kept his voice low so that there was no chance Tia could hear them.

Gavin lowered his voice, too. "I did. You didn't answer, but your car was in the drive, so I assumed you were sleeping— until I checked your bedroom. When you weren't in there, I thought for sure you'd be working."

"With Maxi's bird talking at all hours of the day and night, I think I've quit paying attention to the sounds in this house. I didn't hear a thing." Hungry, Seth opened the refrigerator to get out the milk.

"You were probably worn out," Gavin said, joking.

Seth shot him a dirty look when he couldn't keep a straight face, which only made Gavin laugh harder.

"What's going on between you two?" his brother asked.

"Nothing." Seth replied firmly to let Gavin know he didn't want to talk about what had happened with Tia.

Gavin lifted his hands as though at gunpoint. "Fine. I'll say no more. But…seriously, I'm proud of you, bro."

Seth didn't ask why. He could guess. His family had been bugging him for a while, telling him that it was time to get back to the business of living. Now Gavin assumed he had. But Seth wasn't sure he was capable of moving on, despite how it might appear.

Purposely changing the subject, he said, "So why are you here? Don't you work today?"

"Mom's having a meeting with the teachers over lunch to get ready for the school play and the big Christmas party, so I came into town to pick up some sandwiches for them. On the way back, I stopped to grab a coffee at the Daily Grind and saw Lois Ivey there."

Seth refrained from grimacing at his mother-in-law's name

as he selected a box of cereal from the cupboard. "And?" He
didn't plan to tell Gavin what'd happened with Shiloh's mother
if he didn't have to.

"She was meeting that guy we saw at The Blue Suede Shoe
who was asking about Tia on Saturday night."

Seth froze. *What?*

"She was there with that guy—Kouretas or whatever his
name is. I saw them at a table in the far corner and thought it
was kind of weird. How would she know him?"

Seth could answer that. She'd run into him at the gate yesterday. He'd probably convinced her to take his card, and she
must've contacted him afterward. "Did she see you?"

"I don't think so. That place is always packed. And they were
deep in discussion."

Seth poured the cereal. "Thanks for letting me know."

"What could they have to discuss?" Gavin asked. "Lois doesn't
know Tia is staying here, does she? Even if she does, it's none
of her business. Maxi can invite whomever he wants to stay at
his place. Her daughter has been gone for three years. She can't
expect you to spend the rest of your life alone."

The matter-of-fact way Gavin addressed something that still
cut Seth deeply was part of the reason he typically steered clear
of the subject with his family. They didn't understand why he
couldn't just pick up and move on, and he was tired of having
them prod him.

Ignoring the last part of what Gavin had said, he took a bite
of cereal and spoke around it. "Maybe word's getting around
town." He spoke as though he was only speculating. But he
knew Lois was aware of Tia. He also knew she wasn't happy
they were staying on the property together. She claimed she'd
stopped by to apologize but had wound up insinuating that he
wouldn't help them out financially because it no longer served
him now that he had his eye on another woman. Which was
preposterous. Giving the Iveys money had never served him.

While he'd been trying to be a good son-in-law and help whenever he could, they'd only ever been using him.

Gavin checked his watch. "I've got to go or I'm going to be late with the sandwiches. I just thought you should know. I mean, she's the worst person Kouretas could team up with, right?"

Seth was more than a little confused by that statement. "You mean because she's my mother-in-law?"

"Because she and Graham are desperate for money, and Kouretas has made it clear—to several people around town—that he's willing to pay for a little help. You know Graham's got a gambling habit, don't you?"

Seth nearly choked on his cereal. "Since when?"

"For a while."

"That had to have started after Shiloh died." Surely, if it was before, he'd know.

Or would he?

Gavin rubbed his chin. "Might've started before that. It's been going on long enough that word's beginning to spread. Savanna works with Lois's sister, who's mentioned on more than one occasion that they're always fighting about money."

"Why didn't you tell me?" Seth asked.

Gavin shrugged. "There didn't seem to be any reason. I figured it was his escape, how he was dealing with the loss of his daughter. I mean...it's their business—until it's not—and now, with Kouretas in town, I think it's not."

Of course. Gavin wasn't much for gossip. And he had no idea that Seth had been giving the Iveys money. Seth had never mentioned that to anyone. Why would he? "Where is he gambling? At the local casinos?"

"I don't think so. Savanna told me he goes to Vegas almost every weekend. It's just an hour-long flight."

Shocked, Seth rubbed his chin. That explained a lot. He should've guessed. But after losing Shiloh, he hadn't kept up with what was going on with his in-laws or anyone else. "That's good information to have."

"I'm surprised it's news to you."

"I don't talk to them much these days." He doubted they would've told him, anyway. That wouldn't be conducive to getting more financial help.

"I'd better go," Gavin said.

"Right." Seth thanked him and walked him out.

"Oh, and don't worry," Gavin said as he climbed into his truck.

"About what?" said Seth.

His brother closed the door and rolled down the window before starting the engine. "I won't tell anyone you're messing around with a freaking movie star, except Mom and Eli and Savanna and—"

Seth scowled as he smacked the door. "Keep it to yourself."

Gavin laughed at his response. "Come on, bro. Your secret's safe with me."

"It'd better be," he grumbled and tilted his head with an *I mean business* look, but that only made Gavin laugh harder, and Seth couldn't help chuckling as his brother swung around to roll down the drive.

Seth felt his smile fade as he watched the gate close behind Gavin, though. Now he understood why his in-laws were always so desperate for money—and what he'd been feeding when he'd written them checks in the past.

"You'd better not be helping Kouretas after all I've done for you," he muttered, thinking of Lois.

But after what he'd learned this morning, he had a strong feeling she wouldn't hesitate.

CHAPTER NINETEEN

Something was different about Gavin. He was always even-tempered—*chill*, as her students would say—but today he looked like the cat who'd swallowed the canary. Aiyana couldn't help watching him curiously once she met him at his truck to help carry in the sandwiches and drinks.

"What's up with you?" she asked as they arranged everything in the teacher's lounge on two long tables covered with butcher paper. The teachers would be arriving in a few minutes. He'd gotten back later than she'd expected. But they were alone for now, so she was hoping to get whatever it was out of him before she had to turn her attention back to work.

"Nothing," he said, but his lips curved into a grin he couldn't seem to hold back.

"It's definitely something," she insisted. "What's going on?" She sat up taller as an idea struck her—a possible answer to her own question. "Oh, my gosh! Are you and Savanna going to have another baby?"

"No." He lifted a hand to stop that guess right away. "We're done having kids, Mom. No more for us."

"But Alia and Branson are getting older—Branson will be a

teenager before we know it—and they've been such a big help
with Crew. Alia told me she would love to have a little sister."
Savanna had had two children from a previous marriage when
she moved to town, and since she and Gavin had been married,
they'd added one more to the family.

"Three kids is a lot in this day and age," he said.

"Three is nothing," she argued. "I can't imagine having anything less than eight."

He chuckled as he slung an arm loosely around her shoulders
and pecked her cheek. "Because you're Superwoman," he said.
"There aren't many people who can do what you do. We're not
even going to try."

"Flattery will get you everywhere—except it won't throw
me off the scent." She eyed him shrewdly. "What are you so
happy about?"

He glanced at the door as if he was afraid the teachers were
about to barge through it.

"We still have ten minutes," she told him, indicating the
clock on the far wall. "You can do a lot of talking in ten minutes," she added playfully.

He laughed again. "I'm just excited to think Seth might be
able to overcome the funk he's been in since Shiloh died."

"That's exciting to me, too, but that's a pretty general statement. What are you referring to? Tia? Did I miss something?"
Lord knew she'd been watching the two of them at breakfast,
had definitely noticed how Seth's eyes had followed Tia whenever they were in the same room and how protective he was of
her. He'd texted before he'd brought her over to tell them not
to even mention the movie, her career or the accident. He'd
been very careful to lay the groundwork so she could feel comfortable and welcome.

"I can't say too much," Gavin said with a scowl.

"Why not?"

"Because…"

"Then, you *do* know something I don't."

His long-suffering expression suggested he couldn't fend her off. "Yes, it is Tia, okay? I suspect Seth might like her more than just a friend. That's all."

A thrill shot through her. "Really?"

"Don't take it too far," he warned. "I'm not sure. Just seeing the right signs."

When Seth had asked if he could bring Tia to breakfast, Aiyana had wondered if there might be something between them. But she was almost too afraid to hope. She'd been so terribly worried about this son in particular. He had such a distrust of love, and since Shiloh had died, he'd seemed to be absolutely convinced the love she'd offered was the only love he'd ever find—at least that he could rely on. "I won't say a word to anyone," she said. "But…what makes you think so?"

"He's been so morose the past three years. So hard to reach. Most of the time I could hardly even get him to respond to my texts or calls."

"It's been that way for all of us," Aiyana reminded him ruefully.

"But now—" Gavin's smile returned "—he's happier. I feel like… I feel like he's healing and beginning to come around."

"And you think Tia might be the reason?" Aiyana couldn't help going right back to that. She liked Tia, thought she might be perfect for Seth. But she didn't want to get her hopes up too high, not without sufficient reason, and it seemed as though Gavin could provide that reason. He was certainly acting as though he'd seen or heard *something*.

"I do."

"Why? Did he say something to you about her?"

"Not specifically. But—" he started to laugh "—let's just say it was pretty…*apparent*."

Aiyana grabbed his arm but lowered her voice. "Are you hinting that he might be sleeping with her?"

Gavin's eyes went wide. "I didn't say that."

It was Aiyana's turn to start laughing. "You didn't have to."

Some of the teachers started wandering in. Gavin shot her a disgruntled look to let her know he wasn't pleased she'd gotten so much out of him and left. He had a lot to do around campus, and he was so good to step up and get it done.

For the next forty minutes, Aiyana was too preoccupied to be able to concentrate on anything besides the events they were planning at the school. But after the meeting ended, and she was sitting alone in the room, she felt lighter than air as she texted Gavin.

Thank you, son.

For what? came his response.

For Aiyana, there simply couldn't be a better Christmas present than Seth finding love and happiness again. For giving me hope, she wrote back.

He didn't ask her to clarify. It'd been almost an hour since they'd spoken about Seth and Tia, but he understood, because all he sent back was a winking emoji.

"Lunch is ready," Seth heard Tia call as soon as he stepped out of the shower.

After he pulled on some jeans and a long-sleeved T-shirt, he went into the kitchen to find that she'd made avocado toast, squeezed some of the oranges from the pile he'd picked and put on some coffee. He was still hungry, despite the cereal he'd eaten when Gavin came over, and the toast was exceptionally good the way she made it, with pesto as a base and hot pepper flakes on top. It was such a simple thing, this breakfast after a night of great sex, and yet it was so fulfilling. Somehow, he'd forgotten how gratifying it was to share a meal with someone he enjoyed.

Or maybe he hadn't forgotten. He'd just thought he'd never enjoy anyone as much Shiloh.

Guilt flared up immediately, but that didn't seem to matter. As he ate, images from last night kept cycling through his brain. It was almost impossible to get those hours with Tia, naked in his arms, out of his head. But he was glad she didn't mention it. They made small talk instead, which felt much safer. She asked how it'd gone with his brother, and he said that Gavin would be cool about everything and took the time to explain why he had stopped by. He didn't want the conversation to become awkward. One night was a random encounter. A second night was...

He refused to finish that thought. Two nights said something more. That was all.

"But even if Lois wants to help Kouretas, how can she do that?" Tia asked, once she knew about the meeting Gavin had witnessed at the coffee shop. "It's not like she can call me up and ask me to meet somewhere Kouretas can ambush me. She doesn't even know me."

"She knows *me*."

"You think she'll try to get you to buzz her in and then hold the gate for him or something?"

"No, he doesn't need her for that. It wouldn't be hard to jump the fence. I'm guessing she'll try to invite me over for dinner one night—under the pretext of talking through what's going on between us or something else—so that I'll leave you here alone."

Tia drew her coffee closer to her. "You really believe your mother-in-law would do that? I mean... I get why she might not be happy to see another woman living in the house with you. She's probably concerned that could change everything, make you less attentive to them, but—"

"Desperate people do desperate things," he broke in.

"They need money that badly?"

"Apparently." He took a drink of his juice. "Maybe I should take away Kouretas's power by giving the Iveys the money they want," he mused.

Tia wrinkled her nose. "No. I don't want you paying his gambling debts—not for my sake, anyway. He needs to get help with the addiction. Otherwise, you'll just enable him."

"But it would be the easiest and quickest way to outmaneuver Kouretas."

"It would also be the most expensive way. I can't afford it, and I won't let you do it for me. Besides, you don't know that'll solve the problem. If they're that down on their luck, they could always go for the money he's offering, too. Besides, thanks to Gavin, we don't need to go in that direction. Now that we know they're in contact, we'll be prepared."

Seth couldn't help feeling as though the Iveys had let him down again, but he supposed he shouldn't have expected much more from Lois and Graham. His relationship with them might've begun to feel sincere right before Shiloh died, but it had fallen apart immediately after. He'd blamed himself for that; he'd withdrawn from everyone. But maybe things would've fallen apart, anyway. He was seeing a side of them he'd never seen before. The only good thing about having Shiloh gone was that she didn't have to see it, too.

The buzzer sounded. Someone was at the front gate.

Tia immediately began to worry her bottom her lip. "Oh, boy. What's going on now? We know that can't be anyone in your family. They just walk in." She smiled to let him know she was joking, and he couldn't help smiling in return. Gavin strolling into the office had to have been embarrassing for her.

"We'll see," he said and got up to answer.

When Tia followed him, he gestured at the stairway. "You might want to get upstairs while you can."

She seemed reluctant to leave him. "I hate that I'm causing so much trouble."

"You're not causing trouble. They are."

He waited until she was out of sight before pressing the button to respond to their guest. "Hello?"

An older, gravelly voice came back to him. "This is Officer Crocker with the Silver Springs Police Department. I'm responding to a complaint we received yesterday. Are you the owner of the property?"

"The owner is Maxi Cohen, who's out of town." Seth suspected they already knew that. "I'm staying here in his absence—with his permission."

"And you are..."

"Seth Turner."

"Aiyana's son."

Everyone knew his mother. "Yes."

"Do you have a moment that I could speak with you?"

Seth could tell that wasn't as optional as it sounded. "Of course. I'll meet you at the gate."

Once he let go of the button, he turned to see Tia standing at the top of the stairs, looking down at him. "Should I go out with you?" she asked.

He grabbed a coat from the closet a few feet away. "No, I've got it."

"What are you going to tell him?" she called as he opened the door.

"The truth."

"Okay." She lifted her phone to show him she had it with her. "If you need me for anything, just text me, and I'll come out."

"If I need you for anything, we'll come *in*," he said wryly and stepped into a blustery, wintry afternoon.

Tia waited anxiously for Seth to return to the house. When it took longer than she thought it should, she went from room to room, looking for a window that might give her a view of what was going on and finally found one in the music room. If she stood on a chair, she could see the back of Seth's head and shoulders: greenery blocked everything else except part of the police officer who was with him, a shorter gentleman with gray hair and a stockier build.

Sadly, she couldn't see well enough to be able to figure out what was going on. But she kept her eyes pinned to the scene. Would Seth bring him in? Would she need to corroborate the story of what happened with Kouretas?

She assumed the answer to that question was yes when she saw Seth reluctantly let the officer through the gate.

She wished she could cover her scars but refrained, because it would make the situation plain. Once the officer saw the damage to her face, maybe he could understand why there might be someone out to snap a picture for the tabloids and how that person might push Seth to the point of breaking a camera.

The sound of the door opening and closing echoed up to her. "Tia?" Seth called. "Can you come down for a moment?"

Quickly pulling her hair into a ponytail, so the officer could get a good look despite her insecurities, she took a deep breath and walked down to the entryway, where both men were waiting for her.

"Tia, this is Officer Crocker," Seth said. "Ray Kouretas has filed a complaint over what happened yesterday when he blocked our driveway."

"Nice to meet you," Tia said.

The officer's expression grew sympathetic when he saw her damaged cheek. "I'm sorry to hear about your accident," he said. Fortunately, he sounded sincere.

"Thank you."

"Would you mind telling me what happened when you encountered Mr. Kouretas at the gate yesterday?"

"Not at all." She told him how they'd come home to find that they couldn't get back onto the property, how Seth had asked Kouretas to leave but Kouretas refused, and how Seth had knocked the camera from his hands when Kouretas pulled it out and started snapping pictures, anyway.

"That doesn't sound like much of an assault," he said.

"Like I told you, I didn't touch him, just the camera," Seth said.

"Is that true?" Officer Crocker asked Tia.

"Absolutely," she replied.

He nodded. "Mr. Kouretas made it sound much worse, but I can't imagine anything will come of it, although he could always try to make a case in civil court."

"I'd be fine with that," Seth told him. "If he shows up and wins, I'll buy him a new camera. I was going to do that anyway, but now that he's involved the police, I think I'll wait to see if he can make me."

"That's up to you. Thanks for your time." He pivoted to leave but turned back before opening the door. "Ms. Beckett?"

"Yes?"

"My daughter's a huge fan." He seemed slightly embarrassed as he added, "Would you mind giving me your autograph?"

"Not at all," she said and accepted the pad and pen he pulled from his shirt pocket.

"I'm sorry that Mr. Kouretas is being such a nuisance," he said as she scribbled her name. "I'll warn him that he'd better not step foot on the property and make it clear that he can't block your driveway. But according to the law, what the eye can see, the camera can photograph. It's all part of the First Amendment. So if you're in a public place, or you can be seen from a public place, there won't be anything I can do."

"I understand."

"I'm going to put this down as a civil dispute," he said as he slid the pad and pen she returned to him back into his pocket. "Nothing serious has happened yet. But I wanted to stop by because I'd hate to see this escalate into someone getting hurt."

"That won't happen," Tia assured him.

"As long as he doesn't cause a problem, there won't be one," Seth clarified.

Officer Crocker arched an eyebrow at this response. "I love your mother, son. Everyone does. But you've been in enough trouble to last a lifetime. Let's not ruin her Christmas, okay?"

"That's the last thing I want to do," Seth said. "But there's no way I'm going to let Kouretas get a picture of Tia before she's ready to let that happen."

Crocker rested his hands on his gear belt. "Sounds to me like you're itching for a fight, and I can tell you that's not the right attitude—"

"I'll make sure there's no more trouble," Tia quickly interceded. Officer Crocker had no idea how angry Seth was at the world. If she had her guess, he'd welcome the chance to stand up for something and fight, as long as he could feel justified. He hadn't been able to defend himself from those who'd hurt him so badly as a child, and he couldn't allow himself to react to the Iveys as he probably wanted to since he met Shiloh. Feeling as though his hands were always tied would only add to his frustration.

Still somewhat skeptical, Crocker looked from her to Seth but finally nodded. "Okay. I'll let you get back to your afternoon."

When Seth made no move, Tia thanked him and showed him out.

"Lot of help he was," Seth grumbled after he was gone.

"There's nothing he can do," she said. "He's willing to let bygones be bygones with the camera incident. That's what matters. We don't want to give the police any reason to side with Kouretas."

"That isn't what I'm concerned about."

She studied the hard set to Seth's jaw. "Then, what are you concerned about?"

He seemed restless as well as angry. "I wasn't there to protect Shiloh. I didn't see the threat," he said. "But I see this one."

CHAPTER TWENTY

Tia was finally feeling more like herself than she had since the accident. If she continued to improve, she thought she might be able to rebound completely and was certainly going to strive for that. She wasn't the only person in the world to suffer. Like everyone who'd ever coped with a tragedy, she had to pick herself up, dust herself off and keep going, assuming there would be better days ahead even if she couldn't imagine, right now, how there could be.

Of course, in order to do that, she had to let go of everything she'd wanted so desperately and quit mourning it. Maybe her future wouldn't involve the fame and fortune she'd imagined when *Expect the Worst* vaulted her onto the international scene. Anyone would grieve the loss of such a promising career. But her life could still hold great value and meaning, couldn't it?

She was beginning to believe it could. There was just one problem. She was afraid this new lease on life might be tied to Seth, even though he'd made his situation clear from the beginning. Not only was he a widower who refused to let go, he was still dealing with issues from his childhood and probably always would be, at least to a degree. Letting herself care too much about him, especially while she was in such a fragile state, would be unwise.

Yet…she couldn't control what she felt. And she was beginning to feel a lot.

She should probably try to put more distance between them by moving back into the guesthouse, at least. Living in the main house made her hyperaware of Seth and everything about him. Even when he was upstairs working, as he was now, she couldn't quit thinking about him. Last night had been all the more satisfying because there'd been an emotional connection, too. He certainly seemed to feel more than he had before. She guessed those emotions weren't all positive—he'd nearly stopped for a reason—but he wouldn't have reacted that way if he hadn't been feeling more than he wanted to feel, too.

Regardless of what he'd been experiencing, she'd felt so close to him that she hadn't even tried to get up and leave after it was over, and neither had he. They'd spent the rest of the night together.

Did that deeper connection mean anything? Would he ever allow it to?

She couldn't imagine he would, which brought her back to trying to protect herself by putting more distance between them. She should move back to the guesthouse, but she knew he'd never let her, not while Kouretas posed a threat. And now that they'd crossed certain boundaries, it was going to be all the more difficult to make sure they didn't cross them again—and again and again.

"I'm heading for another crash," she grumbled to Kiki as she fed and played with Maxi's pet. "Only this one is going to shatter my heart instead of my face."

Kiki was beginning to recognize her and vocalize more often. Tia found it funny that the bird had said hello when she entered the atrium today. She doubted Kiki understood the meaning of the sounds she made, but the bird had impeccable timing.

After spending two hours trying to teach the parrot some new words—again without success—she let herself out of the atrium. She wished she could go swimming. The pool was heated, and she was itching to do something—another sign that she was healing. But she didn't dare. For all she knew, Kouretas was perched on the fence with a telephoto lens just waiting for her to step outside.

She wasn't going to make it that easy.

Instead, she used her ear buds so she could listen to music without disturbing Seth and carried her laptop to one of the recliners in the living room. She couldn't go out in the real world, but she could venture into the virtual one, as long as she was brave enough to face whatever she might read about her role in the movie, her accident and public speculation as to the cause and aftermath. As much as she tried to convince herself that she didn't care who was nominated for an Oscar this year, she couldn't help being interested. What names were being bandied about? And was hers one of them?

She checked her email first. She'd received hundreds of messages. Most were spam, but there was also a decent outpouring of support from people she'd gone to acting school with and various other people she knew in the industry and from other jobs where she'd worked. There were even some messages from people in her hometown—an elementary schoolteacher and the owner of the feed-and-tackle shop where she'd worked after school and on weekends for two years.

She could get past this, she told herself. She had no choice.

Finally, she checked to make sure the date for the Oscars hadn't changed. It was still scheduled for February 27 at five o'clock, and the nominees were to be revealed mid-January, which was less than a month away.

After twisting around to make sure that she was still alone, she typed the title of her film into the search engine and began to read the reviews. Some she'd seen before; others were new.

But she took the time to look at every one, because she was working up the nerve to Google her own name.

Seth had finished his painting of Tia. It'd come together faster than anything he'd done in recent years—at least since Shiloh died—and he really liked it. He thought it was some of his best work.

As he stood back, he wondered if she'd recognize herself. He covered it, just in case, but doubted that was necessary. To other people, even to her, it would simply look like a modern depiction of a nude woman. No one besides him would be able to recognize the things that were unique to her. That was the beauty of expressing himself the way he did: there was still plenty of ambiguity.

He had little doubt this painting would fetch a high price if he was put it up for sale, but he had no plans to do so. He was going to keep it as a reminder of the Christmas he'd been dreading but was actually beginning to enjoy.

He went over to the bar to clean his hands and brushes. He really needed to work on the sculpture for San Francisco—this morning he'd yet again had to put off the lawyer who'd hired him—but he was done for the day. Not only was he getting hungry, he was eager to see what Tia was doing. She'd been so quiet.

She didn't look up when he walked into the living room. She probably couldn't hear him. She had ear buds in and seemed to be concentrating on her computer.

Because the entry into the living room was behind her, he could see that she was reading about Oscar predictions for the year and wondered how it was making her feel.

"Do you think you'll make the list?" he asked.

Startled, she closed her laptop and removed her ear buds. "Oh, hi. I didn't hear you come in. Are you all done for the day?"

"I think so."

"Did you finish what you were working on?"

He almost said yes but didn't want her to ask to see it, so he said, "Not yet."

"How long does it normally take you to create a painting?"

He shrugged. "Depends. If it comes together easily, it might only take a few days."

"And if it doesn't?"

"I can fight with it for months."

"Have you ever created something you didn't like and gave up on it in the end?"

"Plenty of things," he said as he went to the refrigerator. "I think most artists are their own worst critics."

"What do you do with the ones you don't like?"

He poured himself a glass of milk and downed it. "I toss them."

"In the trash?" She set her computer aside and got up. "I hope you're kidding. There's got to be a lot of people who would love to have what you cast off."

Did she want one of his paintings? She'd been complimentary of his work, especially last night. She'd had some nice things to say about him, too, but he was trying not to think about that, because then he started thinking about what'd happened right after. "I have to be happy with it, or it doesn't leave my studio," he said, unapologetically. To him, his work had to have some integrity. He wasn't going to lower his standards.

"I can understand why you'd only want your best out there," she conceded. "Just seems like a waste, given that what's bad to you is probably still very good to others."

He gestured at her laptop. "What'd you learn?"

"About?"

He raised his eyebrows. "The Oscars."

Obviously not pleased that he'd caught her, she scowled at him. "My name is on some lists, but it's all just speculation. Doesn't mean anything. I wouldn't be surprised if the film was

nominated, though. It was an excellent script, and our director did a fabulous job."

He could tell she was trying to talk herself down so that she
wouldn't be disappointed later. She'd faced so much disappointment of late. "Whether anyone else recognizes it or not, Maxi
told me you were the one who brought the script to life, that
it was your performance that set the tone for your costar, too,
even though he's a big deal in Hollywood right now."

A blush crept into her cheeks, but he could tell she was flattered, which had been his intent. She deserved to enjoy at least
some accolades for what she'd accomplished. How many people
ever made it to the level of acting she had? "Maxi's giving me
too much credit," she said.

"Why don't we watch your movie together tonight?" he
asked.

"No way."

"Why not? I haven't seen it."

"You don't need to see it. You're not a big movie buff. You've
said so before. And that's fine."

He was suddenly much more interested in viewing the film.
But in case it would only remind her of what she might have
done *if only*—he didn't push. "What should we do tonight,
then?"

"You don't have to see your family?"

"Nope. My mother said she needed to spend some time with
Cal, that she's been so busy she feels as though she's been ne-
glecting him—which is just as well, because I wouldn't leave
you here alone with Kouretas around, anyway."

"You don't have to babysit me," she said. "You can go hang
out with your brothers at the bar and play some pool or whatever. I'll stay in and keep the doors locked."

"It's a weeknight. Gavin and Eli are both with their families."

"We could have a glass of wine and sit in the hot tub," she
suggested.

"What about Kouretas?"

"It's dark. If we keep the lights off, he won't be able to get anything—not from beyond the fence."

"And if he comes in the yard?"

"I'll wear one of your ball caps and my big sunglasses. Even if he gets close, he can't snap anything worth selling, not without sufficient lighting."

Made sense. "Okay. That just leaves one thing."

"What's that?"

"Who's making dinner?"

She laughed. "I guess I will, but I miss the good old days when you did it without me asking."

Unable to resist her smile, he grinned back. "How about we do it together?"

Tia was in trouble. It was a different kind of trouble than she'd ever been in before, but it was trouble all the same. She realized that when she enjoyed cooking with Seth as much as doing anything else with him.

While she chopped vegetables and he made the stock for chicken noodle soup, they talked about his home in San Francisco and how much he liked the Bay Area. They also talked about the projects he needed to finish for work in the next six months, and he told her a little more about Aiyana, his brothers and their families. He asked where she lived in LA and if she planned to stay there—she had to say she didn't know—but they were both careful not to bring up Shiloh or the accident, except to crack a joke about the possibility of Kouretas being crouched outside the window, frustrated that they'd lowered the blinds.

Blocking out the outside made Maxi's mansion feel much more intimate. Being around Seth also had the tendency to make Tia feel as though the rest of the world had faded away and the terrible things that were so upsetting didn't matter anymore—another sign that she was getting in over her head. She worried about what was happening to her, but she wasn't going to let those worries ruin this night. She had the chance to feel good again, for a while anyway, and she was going to take it.

They cleaned up after they ate and changed. Seth brought her a ball cap and laughed when it was so big he had to keep adjusting the back.

Once she'd donned her sunglasses, too, and he seemed satisfied that even if Kouretas got a picture it wouldn't be good enough to sell, he stuck his head out into the yard. "Looks clear, but…let me double-check first. I'll come back for you."

He didn't give her the chance to argue. He strode out, and she peered through a crack in the blinds, trying to see as much as she could while he walked the perimeter.

The light in the pool and hot tub suddenly went off. Immediately afterward, the low lighting in the yard went dark, too. It was pitch-black when he came back for her.

"All clear," he murmured, keeping his voice low, and took the wine bottle, since she was carrying both glasses.

Using the flashlight on his phone, he guided them to the hot tub.

Chills ran through Tia's body when she first got in. With a deep sigh, she tilted her head back to gaze up at the stars as Seth poured the wine. "It's gorgeous out here," she said as she accepted a glass.

"I like Silver Springs."

"Maybe you'll move here at some point in the future."

"Maybe. One day. I've always thought I might come back, when the timing is right. How'd it go with Kiki today?"

"Pretty good, although she refuses to let me teach her anything new. I think she's just being stubborn."

"You've only been here a week or so. Maybe it takes longer."

"It must," she allowed.

He gazed around. "I wonder how long Kouretas will stay in town."

"I can't imagine getting a picture of me is important enough that he'll last more than a few days," she said so Seth would quit worrying about him. But knowing the persistence of the paparazzi, she wouldn't put it past Kouretas to last a week or longer. It could even be that their encounter at the gate had made him that much more determined to win the power struggle that'd sprung up between them.

"Tell me a little more about your family," Seth said. "You don't seem eager to talk about them."

She wasn't. "There's really nothing to say."

"They live in Iowa?"

"Yeah. In a small farming community."

"When I had my first showing in New York, Shiloh and I couldn't afford to fly there. So we drove clear across the country."

"Didn't that cost more than flying?"

His grin slanted to one side as though he was slightly embarrassed. "No, because we slept in our car."

She chuckled. "You climbed up the hard way, too."

"I started with nothing. Actually, I started in the negative on most counts."

"And look where you are now."

"Look at *you*," he said.

"I almost got somewhere. And I started in the negative, too," she said, jokingly.

"In what way?"

Should she tell him? If she did, he'd be the first person she'd told since leaving Iowa—other than Barbie. "You know I grew up on a farm."

"Yes."

"Well, it wasn't just any farm."

"What does that mean?"

"I grew up a Mennonite."

He sat forward. "A what? That's Amish—or something similar—isn't it?"

"Sort of. They both have Anabaptist roots."

"How is an Anabaptist any different from a regular Baptist?"

"Mennonites believe in baptizing as an adult, not as an infant."

"Is that the only difference?"

"For the most part. That and some other very small differences in the way they practice their religion."

"Like…"

"Mennonites typically meet in a church instead of a house or barn, for one."

"Your parents don't drive a horse and buggy, do they?"

"No. My parents have a car. It's a black jalopy. We've never been able to afford much. But it's a car. Old Order Mennonites reject certain technologies, but most drive cars, use electricity, have a house phone, and so on. And my parents went through periods when they were more progressive than others of their faith."

"In what way?"

"Well, we had a TV."

"That's walking on the wild side?"

She laughed. "Yeah. It's letting Satan into your home."

"Doesn't that depend on what you watch?"

"They don't really see it that way. We only had it for a few years, anyway—until I started talking about becoming an actress."

"And then?"

"I came home from Bible study one day to find it gone."

When Seth didn't say anything right away, Tia wondered if he thought that was crazy. To a more modern, secular ear, it had to sound totally nuts, if only because it was so foreign. "What about cell phones?" he asked.

"My father has one. So does my sister's husband."

"What—women can't have them?"

"According to the men, they don't need one, since they're primarily for business."

"And only men do business."

"Right."

"Do you have to call a landline to talk to your mother, then?"

"Unless it's at night, after my father's gone to bed. Then she'll text me sometimes—and delete it afterward so that he doesn't see it."

"Would he get mad?"

"He wouldn't like it, and it's a sin to displease your husband."

"Hm. Maybe I need to look into this religion."

She scowled at him. "Not funny."

"And your sister, who's younger, goes along with this?"

"For the most part, although she uses her husband's cell phone more often than my mother uses my father's. I think it's one of the compromises he's made to try to keep her happy."

He wiped away the drops of water condensing on his face. "I wasn't brought up with religion. I admit that whole world seems strange to me."

"You're not alone. That's part of the reason I don't talk about it. If you haven't lived as part of a similar community, it's hard to imagine what it's like, but the pressure to stay and conform is enormous."

"The Mennonites aren't as strict as the Amish, are they?"

"Not really. But it can be hard to tell the difference between them, especially because they can dress and look so much alike."

"Are the pictures shown in the media accurate?"

"If they depict the men with a bowl cut and a beard—but no mustache—wearing black pants, any color of shirt and a straw hat. The women wear long dresses with aprons and bonnets and put their hair in a bun each day."

His eyes widened. "That's how *you* dressed?"

"Of course."

"But dresses can be so impractical."

"They symbolize the gender roles. By wearing a dress, a woman shows her submission to God, and to men in general—and to her husband in particular."

"That's so…opposite to how I've been taught to think about women."

"It doesn't sit right with me, either. But I never fit in. I couldn't believe what they believed—not only about a woman's role but that God cared about whether or not I owned certain technologies or wore colorful clothing or wanted to be an actress instead of a stay-at-home wife and mother."

He rubbed his chin as though he was considering what she'd told him. "How have your parents responded to you becoming an actress? I can't imagine they were excited about it."

She winced. "Definitely not. They think I'm going to Hell. When I told them becoming an actress wasn't just a childhood dream, that I meant to move to LA and take acting lessons…" She let her voice drift away as she remembered that night. Mennonites didn't practice shunning quite like the Amish. But her parents had threatened to disown her. And for the first five years, they'd made good on that promise. She assumed they thought it would eventually force her to bend to their wishes and come back. But she was so relieved and happy to be free at last, she knew she'd never do that, and eventually, they called to tell her about the birth of her sister's fourth child, and she started communicating with them again, on a limited basis. "It was rough," she continued, knowing even as she said the words what an understatement that was. It'd almost torn her heart out. She'd had to leave everyone she knew and loved and accept that they would not think well of her. "I stayed for eight months after that, trying to 'get the devil out of me' once and for all, while they prayed for my soul, but I guess the devil wouldn't *depart*, as they say."

"So you left the group, anyway."

"I finally figured out that I had no choice. I'd suffocate if I didn't. In the most basic sense, it came down to them or me, and I couldn't live my whole life for them. Sometimes I still feel guilty about that," she added softly.

"You deserve the right to lead your own life," he murmured. "Everyone does."

"I believe that now. I just wish… I don't know. If I was more like them, maybe I could've been satisfied with such a simple life, too."

"It's not just simple. You structure your whole life around your religious beliefs. If you can't buy in, it's no wonder you couldn't stay."

"I tried to believe, to conform. But it was impossible for me."

"What about your brother and sister? They're true believers? And they're happy?"

"My brother is. He's the oldest, and he's following in my father's footsteps. One day, he'll inherit the farm. But my sister… She married at seventeen and started her family about the time I moved to LA. After she'd had her second child, she contacted me, secretly, in tears. She told me that she had to get out, too, that she was miserable. And I felt so sorry for her. Despite what I'd been through, and how much I missed my family, my freedom was the most important thing to me. So I felt like it was my responsibility to help her—and I tried."

"In what way?"

"Eventually, I managed to save up enough to send her plane fare for her and the kids."

"What about her husband?" he asked in surprise.

"I figured they'd divorce and he'd find another Mennonite wife, one that might be more satisfied. Then, everyone would be happier."

"Divorce isn't a sin?"

"It is, but it's…more of a gray area."

"Yet she's still with him."

"Yes. And Phil, my brother-in-law, hates me to this day. The rest of my family will never forgive me, either."

"What happened?" he asked. "Did she ever come?"

"She tried a year ago. But her oldest daughter, Anna, refused to leave with her. She told her father what was going on, and there was a big fight and a family-and-church intervention. Everyone joined forces and told her if she left, she had to leave alone."

"Without her kids."

"Yes."

"And?"

"She wouldn't do it. I would've made the same choice."

"I wish my mother had been more like her," he said bitterly.

She stared at him through the steam rising from the hot, bubbly water. "Do you think she regrets what she's done?"

"Not at all. That would require too much self-awareness."

"Do you ever hear from her?"

"Never."

"The guilt would have to be terrible, at least for someone like me," Tia explained. "Maybe it's just…easier for her to leave the past in the past, pretend she never even had another son. What about your brothers? Do you ever hear from them?"

"Occasionally—and of course it's at my favorite time of the year."

"Christmas," she guessed.

When he nodded, she understood he had many reasons for hating the holidays. He probably hadn't received much for Christmas after his mother abandoned him. When others gathered happily with their families, it was probably just a reminder of the family he didn't have. No wonder he couldn't hear a Christmas carol without wincing. "One or both of them?"

"Both of them. One usually tries to call or text and does so at other times of the year, too—occasionally on my birthday. The other just sends me a card with a picture of his beautiful family."

Maybe coming to Silver Springs was as much an escape for him as it was for her. "Do you ever respond?"

"No," he said.

"Why not?"

"I don't know." He took a drink of his wine. "Anyway, back to your sister. How's she doing now?"

Changing the subject was an evasive maneuver, and Tia knew it, but Seth was so sensitive about his past, she didn't want to force him to discuss it. "I wish I could tell you. She doesn't confide in me anymore. Her husband and my parents have her convinced I'm trying to tempt her away from all that is good and holy, even though she was the one who came to me for help to begin with."

"That's probably the only way she can hang on."

Tia understood that, but it didn't make the situation any easier. "I guess." Since she was getting too hot, she got out of the water and sat on the edge. "Maybe I was wrong to help her. I was just doing what I thought was best at the time, but...what happened couldn't have helped her relationship with her husband."

"Sounds like she's angry because you got away and she didn't," he said.

"And now my attempt to help her has made her life that much harder."

He got out and sat on the edge, too. "When I looked you up online, I didn't learn any of this. I'm surprised there isn't more in the media about your background."

"I've been careful to keep my family out of the news," she explained. "Not because I'm embarrassed of them, although I would hate having every media interview focus on the way I was raised. I've tried to keep them out of the spotlight because they're embarrassed of *me*."

"Given the way most people would react, that's ironic."

"I even changed my name once I got to LA."

He gripped the edge of the hot tub. "You *what*?"

"My birth name is Sarah Isaac." She couldn't believe she'd just told him that, blurted it out as if it wasn't anything. She hadn't even told Barbie that part.

"I'm blown away right now," he said.

"I chose *Tia* because I thought it would be a good name for an actress."

"That's how the press doesn't know."

"They haven't caught on yet, thank goodness."

He scooped warm water into his hands and poured it over his legs. "How often do you talk to your family these days?"

"More since the accident."

"Because they're concerned about you."

"Because they think God had a hand in the accident. That he was trying to block my path forward and bring me home."

He stopped messing with the water. "You've got to be kidding me."

"No. This is the answer to their prayers. With my career in shambles, where else will I go? At least, that's what they're thinking."

"Wow. I don't even know what to say. Will it force you back?"

Part of her anger and depression over the accident stemmed from the thought that it might. But she was beginning to realize that she still had control over her life. She'd worked three jobs to survive on her own the first time. If she was determined enough and she scrimped and saved, she could find a way to survive on her own this time, too. "No," she said. "It won't."

He studied her for several seconds before saying, "Good."

CHAPTER TWENTY-ONE

Seth had assumed Tia had an unremarkable background. There'd been nothing to indicate otherwise. But he supposed he shouldn't have taken that for granted. He'd had nothing but her looks and current situation to judge by—two things that could easily be deceiving. She was so beautiful and had met with so much success in such an unlikely industry. It was shocking to learn what she'd had to sacrifice just to live in LA and pursue her dream.

Learning about her background gave him a newfound appreciation and respect for who she was as a person. In some ways, she hadn't had it any easier than he had.

"You've grown quiet," she said as they got out of the hot tub.

He checked as much of the yard as he could see in the dark—fortunately, all seemed well—as he handed her a towel. "I'm just thinking."

"About…"

"You."

She seemed surprised that he would be so direct. "What about me? Did I shock you too much?"

"No. You taught me a valuable lesson—one I shouldn't have needed to learn."

"What lesson is that?"

"Not to make assumptions about people. When you told me you grew up on a farm—well, that's about as normal, wholesome and all-American as you can get."

"The wholesome part is still true," she said jokingly.

He cleared his throat. "The normal part isn't."

"I typically leave what I say about my past right there for just that reason."

"You're hoping people will accept it and not look any closer."

"Of course. Because that's when the illusion unravels."

"I can't imagine you wearing a long dress with an apron and a bonnet to cover your hair."

"There's nothing more American than religious freedom," she quipped.

"I support that. It's just strange to think that something meant to be good—religion—can also act like a spider's web."

She hugged her towel closer. "That's a good analogy."

"Growing up I was jealous of those kids who had the type of family who attended church every Sunday."

"Religion can be a blessing."

"But it's not for you."

"Not after what I've been through."

"I understand, and I hope you know that I won't tell anyone what you told me tonight," he said as he used his flashlight to light the way.

"Except your family?" she teased.

"*Including* my family. We've both seen that they aren't very good at keeping secrets," he added with a laugh.

She chuckled with him. "They mean well."

"They do." He stopped at the door and turned to face her. "Can I ask you something?"

She seemed startled by the question. "What?"

"What does beauty mean to you?"

Her eyes widened as she groped for a response. "Beauty is…a lot of things, I guess. Is this a trick question?"

"No. I'm looking for your honest opinion."

"Okay, well…integrity is a form of beauty, I suppose. Sacrifice. Summoning the strength to conquer a big challenge. Fighting to the death and never giving up—for the right reason. Making a difference in the world. How philosophical do you want to get?"

"No need to go overboard. I just want to make sure that…"

"What?" she prodded.

"That you understand it has very little to do with a pretty face."

"You're pointing out that those other options are still available to me."

"No," he said. "I'm saying you've already got those things nailed. So…what happened to your face doesn't really matter. That's not what I see when I look at you. And if that's what other people see—they're missing out on something even more beautiful."

He opened the door for her, but the moment he followed her into the house, she turned, slid her arms around his neck and rose on tiptoe to press her lips against his. "Good night," she murmured as she pulled away.

His head and his arms were full of her, and he didn't want to let go. He'd hoped what she'd already given him would be enough, but the fact that they'd made love several times only made his desire grow stronger. "You're sleeping in your own bed tonight?" he asked when she pulled away to leave him.

She hesitated. "Is that an invitation?"

"It is," he murmured.

She stared at her bare feet for several seconds before looking up at him. "I can't sleep with you again."

Disappointment hit him harder than he'd expected it to. "Why not?"

Her chest lifted as she drew a deep breath. "Because I'm falling in love with you," she replied.

He didn't know what to say. They'd become what he considered *good friends*. They'd been there for each other during a difficult time; they'd confided in each other and supported each other. Already, he admired her, cared about her, wanted what was best for her. And there was no question that they were good together in a physical sense. But...

When she gave him a second before walking away, he could tell she was hoping he'd stop her.

He wanted to. He couldn't. That would be too selfish. He couldn't risk hurting her. His heart belonged to Shiloh.

It would always belong to Shiloh.

"I'm sorry," he whispered, and she cast him a sad smile before going upstairs.

Seth couldn't sleep that night. He kept listening for footsteps outside his door, hoping Tia would join him despite what she'd said earlier. She'd accepted the terms he'd offered before. But deep down he knew she wouldn't be able to accept them tonight, and he couldn't let himself go to her, either.

After a couple of hours spent tossing and turning, he went upstairs and tried to work, but he couldn't concentrate and soon found himself staring at the picture he'd created of Tia, wanting to be with her all the more.

Finally, he cleaned up and returned to the first floor, where he ordered *Expect the Worst* on Apple TV and started watching it using headphones so that it wouldn't wake her.

The movie was quirky and clever. He especially enjoyed the dialogue, but watching her fall in love with the man on the screen felt strange, even though he had no claim on her. And he certainly hadn't anticipated how the love scenes would affect him.

At one point he got up and started to pace around the room just to blow off some sexual energy. Already, he knew her kiss, her body and how she liked to be touched, and while he didn't enjoy seeing another man touching her in that way, it reminded him of what he was missing.

Finally, he turned it off. He knew if he didn't, he'd go upstairs to her room, and he'd already decided he couldn't do that.

To distract himself, he surfed the web on his phone. At first, he was reading sports articles, but before long his thoughts reverted back to Tia, and he entered her real name—Sarah Isaac—into his browser just to see what might come up.

Only links about random women with the same name populated his screen. So he started to search *Mennonites* and *Mennonites of Iowa* to learn more about what she'd been taught as a child. He couldn't believe that she'd been someone else, a young Mennonite girl who, from what he was reading, likely only went to school through the eighth grade and was expected to marry a man with a bowl cut who would most likely refuse to allow her to have her own cell phone.

How had the modern world not corrected such traditional behavior? He found no answer for that. But he learned that most Amish and a lot of Mennonites spoke Pennsylvania Dutch and wondered if Tia knew the language. Was that how her parents communicated with her? Was that the language her nieces and nephews were being taught?

According to various sources, Anabaptists were part of the Protestant radical reform movement of the sixteenth century, when some Christians broke off from the Catholic Church. Any religion, let alone one so all-pervasive it was actually a culture, was completely foreign to him, which was partly why he found Tia's background fascinating.

He was so caught up learning about the Mennonites that several hours passed while he followed link after link, reading facts he'd never heard before. Some Mennonite groups didn't have to pay social-security taxes because they pulled together as a community to take care of their elderly. They were Christian but didn't celebrate Christmas the way most other Americans did. And they believed so strongly that vanity was a sin they often pulled out their own teeth rather than pay to maintain them.

No wonder Tia's parents were mortified that she'd become an actress and felt God had intervened to stop her. If she were Amish instead of Mennonite, she'd probably never be allowed back, even for a visit.

Given how insulated and restrictive the Mennonite communities were, he would've assumed the number of people in them would be shrinking, maybe even hanging on the brink of extinction. But he was surprised to find that wasn't the case. The opposite was actually occurring. These communities were growing, largely due to the huge size of their families. Many had ten or more children, and because their children were only educated to the eighth grade and were effectively cut off from the outside world, leaving wasn't much of an option.

How had Tia been able to mesh such a past with LA, a city full of people who focused on physical beauty, fame and fortune to the exclusion of almost everything else?

The move must've been quite a culture shock. And yet she'd not only managed to adjust, she'd managed to flourish all on her own—until the accident.

So what was going to happen to her?

She said she wouldn't return to Iowa, and he was glad of that. But now she had something else that was huge to overcome. He hated to think of how Hollywood would react to her scarred face.

With a sigh, he navigated to his messages and found the contact for his mother-in-law. He hated to be drawn to Tia's defense, especially against Shiloh's parents, but he would not allow them to do anything that could make what she had ahead of her any more difficult.

You'd better not try to help Ray Kouretas.

"What are you doing today?"

Aiyana sounded wide-awake and cheerful, but Seth was still half-asleep. He wasn't even sure why he'd answered the phone. His eyes could barely focus as he squinted at the light streaming into the living room through the gaps around the window coverings. Apparently, he'd spent the night on the couch. "Just... working, I guess," he said.

"Did I wake you?" she asked when she heard his raspy voice.

He cleared his throat. "What time is it?"

"You *were* sleeping. Sorry about that. I thought I'd be safe to call at eleven."

He pushed himself into a sitting position. It was almost noon? Was Tia still asleep? He didn't hear her moving around the house... "It's fine. I was up most of last night, that's all."

"Again?"

"Story of my life, right? What's going on?"

"I was hoping you could come meet your students today."

He covered a yawn before responding. "Why can't I do it on Friday, when I speak at the assembly?"

"We need to pick the winners of the art contest you sponsored. We're announcing them on Friday."

"Oh. That's right." He got to his feet and went over to raise the blinds. As the motor whined and they went up, the room was flooded with light. The weather had cleared; it was nice to see the sun. "Can't you just take a picture of each one and send it to me?"

"Seth, there're over one hundred entries. I don't have the time, and I don't think a picture will do them justice, anyway."

He couldn't ask her to bring them all over to him, either.

That would take as much time, and the kids had worked too hard to treat them that casually. "True. My bad." He heard Kiki bark like a dog and went over to peer into the atrium. He thought he might find Tia there, but the bird was alone. "Why can't *you* choose the winners? I'd be happy to work with anyone you recommend."

"I'm not the artist, you are. I don't know what to look for, which was why we set you up to judge from the beginning. Why don't you want to come over?"

"It's not that I don't *want* to come over," he said. "It's that… there's a guy in town who's part of the paparazzi. He's being aggressive and intrusive, trying to get a picture of Tia. He even blocked the gate when we were trying to come home the other day. I'm reluctant to leave her alone, because I have no idea what he might try."

"I heard he was in town. Gavin and Eli both mentioned him. Name's Kouretas or something, right?"

"Yeah. Ray Kouretas."

"Won't Tia be safe inside, as long as she keeps the doors locked? He might not even realize she's in the guesthouse."

"She's not in the guesthouse any longer," he said. "After he got so belligerent, I had her move into the main house with me, just to be safe."

When Aiyana cleared her throat before responding, he said, "Don't read too much into that."

"What do you mean?" she asked innocently. "I'm glad you're looking out for her. But…why can't you bring her with you when you come? Kouretas would never expect her to be here, so it should be easy to avoid him."

"You know she won't allow herself to be seen—by anyone other than you and some of the other members of our family."

"She can't stay behind closed doors forever, Seth."

"She'll come out when she's ready."

"I respect that. But the sooner she forgets about her scars, the sooner everyone else will, too."

"Like I said, she will when she's ready."

She sighed. "What do you want to do about the contest?"

"I'll come. What time do I need to be there?"

"Is one thirty okay?"

"Yeah. See you then." He was just disconnecting when his phone dinged with a text. Lois had responded to his late-night message.

How could you choose some woman you've barely met over us?

If you're talking about Tia, I'm just trying to help her out, he wrote back.

You'll help her but not us?

Helping them and allowing them to use him were two different things.

"Morning."

Seth lowered his phone as Tia walked into the room, freshly showered and dressed for the day. "Morning."

"Sleep well?" she asked, giving his rumpled T-shirt and basketball shorts the once-over.

He couldn't help noticing that her eyes were brighter, she had more energy in her step and her voice contained confidence that hadn't been there since he'd met her. Those slight adjustments made a huge difference. It was almost as if he could see the beautiful and capable woman he'd watched on-screen last night begin to overtake the hurt and angry person he'd encountered in the guesthouse when he'd first arrived. "Not really," he admitted. "You?"

"Like a baby."

Was she rubbing it in that last night could've gone much differently for him? He had no doubt he would've had a far better time with her, but she deserved more than he could give her. He couldn't trust love again even if he could get over Shiloh. "Now you're just being salty," he grumbled.

"Salty about what?" she asked, but he could tell she was only pretending not to understand.

"You're not going to make this easy on me, are you?"

She didn't answer. After studying him for a moment, she moved into the kitchen. "What would you like for breakfast?"

He followed her. "You're doing the cooking?"

"I am."

"Then I'll have whatever you make."

She burrowed around in the refrigerator and pulled out some blackberries, raspberries and blueberries. "Oatmeal okay? With fruit on top?"

He wrinkled his nose. "Oatmeal? That's the best you can do?"

"For now, yes. I'm going on a diet. I have to get off the weight I've gained."

"Why?"

"So I'll feel better about myself. Maybe I can't fix the scars on my face, but there are other things I can fix, and this is one of them."

"Your body's already perfect. It's all I can think about."

Obviously surprised by this comment, she looked over at him. "If you're trying to get me back into bed with you, it won't work. I hope," she added with less certainty.

Her equally honest comeback made him chuckle. "Okay, but I'm not gonna lie. If you changed your mind, I wouldn't be disappointed."

When their eyes met and held, several images of her naked in his arms paraded before his mind's eye. Those encounters weren't something he'd soon forget.

"Maybe I should move back into the guesthouse," she muttered as she tore her gaze away.

He lowered his voice. "I'm flattered to think I might be that much of a temptation."

"I've made plain what I want," she said.

"I know. And I'm sorry. I don't want to make your life harder. That's the truth."

"I know," she said with a sigh.

There was so much more he wanted to say. Their time together had been good for him, and he was grateful—for the way she'd crashed into his life and made this Christmas different than the last three, which had been almost impossible for him to get through, and for the conversation and companionship and the physical and emotional intimacy. He'd needed to feel connected to someone again—although the urgency scared him—so that had made more of a difference than anything.

Maybe she had a few things to say to him, too. But where did they start? And where did they leave that conversation once they had it?

He folded his arms and leaned up against the wall as he watched her prepare their food.

"What?" she said as she put a pan of water on to boil.

"I have to go over to the school today."

"Okay."

"I take it you won't go with me."

She cocked an eyebrow at him. "You're kidding, right?"

"I'm not. I don't want to leave you here alone."

"I'll be fine," she said, adding a dash of salt to the water.

He moved closer, simply because he couldn't seem to stay away. "I don't trust Kouretas."

She glanced over her shoulder when she realized he was standing right behind her. "I had to deal with a whole army of paparazzi at my condo. I can handle one man."

He was tempted to put his hands on her shoulders. He wanted to touch her so badly it was a struggle to overcome the impulse. He walked over to put some bread in the toaster so that he wouldn't. "I hope by *handling him* you mean you'll stay inside and not answer if someone comes to the gate."

She looked back at him again. "If Kouretas returns, he's not going to buzz the intercom. He already tried that."

"*He* might not, but Lois could. Just promise me you won't answer."

"Fine. I won't answer. That's an easy promise to keep."

Her agreement should've made Seth feel better. What could go wrong in just a few hours? he asked himself.

But he couldn't seem to rid himself of a certain uneasiness. Shiloh should've been fine when he'd left her, too.

"You've got to be kidding me." Kouretas gripped his phone that much tighter. He was dying to escape this Pollyannaish town, to get home and get paid before Christmas. But Seth Turner wasn't making his job easy, and now he'd just received another setback.

"I wish I was," Lois Ivey said, her voice slightly tinny as it came through the phone. "Someone must've seen us at the coffee shop."

"Who?"

"I don't know."

"You're the one who suggested we meet at there," he said, irritated that she'd been so shortsighted. "Why didn't we go somewhere else?"

"Because I didn't expect it to be a problem. I didn't think anyone would know who you are, let alone tell Seth we were together."

"If it was even a possibility, you should've protected against it."

"What'd you want me to do? Invite you over to my house? I don't even know you!"

He rolled his eyes. "Believe me. You have nothing I want."

"Except access to Tia," she said, coming right back at him.

"Which you can no longer give me," he pointed out.

There was a moment of silence. Then he heard her draw a deep breath. "We can think of something."

"What?" he snapped. "You've blown it. Now I won't get paid, and neither will you."

"I did my best!" she cried.

"Well, your best wasn't good enough. Now you've ruined it for both of us. Thanks for nothing," he said and hung up.

Calling Lois Ivey every name in the book, he was about to toss his phone onto the bed when he realized that she might be useful to him after all. Just because she couldn't draw Seth over to her house under the pretense of giving him something that had once belonged to his dead wife, like they'd planned, didn't mean something else wouldn't work. Ray had spent his life cutting and jiving. If anyone knew how to overcome an obstacle, he did.

"This'll be even better," he muttered with a smile as he imagined the outcome for all parties.

When he called Lois back, it took her so long to answer he was afraid he'd made her so mad she wouldn't. But on the second try, he heard her say, "What do *you* want?"

He ignored her waspishness. He didn't care about her—she was just a means to an end—so it didn't bother him in the least. "I just thought of something," he said.

"What?" She still sounded sulky.

"Do you know any of the police officers in this town?"

"Of course. I know them all—at least by sight. I've lived here for thirty-six years."

"Have you ever been in trouble?"

"What kind of trouble?"

"With the law!" he said in exasperation. "Traffic tickets, parking tickets, DUI, a dispute with a neighbor, shoplifting. Anything?" She looked innocent enough, but looks could be deceiving. If there were young actresses with the face of an angel who'd do anything for a dime bag of cocaine, there could also be middle-aged nobodies like Lois Ivey with more than a few skeletons in the closet.

"Of course not!" she said, indignant. "What kind of a person do you think I am?"

Bingo. That told him all he needed to know. "A credible one. And that's what it's going to take to make this whole thing work."

"What whole thing?"

"My new plan."

"Will I still get paid?"

"That depends on how well you play your part."

CHAPTER TWENTY-TWO

Aiyana couldn't help watching Seth closely. What she was looking for she couldn't really say—some change in him, fresh enthusiasm for life, the loss of the black cloud that'd hung over him since Shiloh's death. Maybe she'd gotten lucky when he agreed to come teach. And maybe she'd gotten even luckier when Tia wound up in the guesthouse on the same property. Although she'd never wish bad luck on anyone and was terribly sorry for what Tia had been through with the accident, she couldn't help feeling as though there might be a few Christmas angels at work.

She knew Seth would laugh at her for thinking so idealistically—and, he'd say, superstitiously. He was far too practical to believe in meddling angels, at Christmastime or otherwise. But there did seem to be some magic afoot, and she couldn't help hoping it was strong enough to make a difference.

"This one's pretty amazing." He was partially turned away from her and fully focused on a dragon clawing its way out of an egg. He called it a *mixed media* piece; to her it was a papier-mâché creation. "This kid has a natural eye for dimension."

"I think so, too," Aiyana agreed, but she must've sounded as distracted as she was because he looked over at her curiously.

"What is it?" he asked.

She spread out her hands. "I don't know what you mean."

He narrowed his eyes. "You're up to something."

"No, I'm not!"

He continued to study her.

"It's Christmastime," she said, blinking innocently.

"This has nothing to do with the holidays."

She'd never been able to get one over on him. No one could. "Well, for one thing, you haven't complained about the music."

He tilted his head as if he'd only just noticed the carols playing on the Bluetooth speaker in the corner of the room, but she knew that was something he would not have missed before. He hadn't been able to endure so much as a chorus of "Winter Wonderland."

"I can barely hear it."

"It's plenty loud."

He shrugged. "So?"

"That says something."

He scowled. "It says I'm concentrating on something else. That's all."

"And you're in a hurry to get back to Maxi's."

"I *am* in a hurry, but not for the reason you're probably implying."

"Can I just…" She caught hold of his arm. "Seth, can I tell you one thing…because I love you?"

He arched a sardonic eyebrow at her. "I have a feeling you're going to do it anyway."

She would've chuckled at his reaction, except this meant too much to her. *He* meant too much to her. If she risked overstepping, so be it. "Life is too short to let yourself go on like you have been."

"Maybe you're right, but I don't know how to change it."

"I do."

He seemed taken aback by her answer. "So how do I do it?"

"Let her go," she said softly. "Let her go at last."

He didn't ask whom she meant. She knew that would be obvious.

Surprisingly, he didn't get angry, as she felt he would've done in the past. He just hung his head for a few seconds before meeting her eye. "It's not that easy, Mom."

"Losing someone we love is never easy. I don't mean to suggest that it is. But—"

"Her love is the only love that's ever made me feel whole," he interrupted. "Without you, I wouldn't even have been half-whole. But she took me the rest of the way, completed me, showed me what it felt like to be truly happy. I don't know how to explain to you how vital she was to me."

"I understand. And I believe you. But you need to consider this—you're not doing her any favors by holding on the way you are. Do you think she'd want you to be lonely or isolated or unhappy? Watching you suffer would be hell to her."

He didn't argue. He just dropped his head again.

"Will you think about that?" Aiyana pressed gently.

And, finally, he nodded.

There he was! His name hadn't been easy to find, but Tia had scoured all the various celebrity-gossip sites, looking at the fine print for a list of editors, contributors and photographers—until she'd found him. Ray Kouretas worked for *The Lowdown*.

Whoever had told Kouretas that she'd come to Silver Springs for the holidays had to have been someone familiar enough with Hollywood to have known how to find him. That meant it couldn't be her family—unless he had tracked them down, and that was even more frightening than the possibility of him getting a good shot of her damaged face.

No, that couldn't be it, she decided. If that was the case, she would've seen or heard something about it.

Or…maybe not. Since the accident, she'd purposely avoided the news in all its various forms, other than a few push notifications on what she considered safe subjects that popped up on her phone.

Steeling herself for what she might find, she put her name into Google's search box.

Link after link appeared, but they were all about the movie or the accident, and there was nothing new except more Oscar speculation.

After an hour spent reading everything recent, she felt mildly encouraged. Either Kouretas hadn't discovered her background, or he hadn't reported it yet. Was he waiting to get her picture for an entire coup de grâce? So his magazine could do a big two-page exposé that ended with her accident and what her family believed was God's way of attempting to reclaim their wayward daughter?

Setting her laptop aside, she wandered aimlessly into the kitchen and ate a banana. Then she let herself into the atrium, where she threw the ball for Kiki. She was trying to piece it all together in her mind, but nothing really made sense. Only a few people knew where she was, and she hated to doubt any of them.

Once she returned to the living room, she took out her phone and called Barbie, hoping a conversation with her friend might provide some answers.

"There you are!" Barbie's voice was immediately filled with concern. "I've been so worried about you. Why haven't you responded to any of my calls and texts? I've been going crazy over here. I don't even know where you are, so I couldn't drive over to check on you."

Would she do that? Was she being sincere? "I'm sorry," Tia said. "I just…checked out for a while. Needed some space."

"Oh, honey! I don't blame you. But I hope you're not taking what happened too hard. You're so beautiful. A few scars won't change that."

"I look significantly different," she pointed out.

"Your heart is still the same. But…when you disappeared on me, I began to worry that… You're not self-medicating or doing anything else that could potentially make things worse, are you?"

Tia wasn't likely to go that way. Mennonites weren't allowed to drink; she hadn't even tasted alcohol until she moved to LA. Even after ten years, the most she ever had was a glass or two of wine. But Barbie had lost a friend to an overdose not long ago; Tia knew where that comment stemmed from. "Of course not. You know I barely drink."

"That's what I kept telling myself, but so much has changed for you, and—"

And she'd be tempted to end it all if she was Tia? That wasn't encouraging, but she knew Barbie meant well. "I don't have any more pain meds, so you don't have to worry about that, either."

"Do you need them?"

"No."

"Good. So…how are you feeling?"

"Better."

"I'm glad! But I hate that you're spending the holidays alone. Why don't you get someone else to house-sit for you so you can come stay with me?"

"I'm sure Mike would love me hanging out all the time, sleeping on your couch," she said, but she knew she would never put herself in that position regardless.

"He won't mind. I promise. And we won't let the paparazzi get anywhere near you."

Did Barbie care as much as she seemed to? Or was there some latent jealousy, or greed, motivating her to stab Tia in the back?

Tia felt terrible even suspecting her. She wasn't sure how

she would've gotten through those early years in LA without Barbie. She probably would've been forced to go back to her family. But *someone* had to have told Kouretas where she was, and Tia had communicated with so few people. "I can't invite someone else into Maxi's home."

"You're house-sitting for Maxi?"

Barbie was familiar with Maxi because Tia had brought her to the movie premiere for *Expect the Worst*, hoping that an introduction to the people she was working with might help launch Barbie's career. Having the right contacts could mean everything in Hollywood. "I am."

"Why didn't you say so? At least now I know you're in a safe place."

"I didn't tell anyone where I was going. I didn't want to be found."

"I understand. I'm just relieved, that's all."

Tia considered mentioning Seth but decided against it. How would she explain what'd happened with him? She couldn't say she'd met someone and fallen for him right away. That would sound foolish, and it probably was.

Maybe she was just grasping at whatever she could to save herself. "Well, I *was* in a safe place—a better place—until a man named Ray Kouretas showed up."

"Who's Ray Kouretas?"

Barbie sounded legitimately unfamiliar with the name, which came as a relief—except it left other, more hurtful possibilities on the table. "He works for *The Lowdown*."

"Oh, no! That gossip rag? What are you going to do?"

"I'm going to stay out of sight, hoping he'll give up and leave."

"You can't hide forever."

"I won't. Just until after Christmas. Then I'll have to come out and face the world, but I'd hate to let him out me before I'm ready."

"That's reasonable. How do you think he found you?"

"That's the thing. There aren't very many people who are even aware that I'm in Silver Springs."

"Oh, no!" Barbie exclaimed.

Tia stiffened.

"You didn't tell your sister, did you?"

"I honestly don't remember. But if I didn't mention it to her, my mother might have."

"Oh." Barbie's voice softened. "Well, I suppose it doesn't *have* to be her."

Now Barbie was just being nice. "Who else could it be?"

"The paparazzi are good at their jobs, Tia. They have to be to dig up the shit they do. You know that. Maybe they tracked you there some other way—using your cell phone or something."

"I've seen police trace a suspect using a cell phone, but I don't think regular people can access those kinds of records."

"You never know," she said. "A good picture of you would be worth a lot of money right now. Everyone's wondering how the accident affected you. It's all anyone can talk about."

"I just don't see how anyone could figure it out. I haven't been here long enough."

"I remember reading about a private detective who bribed police and telephone-company employees to be able to gain private information on a vast network of movie stars," Barbie said. "Sylvester Stallone was one of them."

"Why was a PI doing that?"

"The right information could be worth a lot of money in LA. Maybe that's why, but who knows? The point is weird shit happens."

Barbie was much more of a conspiracy theorist than Tia was, but Tia, too, remembered hearing something about the PI involved in the scandal. He went to prison. "It's hard to believe anything that nefarious is going on."

"If money's involved, you can't count it out."

The buzz of the intercom made Tia jump. "Barbie, I'll have to call you later," she said.

"Okay. But if you won't come here for Christmas, at least stay in touch so I know you're okay."

"I'll be better about that. I promise."

Keeping her phone handy, in case she needed to dial Seth or even 9-1-1, she hurried to the intercom. Seth had told her not to answer if someone came, but whoever it was wouldn't lay off the buzzer. Certainly there had to be a good reason.

She pressed the button. "Can I help you?"

"Ms. Beckett? This is Officer Crocker. Is Mr. Turner there?"

"I'm afraid not," she replied. "Is…is something wrong?" She could tell there was; she was just afraid to find out what it could be.

He didn't answer the question. "Can you tell me where he is?"

She was hesitant to reveal anything until she knew what Crocker wanted. "I can't," she lied. "What's going on?"

"I have a warrant for his arrest."

The student Seth suspected of having the most talent would hardly say a word. Aiyana had told him that this particular boy—Jaden Kaplan—was new to the school as of three months ago and came from a mother who wouldn't or couldn't protect him from an abusive boyfriend, which was why the state had stepped in and removed him from the home. He had long brown hair he hadn't bothered to comb today, was wearing a ragged heavy-metal T-shirt with jeans and could stand to gain about fifty pounds. But the most noticeable thing about him was the distrust in his dark eyes.

That distrust hit Seth in the chest as hard as a defibrillator and made him want to try to reach this kid, if possible. In the past, he'd been reluctant to meet Aiyana's students or teach at the school because he was afraid of what he'd see. He was terrified of the inevitable empathy, didn't want to feel those hard emotions. And he didn't want to be reminded of his own childhood. It was difficult enough to leave his past behind.

But art had helped him so much he couldn't avoid wanting to share it as a coping skill with others who might be struggling, especially because he saw so much of himself in this boy. Although he'd been tall, even at that age, and not nearly as underweight as this small boy, he'd been just as angry, just as disillusioned and just as scornful of adults. The ones who'd really mattered had let him down.

"Your chess set is impressive," he told Jaden.

The boy said nothing, just stared down at the hole in the toe of one tennis shoe.

"Have you ever had any art classes?"

He glanced up. "Who would pay for those?"

"What about in school?"

He dropped his head again. "I was always grounded. I hardly ever went to school."

Seth handled the cool gadget the boy had fashioned out of cherrywood into one of his pawns. "What made you go with steampunk?"

He shrugged.

"You have genuine talent, Jaden, and I'd love to work with you. Are you interested in being part of my class?"

"It sounded like fun in the beginning," he mumbled. "That's why I made the set. But…what's the catch?"

"There is no catch," Seth told him. "We'll explore what you're good at and how you can get better. That's what we're all here for," he told the others, who were looking on.

"But…you've already made it," Jaden said, surprising Seth by engaging him again. "Why would you teach kids like us?"

"Because I went to this school, too, and it helped me a great deal."

Jaden's gaze shifted to Aiyana, who was standing near the door. "You went here because Ms. Turner's your mother."

"No. My birth mother gave me up for adoption, and I didn't exactly thrive in the foster system. That's how I came here."

"Does anyone thrive in the foster system?" one of the other kids said under his breath and several snickered.

Seth ignored the comment because he was trying to make a connection with Jaden. "A lot of my foster parents were good people. But I was pretty angry, and I wasn't behaving the way I should."

"So Ms. Turner adopted you after you came here?" someone else asked.

His mother must've made that clear to the student body at some point. "That's right."

"Is she the one who got you into art?" asked a somber girl with a long ponytail.

"Not really. It was always an interest of mine. But once she realized that I loved it and I might be good at it, she did everything she could to support me, and now she's trying to foster your love of art by having me come back to teach you what I've learned. Are you interested?"

All the other kids readily agreed. Only Jaden still seemed skeptical.

"Well?" Seth said, focusing on him.

He toyed with the various pieces of his chess set. "If I go to your class, will I get to create for a living, like you do?"

"You can do whatever you want for a living. It's possible you won't need me to make it in the industry. But why not take the help I'm here to offer you?"

The tension in the boy's shoulders eased. "Okay. I'm in."

Seth went over some of the basic things he'd be teaching. Most were happy to hear there'd be no tests, just projects that would be due by certain deadlines. "I'll assign your grade, but we will have peer reviews as well," Seth said. "As an artist, it's important to learn how what you create affects others and how you can improve. It's also important to separate yourself from your work."

They each signed a contract Aiyana had created, which stated that in order to attend the class they would keep up their other grades, and they turned those in on their way out.

"Well?" Aiyana said after the last one left.

"I think it's going to be an interesting class," Seth told her.

"You've never taught before. Are you comfortable with what's ahead of you?"

He thought about Jaden and what'd held him back in the past. His reluctance to experience the pain he'd feel for some of these kids hadn't gone anywhere. But now there was something bigger to counteract it: his desire to teach Jaden and others like him how to express themselves in a much healthier way. "It'll be okay," he said.

Tia's palms were sweating by the time she opened the door for Officer Crocker. "Would you like to come in?" she asked nervously.

He cleared his throat as he stepped inside. "I'm sorry to bother you again. I honestly didn't anticipate having to come back."

She hadn't expected to see him again, either. "What's going on?"

His chest lifted as he hitched up his gear belt. "I'm afraid we've got a problem."

The last thing she needed was another problem. "And that is…"

He peered closer at her. "You don't know?"

"How would I?" she asked, spreading out her hands.

"What did Seth look like when he came home last night?"

This question confused her even more. "What do you mean? I don't think he ever went out. Why?"

This seemed to throw him. "Kouretas is saying that Seth assaulted him at The Blue Suede Shoe."

She'd heard Seth refer to that bar before. That was where
he'd seen Kouretas for the first time. But...had he gone there
again? "When? What time?"

"According to the report, it was late, almost midnight."

Tia's mind was racing, trying to determine if it was possible
that Seth had left the house after she went to bed. When she'd
first seen him this morning, it looked as though he'd crashed
on the couch. But...was that after he got back from the bar?
"And?" she prompted, a hard knot forming in the pit of her
stomach. "What happened?"

"There was an altercation in the parking lot."

"A fight."

"Yes. Seth was just arriving and Kouretas was leaving when
they ran into each other and had a few words."

"Words," she repeated hopefully.

"That was how it started. Then it got physical. According to
the report, Seth attacked him."

"If that's true, there must be a good reason."

"I hope so, because he'll have to explain that reason to the
judge."

"This is crazy," she said. "I—I don't believe it."

"You might believe it if you saw Kouretas's face."

"How bad was he hurt?"

"See for yourself." Crocker handed her a picture that showed
Kouretas with a swollen eye and a cut lip.

She blanched as she gazed at the damage. "No. Whoever
did this, it wasn't Seth. Like I said, I'm pretty sure he was here
all night."

"*Pretty sure?*" he said skeptically.

She wished she would've stated that with more conviction,
but she didn't know. Not really. She'd assumed Seth hadn't left
the house. The alarm would've announced if the front door had
been opened. But maybe he'd left after she was asleep and she
didn't hear him. He had been at that bar before. And he was

angry with Kouretas. "If…if something like that happened, Seth would've said something about it this morning."

"He didn't?"

"No. Not a word." This, she could state with absolute conviction. "He…he seemed the same as he was last night. And there wasn't a scratch on him."

"That's because he used a board he grabbed off the ground."

Tia swallowed hard. "No way. I don't believe Seth would ever do that."

"For Aiyana's sake, I'd like to believe you," Crocker said. "But we have a witness."

Tia was so shocked by this news she nearly dropped the photograph. *You do?*

"We do. And it's someone I've known for years, someone who'd have no reason to side against Seth."

Tia gaped at him. "Who?"

"His late wife's mother," he replied. "Lois Ivey saw the whole thing."

CHAPTER TWENTY-THREE

Aiyana was so angry that she could barely keep her foot from pressing the gas pedal to the floor. That Seth would assault Ray Kouretas made no sense. He had a temper but would never get violent, not unless he was provoked. If Kouretas had swung first or threatened Tia, she could see how a fight might break out, but even then, Seth would never use a length of board or any other weapon on an unarmed man. Not only that, but she'd been with him for several hours this afternoon. He'd acted as though nothing had happened—because, she had no doubt, nothing *had* happened. The only witness was Lois Ivey, and after what Seth had told her when he called from the police station a few minutes ago, Aiyana knew Lois wasn't reliable.

Had Graham been at the bar, too? If so, what was his story?

Aiyana was planning to find out. She couldn't believe Lois would be there alone.

She parked in front of the Ivey home and marched to the front door.

At first, no one would answer. She guessed Lois or Graham had spotted her car from one of the windows and knew it was her. But she wasn't going to give up that easily. If she had to, she'd bang and bang and keep banging until they had to deal with her.

It took fifteen long minutes, during which Aiyana used her purse to save her hands so she could keep pounding. Even then, it was only after she started yelling, "I know you're in there. Open up!" that Graham finally answered.

"If someone doesn't come to the door, it's usually because they don't want visitors," he barked.

"And why wouldn't you want to see me, Graham?" she snapped. "We've always been on good terms."

"We're—" he struggled to finish his sentence "—busy."

Again, she came right back at him. "I don't care whether you're busy. I want to know what the heck is going on."

"Your boy assaulted a man at The Blue Suede Shoe last night. That's what's going on."

"*You* saw it, too?" she challenged.

He paused for only a millisecond, but that was enough to tell Aiyana he was lying. "Of course," he said. "What would Lois be doing at a bar at midnight if I wasn't with her?"

"That's what I was thinking. Glad to hear you were there, too. Why don't you tell me exactly what you saw?"

"I don't have to tell you anything," he said. "Lois has already gone over it with the police."

"And they've arrested Seth. Did you know that? Is that what you wanted? To lie about your son-in-law and have him arrested for something he didn't do—at Christmas, for crying out loud?"

A flicker of uncertainty flashed in his eyes, but he attempted to wave off her words. "It won't be a big deal. He has the money to get out of it."

Aiyana felt her jaw drop. "That's all you have to say? If you really saw what you claimed to have seen, I think you would've given me a much different response."

The grooves in his forehead deepened. "What do you mean?" he asked with less surety.

"You know he *didn't* do it. You're simply justifying your actions by telling yourself it won't really hurt Seth."

"I'm done talking to you," he said and started to close the door.

Aiyana stopped it with the palm of her hand. "If you shut me out, I'll stand out here and pound all day if I have to."

He rolled his eyes. "Jesus Christ! What is it you want from us?"

"The truth!"

"With Seth's reputation, how do you know he didn't do it?"

"Because I know my son. I know the man he has become. I can't believe you'd falsely accuse him. I thought you were better than that."

The last part of her statement seemed to really bother him. "I'm getting Lois," he said in a huff. "I didn't want to get involved in the first place."

After he disappeared, Aiyana heard raised voices coming from inside. *You talk to her! You're the one who wanted to go to the police.*

Just tell her to leave.

She won't!

When Lois cracked the door open, she was already on the defense. "Maybe you should be over at the station, bailing out your son," she said, "instead of banging on our door, trying to cause trouble."

Cal was over at the station, taking care of Seth's bail and getting him released. Aiyana felt her time was better spent trying to get the Iveys to recant. "*I'm* trying to cause trouble?" she echoed. "I'm not the one who's falsely accused an innocent man."

"I saw what I saw," she insisted.

"And what was that?" Aiyana challenged.

"It's just like I told the police. When I got out of the car, I saw Seth arguing with Mr. Kouretas. He was mad that Mr. Kouretas wouldn't leave town."

"Even though Seth was there without Tia, so there was no risk of her being photographed?"

As she blinked, Aiyana could almost see her mind scrambling to come up with a credible response. "Sh-she may have been in the car."

"Now Tia was there, too?"

"I don't know. I didn't see her. But that part doesn't matter."

"The details *do* matter, Lois. And you and Graham were just arriving at the bar—at *midnight*?"

"What are you implying? A lot of people go out late at night."

"Not at your age. Have you ever done it before? Has anyone *ever* seen you at The Blue Suede Shoe at midnight?"

"Just because we've never done it before doesn't mean we didn't do it last night."

"Okay. So let's say you did. You go there at midnight, for the very first time, and witness a fight. Did you try to stop it?"

"I—I was yelling for Seth to stop."

"Yelling. Then, there must've been others who heard you. The Blue Suede Shoe is a very popular place. Who else was there?"

"No one. We were in the parking lot."

"Did you run into the bar to get help?"

"N-no."

"Why not?"

She had to think about her answer. "It happened too fast."

"So what did you do after? Go in and have a drink? If so, there must be someone who can place you there. Who'd you see?"

"No one," she said, her voice no longer so strident. "We didn't end up going in."

"Because..."

"I was too upset."

"You weren't even there," Aiyana said with disgust. "And if you don't think it'll all come out in court, you're wrong, because Seth won't stand for what's happening. He'll fight this. I hope you know that."

"You need to leave now," Lois said in exasperation. "I don't have to stand out here in the cold while you call me a liar. I've told the cops everything I know."

"You told them when you called them last night?"

"No, not last night. Kouretas said he was okay. This morning, he must've decided to go to the police, because they called me a few hours ago to see what I witnessed."

"What *you* witnessed? Or what you and Graham witnessed? Because sometimes it sounds like you were there alone."

"We were there together," she reiterated.

"Then, let me get this straight. Kouretas was hurt and angry, and yet he just…got in his car and drove away? And you did the same?"

She seemed stumped, so Aiyana kept pressing. If she could get Lois flustered enough, maybe she'd break down and admit the truth. "Did you tell anyone else what you saw?"

"Just leave us alone!" she snapped and slammed the door.

Aiyana didn't expect either Lois or Graham to return, but she pounded on the door again, just to make sure they were listening. "Your daughter loved Seth more than anything in the world. And this is how you treat him after she's gone? I bet she's rolling over in her grave." She started to leave but turned back for one last parting salvo. "Or maybe, since she knew you so well, that's all she would ever expect of you."

There was no response, so she returned to her car and called Cal. "Do you have him?"

"Not yet. I'm working on it, though. How'd it go with the Iveys?"

"I'm not overly optimistic they'll recant like they should," she replied. "But I left them with a few things to think about."

★ ★ ★

Seth jiggled his knee in an attempt to relieve some of his agitation as Cal drove him home. Cal was an old cattle rancher, a true cowboy, who took excellent care of Aiyana. Seth would've liked him for that reason alone, but he was good to everyone else, too.

"Sorry about all of this," he'd said as soon as Seth climbed in the truck with him. "It's not fair to you."

"It'll be okay," Seth had assured him. He was angry, of course, but he believed any good lawyer should be able to get him out of such a bogus battery charge. If nothing else, Maxi's security system would prove he didn't leave last night. He'd tried to tell the police that Maxi probably had a way to check it, but they wouldn't listen. They couldn't believe longtime residents like the Iveys would ever lie. Apparently, no one on the force had heard about Graham's gambling problem. But there might even be cameras at The Blue Suede Shoe that could prove Seth hadn't been there—if they covered the parking lot. Kouretas was just messing with him, trying to use a little leverage to get Tia to agree to let him take her picture.

But she wasn't going to agree. At least, Seth hoped not. He hadn't spoken to Tia since he'd left the house earlier. Crocker had been waiting for him at the gate when he returned home, had barely let him park his car in its usual place before hauling him over to the police station, where they'd taken away his personal possessions, including his cell phone, when they booked him. He'd tried to reach her numerous times since being released, but she wasn't picking up.

Cal glanced over as they reached Maxi's property. "Still nothing from Tia?"

Seth shoved his phone back in his pocket. "No." He tried to spot her car as Cal punched in the code, but it wasn't until they'd rolled through the gate and wound down the drive that he could see she was gone.

"Damn it!" Seth jumped out the moment Cal came to a stop and then rushed into the house. Tia's things were still in her room, so she hadn't left permanently. But he was afraid of where she might've gone. He hoped she hadn't agreed to meet Kouretas in exchange for dropping the battery charge.

The security system announced activity at the front door, so he came to the banister to look down at Cal.

"She here?" Cal asked.

"No."

"Where could she have gone?"

"I have no idea." Seth jogged down the stairs so he could check the kitchen for a note or anything else that might provide more information.

Cal trailed after him. "Anything?"

"No." He slammed one of the drawers that had been left open, suggesting Tia had left in a hurry. "I hope she didn't walk right into Kouretas's hands, thinking she was helping me by doing so."

Cal began jingling the change in his pocket. "How can we find out if she did?"

Seth scrolled through the many attempts he'd made to reach her on his phone. Should he try calling her again? Was she even getting his voice-mail messages?

He'd left her plenty, telling her not to let Kouretas get anywhere near her. He'd wanted to speak to her, to hear her voice so he could talk her down and explain. But maybe she'd be more likely to respond to a text.

Although he planned to tell her pretty much what he'd said in his voice mails—to stay away from Kouretas because it was all a ploy, and there was no way he wanted the paparazzo and the Iveys to get away with it—his wild accusations suddenly seemed less important than simply hearing that she was okay. Can you answer my calls? he wrote instead. Please? I'm worried about you.

He waited, but when he didn't get a response, even to that, he started to search for Kouretas's business card.

"What is it?" Cal asked when he came around the corner to find Seth searching the counters.

"Kouretas's card. I had it here. I know I did."

"And now it's gone?"

The second Cal said that, the obvious occurred to him, and he groaned as he straightened.

"That doesn't sound good," Cal said.

"Tia must've taken it," he replied. "How else would she reach him?"

The studio where she'd been told to go looked like an up-scale warehouse. Tia's stomach did a few somersaults while she was still out in the street. She'd disguised herself with her scarf, beanie and sunglasses, but she still ducked her head when she saw a group coming toward her.

After they passed, she walked in.

Despite being raised in a religion that eschewed physical beauty, she'd taken great pride in her looks. Since coming to LA, she'd learned they were extremely important, at least to some people. Now the accident was forcing her to decide just how important they were to *her*. Was she going to let the loss of her pretty face ruin her life?

She told herself it wasn't just her looks. It was her career, too. Her beauty had been her stock-in-trade. So getting in front of a camera to show the world what Tia Beckett looked like now wasn't going to be easy. But she was going to do all she could to get Seth off the hook for trying to protect her. He didn't deserve the blowback he was getting.

Besides, if she had to show her face at some point—and she did if she ever wanted to live a normal life—she figured she might as well do it now and get it over with. She could only imagine how much it must've stung for Seth to hear that Shiloh's parents were involved with Kouretas's false claim. Just the thought of him being arrested and taken to jail, for an assault that never occurred, enraged her.

She kept asking herself how the Iveys could do such a thing. Even if they were desperate, it wasn't Seth's responsibility to pay their gambling debts.

But they wouldn't get away with what they were trying to do. Not if she could help it.

The woman who came to greet her as she waited in the lobby was a complete stranger. She introduced herself as Nina Miles, said she was the art director and smiled warmly as she invited Tia into an inner room that was already set up with props—a stand of leafless birch trees with fake snow on the branches, the corner of a stone building that looked sort of like a cottage and a wind machine.

"Looks…wintry," Tia muttered.

"We're going to give the shoot some wow factor—make it as glamorous as possible, and I think the white bark on the trees and the white of the snow will be gorgeous."

Glamorous. Gorgeous. Such words stuck out, given the situation, and hung heavy in the air. "Something that gorgeous might be difficult to accomplish," Tia told her. "You haven't seen my face."

"Then, why don't we have a look?" she said without any apparent concern.

Tears sprang to Tia's eyes, making her grateful she was still wearing sunglasses and could hide it, but she was able to blink them back when the woman's gentle yet professional manner didn't falter.

"Do you mind?" she asked, and Tia let her unwrap the scarf from around her neck, which she set aside as Tia removed her sunglasses and pulled off her beanie.

Nina Miles's expression grew somber as she used Tia's chin to tilt her face one way and then the other. "Give me a moment," she said and left the room.

Tia wandered to the window and looked out on the bustling streets of downtown LA. Had Ms. Miles been so shocked by what she'd seen that she was calling someone to report how terrible it was? Or to ask her superior if they should cancel the shoot?

She winced at the possibility but reminded herself that was insecurity talking. Almost any magazine would be eager for the chance she'd just given *People*.

True to her word, Nina reappeared a few minutes later. "Why don't we have you come over here and take a seat? Katherine Stewart's on her way. She's one of the best makeup artists in the industry."

Tia doubted makeup could fix the problem. She'd tried that herself. But she'd resigned herself to the process, and, of course, any professional shoot would start with hair and makeup, so she allowed Nina to lead her to the mirrorless vanity.

"Would you like a cup of coffee or tea while you wait?"

The lump in Tia's throat made it difficult to speak, so she shook her head. All she wanted was to get this over with as soon as possible.

"Okay. It shouldn't be long," Nina said and left again.

While she was alone, Tia pulled out her phone and stared down at the many calls she'd missed from Seth. She could've answered while driving to LA. She'd heard her phone ring. But she was afraid he'd talk her out of what she was about to do, and she didn't want to give herself an excuse to procrastinate this any longer.

But his latest message, a text, was new.

Can you answer my calls? Please? I'm worried about you.

Worried suggested he cared, but she was careful not to let herself believe he cared too much. They were just friends. He'd made that clear.

She considered texting a response to let him know there was no reason to be concerned, but once she allowed him to engage her, she'd have no excuse for not picking up the phone. And she couldn't start a conversation with him until this was over.

She was just sliding her phone back into her purse when Nina came in. "It's official. You've made the cover!" she announced. "We had to make some adjustments and rearrange a few things, so now we're under a strict deadline and can't waste a second."

Tia had always viewed the cover of *People* as the epitome of success. When she was a girl, she'd saved any money she was given to be able to get a subscription without her parents knowing and used a friend's address instead of her own—someone whose mother sold the handmade quilts the Mennonite women created at her gift shop. Each month, she'd eagerly await the release of the next issue. Then, once she took possession of it, she'd hide the magazine in the hayloft, and whenever she could get her chores done early, she'd sneak away and pore over each page, examining with envy the stars who graced the cover.

Now she was going to be on the cover herself—but only after an accident had destroyed everything she'd built since leaving her family.

At least it would be *People* that would reveal her new face for the first time and not the gossip rags. Kouretas might be able to come up with a story—possibly about her seeing a famous artist—or get a second-rate picture he could put in *The Lowdown*, but the big prize would be gone. He wouldn't break the story like he was hoping to, and he'd have no reason to continue to try to hurt Seth—except out of spite, of course, and once he realized he no longer had a strong hand and faced retribution by someone who could afford to defend himself and even countersue, if necessary, she was willing to bet he'd back off that, too. She was consoling herself with those thoughts when Katherine rushed in, apologized for being late and shoved her purse under the vanity before examining Tia's face.

"What do you think?" Nina asked, standing behind her and looking on.

"It'll be difficult to cover the scars entirely, but I'll see what I can do."

"I have every confidence in you." Nina turned to Tia. "I have someone coming to do your hair, too, but first I want to go over what you'll be wearing. With so little warning, we don't have a lot to choose from, but fortunately, I have someone at Neiman Marcus who helps me out when I'm in a pinch. She sent over an elegant ecru knit dress I believe will be spectacular on you. Why don't we have you try it on now so that I'll know if it's a go before we do makeup and hair?"

Tia was impressed by how quickly they'd been able to mobilize their resources since her call. "Of course."

She stepped behind the screen that was there to allow her a modicum of privacy, but she shouldn't have bothered, because Nina followed her behind it as if it was nothing.

The dress had fur around the wrists as well as the drop-shoulder décolletage, and a short train, and it fit a little snug, but Nina was ecstatic about it. "Oh, my god! When we add the boots, it's going to be every bit as spectacular as I was hoping. You look curvy, sensuous."

Curvy and *sensuous* were two words her family would find cringeworthy, but Tia didn't say anything.

With that hurdle cleared, they moved directly on to hair and makeup.

Tia's heart raced the entire time she sat in Katherine's chair. Her makeup seemed to take much longer than it ever had before, so she couldn't help wondering if Katherine was struggling with her scars. But there was no way to tell. The other woman was too intent on what she was doing to speak.

When Katherine finished, Tia couldn't help feeling slightly hopeful. The makeup artist stepped back as though satisfied with her work, and Nina nodded appreciatively. But Tia couldn't see what they were seeing. At her request, there wasn't a single mirror in the room. She didn't want to see herself, get scared and back out. They didn't want that, either, so they were happy to oblige her.

"Do I look okay?" Tia asked Nina while they were getting ready for the photographer.

Nina nodded. "Definitely."

The shoot wasn't exactly excruciating, but it was long and tedious. The photographer, a man named Miguel, was extremely particular. He had her move this way and that and told her to angle her face just so and to hold her hands in a certain way. She almost said, "What does it matter? All anyone is going to be looking at is my face." But he took his work seriously, and he had the right to capture something he was proud to take credit for.

Besides, she'd already signed the agreement they'd pushed in front of her before he started shooting. They were paying her handsomely. All she could do was grin and bear it.

"That's a wrap," Miguel finally said, checking his watch before rushing off to get them in before the deadline, and Tia sagged in relief.

As Nina helped remove the dress, Tia was glad to have the shoot behind her. She felt she'd done the right thing in making it happen and making it happen now. But she couldn't help being anxious about the results, because she had no idea how it would play out with her fans, her peers or the media.

She had to speak with one of their journalists after that, which took another hour, but it was soon over, too. And once it was, she felt she could talk to Seth. But she waited until she was back in her car, safely disguised by her beanie, her sunglasses and her scarf, before taking out her phone.

Another text had come in from him. Where are you? Don't make me file a missing person report. I'm not feeling very good toward the police right now.

With a sigh, she let herself respond. Sorry. It's been crazy. I'll explain when I get home. Just wanted to let you know I'm okay.

Can't you call me? came his immediate response.

In a minute, she wrote back and pulled Ray Kouretas's card from her purse.

CHAPTER TWENTY-FOUR

Kouretas couldn't imagine he'd have to hang around Silver Springs much longer. He was so confident he was close to getting what he wanted that he was at the gas station, filling his tank so he could head home. His wife was expecting him. She'd had another blowout with their teenage son, who'd taken off with his loser friends even though she'd said he couldn't go anywhere.

"Who cares about Seth's mother?" he said to Lois Ivey, who'd called him just as he'd pulled up to the pump.

"*I* care," she said. "Everyone in town respects Aiyana. And you should've heard her. She was angrier than a hornet. She stood on my front porch, shouting questions at me like a lawyer—questions I had trouble answering and certainly couldn't handle in court."

"Don't be ridiculous," he said. "I told you this thing isn't going to last that long. It's a misdemeanor, anyway. It's not going to court."

"She said Seth will fight the charges, and I believe he will."

"We're going to *drop* the charges, remember? Just as soon as I can get a good picture of Tia. She has to let someone take one sooner or later. It might as well be me. Then she can save her new boyfriend at the same time. Believe me, this will be over before he can even hire an attorney."

"But you said you haven't heard from Tia."

He grabbed his phone since it was starting to slip, and he didn't want it to fall and crack on the cement. "I haven't. Not yet. But I will."

"Surely, she knows Seth is in legal trouble by now. Maybe we were wrong, and she doesn't care. Maybe there really *is* nothing going on between them."

"Don't kid yourself," he said. "The way he defended her? You should've seen it. I know what that kind of protective behavior means."

"Seth is still in love with our daughter."

"Which is why you should be pissed that he's fooling around with someone else." He hated having to hold Lois Ivey's hand like this. She was what he termed a *Nervous Nellie*, all uptight and atwitter and constantly fearful and whining. But if he didn't talk her down she might go to the police and admit she'd lied, and he couldn't allow that. Not yet.

"Shiloh's dead," she said flatly. "I've already told you that."

So? Was he supposed to care? He hadn't even known her daughter. "Right. Sorry."

"I don't like doing this to my son-in-law," she said. "Shiloh would never forgive us."

"If your daughter's dead, she has no idea what you're doing, for one. And for another, I'm not even certain Seth would still be considered your son-in-law. They didn't have any children together, did they? If not, he's technically no relation."

"They would've had children. They weren't married long enough, before—" she choked up "—before it happened."

She was growing maudlin, and he had no time or patience for that. After today, he never planned to talk to her again. "Look, now's not the time to grow a conscience. Just sit tight. Like I said, this will all be over soon."

"*Grow a conscience?*" she echoed.

"You know what I mean."

She sighed into the phone. "Just let me know the minute you hear from her."

Another call came in before he could say anything else. He returned the gas nozzle with his left hand while pulling the phone away from his ear with his right so he could see who it was. It was a blocked number. That didn't necessarily mean it was Tia, but it was a definite possibility.

"This might be her now," he said, with a surge of excitement, and switched over before Lois Ivey could even respond. "Hello?"

"Mr. Kouretas?"

"Yes?"

"This is Tia Beckett."

As he'd guessed. He couldn't help grinning triumphantly as he said, "Am I happy you've called!"

"Actually, I don't think you'll be very happy when you hear what I have to say."

He sobered. This wasn't how he'd imagined it going. "I'm sorry if you're upset. But what I want won't take more than a few minutes. It can be that easy. Then you'll be rid of me for good."

"Except it won't be that easy after all."

"Excuse me?"

"It's too late."

"For…"

"That picture you want."

"Maybe you don't understand. The only way you're going to get me to drop the charges against Seth Turner is to allow me to take one good photograph. That's it. Just one."

"You'd be stupid to continue to press charges against Seth."

This took him aback. She didn't sound upset, which was odd.

She sounded determined, and that was never a good thing—not in a game of chicken. "Because…"

"There's no longer anything to be gained. Well, the big prize is gone, anyway. You'll have to decide if you're willing to continue to stay in the fight, hoping for a few scraps."

He began to sweat despite the cold weather. "Scraps? What are you talking about? All I need is a picture," he reiterated.

"You're not going to get it—not if I can help it. And whatever picture you get without my permission certainly won't be the first. I just had a photo shoot with *People*. I'm going to be on the cover of their next issue."

Shit. Pressing his eyes closed with a finger and thumb, he bowed his head as he leaned up against his car.

"Mr. Kouretas? Are you there?"

"A more candid shot might still be worth something," he said. "Just give me that much, and I'll drop the charges."

"After what you've done, I'm afraid I won't work with you at all."

"You don't care about your new boyfriend?"

"I suggest you drop the charges against Seth and get out of town. There's a security system on Maxi's house. We have proof that Seth never went to The Blue Suede Shoe the night you claim he was there, and giving false information to the police is a crime. You might be interested to learn, ironically enough, that the penalty happens to be the same as the battery charge you now have against Seth—up to six months in county jail. Only there's one important distinction."

"What's that?" he said dully.

"You're guilty, so you won't be able to win, even if you try to fight it."

"I have a witness. A credible one."

He realized he wasn't going to be able to bluff his way out of this when she said, "Video footage is much more reliable."

As he thought of his last call with Lois, he knew Tia was

right. Lois wouldn't hold up under any kind of pressure, anyway. She had to live with the folks in this town after he was gone.

He'd made a valiant effort, but he'd tried and failed. "Fine. It's over," he said. "I'll drop the charges."

"Great, because that's what your editor said, too."

He was used to confrontations with various movie stars that sometimes turned nasty, was used to losing more fights than he won, too, but this statement caused him to jump to attention. He couldn't let her talk to Eddie. It was going to be bad enough that he didn't get the shot. "I don't have an editor. I—I freelance."

"That's not what I found out."

His mind raced as he tried to imagine how she'd come up with this information. He hadn't told anyone in this town that he was associated with *The Lowdown*. It wasn't on his card. He'd searched his own name on the internet, several times, and nothing had come up. *"Where?"*

"Maybe you should've checked the small print on your magazine's website."

He tightened his grip on the phone. "Look, there's no need to contact the magazine—"

"Too late," she broke in. "I just hung up with a man named Eddie Hoffman. He was pretty disappointed to hear what I had to tell him. Apparently, he doesn't condone lying to the police. He promised me if I didn't file suit against the magazine, he'd make things right."

Ray's heart sank. "You didn't…"

"I did."

With a groan, he dropped his head in his hands. He was *so* screwed. "What, exactly, did you tell him?"

"The truth," she said and disconnected.

Ray let his hand fall from his ear and barely managed not to drop his phone at the same time. What was he going to do now?

He stared at the people who were coming and going at the

gas station, without really seeing them. He had to come up with a good excuse, something he could say when Eddie called. But before he could even climb into his car, his phone buzzed with a text message.

He held his breath as he looked down at it. Sure enough, it was from his editor.

You're fired.

After Tia hung up with Kouretas, she sat back in her car and stared out at the quiet city street where she'd parked. It'd grown dark since she'd arrived, which made her feel strange, but she could see Christmas lights and decorations not far away and found the sight comforting. Everyone who worked downtown had left for home, that was all. Christmas was right around the corner, so they had shopping and baking and wrapping to do. With a two-hour drive ahead of her, she needed to get on her way, too. But while she was alone and feeling empowered after conquering what had become one of her worst fears, she had another call to make.

She tried to reach her sister, but it was Rachel's husband who answered.

"What do *you* want?" he barked into the phone without even saying hello.

She did her best to ignore the pique in his voice. "Is Rachel there?"

"Of course she's here—no thanks to you."

"If you want to blame me, Abram, that's fine. But your marriage would probably be better served if you took a hard look at why she wanted to leave in the first place."

Click. He'd hung up.

Tia leaned back and blew a long breath toward the ceiling. "That went well," she muttered. But before she could start the car, her phone vibrated, signaling an incoming call.

She assumed it would be Rachel, that maybe her sister had overheard what Abram had said and called back. But it was her mother.

"Tia? Did you just call Abram?"

"I called Rachel," she said. "Last I checked, she was still my sister."

"And that would be fine if…if circumstances were different. But I'm going to have to ask you not to contact her again."

Tia's stomach knotted. "What do you mean?"

"It made Rachel mad that Abram won't let her talk to you, and now they're arguing again."

Tia sat up straighter. "It *should* set her off. He has no right to decide who she can talk to and who she can't."

"He's her husband!" her mother cried as if he had every right.

"That doesn't make him her prison warden!"

"Listen to you! Listen to how you're talking! We taught you better than this."

She let her head fall against the steering wheel. She could try to explain, but her mother would never understand. She'd assume that Tia was in the wrong, that the devil had hardened her heart and made her reject their beliefs and traditions.

"Tia?" her mother said.

Tia summoned as much calm as she could muster. "Never mind. I won't try to call her again."

"You could write her a letter. I don't think anyone could have any complaint about that."

"So Dad and Abram could read it and censor it before giving it to her? No, thanks." She almost hung up but stopped herself at the last second. "Before Dad gets mad at you for talking to me, can I ask you one question?"

Her mother hesitated. "What is it?"

"Have you told anyone where I am?"

"Told anyone? Like who? Our friends all know you're in LA. They knew where you were going when you left."

"I'm not talking about Mennonites, Mom. I'm talking about the paparazzi."

"The what?"

Tia felt ridiculous for even asking. Her mother couldn't have contacted Ray Kouretas. She had limited access to technology, didn't even own a TV anymore. Naomi wasn't sophisticated enough to figure out how to find him. "There's a man named Kouretas. Ray Kouretas. Have you ever heard of him?"

"No. Never."

"What about Rachel?" Tia said. Every once in a while, her sister pushed through the oppression. It wasn't beyond belief that she'd picked up a copy of *The Lowdown*, or seen one at the grocery store they frequented on occasion, and asked the checker to Google the number for her. From there, the receptionist at the magazine could've patched her through to Kouretas.

"Tia, Rachel wouldn't know him, either. What business would she have with a strange man? Why are you trying to start trouble?"

She could hear screaming in the background and knew that her mother hadn't been stretching the truth when she'd said that Rachel and Abram were having one of their many arguments. "I'm not trying to cause trouble," she said and hung up.

She sat there for a few minutes before picking up her phone again, this time so that she could send a text message to her sister's husband:

Did you do it?

But, of course, he was otherwise occupied, so she received no response.

Tia began to feel lighter and lighter as she drew closer to Silver Springs. As negative as her conversation had been with her mother, she'd spoken to Seth right after, and that had been much more enjoyable. She'd also conquered her fear and allowed her picture to be taken for the world to see, and now that hurdle was behind her. It felt as if a huge weight had been lifted off her shoulders. She had no idea how the public would respond. She couldn't even say if Miguel had gotten a decent picture. But she was grateful for the professionalism with which Nina Miles and her team had handled the shoot. None of them had shown her an ounce of pity. They acted as if pity wasn't even warranted, and that had made Tia feel more normal than anything else.

Although this part of California didn't get snow, even at Christmas, the cold air coming through the vents of her car smelled crisp and clean. She filled her lungs and let her breath go. Although she'd never experienced the kind of excitement most children did at the approach of Christmas—there'd been no Santa, decorated tree or presents where she came from— she was beginning to feel the stirrings of a childlike wonder.

She was alive. She had her whole life ahead of her despite the accident. She had enough savings to carry her for a couple of years, if necessary, until she could find work she enjoyed, even if it wasn't acting. And she was free of the ties that bound her poor sister to Kalona, Iowa. As much as she missed her family and some of the other members of the community and mourned the loss of those connections, at the end of the day, she was grateful to be where she was. She had to forge her own path. At least she'd managed to escape the constant guilt and shame that her parents and their strict teachings had heaped upon her. That was more than she could say for a lot of Mennonites. It wasn't easy to overcome the indoctrination, the lack of education and a general unfamiliarity with how the rest of the world worked. And yet she'd done it.

The holiday decorations blinking brightly in store windows and the manger scenes in the yards of the houses she passed made her want to buy a few gifts—a complete reversal from trying to hide from the world and ignore the season entirely. Tomorrow was the twenty-third. She was running out of time.

If she was still feeling as brave in the morning, she'd visit a few stores and get some shopping done, she decided. Maybe she'd even go to Aiyana's on Christmas with Seth. She might as well enjoy him and his family while she could. She had a feeling her days in Silver Springs would come to an end long before she wanted them to.

The closer she got to Maxi's place, the more anxious she became to see Seth. She expected him to be in Maxi's office sculpting or painting when she arrived. He already knew what'd happened with Kouretas and *People* magazine, and it was night, when he usually tried to get some work done. But as soon as she let herself inside, he came from the living room to greet her.

"Finally," he said.

She didn't respond. She just walked into his arms as if it was the most natural thing in the world.

"I'm glad you're back safe," he murmured, his lips at her ear as his arms closed tightly around her.

"I did it," she told him. "It's over."

His fingers slid into the hair at the back of her head as he looked down into her face. "You got the cover of *People*, Tia. That's no small thing. And I bet you're going to look great."

"I might look okay," she allowed. "Thankfully, they took a completely different approach than the one Kouretas and his rag would've used."

"How so?"

"They weren't looking to make it too sensational. They were actually trying to make me look good, as if my face isn't everything, you know?"

"It's *not* everything. There's so much more to who you are. But you don't have to worry, regardless, because there's no way you could ever look bad."

He seemed so sincere she was tempted to believe he really

thought so. "I'm relieved Kouretas is going to drop the charges. Have you heard anything?"

"Not yet. But I'm not worried. From what you told me, his editor won't let him renege." He tucked her head under his chin as he continued to hold her. "Did you ask him who told him you were in Silver Springs?"

"No. I was reluctant to let him know he had something I wanted. I didn't want to provide anything for him to gloat over. I doubt he would've told me, anyway."

"It might be best just to let it go. It'll only hurt you to find out."

"I'm pretty sure I already know who it was."

"Who?"

"My brother-in-law. He hates me," she said, but if Abram was the one who'd called Kouretas, he must not have revealed anything about himself or her background, or Kouretas would've tried to hold that over her head.

"Better him than your sister or your friend," Seth said.

"True," she agreed, trying to convince herself it was possible that Abram had called anonymously.

"You tired?"

"Yeah." She covered a yawn. "It's been a long day. I think I'll head to bed. What are you going to do? Are you going to work?"

He rested his forehead against hers. "That depends."

"On…"

"Whether or not you'll let me join you."

CHAPTER TWENTY-FIVE

Seth had told himself he'd leave Tia alone. He'd said he didn't want to hurt her, and it was true. But having her in the house with him made it almost impossible to keep his distance. She was all he'd been able to think about today. He would've blamed that on the drama Kouretas had caused, except he hadn't been able to focus on anything else even after he heard from her and knew she was safe and hadn't succumbed to Kouretas's pathetic attempt to strong-arm her. If he could focus on something else, he would've gotten some work done.

Instead, he'd surfed through TV stations while waiting for her to return. And now that she was home, they were in bed together—within a few minutes of her walking through the door.

He told himself he'd get it all figured out in the morning—somehow regain his footing. He couldn't be expected to think coherently right now. The concern he'd felt today had wound him up, and now that he had her naked body beneath him there was no going back.

She threaded her fingers through his as he settled between her thighs and, closing his eyes in relief, pressed inside her. He'd been without this kind of intimacy for too long, he decided. No way was he going to be able to give it up again, not until Tia left Silver Springs and the temptation went with her.

He dipped his head and kissed her, pulling her lower lip into his mouth for a moment while luxuriating in the taste of her. He planned to take his time tonight, make it last as long as possible, but she surprised him by shifting so that she could be on top.

Once she took control, such a devilish smile tugged at the corners of her mouth that he couldn't help grinning back. He loved that she was enjoying herself and that she willing to be bold about her own wants and needs. And the sight of her straddling him, with her hair falling over her bare breasts, drove him crazy. She rested her hands on his chest as she began to rock, nearly bringing him to climax, only to stop at the last second and start again, which took him even higher. She did that twice, and might have done it a third time, but he heard her gasp as though her own climax had taken her by surprise.

She dropped her head back as goose bumps covered her body, and, with a groan, he let himself go over the edge with her.

Tia could smell coffee when she woke up. Shoving the hair out of her face, she leaned up on one elbow to check the time on her phone and was shocked to see it was almost eleven. Rolling the other direction, she stretched out a foot, searching for Seth in the tangled bedding. With the blinds down it was too dark to see much, and when she didn't find him, she guessed, from the coffee aroma, that he was down in the kitchen.

How had she slept so late? Had he slept in, too?

"Wow, what a night," she murmured and couldn't help shaking her head as she remembered how intense it had been at various points. Every night she spent with Seth was better than the one before, because they were growing more and more comfortable with each other.

She was also falling in love with him. But she refused to think about that. Now wasn't the time. For once, she was going to be like everyone else and embrace the holidays—celebrate life and love and the beauty of sacrificing for others.

Shoving the pillows behind her back, she checked her phone again. She wanted to be sure Nina at *People* didn't need anything else.

There was nothing from Nina, but she found a message from her brother-in-law. He'd finally responded to her text asking if he'd betrayed her.

What are you accusing me of?

She'd received that message at six o'clock his time, which was probably right before he headed out on the farm. Had he and Rachel made up after their argument last night? Were they going to be able to hold their marriage together? She didn't understand how they could. And yet she didn't see any way out for them, either.

For the first time, she felt sorry for both people. She sort of wanted to convey that to Abram to offer him some sympathy, too, but she had no idea how such a sentiment would be received. If he blamed her for his troubled marriage, she couldn't imagine that anything she had to say would bring him any solace.

It certainly wasn't going to help their relationship that she'd now accused him. She wished she could just let it go; she got the creeping sensation that she had the wrong person. But she was the one who'd put it out there. He deserved some clarification.

Did you tell the paparazzi where they could find me?

She thought it might take some time to get a response. For all she knew, he didn't even have his phone with him. He left it at the house a lot; he had little need of it out on the farm. That was how Rachel had contacted her so often. But he surprised her when he messaged right away.

How would I do that? First of all, I don't know where you are. I've heard Rachel say the name of the place, but it has no meaning to me. It's somewhere in California. That's all I know. And even if I wanted to contact a paparazzi person, I couldn't. I wouldn't know where to look for one.

A paparazzi person. She chuckled because his gaffe actually lent him some credibility.

But you're the only one with the desire to hurt me, she wrote.

I won't lie. I don't appreciate the worldly influence you've had on my wife. It's hard not to hold that against you. But I would never try to hurt anyone. I'm a pacifist. All Mennonites are pacifists. The Bible teaches against that kind of evil. Or have you forgotten?

She could feel the umbrage in that response. She'd accused him of something he considered beneath him, and maybe it was. Perhaps she thought worse of him than he deserved. After all, he was a product of how he'd been raised and what he'd been taught. In the Mennonite world, the man was the head of the house, and his word was law. The woman was supposed to support him and obey him as her master. No matter how that clashed with her modern principles, she'd been part of the community once. She understood how strongly they believed the patriarchal system to be ordained by God.

Do you have any idea how the paparazzi found me?

Come on, Tia. You know what it's like here. We don't take our problems to outsiders. We handle everything among ourselves.

That was true. And as she'd realized last night, if Kouretas knew about her background, he would've said something. He was the type of person to strike back.

Then I owe you an apology, she wrote to Abram.

You owe Rachel and your parents one, too, he wrote back.

She didn't believe that was true. She'd never meant to hurt any of them—and with Rachel she'd only been trying to help. For what? she wrote. All I've ever done is live my life according to my own conscience.

When she didn't get anything back from him, she thought that was the end of the conversation. But just as she was climbing out of bed, she felt her phone vibrate.

You'll never come back here—not to stay—will you?

As she considered Abram's assessment, she realized just how wide the gap between her past and her present had become. He obviously recognized it, too. Although she'd never come right out and said this to her family before, she felt it was time to be totally transparent. No. Never.

"Hey."

Startled, she looked up to find Seth filling the doorway. "Sorry, I… I didn't hear you coming."

He jerked his head toward her phone. "Don't tell me Kouretas is causing trouble again."

"No, it's not him."

He carried the cup of coffee he'd brought up into the room and put it on the nightstand before sitting next to her on the bed. "Then, is everything okay?"

"Of course." Putting her phone down in favor of taking a sip of coffee, she forced a smile. "I was thinking… It might be fun to go shopping today."

"Did you say *shopping*? As in leaving the house and going to a store? Or are you talking about ordering online?"

She could understand his shock. "I mean going out. It's too late to have anything shipped, and I'd like to get your mother a gift for Christmas."

"Wow. Now you're just getting cocky," he said jokingly.

"I don't want to let the accident hold me back. She was the one who told me not to let it, remember?"

"My mother's always got good advice."

"I'm going to take it."

He reach out to touch her face and ran a thumb over her bottom lip. "Thanks for last night."

Tia had enjoyed it, too. Just the way he was looking at her right now made her want to pull him back into bed. Which was frightening. She couldn't remember feeling this way about anyone else.

If she wasn't careful, she was going to have a hard time letting him go. "Want to go shopping with me?" she asked.

"Sure." Still holding her chin, he pecked her mouth. "As long as we go for a run first."

That effectively dispelled the moment.

"Ugh! You can't be serious."

"We're setting healthy habits, remember?"

"Tomorrow will be soon enough to start," she grumbled.

Playfully pushing her back onto the bed, he pinned her down while tickling her, making her laugh so hard she didn't have the strength to even try to fend him off. "Are you ready to go running today?" he challenged. "Huh? What do you say?"

"Okay," she finally gasped so that he'd stop and let her catch her breath. "Yes, I'll go today!"

Running didn't turn out to be nearly as bad as Tia had expected. She enjoyed being with Seth no matter what they were doing, and he was especially charming when he was coaching and encouraging her. He was also eager to take a shower with her when they got back, which made the effort well worth it.

"Can you tell me why you've been on the pill since you were just a girl?" he asked afterward, standing in the doorway of the bathroom while she was getting ready. "Especially when you were in such a strict religious sect and probably didn't have much sexual contact with boys?"

"I had *no* sexual contact with boys," she clarified, looking at him in the mirror. "Until I reached LA, I hadn't even kissed a boy. I had my eye on leaving as far back as I can remember, and I wasn't about to let anything happen that might make my exit that much more difficult."

"Like an arranged marriage? Is that something Mennonites do?"

"No, but approval from both families is typically sought. And I didn't want to go anywhere near that. I knew I wanted out."

"That's a pretty mature thought process for someone who was as young as you were."

"After sneaking around just to be able to read *People* magazine, I understood what I was up against."

He shoved his hands in his pockets. "So no first love from back then?"

"Not back then, no. I can't call him my first love, but there was a guy living in the same place I was after I reached LA—a fellow tenant—who was my first kiss. There were so many of us sharing the same house," she said with a laugh. "It's crazy to think about what it was like in those days. But I was lucky to have a place to sleep."

"I can't imagine you in LA not knowing a soul—not even understanding much about how the outside world worked."

"It was a steep learning curve."

"Did he become your first boyfriend?"

"Not really. We hung out a lot at first. But it didn't last. There wasn't any spark. After a while I felt like it was more about studying how people outside the Mennonite community behaved. Then I got with a guy I met at the comedy club where

I worked hawking tickets. Jack Lippy. He was the first man I ever slept with. I remember feeling so guilty afterward that I broke up with him."

"How many men have you been with?" He raised his hands. "You don't have to answer that question if you don't want to. I'm just curious if you went hog wild once you realized what you'd been missing, or if your upbringing or something else still held you back."

She smoothed concealer over her scars. "I've only slept with three people."

His jaw dropped. "Including me?"

She nodded before widening her right eye so she could apply some mascara. "I was too busy working, taking acting classes and going to auditions. I didn't have time to sleep around."

"Most people in their twenties make time for sex," he said wryly.

"Okay, I also didn't want to disappoint my family. I knew they believed I'd fallen from grace, and feeling their disappointment and disapproval has never been easy. I guess that held me back, too."

Their eyes met in the mirror. "I can't believe you were willing to sleep with me."

In a way, neither could she. She'd always been so careful to look before she leaped. She knew how fragile her existence was and had never had much margin for error. But she honestly didn't see how she could've refused him. There was just something about him that made him different than every other man. "You're irresistible." She grinned as though it was a joke; he didn't need to know it was actually the truth.

He folded his arms as he leaned against the vanity. "So how does birth control come into this picture?"

"I have endometriosis, so my periods have never been regular." She switched to her left eye so she could finish with her mascara.

"And your parents let you go on the pill?"

"Shocking, right? My father didn't want to do anything about it. He said it was God's will. But the pain was so intense that, for once, my mother insisted on getting me to a regular doctor, who insisted that I needed this prescription. I don't think she even realized it was the pill."

He chuckled before sobering when he asked, "Is endometriosis bad?"

"There are worse things."

"What does it mean?"

"Hopefully, nothing." Finished with her mascara, she put on some blush, being careful to avoid the side of her face that was too red to begin with. "The doctor thinks I can probably still have children." She'd added that last part because she felt it would be natural for anyone to wonder. But considering how she felt about Seth and that they were sleeping together, she wished she could take it back. She didn't want him to think she was trying to entice him into a commitment.

Clearing her throat, she dug a pair of earrings out of her bag and put them on. "How do I look?"

"Perfect," he said without hesitation.

"My scars don't bother you?" she asked earnestly.

"Everyone has scars, Tia. Some are just more visible than others."

"But...if they don't have to hold me back, they don't have to hold you back, either."

"I'm working on it," he said.

She smiled. "I know you are."

"Ready?"

She indicated she was, but he didn't head out of the bathroom. He pulled his phone from his pocket instead.

"What is it?" she asked when she saw him frown.

"Lois Ivey just texted me."

"Has she heard about Kouretas dropping the charges?" Tia asked. "How's she reacting?"

"She's in a panic. She says the police plan to press charges against her for providing false information."

"Really?" Tia said. "I didn't think they'd do anything, since this didn't end up going anywhere. Are they going after Kouretas, too?"

"I don't know. But she's begging me to step in and talk to the Silver Springs Police so that she doesn't wind up in jail."

"And? Will you?"

"I don't know." He squeezed his forehead as though just seeing Lois's text made him tired. "She didn't seem to care much if I went to jail, but—" he dropped his hand "—I'll probably end up doing what I can."

Tia would've guessed that. Unable to resist a wave of tenderness, she slid her arms around him and kissed his cheek. "You're such a good guy."

It felt wonderful to see Tia having fun. Seth held her hand as they ambled from one store to another to give her added support, and she turned her face toward him so that she wouldn't be recognized whenever someone walked by. But with her scarf, beanie and sunglasses, and most people busy doing their own holiday shopping, no one seemed to be paying them any attention.

"Do you think your mother would like this?" she asked, holding up a set of whale bookends at a gift shop a few doors down from Sugar Mama. "She has those shelves in the living room with plenty of space to display them."

"I bet she'd love them," he said.

"What would she like better? Any ideas?"

He wanted to help her look. For a change, he was feeling the Christmas spirit, too. Even the carols that played in every single shop didn't grate on his nerves like they usually did. The colorful lights, the scent of evergreen that permeated the nicer gift shops, the man roasting chestnuts with an old-fashioned cart at one end of the street—he had to admit it was all quite pleasant. The only thing that bothered him was Lois Ivey. His phone vibrated again and again, and every time he pulled it out, he found another text or incoming call from Shiloh's mother.

"She won't quit?" Tia asked, grimacing when he checked his phone yet again.

He scowled at the screen. "Apparently not."

"Have you decided how you're going to handle the situation?"

"No. I don't even want to think about it today. This is our time to relax and have fun."

He was almost certain Tia was smiling under the scarf that came up to cover half her face, because she hugged him impulsively before allowing herself to be distracted by another potential purchase.

He was looking for a gift, too, something she lingered over and seemed to want for herself, which was why, when his phone finally went silent for half an hour, he was relieved. He thought maybe Lois had finally exhausted her efforts, but they'd just entered a shop like a Williams-Sonoma when his phone went off again.

Irritated to think she was back, he almost answered it just so he could tell her not to bother him, that he'd get back to her when he was good and ready.

Except this time, it was his mother.

Tia was a few feet away, examining some trees made out of mirrors. "Aren't these gorgeous?" she said.

He didn't have a chance to respond. He signaled that he'd be outside and answered his mother's call as he passed through the door. "Are you checking in about the assembly tomorrow?" he asked without preamble. "If so, you don't have to worry. I'll be there."

"I was actually calling about something else," she said.

"What is it?"

"Lois Ivey just left my office."

"She was at the school?"

"She said she's been trying to reach you but you won't speak to her."

"It's not that I won't speak to her. I'm still trying to decide how I feel about the whole thing and what I'm going to do about it. What do you think I should do?"

"I'm still so angry over what she did that I'm tempted to say you should let it run its course. Maybe it'll teach her a good lesson."

"Wow! This is coming from *you*? You're the most forgiving person I know."

"Not when someone threatens you," she said.

His own mother hadn't done much to protect him, but Aiyana had always been a fierce defender. "I guess I'll call the police and try to get them to back off," he said. "She's already lost her daughter. And having to pay Graham's gambling debts—or face bankruptcy—won't be easy."

"That's nice of you, son."

"It's what you would do," he said with a laugh.

"I guess you're right. Like you say, the Iveys have already lost a daughter. And the gambling debts might be a problem. But it's even worse than that."

"Worse? How?"

"They might not realize it yet, but they've also lost a son—one who would've continued to be good to them if only they had treated him fairly."

As Seth watched a group of carolers set up across the street, he realized that his mother was right. He was going to do everything he could to get the police to let the Iveys go.

But then he was going to walk out of their lives for good.

CHAPTER TWENTY-SIX

Friday, December 24

"What do you think?" Seth asked Aiyana.

Aiyana touched one of the trees with the leaves made of tiny mirrors Tia had admired at the gift shop yesterday. Seth had swung by to purchase a set of three on his way to his mother's so that he could surprise her with a gift for Christmas. "They're gorgeous," she said. "So artsy and different."

"I like the way the light makes them shimmer."

"Reminds me of standing in a forest of aspens and seeing the leaves quake in the wind," she agreed. "They look expensive. How much were they?"

"Three hundred bucks."

"That's a nice gift."

He shrugged. "Not that much."

"Maybe not for you," she said with a laugh. "Anyway, I have some pretty paper. Want me to wrap them up?"

"The package will look a lot better if you wrap it than if I do," he said.

"I'll add a big bow and put it under the tree. I can't believe she's coming to Christmas tomorrow."

His younger brothers—the twins, Ryan and Taylor, who both worked for the same tech firm in Denver, and Liam and Bentley, who were in college at San Diego State—had arrived late last night. Eager to see them, Seth had come over early, before he had to speak at the assembly on campus. But no one, except Cal, who had just left for his cattle ranch, and Aiyana, was up yet.

"You wouldn't believe how much better Tia is doing," he told Aiyana as she put the trees back in their box.

"I can't tell you how happy I am to hear that."

"We went shopping yesterday and everything." He gestured at his purchase. "That's how I found these."

"Did anyone recognize her?"

"Nope. She was disguised, of course, and just kept her face averted when we were near others."

"That should give her some confidence."

"I think so."

She set the trees aside for the moment and reclaimed the coffee she'd been drinking when he arrived. "So what did the police say when they contacted you about the Iveys?"

"They said they'd let it go. Officer Crocker was just angry they'd caused him to make a fool of himself. But I said it was Christmas and mentioned that they've had a rough go of it, and he relented."

"Do they know they're in the clear?"

"They do. I texted Lois before I drove over here. She thanked me and invited me to dinner next week."

"What did you say back?"

"That I wouldn't be coming."

Ryan shuffled into the room wearing nothing but a pair of sweat bottoms. "Thought I heard voices down here," he said. "How you doin', man?"

Seth gave his brother a hug. "'Bout time you got up."

Ryan scratched his head, which did little to relieve his bed-head. "We were up late."

"Gaming?"

"Of course. Taylor and I had to show the younger bros how it's done."

"What game?"

"We were playing the new *Oculus*. You here for breakfast?"

"I came to see you and everyone else before the assembly."

"The one at New Horizons? *You're* going?"

"I have to speak."

"About what?"

"Art. What else? Mom set me up to teach a class the first block of next semester, and we're awarding prizes for an art contest we sponsored."

"Oh, that's right," he said. "I think she told me about that."

Aiyana added a splash of cream to her coffee. "I definitely told you about that."

Ryan opened the fridge and gazed inside. "What's for break-fast, Ma?"

"Whatever you decide to make for yourself," she replied.

He shot her a wounded look as he closed the fridge. "Re-ally? I thought you'd make some French toast or something."

Aiyana rolled her eyes in exasperation. "The assembly starts in twenty minutes, and I need to finish getting ready. Why don't you grab a quick bowl of cereal and a shower and join us?"

"Not too excited about going to a high-school assembly," he said.

"It's more of a Christmas party for the kids who couldn't go home. You know that. I've been sponsoring activities for them all week so they won't feel left behind."

"Is this the one where Sam Butcher shows up as Santa?" he asked.

Cal's farmer friend, who had the right body type, had played Santa for Aiyana and the boys and girls at her school for years.

"No," she replied. "That one was last week, before any of the students left. But today is still going to be fun."

"Yeah. No, thanks," he said. "I'm still tired. Think I'll go back to bed." He turned to face Seth before leaving the room. "Hey, when Eli picked us up at the airport last night, he said you were bringing Tia Beckett to Christmas tomorrow. That true?"

Seth poured himself a cup of coffee. "She says she's coming, so...we'll see."

"That's dope! I can't believe I'll get to meet her. She was so freaking awesome in *Expect the Worst*."

"You saw that movie?"

"*Everyone* saw that movie."

Seth took a sip of his coffee. "Well, try not to mention anything about Hollywood—the movie, the Oscars, anything—when you see her. Or the accident, either."

Ryan grimaced. "Eli says she has a few scars on her face. How bad are they?"

"You can see them, but they're not that bad."

"Who would've guessed that the hermit in the family, a guy who will barely leave his house, would wind up dating a freaking movie star," he marveled.

"Tia and I aren't dating," Seth clarified.

Aiyana sent him a glance. "Does *she* know that?"

A wave of guilt swept over him as he remembered how he'd spent the last two days—by her side and in her bed. Although he'd made his position clear in the beginning, the lines had definitely begun to blur. "She knows how I feel about Shiloh," he replied.

Aiyana didn't seem pleased by his response. "Shiloh's dead, Seth. Don't let what you feel for her stop you from moving on and loving someone else."

He dumped his coffee down the sink because it was suddenly making his stomach sour. "If only that was something I could control, Mom."

Tia was nervous as she settled into a plastic chair along the back wall of the gymnasium. Seth wasn't expecting her to be there, but as private and contemplative as he could be, she knew he wasn't particularly excited to speak in public, and she wanted to support him in doing what he could for Aiyana and the school where he'd finally found a home.

Because she'd slipped in after the assembly started, she hadn't encountered anyone who'd paid her any mind. And she was wearing her beanie, glasses and scarf, so even if someone did notice her arrival, she didn't expect to be recognized on sight. The students were playing some Christmas trivia as she shoved her purse under the chair and glanced around, relieved to find that no one was looking at her. No one was even sitting close by. The students were in a tighter group, closer to the stage. Only the teachers lingered in the chairs that were strung out like beads falling from a broken necklace in back.

Eli spotted her first. He wasn't on stage with Seth and his mother; he was leaning against the wall not far from where she'd sat down. He nodded when he realized he had her attention, and she gave him a subtle nod in return.

As Aiyana started to award prizes to those who'd gotten the most correct answers on the holiday trivia, Tia knew she had to take off her sunglasses or she'd stand out for wearing them inside the building. She was just working up the nerve to do that when Eli strode over, pulled up a chair and sat down.

"Hey," he whispered.

She glanced around again before finally removing her sunglasses. "Hey."

"It's nice of you to come."

"I wanted to hear what Seth has to say. He's such a natural at what he does. I know he'll be an inspiration to these kids."

Eli grinned.

"What?"

"Nothing. He's definitely talented," he said, but that grin only broadened.

She got the impression Eli knew how she felt about Seth, but she wasn't trying to deny it. She knew that would probably only make her more transparent.

Taking a deep breath, she unwrapped her scarf so that she could breathe easier in the warm room. "What comes after this?" she whispered.

"Just some announcements. They won't take too long. Then Seth will be up."

She noticed another teacher looking at her. When his eyes widened, she knew he'd recognized her and had to steel herself so she didn't bolt—especially when he slid to the left, nudged the woman closest to him and jerked his head in her direction.

"I think the word is out," Eli said. "Are you going to be okay?"

"Sure," she said with a nervous laugh. "What can they do?"

"Ask for an autograph and try to get a picture," he replied, stating the obvious as if he understood that would not be enjoyable for her.

"I hope to get out of here before the assembly's over and they have the chance."

"I'll make sure of it," he told her.

Although her presence caused a small stir, none of the kids seemed to realize what was going on behind them, and she stubbornly maintained her smile.

"Fame has to be hard," Eli muttered as he shook his head at the man who'd started to spread the word that she was there as if to tell him not to do anything more to draw attention her way.

"It is when it goes bad," she said, joking.

"It says something that you're willing to brave coming here."

It said she cared a great deal about Seth, and that was true. He knew it as well as she did. Still, she wondered if she'd been crazy to take this on. She was just considering telling Eli that she was going to duck out, when Seth came to the podium.

He started by telling the kids it was art and the ability to create and express himself that had provided him with a lifeline through a really difficult childhood. What he shared was more intimate than she would've expected, and she could tell the kids really responded to it. There was no more fidgeting or talking. They were all drinking in his words, and she loved seeing this window into a period he didn't generally like to talk about.

He was almost finished by the time he saw her. When he realized she was there, he paused as though he couldn't believe it, and it took him a moment to remember what he'd been about to say. He got back on track, but his eyes kept flicking in her direction.

Suddenly, she forgot about being self-conscious and simply smiled at him. She was so caught up in who he was and what he'd been able to accomplish, despite his rough beginning, that Eli had to lean over and nudge her as Seth brought his remarks to a close.

"If you don't go now, you'll be caught in a throng," he warned.

She blinked and pulled her eyes away from Seth just as he started naming the students who'd won the art contest. "Right. Of course. Thanks." Retying her scarf, she donned her sunglasses and felt him squeeze her forearm in a quick goodbye as she hurried out the door.

Eli was waiting for Seth when the assembly was over. "Great job," he said as he approached. "The students loved it."

Seth had enjoyed speaking more than he'd thought he would.

After what New Horizons had done for him, it was gratifying to be able to give back. "I hope so."

"I heard one of the kids say he couldn't wait for your class to start."

"Which one?" Seth asked curiously.

"Jaden Kaplan."

"*Jaden* said that? I wasn't convinced he was glad to be selected."

"Oh, he's glad, all right. He's just reluctant to show it."

"I can understand why."

"You're going to be good for him."

"We'll see." He waved as Gavin called out a goodbye. He knew his other brother had a few things to do before heading home for Christmas Eve.

"Want to grab some lunch?" Eli asked.

Seth was too eager to get back to Tia, but he knew better than to admit that. "I need to get ready for Christmas."

Eli blinked in surprise. "What'd you say? *You're* getting ready for Christmas? What happened to giving everyone money so they can get their own present and trying to otherwise ignore the holidays?"

"I'm feeling a little more festive this year," he said, not entirely pleased to be called out.

"Does Tia have anything to do with that?" Eli asked.

"I have the sculpture you gave me to repair," he said instead of answering. "It's in my car. Why don't you walk out with me?"

"Sure. Thanks for taking care of it."

"No problem."

"So... Mom said you're bringing Tia to Christmas tomorrow," he said as they made their way to the parking lot.

"If she doesn't change her mind."

"I can't believe she braved coming to the assembly today."

"That took me by surprise, too."

"You weren't expecting her?"

He hadn't asked her to come. He'd assumed there was no way she'd want to be seen in public. "No. Do you think anyone recognized her?"

"Not long after she came in, a couple of the teachers in back realized who she was."

"Did they say anything to her?"

"No. She left before they could."

"No doubt word of her being in town will spread through the school quickly."

"Probably," Eli agreed. "But Kouretas already let that cat out of the bag."

"True."

After they reached the Porsche, Seth got the statue from his back seat and handed it over.

"Thanks again."

"No worries."

Eli obviously had more on his mind, because he didn't say goodbye and leave. He kicked a small pebble across the pavement. "So what's going on between you and Tia? Given how excited Mom is, it seems it might be getting serious."

"No, we're just friends," he said.

"*Friends*?"

"Yeah." Afraid Eli would say something else—something he wouldn't want to hear—he looked down as soon as his phone signaled a text message, hoping the shift in attention would put an end to the conversation.

But when he saw who'd sent the message, he sort of wished he hadn't bothered.

Some of what he felt must've shown in his expression, because a look of concern came over Eli's face. "That's not Kouretas, is it? Mom said you were rid of that dude."

"It's not Kouretas."

"Is it the Iveys?"

"No, it's Brady."

"Your biological brother?"

"Yeah. It's that time of year," he said with a sigh.

"Are you going to respond?"

Seth didn't know if he could. Part of him wanted to. Part of him had always wanted to. But he hadn't been able to make himself so far. Just thinking about letting Brady and Derrick back into his life dredged up too many bad memories. "I don't know yet," he replied.

CHAPTER TWENTY-SEVEN

"I was shocked to see you at the assembly," Seth said to Tia once he returned to Maxi's. "What were you thinking?"

"I didn't want to miss your big speech." As she slid into his arms, he couldn't avoid the memory of telling Eli only half an hour ago that they were just friends. Maybe he would've been able to convince himself it was true, except he'd come straight home from the assembly instead of hanging out at his mother's with his younger brothers, whom he didn't get to see very often, because he couldn't wait to be with her.

It wasn't that they were just friends. He had to acknowledge that. It was that he couldn't trust love. Not after what his birth mother had done, and not after losing Shiloh. Love sucked. It wasn't to be trusted, and he was done letting it mess with his heart.

That was also why he wasn't going to reply to Brady this year, either. Brady's text had swirled around in his mind the whole way home, reminding him of the hope he used to harbor of reconnecting with his biological family—and making acid churn in his stomach because what he wished for and what he could allow himself were two different things.

"Are you happy with the way it went?" she asked.

"I think so." The moment he buried his face in her hair and breathed deeply, he began to feel better. What they had couldn't last, but he was going to enjoy it while he could. He needed to remind her not to count on too much from him, but he'd be a jerk to initiate that conversation on Christmas, which gave him a pass for the next two days. He would deal with reality later and continue to live in this bubble.

"You smell delicious," he murmured as he began to kiss her neck.

"Are you sure it's me and not the broccoli cheddar soup I'm making?"

He could smell that, too, although he hadn't been able to identify what it was. "You're making broccoli cheddar soup?"

"I am. And some dinner rolls."

"From scratch?"

"Of course. You can't be a Mennonite girl without learning a few things in the kitchen. I can make the best jelly you've ever tasted, mouthwatering pies, which is why I'm making two pecan pies to take to your mother's tomorrow, and turkey and stuffing and gravy and...lots of stuff."

"You've been holding out on me," he said jokingly.

"I was channeling movie star Tia Beckett. But I realized Christmas calls for some of the skills I learned as Sarah Isaac."

"Do you ever feel like two separate people?" he asked, lifting his head.

She nodded. "Sometimes."

He thought about his childhood, the boy he'd been and the man he'd become. "So do I."

"Which person do you like better?" she asked.

"Definitely this one. You?"

"I miss some things about my life back then. The simplicity. The safety. Thinking my parents and those around me had the answers to life's toughest questions. Being able to rely on a whole community to come to my aid, if necessary. It can be colder and harsher and lonelier on the outside. But..."

"What?"

"I think this version of me is better. At least I don't feel pressure to conform or try to believe something I can't." She suddenly let go of him. "I'd better stir the soup so it doesn't scorch on the bottom."

Reluctantly, he let her go and was surprised to find a small Christmas tree on one of Maxi's expensive tables when he walked into the living room. "Where did this come from?"

"I saw a tree lot on the way home and had to stop. But that's probably silly, right? It was sort of impulsive."

"It's not silly at all. Are you going to decorate it?" he asked.

"I don't have anything to decorate it with. I've never done the whole Christmas thing, but this year I... I don't know... I sort of felt like trying it. Maybe it's part of letting go of Sarah Isaac and more fully embracing who I'll be in the future."

He smiled because she was going to be okay. She was stronger than she knew. She would overcome the accident like she'd overcome all the other challenges in her life so far.

"I know you're not that excited about Christmas," she added. "Do you mind having a tree here?"

"No," he said. "But we have to get some ornaments."

"We do?"

"We can't leave it like that. That's not doing the 'whole Christmas thing.'"

She grinned. "Then, we'll go as soon as the food's done."

He checked his watch. "It's nearly three. We have to hurry if we want to buy anything. The stores close early on Christmas Eve, especially here in Silver Springs."

"I can leave the rolls to rise and turn off the soup. The pies haven't gone in the oven yet, so we're good there."

"Perfect." Since he hadn't gone back to the house with Aiyana, he hadn't eaten since the bowl of cereal he'd had for breakfast. He was hungry, but he figured he could pick up a small snack to tide him over while they were out. It was suddenly important to him that Tia have the kind of Christmas she was looking for. "I'd better line up Pentatonix for some Christmas songs while we drive over."

"You don't mind Christmas music, either?"

Not if it was for her.

Tia held one of the small arm baskets that'd been stacked by the door of the local gift shop as Seth helped her load it, and they spent almost thirty minutes choosing ornaments they liked. Tia had a feeling it didn't go like this for most people—where every ornament was expensive and unique—but they didn't have a lot of other options. There were no large stores in Silver Springs where they could buy more standard decorations, and there was no time to drive anywhere else before everything closed.

She was wearing her beanie, but she'd removed her sunglasses so she could see in the dim shop, and she'd untied the scarf so that Seth could hear her when she spoke. "What about this one?"

Although there were quite a few people out on the street, rushing here or there, trying to get last-minute preparations in place, there weren't many people in this particular store, so the shop clerk had been watching them for a while. She flashed Tia an eager smile whenever Tia looked up, giving Tia the impression the woman knew who she was, but after approaching just once when they came in to see if they needed assistance, she'd left them alone, and for that Tia was grateful.

Seth looked at the fat snowman holding a top hat in its hand. "That's a definite yes," he replied and put it in her basket.

"If we keep going, we're going to need a bigger tree," she remarked.

He shrugged. "Then, we'll get a bigger tree."

"It's too late. The lot was shutting down when I bought the last one."

"Fine." He moved to another display. "But we have to get these lights and this star for the top."

"Why?"

"If you're going to do this, you need to do it right," he said and laughed. "Every tree has to have lights and a topper."

He pushed Tia aside when she tried to pay at the register and bought them himself, but before she left, Tia turned over one of the business cards by the register, signed it and gave it to the woman who'd been so respectful of her privacy. "Thank you," she murmured.

The woman's smile stretched from ear to ear. "No, thank *you!*" she said excitedly. "I didn't want to ask, but... I thought it was you."

"Merry Christmas."

When they came out of the store, Seth took Tia's hand. "That was nice of you."

"I could see her watching me."

"I could see it, too," he said as they strolled down to Sugar Mama and bought cookies and mint hot chocolate they then carried to the park.

"So...what do you think?" he asked when they reached the giant Christmas tree he'd wanted to show her.

She'd left her scarf untied so she could drink her hot chocolate but felt far less self-conscious than she had in a long while. She smiled as she gazed up at it. The sun was beginning to set and the lights were just coming on. "It's spectacular."

"I thought you should see it for the sake of inspiration," he said.

She fit comfortably against him when he put his arm around her. "I'm definitely inspired."

They took a selfie in front of the tree. It was the first picture Tia had taken since the accident—not counting the cover of

People—but she was so happy she didn't care that her face wasn't what it had been before, especially when Seth held a piece of mistletoe he'd purchased at the gift store over her head and said it was a tradition to kiss beneath it.

They took a selfie of them trying to do that, too, but keeping the mistletoe overhead and one arm stretched out far enough to fit them both in the frame wasn't easy. They came away laughing at the shot they'd gotten as a result.

A group of people passed by, wishing them a Merry Christmas, and Tia responded in kind, but none of them seemed to recognize her. She didn't think any of them had looked too closely. Busy celebrating themselves, they hurried on.

By the time she and Seth started back to the car, they could see their breath misting in front of them.

"It's getting cold," he said.

"We need to start a fire in the fireplace when we get home."

"You mean *turn on* the fire? Maxi only has a gas fireplace."

"Hm." She wrinkled her nose. "Won't smell like a real fire. But beggars can't be choosers."

"You're really trying to experience it all, aren't you?" he said, smiling.

She supposed she was. She wished she had his present to wrap tonight. Because she hadn't been able to find anything for him in town, she'd gone online while he was at New Horizons and purchased a monogrammed leather carrier for his expensive brushes. Because of the personalization, it would take two weeks to arrive, but she figured she'd just print out a picture of what she ordered and wrap that so he could at least see what it was.

Once they got back to Maxi's, they put off finishing dinner until they could decorate the tree, since they'd eaten half a sandwich before buying the ornaments and had cookies and hot chocolate after.

"It's a masterpiece, right?" he said, standing back when the tree was done. "Is this a tradition you'd like to incorporate from now on?"

She watched the lights twinkle between the many ornaments Seth had insisted on purchasing for her and felt, for probably the first time, the magic other people talked about experiencing at Christmas. "Absolutely," she said. "I don't think I've ever had a better day. What about you? Don't you think it's been wonderful?"

When he didn't answer right away, she turned to look up at him. She thought that maybe he was struggling with the whole Christmas thing. But he wasn't looking at the tree—he was looking directly at her when he said, "I do."

Seven of Aiyana's eight sons were home for Christmas—Eli and Gavin with their wives and kids—which made it absolutely chaotic. Sometimes they all talked at once, and they teased, hollered, groaned and laughed as they competed in online games, card games, board games, even who could eat the most pie. Tia was both a little intimidated by the hubbub and enchanted by it. Although there were only three kids in her family, because her mother had had difficulty getting pregnant, most of the Mennonites she'd known had a great deal more children. She was used to big families. But she hadn't been part of that world for eleven years, and the celebration here was on an entirely different level.

"How are you holding up?" Aiyana asked when she found Tia standing off to one side, watching Seth try to beat Bentley at a new virtual-reality game.

"I'm doing good," she said.

"It probably seems a bit crazy here."

Tia had helped pick up the wrapping paper after they'd opened gifts. But the floor still wasn't clear. There were unwrapped presents stacked everywhere, including what she'd received—the beautiful mirrored trees from Seth, a gold bracelet

from Aiyana, a scented candle and matching lotion from Eli
and his wife, a pressure cooker from Gavin and his wife and a
box of See's Candies from the younger boys. "It's magical," she
said. She understood what her family meant when they said that
Christmas had become too commercial in the outside world.
She supposed a case could be made for that. But she loved the
holiday, anyway, and preferred to focus on the beauty of spending time with family, making and enjoying a good meal and
celebrating peace on earth and goodwill to all. "It's not too
much for you?"

"Not at all." She almost admitted that it was very different from the Christmases she'd experienced as a child, but she
hesitated to take the conversation in that direction. Aiyana had
asked about her family while they were getting ready to open
presents, and she'd answered honestly. She'd said they lived on
a small farm in Iowa and that she had two siblings. The only
thing she'd left out was the Mennonite aspect. She figured she
might tell Aiyana one day that she'd been born Sarah Isaac, if
Aiyana was still part of her life. But she had no idea what the
future would hold. Although she couldn't imagine her time
with Seth coming to an end, she could tell he was still holding
back—and she knew why.

Maybe he'd never get over Shiloh. Maybe she wasn't everything Shiloh was or she wasn't enough to satisfy him in any
kind of permanent way.

She was about to excuse herself so she could step out of the
room and go somewhere quieter to call her family to wish them
a Merry Christmas, when she got a text from Nina at *People*.

Did you get it?

Get what? she wrote back.

Sent you the mock-up for the cover. Check your email. It's beautiful. Merry Christmas!

It was touching to Tia that Nina would take the time to message her on Christmas Day. She couldn't help feeling gratitude for how Nina had handled everything—although she was hesitant to feel too much gratitude when she didn't yet know how the cover had turned out.

"Is that your family?" Aiyana asked when she noticed Tia using her phone.

"I need to call them," she said instead of answering directly. "Is it okay if I go into another room so it'll be easier to hear?"

"Of course," she said and took Tia down the hall to a room at the back of the house she said was Cal's and her office.

Tia stood between the two desks as she used her phone to navigate to her in-box. The dress she'd been wearing for the photo shoot was gorgeous. She had no doubt it had photographed well. It was her face she was worried about. Had Miguel been trying to enhance or hide her scars?

Butterflies rioted in her stomach as she found the email Nina had been referring to and downloaded the attachment.

The cover had a wintry theme, as she'd expected. She saw that in a general sense right away but wouldn't allow herself to look directly at her own picture. She was so nervous she had to ease into it.

First, her eyes ran over the shout lines that touted the content. *A new year of fit and healthy, The best of plant-based eating* and *Oscar hopefuls* were three she read before coming to the blurb that corresponded with the cover: *Tia Beckett. Accident. Recovery. And an Oscar nod for* Expect the Worst?

It all sounded so matter-of-fact. So…possible.

At last, she allowed her eyes to focus on the subject of the cover, and because her knees suddenly went weak, she had to lean on one of the desks.

The thud of her own heartbeat filled her ears as she stared at herself for several seconds. Then she felt a huge smile spread across her face. She wasn't as beautiful as she used to be. But she didn't look as bad as she'd expected, either. As a matter of fact, given the circumstances, she looked pretty darn good. The team at *People* hadn't hidden her scars, but they hadn't done anything to make them more apparent, either.

Hugging her phone to her chest, she let her breath seep out in relief. She'd made the cover of *People*, just like she'd dreamed about when she was a little girl. She was going to take a moment to celebrate that accomplishment, to be grateful for it.

When she was ready, she finally turned to the article inside and perused the photographs they'd included with it, before reading the headline: *Up-and-coming actress Tia Beckett. After surviving a near-fatal accident, Tia looks forward to mental and physical healing and, possibly, an Oscar for one of the best performances of the year.*

"What are you doing? Are you okay?"

Tia looked up to see Seth.

"Nina sent me the cover," she explained.

"The woman you've been dealing with at *People*?"

With a nod, she held up her phone, and he strode over to take it.

"Wow," he said on a long exhale. "You gotta be proud of that, Tia. It's drop-dead gorgeous. *You're* drop-dead gorgeous."

Tears sprang to her eyes. "You really think so?"

"Are you kidding? There's no question."

He seemed absolutely committed to his answer; she didn't get the impression he was just being nice.

"What does the article say?" he asked.

"I haven't had a chance to read much of it yet. There are some other pictures I was looking at first. Those show close-ups of the damage to my face, but they could've been a lot worse."

"Mind if I read it out loud?"

She was feeling encouraged enough that she didn't hesitate. "Go ahead."

As Seth began to read, Tia hung on every word. The article talked about the crash and how she'd had to put her career on hold while she recovered. It went over all the things she'd told them during the interview, but it also indicated that she might be able to return to acting some day and suggested that she was almost a shoo-in for the Oscar for Best Actress.

When he finished, Seth set her phone aside and looked over at her. "How are you feeling?"

"I'm good," she said and realized it was true. The road ahead wouldn't be easy, but she was a fighter, a survivor.

"I'm so happy for you," he said. "Merry Christmas."

CHAPTER TWENTY-EIGHT

After spending the day in a house packed with happy, talking people, and kids loaded up on sugar and excitement, the quiet at Maxi's seemed exaggerated.

"I love what you gave me," Tia told Seth as she put the leftovers Aiyana had sent home with them in the fridge. "Thanks so much."

"I love what you gave me, too," he said. "That pouch is going to be perfect for me."

"I'm sorry I couldn't get it right away."

"No worries. It'll come." He put down the sack of gifts he'd carried in and turned on the fire. "Did you ever get ahold of your family?"

Tia had tried calling her parents three times. No one had answered. This Christmas had been special in so many ways—she was trying not to let their lack of response ruin it for her. But now that she was no longer distracted by Seth's family and all their festivities, she couldn't seem to keep from feeling that slight. "Not yet," she said, infusing as much cheer into her voice as she could so he wouldn't know how bad it hurt.

But she didn't fool him. His next words proved it. "I'm sorry."

"It is what it is," she said. "We've struggled to understand each other for some time now."

He came over and pulled her into his arms. "That doesn't make it any easier."

She rested her head on his shoulder, letting the warmth and comfort he offered buoy her spirits. "I'll try again tomorrow."

"It's only eight there. Why not try again tonight?"

"I guess I'm holding out hope they'll think of me and want to respond."

He kissed her forehead before drawing away. "I have something else for you."

"Something else?" she echoed in surprise.

"Another gift. I didn't give it to you at my mother's because I didn't want my family to make a big deal of it."

"What is it?"

He went to the coat closet and got a small velvet box from the pocket of his coat. "Take a look."

They sat in front of the fire as she opened it. It was a pair of diamond stud earrings that had to be almost a karat each, and she could tell from the box they'd come from a fine-jewelry store. "They're gorgeous!" she said. "But unless they're fake I can't accept them."

He laughed. "They're not fake."

"Then, they must've cost a fortune!"

He took them from the box and helped her change from the much cheaper earrings she was wearing now. "I can afford it, and I wanted you to have them."

Seth was more than generous. She loved that about him. But she wasn't sure how to interpret this gift. Was it as simple as wanting her to have something he thought was beautiful? Something she might like and would never buy for herself? Or had he bought them out of guilt, because he couldn't give her what she really wanted?

"Thank you. I wish I had something else for you."

"I don't want anything else. You've already made this Christmas so much better than it would've been," he said and kissed her.

Her phone rang over on the counter where she'd set it while putting away the leftovers.

"That might be your family," he said, sounding as hopeful as she immediately felt.

She hurried over to see. "It *is* them," she said in relief and answered.

"Tia?"

It had taken her mother years to get used to her new name. It still sounded foreign on her lips, but at least she was trying. "Merry Christmas!" Tia said. "How was your day?"

"We enjoyed it."

"What'd you do?"

"We had dinner with the Parkers."

After the day she'd spent at the Turners', the contrast between her old world and her new one had never seemed greater. "That sounds nice."

"It was. We are truly blessed."

"I'm glad you feel that way. I wanted to send gifts to my nieces and nephews, but—"

"It's better not to get that started," her mother broke in. "You know your father would not approve."

Tia didn't see the harm in sending each of the kids a small present, but she wasn't willing to put up a fight today. She wanted peace where they were concerned. "Okay."

"Abram said you thought he called the paparazzi and told them where to find you. I can't believe you would accuse him of that."

"I realize now that I was wrong, and I'm sorry. I apologized to him, too. But...who else would do it?"

"No one here. We're your family, Tia. We would never do something like that. The reason we want you to come back is because we want you to be happy, and this is the only path that leads to happiness."

"Does that go for Rachel, too?" she asked.

Suddenly, the phone switched hands. "Sarah?"

Her father refused to acknowledge her name change. "Hi, Dad."

"Rachel's right here. Tell her," he demanded aside. "Did you call the paparazzi?"

"Of course not," she heard her sister say. "I wouldn't even know how to find one."

"Did you hear that?" he said. "She didn't call the paparazzi. Abram didn't call the paparazzi. No one here called the paparazzi. You may not think much of the way we live, but you have to respect our honesty."

"Okay, Dad. I've handled it, so it doesn't matter anymore, anyway."

"It matters to me," he said. Then her mother came back on the line.

Tia made small talk with Naomi, asking about the quilt she was making and how sales were going in the local gift shop. Naomi told her the Harders had broken down and purchased their very first car, but the Wiens had gotten rid of their TV after realizing that the content it was bringing into their home wasn't conducive to the worship of God.

Tia did her best not to say anything when she disagreed and, instead, focused on trying to make the conversation a positive one.

"How was your Christmas?" Naomi finally asked.

Tia was surprised by the question. Her mother was usually careful not to inquire about her life because she didn't want to imagine her daughter living in a way she couldn't approve of.

Tia glanced over at Seth, who was watching her closely, obviously hoping that the call was going well. "Now that I've had the chance to speak to you, I can say it's been the best Christmas I've ever had," she replied.

After a startled pause, her mother said, "Despite the accident and what it has done to your career?"

"Yeah. Despite that."

"I'm glad," her mother said. "We love you, you know. Your father has a hard time showing affection. It's just not his way. But I can tell how much he cares about you. I hear him pray for you every single day."

"I appreciate his prayers," she said, but what she really needed he couldn't give her. "Please tell him I love him, too."

After she hung up, Seth poured two glasses of wine and carried one over to her. "You okay?"

She nodded. "For us, that was a good conversation. I hope it'll be the first of many more."

"So do I."

"They said they didn't call Kouretas."

"Do you believe them?"

"I do."

"Which means…"

"Barbie had to have done it."

After they finished their wine and put away their gifts, Tia went into the atrium to take care of Kiki, and Seth went up to work. But he was too distracted by the text he'd received from Brady earlier to accomplish anything. He stood in front of the wall of windows, holding a second glass of wine while staring out at the starry night and trying to imagine what allowing his biological brothers back into his life might mean. This was the fifth year in a row he'd heard from Brady. The year before Shiloh died, he'd actually responded. But then he'd lost her, and he not only retreated from Derrick and Brady, he retreated from everyone else, too.

He recalled the conversation he'd overheard Tia having with

her family thirty minutes or so ago. She could probably save herself a lot of grief if she walked away from them. They were never going to change their minds about her, were never going to approve of who she'd become or what she was doing with her life. But she kept trying to make those difficult relationships work and wasn't willing to give them up entirely.

He admired that. He admired the long-suffering and vulnerability it required. *She* was the injured party—not them. But if she treated them the way they treated her, they'd lose each other for sure.

Did he owe it to Derrick and Brady to do what he could to try to rebuild what they'd lost? If he did respond, where would it lead? Would they expect him to associate with their mother?

Because Seth already knew he couldn't do that. Maybe Sandy had good reasons for what she'd done. Maybe she couldn't cope with life any other way. But what he'd gone through during those early years had left an indelible mark, and he refused to have anything to do with her—ever. He felt as though he owed himself that much, at least.

He was less clear about what was fair when it came to Derrick and Brady, however. Jealousy nearly ate him alive when he thought about how they'd gone home while he remained in the foster system. But it wasn't their fault Sandy loved them more. They were just guilty by association.

He pulled out his phone and read the message again.

Merry Christmas! I don't know if this is still your number. It's been a long time since I tracked you down in San Francisco and Shiloh gave it to me, but...trying again. Just wanted to let you know I would love to be part of your life if you're interested. If I don't hear from you, please know I wish you well and always have.

He rubbed his forehead as he mulled those words over.

Brady sounded like a decent guy. What was his life like these days?

Seth knew almost nothing about him—had purposely steered clear of anything and anyone who could tell him more.

This is the right number. Merry Christmas. I wish you well, too, he wrote.

But he couldn't bring himself to send it.

"Pretty girl," Tia said, trying to get Kiki to copy her.
Instead the bird said, "Shh, be quiet," which made Tia laugh.
"Okay, you got it," she said and began tossing the ball.
Kiki brought it to Tia before landing on a nearby branch to await another throw.
"Shh, be quiet," the bird said again.
Tia took a picture of Kiki to send to Maxi.

Kiki hasn't learned any new words. I must be a terrible teacher. But she's happy and doing well. I hope you're having a wonderful trip. Thanks for letting me stay in your gorgeous home. Merry Christmas.

When her phone buzzed a few minutes later, she assumed Maxi was responding to her, even though it was the middle of the night in Europe. But when she checked, she found a message from Barbie instead.

You doing okay? I texted you earlier to wish you a Merry Christmas but I haven't heard back.

Tia hadn't known how to respond. And while she was trying to figure out what she should say now, Kiki flew down, picked up the ball Tia had let roll to the ground and dropped it in her lap.

"Okay, okay," Tia muttered and threw it, but her mind remained elsewhere. Did she pretend not to know that Barbie was the one who'd told Kouretas she was in Silver Springs? Could there be *any* possibility she was wrong?

She tried telling herself she didn't really *need* to know if Barbie had done it or not. She could choose to believe her friend and assume that Kouretas must've used a private detective or something.

But she knew that was highly unlikely. Unless there was a GPS tracker on her car, how would a private detective trace her? Especially so fast? And if there had been something like that going on, Kouretas would've come right to the house.

I know you did it, she wrote.

Did what? came Barbie's immediate response.

Tia shifted on the small wooden bench. Had she just accused another innocent person?

Possibly. But without this conversation, the doubt she now harbored would always stand between them. If they were going to remain friends, Tia had to know she could trust her.

Stop playing games, Barb. Kouretas told me.

I don't know what you're talking about. Kouretas is lying. It wasn't me.

Then how did he give me your name?

It was a bluff. Tia hated to use it, but she knew Barbie would just continue to deny it if she felt as though she could.

There was no response. Tia's heart sank as one minute ticked into two and two into three. If Barbie was innocent, she would've texted right back to say that there was no way Kouretas could've named her because she'd never so much as spoken to him.

The door opened, and Seth poked his head in. "You just about done in here?"

"Almost. You finished working?"

"It's Christmas. I decided to tackle it tomorrow. Want to get in the hot tub?"

Tia's phone rang before she could respond. "It's Barbie," she told him. "I accused her of telling Kouretas, and this is where she tries to convince me that I'm wrong."

He came in and began throwing the ball for Kiki so that she could answer and concentrate on the conversation. "Hello?"

"It wasn't me," Barbie said.

Tia closed her eyes and dropped her head into one hand, because Barbie didn't sound very convincing. "Then, how would Kouretas know your name?"

"He's just…throwing me under the bus, trying to ruin our relationship."

"That still doesn't explain how he would know your name."

"He must know more about you than you think. Must know we're friends."

It was easy to tell Barbie was lying. "Stop," Tia said. "You're only making it worse."

When Barbie spoke again, her voice was barely above a whisper. "I'm sorry. I didn't mean to hurt you. You have to believe that. It was Mike who came up with the idea. He said we'd make a lot of money and…and you deserved it, anyway."

"Deserved it?" Tia echoed. "How could anyone deserve what happened to me?"

"He said you had to have been texting or something when you ran that red light."

"You've got to be kidding me. I wasn't texting, Barbie. I was upset. Do you want to know why?"

"Why?" she said.

"I had just run into Mike at the acting academy. I'd gone

back there to thank our old instructor for all he had taught me. You remember Mr. Arzaga, don't you?"

"Of course. But what does Mike have to do with that?"

"He was there, still taking lessons. And as I was getting in my car to go, he hit on me."

"That's a lie!" Barbie exclaimed.

"Whether or not you believe it is up to you. But I was crying when I ran that red light. I couldn't figure out what to do— whether to tell you or to…to hope Mike had just gotten a little starstruck after my success with the movie. I was so distracted, trying to justify his behavior so that I wouldn't have to hurt you, that I didn't even see that light when I blew through it."

"That can't be true," she said, but the tone of her voice suggested she did, in fact, believe it.

"It *is* true, Barbie. You know me. I would never lie about that. Mike had just cornered me in the back parking lot and told me that he'd always had a thing for me."

After several seconds of tense silence, Barbie said, "So…you were never going to tell me? You've been asked over and over again what made you run that red light. And you've never said a word about this."

"After the accident, I was pretty sure whatever he'd felt before would be gone. We were all in an odd situation, all wanting to attain something that is almost impossible to attain, and I was the only one who was getting it. I was trying to give him the benefit of the doubt because of that. And then you sic the paparazzi on me, knowing how badly I was struggling to cope?"

"Don't make it a bigger deal than it has to be. I wouldn't have done it if I didn't need the money. And it's not like I told Kouretas you come from a Mennonite family and changed your name. He only wanted to get your picture—something that was going to happen eventually, anyway," she said and then hung up.

Tia groaned as she dropped her phone in her lap and began to massage her forehead.

"So that's what happened when you ran that light," Seth said, holding the ball Kiki was waiting for him to throw. "Why didn't you tell me?"

"Because I wanted to forget it, pretend it never happened. I couldn't hurt Barbie that way. She loves Mike too much. So I convinced myself he was just a little too eager to be part of my success. And even if I decided to tell her later because she needed to know, I wasn't going to allow her to be publicly embarrassed on top of it—or to feel as though the accident was in any way her fault."

"It was Mike's fault," Seth said.

"He was also the one who hatched the plan to cash in on the aftermath," she added sadly. "And cost me my best friend."

CHAPTER TWENTY-NINE

Friday, December 31

The week after Christmas flew by. Seth didn't hold himself to a strict work schedule. He was enjoying his time with Tia too much. But he did spend a couple of hours a day fundraising for the humanities center he was planning to build. Tia called some of her wealthier associates in the movie industry too, and most were so relieved to hear from her they were overly generous in contributing, especially Christian Allen, her costar from *Expect the Worst*. Seth planned to make the building itself into a work of art and have the names of all the donors who'd given a certain amount featured in a colorful banner going up one side, so that helped to encourage donations, too. Everyone liked to be recognized for doing a good deed.

By the thirty-first, they'd been able to raise four million dollars. According to the architects and contractors Seth had talked to, he needed twenty, so he still had a long way to go, but he was willing to contribute a sizable amount himself, so he had a great start.

Between going running every day, cooking, enjoying the

pool and hot tub, and watching movies with Tia, he also managed to finish *The Businessman*. Once he could concentrate on it, it took only one night. To make up for how long he'd made his client wait, he borrowed Cal's truck and took Tia with him to San Francisco to deliver it in person. The attorney who'd requisitioned it—a Mr. Li Chen—was so excited he even made a donation for the humanities center.

"I think I'll create something special for the entrance to the building and sell signed, limited-edition prints to help raise the rest of the money," Seth said as they drove away from the attorney's house.

Although Tia was wearing her beanie and her sunglasses with a sweater and a pair of jeans, she hadn't bothered with her scarf. She seemed to be growing less self-conscious about her scars every day. "That's a great idea! Then, people who aren't rich can contribute, too, and have something special to show for it."

The painting he'd done of her came to mind. It was still covered with a cloth and hidden behind another canvas at Maxi's, so she hadn't seen it, but he was keenly aware of it. Easily the best thing he'd created in some time, it seemed like a prime candidate for the humanities center—at least in some regards. He'd met Tia in Silver Springs. She'd helped make the building a reality. And prints of such a beautiful and sensual woman would be broadly appealing.

But he was strangely reluctant to share it with the world. Despite being purely conceptual, it was somehow too private. He would feel oddly exposed—and he didn't care to discover why.

"I'm starving," she said. "Where are we going for dinner?"

"I thought I'd take you to Scoma's on the wharf. It's where Boudin started—if you've heard of that restaurant."

"I haven't."

"They're famous for their crusty sourdough bread."

"I love sourdough bread."

"Me, too. Scoma's isn't overly fancy, but it's been around

since the midsixties, and the food is consistently delicious. Do you like scallops?"

"Sometimes. Depends on how they're cooked."

"You have to try them at Scoma's. The shrimp pasta, too."

"I'm down for that."

He turned toward the water. "Are you afraid of being recognized? Would you prefer we get it to go so that we can eat on the wharf?"

She didn't look too pleased with that suggestion. "It's pretty cold outside."

"We could eat in the truck."

"On New Year's Eve?"

"I'm willing to do whatever makes you comfortable."

She frowned at her jeans. "Am I dressed nice enough for indoor dining?"

They'd chosen to be comfortable for the long drive. "We might be slightly underdressed but only because it's New Year's. The restaurant is more about the fresh seafood it serves than the ambience. It's very casual."

"Then, let's risk it," she said. "It's been a long time since I've been out to eat."

"Okay," he said and took her hand.

Seth was right about Scoma's. Tia didn't feel out of place, and if the host who'd seated them recognized her, he didn't let on. He was an older gentleman—not part of the movie's main demographic—so maybe he hadn't even seen it.

"Everything looks good," she said as she browsed the menu. It felt wonderful to be dining out again, especially with Seth. For the first time in her life, she understood how all-consuming love could be. He treated her as though he cared about her, too. Even the way they'd made love had somehow grown more meaningful. But he hadn't made any promises. Although she'd told herself not to worry about that, to let it come naturally and just live in the moment, there were times when she was afraid she'd unwittingly pulled the pin out of a grenade and was still standing there, holding it.

Seth pointed out the menu items he felt were best, and they ordered, but before their food could come, a woman and a man, who were being guided to a table just beyond theirs, noticed them and suddenly stopped.

"Oh, my gosh!" the woman cried.

Assuming she was about to encounter an excited fan that might alert the whole restaurant to her presence, Tia stiffened. But the woman wasn't gaping at her; she was gaping at Seth.

"Is it really you?" she asked. "It's been so long!"

If Tia hadn't known Seth as well as she was coming to know him, she might not have noticed the subtle tightening around his eyes and mouth that suggested he wasn't happy to encounter these people, especially because he smiled warmly and immediately got to his feet to give her a hug and shake the hand of the man standing beside her. "Amy. Serge. How are you both?"

"We're good," Amy replied. "It's you we've been worried about. We haven't heard from you since Shiloh died. What's it been? Three years?"

"My work has been…crazy," Seth said, lamely.

The woman's eyes cut immediately to Tia. "Is this your new wife?"

"No. This is…this is just a friend," he replied.

Amy covered her mouth, obviously embarrassed by the gaffe. "I'm so sorry," she said. "We didn't recognize you from behind, but we saw you when you came in and…" She let her words fade away. They'd been holding hands when they came in. That was what she was trying to say. It wasn't her fault she'd assumed there was some romantic interest. They'd given the impression they were seeing each other.

Tia had been under that impression, too. They'd spent almost every minute together for the past few weeks. They'd slept together, ate together, visited his family together. They'd even done the fundraising for the humanities building together. The only time they'd been apart was when Seth was working and she was taking care of the houseplants or Kiki.

Her mind flashed back to the diamond earrings he'd given her for Christmas—the earrings she was wearing now—and she knew she'd been right to feel some suspicion. He was trying to use his money to compensate for what he couldn't or wouldn't give of his heart.

Suddenly, it sounded as if Tia had a helicopter inside her head that drowned out everything else. *Whoosh…whoosh…whoosh…* She'd been so stupid! She'd allowed herself to believe things had changed when they hadn't.

Suddenly she realized the woman was holding out her hand. Tia seemed to have blacked out for a moment, and now everything was moving in slow motion. *You can get through this*, she told herself. *You're an actress—so act.*

Forcing a broad smile, she accepted Amy's hand and then her husband's. "How nice to meet you both. Yes, Seth and I don't mean anything to each other at all." She laughed as if it was a joke, and they did, too. "How do you know him?"

"Shiloh was my best friend," Amy said. "We moved to San Francisco about the same time and didn't know anybody else when we met at a Zumba class." She smiled nostalgically. "We hit it off immediately and later found out that we lived only two streets apart. I'm an interior designer, so I helped decorate her house, and she dragged me into all of her do-good schemes, like saving the feral cats in the neighborhood. I'm still doing that, by the way," she added for Seth's benefit.

Seth was too quiet, but Tia ignored that. She just had to get through the next few minutes without making a scene, she told herself.

"Are you an artist, too?" Serge asked Tia.

"No. I'm an actress. Or… I used to be."

"You're not Tia Beckett…"

At this point, she was grateful they'd recognized her because it swung the conversation in a more bearable direction—and that said a lot. "Yes."

"I saw *Expect the Worst*," he said. "It was wonderful."

"Oh, I loved that movie!" Amy added. "I think it should win an Academy Award."

Tia felt no warmth from the compliment. It was almost as if she was standing to the side, watching what was going on at the table instead of participating in it. "I guess we'll find out in January if I'm nominated or not."

Amy turned to Seth. "So…how did you meet a movie star?"

When Seth hesitated, Tia couldn't help jumping in. "We were introduced by a mutual friend just after my accident." She figured that explained it simply enough.

"You were in an accident?" Amy asked.

"Yes. That's what happened to my face."

"Oh! I'm so sorry. I hadn't heard."

"No problem," Tia said. "Bad things happen sometimes. I'm sorry you lost your best friend. Shiloh was obviously an incredible person."

"She was," Amy agreed. "*So* special."

"No wonder Seth can't get over her," Tia said. "If you will excuse me, I have to use the restroom. Why don't the two of you sit down and join us?"

"*Really*?" Amy said.

Seth's gaze cut to Tia—it was obvious he didn't want that to happen—but she didn't back down. "Of course. We'd love it!"

"Okay," Serge said, and Tia slid out so they could take her side of the booth.

"I'll be right back," she promised. But she didn't go to the restroom. She walked out of the restaurant and into the jumble of tourists crowding the wharf.

Tears rolled down her cheeks as she hurried along. She'd left her coat behind. But she couldn't feel the cold. She couldn't feel anything.

At some point, once she was well away from the restaurant and didn't have to worry about Seth coming after her, she used her phone to call a cab and had it take her to the airport.

Seth knew he'd made a huge mistake as soon as the words *This is just a friend* were out of his mouth. But he'd been taken off guard seeing Amy after so long. She was so strongly associated with Shiloh; it had jerked him back three years. And once he'd said what he'd said, he hadn't been able to gain his footing enough to figure out how to fix it—not in the moment.

Knowing Tia was upset, he kept looking over his shoulder toward the bathroom. He did it so often that Amy noticed and said, "Do you want me to go check on her?"

"Would you, please?"

"Of course."

She circumvented Serge and strode down toward the entrance. While she was gone, the waiter brought the food he and Tia had ordered, but Seth had completely lost his appetite. He tried to keep up small talk with Serge, but even that was impossible. For the most part, he just sat there, feeling sick inside, as he waited for Amy to bring Tia back.

But when she returned, Tia wasn't with her.

"She's not in there," she said, alarmed. "I asked the host if he'd seen her, and he said she walked out right after we were seated."

The pressure on Seth's chest was so great it felt as though an elephant had just sat on it. *"Walked out?"*

"Yeah. And he hasn't seen her since."

"You'll have to excuse me." Seth threw two hundred bucks on the table and hurried out after her. Where would she go? he asked himself. How would he find her?

He used his phone to call her, but she didn't pick up. Her voice mail came on.

"Hello! This is Tia. Leave me a message, and I'll get back to you as soon as possible."

"Tia, I'm sorry," he said. "Please…come back. Let's talk about it. I didn't mean… It caught me off guard, that's all. I was stupid. I'm sorry."

His heart was racing when he gazed out over the crowded wharf and didn't see her. He jogged to Pier 39, which was the most popular pier, checking faces as he ran, and when he got there, stood on a wooden bench and searched the sea of people for her beanie.

Unfortunately, she wasn't there. It was crazy to think he'd be able to find her even if she was still at the water's edge. The piers ran from 1 to 45. She could be anywhere.

He checked his phone. She hadn't called back.

He tried a message. I'm so sorry. Please answer your phone. Don't leave like this.

Again, there was no response. All he could do was continue to search. He looked for over two hours, walking up and down each pier and checking every store and restaurant.

He kept texting and calling her, too.

But she wouldn't pick up.

Tia refused to allow herself to think of anything except what she had to do next.

After she landed in Burbank, she had to take a rideshare to Maxi's.

Once she got to Maxi's, she would have to pack her clothes and write out detailed instructions for Seth to be able to take proper care of Kiki. But he'd watched her and helped her enough with Maxi's bird that she had no doubt he'd be able to do it. Maxi would be back before too long, anyway.

She also refused to let herself feel anything.

She refused to picture Seth sitting at the restaurant where she'd left him, wondering where she'd gone.

She refused to imagine how much she was going to miss Kiki and Silver Springs and Aiyana.

She'd been a fool to let herself get so involved with a man who wasn't emotionally accessible. She'd known the danger from the beginning, and yet she'd *still* pulled the pin from that grenade.

And now it had exploded.

But all she could do was pick up the pieces and, once again, try to move on. She wasn't sure how she would do that. She was out of her depth.

You'll figure it out. Just put one foot in front of the other.

That was how she'd gotten through everything else, wasn't it? Except the accident.

It was Seth who'd pulled her through that.

After her Uber driver dropped her off, she rushed into Maxi's house and threw her clothes and other belongings into her suitcase. The flight from San Francisco to LA had only taken an hour, but she'd had to wait quite a while before she could even get on a flight, and it'd taken almost two hours to reach Silver Springs from LA once she landed. If Seth had left San Francisco after eating with his friends at Scoma's, and it was a six-hour drive to bring Cal's truck back, he should arrive around midnight.

She'd only be two hours ahead of him, and she was *definitely* hoping to be gone when he arrived.

She should've left well before Christmas—as soon as she felt herself falling in love with him.

After she carried her suitcase out of the house, she removed the expensive diamond earrings he'd given her, returned them to the velvet box they'd come in and set them out along with the mirrored trees, instructions for Kiki and a note that she hoped would be the last communication they'd ever need to have.

Then she went to the atrium to feed Kiki, just in case Seth didn't get back as soon as she thought he would.

"You're going to be okay in Seth's hands," she told the bird as she poured fresh birdseed into the feeder. "He'll take good care of you. I'll alert Maxi that I've left, too, so he can follow up and make sure of it."

As usual, the bird was more interested in playing than eating. Kiki was smart enough to realize that the food stayed even after her human friend was gone, so Tia started throwing the ball. "I can't hang out for very long," she told Kiki, but she spent twenty minutes playing with Maxi's parrot anyway, just because she wanted to be fair and do her part, before adding some extra pumpkin seeds to Kiki's feed, for good measure.

"I have to go now," she told the bird. "I know you don't like Seth as much as me, but Maxi will be back before you know it."

She was just letting herself out when Kiki squawked as though she was distressed and said, "I love Tia."

The bird had learned what she'd been trying to teach her all along? Anyone with any knowledge of parrots would say Kiki had no understanding of what she said. She was just mimicking what she'd been painstakingly taught the past few weeks. Tia understood that. But it brought tears to her eyes, anyway.

"Thank you, Kiki," she murmured. "That's exactly what I needed to hear. Happy New Year."

CHAPTER THIRTY

On the off chance Tia was still in the Bay Area, Seth had a hard time making himself leave. He couldn't imagine driving home without her. But he'd searched for so long, with no results. He had to assume she was the one who'd left without him.

And if that was the case—what did it mean?

He was afraid to find out.

I don't know what to do. Please let me know you're okay.

He'd texted her that message just before he left, but despite checking his phone over and over again, he hadn't gotten a response to that, either. She must've turned off her cell—or it was out of battery—because now when he tried calling her, it didn't even ring before transferring to voice mail.

If something had happened to her, he'd never forgive himself.

He tried calling Maxi to ask if he'd check the security system on his phone to see if Tia had entered the house, but it was New Year's Eve. Maxi had probably stayed up to ring in the New Year and was now sleeping off the champagne. Aiyana didn't answer, either. She'd invited her grandchildren over for a New Year's party so that the adults in the family could go out and was, no doubt, caught up in the kitchen making hot chocolate bombs or something else to show the kids a good time.

All he could do was rush back to Silver Springs and hope to find Tia safe and sound. If she hadn't beaten him there, he'd call the police in both places and get some help trying to find her.

The drive seemed interminable. He tried to distract himself by listening to music, but certain songs were too hard to hear. When "Without You" by Harry Nilsson came on, he had to switch it right away. He didn't even know how that song had gotten on his playlist. He could only guess that Shiloh had put it there, and he'd never noticed because he had such an extensive library.

But the weird thing was that it didn't make him miss Shiloh—it made him miss Tia.

"What have I done?" he muttered, over and over.

When he finally pulled through the gate at Maxi's, it was after one. As he'd come through town, he'd seen a few revelers who were still celebrating New Year's. The Blue Suede Shoe had been packed. But there wasn't a lot going on anywhere else.

He couldn't believe he'd started the New Year by hurting Tia. He couldn't have felt worse, especially after he drove down the driveway and found her car gone. "No!" he exclaimed and smacked the steering wheel as he brought the truck to a stop and cut the engine.

Although he knew the chances were highly unlikely, he'd hoped someone had stolen it and that he'd find her inside. He could buy her a new car.

He raced into the house calling her name, but she wasn't there. Neither were her things. He found the earrings he'd given her laid out on the counter, along with the mirrored trees, some instructions on how to care for Kiki—as if he hadn't helped her do it the past couple of weeks and wouldn't already know—and a note.

His throat tightened, making it hard to swallow, as he opened the envelope.

Dear Seth:

I'm sorry I had to leave early, but it'll be easier this way. Please don't feel bad. You didn't do anything wrong. After all, you warned me from the start. I just didn't listen as well as I should have, I guess. I let go, trusted what I was feeling, because it honestly didn't seem as though Shiloh was still standing between us. What we had felt authentic—at least to me. But I'm just a naive Mennonite girl at heart, and I obviously misread the clues. Maybe it's because I've never loved anyone else.

Thanks for helping me through the aftermath of the accident. Please don't think I'm angry, because I'm not. What happened at the restaurant was a wake-up call that needed to happen, but I do ask you to please give me some space so that I can heal and pull my life back together.

Regardless of anything else, I wish you every happiness.

Tia.

P.S. Please sell the trees and the earrings and donate the proceeds to the humanities center. I don't have a lot of money right now—I don't know how long my savings will have to last—but I would like to contribute in this way.

"Fuck," he muttered as he sank onto one of the barstools. Her inherent kindness came through even now, which cut him even deeper.

His vision began to blur with tears. Propping his head on his fist, he squeezed his eyes closed and pushed the note away. He'd been a fool to do what he'd done. He hadn't even meant it. It'd been a stupid, knee-jerk reaction to seeing people he associated with his former life, when he was married to Shiloh. But that one thoughtless moment had cost him the best thing to happen to him in a long time.

Fortunately, she'd been gone long enough that there were no paparazzi camped outside her condo—although Tia couldn't imagine they'd be there at one in the morning on New Year's Day, even if she hadn't left the area.

Breathing a sigh of relief to see everything so dark and quiet, despite the revelry associated with this particular holiday, Tia let herself through the gate, parked in her spot and hauled in her stuff.

"I'm home," she called out for no particular reason. She was entirely alone, didn't own so much as a plant—she'd given her succulents to her neighbor before she went to Silver Springs—but it seemed appropriate.

She dumped her suitcase in the middle of the floor and told herself to get in bed and try to sleep. She needed to shut out the memories banging around in her head of Seth and what Christmas in Silver Springs had been like and gain some relief from the pain in her chest.

But her feet wouldn't carry her past the living room. Instead, she curled up on the couch, put her hands beneath her scarred cheek and stared at the blank TV screen, unable to hold back the tears that dripped onto her fingers.

Seth couldn't sleep. He rambled around Maxi's house the way he'd rambled around his own in San Francisco after Shiloh had died and was still awake when the sun peeked over the horizon. He thought of what he'd be doing right now if Tia was around and knew he'd be in bed with her. They'd get up and have coffee together and talk about anything and everything while she cooked something for breakfast, like biscuits and gravy. Although she made a mean avocado toast, she said her cooking skills didn't extend to the trendy stuff found in most LA restaurants these days. She'd been taught to cook with meat and potatoes, but he was perfectly fine with that. He liked comfort food.

After breakfast, they'd go for a run or a swim and maybe they'd wind up making love in the shower.

He wandered outside to the pool, feeling disconnected from everything and everyone, not to mention rumbled, exhausted and so angry with himself that he felt he deserved to be this miserable. He wished he could shut off his brain and go to sleep or bury himself in work to escape what he was feeling; he'd been so careful not to allow himself to feel anything the past three years.

But he couldn't even make himself try. All he could think about was the way Tia had looked when he'd said she was just a friend. The color had drained from her face, except for where her cheek had been cut and stitched back together, and the scars had stood out more than he'd seen in a long while. He'd felt oddly compelled to trace the crooked lines with his finger, as if that could somehow make them disappear—like he could when working with paint. But, of course, that was impossible. Just seeing her look so stricken had made him hate himself.

He pulled out his phone. Just tell me you're okay. That's all I need to know, and I'll leave you alone. He sent her that text message, but he knew she wouldn't respond. She hadn't answered any of his other messages, and he couldn't blame her.

"Seth?"

It was his mother, but he didn't turn to face her. "What?" he said.

"I've been ringing and ringing the bell," she said in confusion. "I couldn't get anyone to answer. Where's Tia? I noticed her car's gone, so I felt it might be okay to let myself in. I brought you both some quiche and mimosas for New Year's Day. If you were gone, I was just going to leave them on the counter."

He finally looked at her. "I think Tia went back to LA."

Concern immediately erased Aiyana's smile. "What happened? Does she have another photo shoot?"

"No. She's gone for good. She took her things with her."

"But…why? I thought she was staying for another couple of weeks."

With a sigh, he faced the sunrise again. "I screwed up and said something I shouldn't have."

Aiyana didn't speak right away. She just pulled on his arm, urging him toward the house. "It's freezing out here. Can we go inside?"

He didn't care if it was cold. He didn't even feel it. But he cared about Aiyana, so he let her lead him back to the living room.

"Maybe this is something we can fix," she said.

He shook his head. "No. I deserve it."

"We all make mistakes, Seth. That's what forgiveness is for. A relationship is never only smooth sailing. You of all people should know that."

He scratched his neck. "I've got too many issues. She'll be happier with somebody else."

"What if she isn't? What if the two of you are meant to be together?"

Normally, he would've said that no one could replace Shiloh. He'd believed that ever since he'd lost her. But something had definitely changed. "There's nothing I can do," he told her. "She won't even talk to me."

"And you're going to give up that easily?"

He didn't answer.

"Do you love her?"

If he didn't love her, would he feel this way?

"You need to decide," his mother said. "Because if you love her, you owe it to yourself to make that clear. You owe it to her, too."

★ ★ ★

Tia was awakened by a knock at the door. Afraid it was her neighbor, using the excuse of asking if she wanted her succulents back to have an opportunity to engage her, she almost didn't answer. She couldn't face returning to her old life quite yet. She needed some time to cope with this latest setback.

Intent on going back to sleep while she was still groggy enough to do so, she grabbed the throw blanket at her feet and drew it up over her. *Shut out the noise. Fade back into oblivion,* she told herself.

But then she heard Seth's voice: "Tia, it's me. Will you answer the door? Please?"

How had he found her?

She guessed it wasn't too difficult. Maxi had her address. He'd probably provided it.

"You don't have to worry," she called. "I'm fine."

"Can you please tell that to my face?"

She didn't want to see him. She knew it would only make her want him more. "Why?"

"I have something to show you."

What was he talking about? Had he brought her earrings?

She sat up and stretched, trying to come to full awareness. "Can't you just tell me what it is?"

"I could, but I won't. You have to open the door."

If she continued to tell him to go, maybe he would. Then, she'd never know what he was talking about. And he'd raised her curiosity.

After scrubbing a hand over her face, she crossed to the door and cracked it open. "What is it?"

"This." He gestured toward a cardboard package he had with him that was about four feet tall and four feet wide.

"You painted something you want to show me?"

"I did."

"And I haven't seen it before?"

"No, but if you'll let me in, I'd like to show it to you."

She stepped back and opened the door wide enough that he could carry it inside. "What's this about?"

His eyes swept over her as though he was eager to reassure himself that she was, indeed, okay. "I hope the fact that this painting means so much to me will tell you something."

She had no idea what he was going for here. Was he giving her one of his paintings to help her out financially? To make himself feel better for having hurt her, even though she knew it wasn't intentional? She had no idea, but she definitely wanted to see what he was talking about. "Then, let's have a look."

When she knelt to unwrap it, he helped remove the tape before lifting off the cardboard that protected the front, and Tia rocked back so that she could take it all in.

It was a conceptual representation of a naked woman and easily the most beautiful painting of his she'd ever seen. "This is gorgeous," she admitted. "Is it of Shiloh? Because if you're here to tell me you'll never be able to get over her, and you want to show me this so that I'll understand, I get it."

He was watching her carefully when he said, "It's not of Shiloh, Tia. It's of you."

"Of *me*?" She pressed a hand to her chest. "But…how? When? We haven't known each other all that long." And she thought she'd seen what he'd been working on while she was living in Maxi's house.

"I painted it after we first made love, and I've been changing and tweaking it ever since. Each time I learned something new about you, or you meant something deeper to me, I had to go back and fix it, make it resemble you more closely, until it became this." He looked down at it himself. "Now I think it's perfect—the best thing I've ever created."

Her gaze shifted from his face to the painting and back again. "I had no idea…"

"Because I kept it hidden," he explained. "I knew it would

make me too transparent, and I was still trying to avoid being that vulnerable." He set the painting down. "I'm sorry about last night, Tia."

"I've already forgiven you. And this is beautiful. I'm glad that what we had meant…*something*. But if you can't get over Shiloh, it's better if we go our separate ways, Seth. I can't—"

"That's just it," he broke in. "What happened at the restaurant didn't have anything to do with Shiloh. Not really. It had to do with *me*. With how hard it is for me to trust love—to trust someone else to give me the love I need."

Tia didn't think she'd ever heard such raw honesty. "Are you sure about this?" she whispered. "About *me*?"

He leaned the painting up against the couch. "I'm sure," he said. "It just took almost losing you to make me accept it. Will you give me another chance?"

Tia wiped fresh tears from her cheeks. When she'd been with Seth in Silver Springs, she'd felt as though she'd found the place where she belonged in the world. No matter where she came from or what her career was or where she was going, he was her safe harbor.

And now she knew it was true. "Of course," she said, and smiling through her tears, she slipped into his arms.

EPILOGUE

Sunday, February 27

Tia was so nervous she couldn't quit fidgeting.

Seth nudged her, looking as sharp as she'd ever seen him in his black tuxedo. "You okay?"

"I'm fine." She straightened the skirt of her gown, which was made of nude netting in parts and nude fabric in others and had a slit up one side. "Just excited."

He grinned at her. "You should be. You're up for an Oscar."

The movie had been nominated, too, as well as her director. In all, *Expect the Worst* had received four nominations, including one for Best Screenplay.

"You've got this," Maxi said. He and his new girlfriend, Amira, were seated to the left of her while Seth's biological brother, Brady and his wife, Cecily, who'd first come to San Francisco to visit them at Seth's invitation almost a month ago, were seated to Seth's right.

"It's an honor just to be nominated," she told Maxi, but she had to admit, at least to herself, that this meant a little more to her than the other actresses in her category. After all, she was the only one who'd probably never have the opportunity to act in another film.

He squeezed her hand as they announced the winner in the category of Best Supporting Actress, and Abigail Hendricks, who was wearing a stunning silver gown, stood when her name was called.

Cecily leaned around the two men between them. "Do you know what you're going to say?"

"I know what I want to say," she replied. "But I might forget every word of it if they call my name."

"Just a genuine thank-you is sometimes best, anyway," she said.

Seth agreed before saying something to Brady that Tia couldn't year. When they both laughed, Tia couldn't help smiling at the resemblance between them. She was so happy for Seth. That he'd taken the risk of responding to his older brother at last—and that it had worked out so well. Now Derrick, his younger brother, was going to pay them a visit next month.

"I never thought I'd be attending the Academy Awards," Brady said. "Thanks for the tickets."

"Of course," Tia said. Seth had invited Aiyana to join them at the ceremony first, but she'd said she preferred to host an Oscar party for Eli, Gavin, their families and anyone else who'd like to attend.

Tia knew she'd done that to open the way for Seth to invite Brady, and that made her love Aiyana all the more.

When the winner of Best Supporting Actor was called, Seth leaned close. "You're up next."

Tia could hardly breathe as they read off the nominees. She thought she might pass out from the anxiety. But when they called her name, she felt Seth stand and help her to her feet.

"Congratulations. I love you," he said with a brief kiss, and by the time she reached the podium to accept her gold statue, she saw that the entire audience was giving her a standing ovation.

★ ★ ★ ★ ★

If you enjoyed this story, don't miss
Brenda Novak's next novel,
Summer on the Island,
coming soon from MIRA.
Turn the page for a sneak peek!

It was too hot to remain so close to the fire. After she'd eaten, Marlow pulled her chair back, away from the others, to the much cooler perimeter, where the bright flames gave way to the softer light of the fading sunset. Her friends Claire and Aida were joking and talking to Reese, her mother's housekeeper's son, as he roasted yet another hot dog. He could eat like nobody else yet still have a perfect body—another testament to his young age—but Marlow couldn't seem to get into the revelry. She was too bugged. She hated the way his brother had acted when they'd run into him on their way back from the beach earlier. She hated the way he'd acted when he'd had a cup of tea with them shortly after they arrived, too. Talk about holding a grudge! She'd been a teenager when they'd had the encounters that'd formed his opinion of her, but he seemed to be holding fast to that opinion, even though she'd grown up a lot since then and they hadn't interacted much in the past ten years.

Surely, he had to wonder if she'd changed.

Or maybe he didn't care. She hadn't handled his interest as kindly as she could have. Maybe she'd even go so far as to say she'd acted a little stuck-up. But it hadn't been *all* her. He'd once called her a rich bitch under his breath when she passed him, and she didn't hold that against him.

She wished he'd give her the chance to wipe the slate clean, so that it wouldn't have to be so stilted and awkward every time they bumped into each other. The island was only seven square miles. As the chief of police, he'd be roving around Teach all summer. And with his mother working at the house, his brother living on the property and her own mother so keen to include him whenever possible, Marlow was bound to encounter him again and again, even if he did his best to stay away.

Claire brought the new bottle of wine they'd just opened to where Marlow was sitting. "This is so nice, Marlow. Thanks for inviting us."

"I'm glad you could come."

It was difficult to tell in the gathering dusk, but Marlow thought she read a sheepish expression on Claire's face. "Even after what I told you earlier—about Dutton?"

"Especially after what you told me earlier about Dutton." She took a sip of the extra dry merlot they'd brought from the house with all their other supplies. "Being away for three months might give you the space you need to decide what you really want for your future."

"I hope I make the right decision." She dropped down in the sand. "I saw you talking to Aida when we were on the beach earlier. Was she...very upset?"

"That you're still talking to Dutton? No. She's handling the news surprisingly well."

"I'm glad. The last thing I want is to hurt her."

Marlow had known Aida much longer than Claire. She hadn't met Claire until Aida had introduced them, and that was after Aida had learned about the affair between Aida's husband and Claire. But Marlow had liked Claire from the start. She was down-to-earth, inherently kind, easy to be around. "I think she understands that you're a victim of the situation, too."

Claire pushed the bottle into the sand beside her so that it wouldn't fall over. "How is it that you're able to keep your life on such an even keel?"

Marlow hadn't had any serious romantic relationships. That was how. She'd been so driven in her career, so determined to get her degree, start her practice and build a name for herself. She'd devoted all her focus and energy to those things. Then the pandemic had hit, and she'd been cut off from almost all other activities. That was when she'd realized just how tenuous human existence was. There had to be more to living than professional success. People said that all the time, of course, and she agreed. It made sense. But she'd been Icarus, flying too close to the sun—was never truly committed to achieving the proper balance until the past year, which was why she was pulling away from work to devote more of herself to her friends and family. Inviting Claire and Aida to the island to spend the summer with her had been part of that effort. "I haven't been through what you've been through. Just losing your house would be catastrophic. But losing your business, too? And finding out the man you're dating is already married? You're holding up well, considering."

Claire grinned at her response. "Well, when you put it that way, I guess I'm lucky I'm still functioning at all."

"Exactly. Things will get easier, though. Don't worry."

Aida and Reese put down their wine glasses and started toward the water. "We're going for a swim. You guys interested?" Aida called as they passed.

"I'm too comfortable," Marlow said. She twisted around to see Aida and Reese plunge into the sea, could hear their laughter as the waves tumbled over them.

"Aida's going to sleep with your housekeeper's son," Claire said, her voice low. "You know that, right?"

"Maybe she *needs* to sleep with someone to reassure her that she's still got it." Marlow grimaced. "I just wish it could be with someone else."

"It won't cause any problems between you and Rosemary, will it?"

"Reese is twenty-two, not sixteen. I'm hoping Rosemary doesn't have to find out."

"What about Walker? What do you think he'll have to say about one of your friends hooking up with his little brother?"

Marlow was embarrassed just imagining what Walker might make of that. "I hope he doesn't have to find out, either."

Claire finished her wine, set the glass aside and hugged her knees to her chest. "I noticed that he avoids looking at you when he's around. Is there a reason? Or am I reading into it?"

This comment surprised Marlow. Aida never would've noticed. But Claire was more thoughtful, more observant. "We have a bit of…history," she admitted.

"And you haven't mentioned that? You've been holding back when you're so intimately familiar with *our* dirty laundry?" she teased.

"There's nothing to talk about. Not really."

"What happened between you two? And when?"

Marlow was feeling a slight buzz, but she didn't put her glass down because she was finally able to relax and start enjoying herself after stewing about Walker through dinner. "We had several…encounters."

"That sounds interesting. What kind of encounters?"

"He had a thing for me while we were growing up. The first time he tried to kiss me, I was sixteen and he was eighteen."

"And you weren't interested?" she said in surprise.

"Not in the least."

"Is something wrong with his personality? Because he's gorgeous."

"There's nothing wrong with his personality. I'm ashamed to admit it, but I thought he was a step down. He'd been around since I could remember, so he wasn't anything special to me. I had big hopes and dreams, and I didn't want any boy, least of all Walker, to get in my way."

"Maybe you weren't ready when he made that move. It was too soon."

"Yeah, well, he made plenty of other moves, both before

and after I went to college. He was *too* devoted to me. That's why I never gave anything back. I was a little bitch when I was growing up."

"You were probably dealing with your own issues—the normal challenges of puberty mixed with trying to grow up so fast. Being put ahead two years in school couldn't have been easy. Having a father who was a US senator probably put a lot of pressure on you, too."

Leave it to Claire to put the best possible spin on it. "It doesn't matter. I shouldn't have acted that way. I really had no excuse."

"You were just a kid. Don't be too hard on yourself. Did he stay in touch after you got your law degree and opened your practice?"

"No. But he was always around for bits of the summer or holidays when I came home. With time, I think he just…started to hate me for real."

"You don't believe he hates you now…"

"I do."

"Have you ever tried to talk to him about the past?"

"No. I'm sure he doesn't want to remember those days any more than I do."

"It's hard for people to move on if you don't address the problem. Get it out in the open. Maybe if you told him you regret not being kinder, and you're sorry if you hurt him in any way, he'd forgive you, and you two could be friends. You essentially grew up together. It seems like you *should* be friends."

Marlow let her breath seep out in a long sigh as she considered Claire's response. That would mean confronting the past. Bringing up an awkward topic. The way he treated her these days—like she was anathema to him—she couldn't imagine he'd have any more interest in doing that than she would.

Or…was she just providing herself with a convenient excuse not to do the right thing? She'd always been too proud for her own good. "I *do* owe him an apology," she admitted, finally acknowledging the truth.

Claire nudged her with an elbow. "Then give him one."